Reaching Out
from the Inside

Reaching Out from the Inside

A Novel

Michele Lewis

iUniverse, Inc.

New York Lincoln Shanghai

Reaching Out from the Inside

iUniverse books may be ordered through booksellers or by contacting:

iUniverse
2021 Pine Lake Road, Suite 100
Lincoln, NE 68512
www.iuniverse.com
1-800-Authors (1-800-288-4677)

Because of the dynamic nature of the Internet, any Web addresses or links contained in this book may have changed since publication and may no longer be valid.

This is a work of fiction. All of the characters, names, incidents, organizations, and dialogue in this novel are either the products of the author's imagination or are used fictitiously.

Cover illustration by Tim Miller
Cover design by Michele Lewis and Tim Miller

Excerpt From THE POWER OF MYTH by Joseph Campbell & Bill Moyers, copyright © 1988 by Apostrophe S Productions, Inc. and Bill Moyers and Alfred Van der Marck Editions, Inc. for itself and the estate of Joseph Campbell. Used by permission of Doubleday, a division of Random House, Inc.

ISBN: 978-0-595-45425-9 (pbk)
ISBN: 978-0-595-69620-8 (cloth)
ISBN: 978-0-595-89738-4 (ebk)

Printed in the United States of America

Sing to me of the woman, Muse,
The woman of twists and turns
Driven time and again off course ... (or so she thought)
Many cities of men and spirits she saw
And learned their minds,
Many pains she suffered, heartsick on the open sea,
Fighting to save her life and bring her people home....
Launch out on her story, Muse, daughter of Zeus,
Start from where you will—sing for our time too.

Adapted from Homer's *The Odyssey*
Translated by Robert Fagles

This book is dedicated to those of you whose journeys have taken you into places of darkness, confusion and loneliness. May you find in these pages a degree of comfort, perhaps healing, and affirmation.

From my heart,

Michele

Note from the Author

This symbol means that Mare is having a dream or vision experience. The spiral indicates a going-within. All of these experiences are from the author's actual dream journals and memories.

Contents

Acknowledgments xi

Book One, Part One 1

1   New Year's Eve 1996 3

2   A Loose Thread 8

3   Emerson District High School 12

4   Dualities 17

5   The Ties That Bind 22

6   House Under Siege 27

7   Day Breaks 35

8   Those First Contractions 45

9   Headlines 49

10   A River in Egypt 54

11   Monkey Business 68

12   Media Appearances 78

13   The Dirt 85

14   First Kisses 91

15   Pairs 97

16   Home 102

17   Slavery and Innocence 107

18   Fallout 117

19   Spring Buds Break Through 126

20   The River and Mare 140

21   Spirals 147

22   The Start of School—September 1997 155

23   Hearing the Music 167

24   Polygraph 176

25   Disasters: Natural and Otherwise 185

26   Punishment, Revenge or Justice 195

Part Two 215

27   From the Soil, Seeds Sprout 217

28   Confinements and Repression 244

29   Releases 274

30   The Waves of Inner Life 302

31   Longing and Disclosure 311

32   Magic and the Power of Words 333

33   Motifs—By Land and Sea 341

34   When the Student is Ready, the Teacher Appears 344

35   Intuition and Contact 348

36   Stuff the Cat into the Box, Honey—and Keep Paddling 361

37   The Goddess, the Bear, the Tree, and the Dragon 369

38   Secret Places and the Spirits Who Reside There 382

39   Affirmation vs. Judgment 402

40   Winter Solstice 409

Questions for Discussion 413

Works Cited 415

Acknowledgments

I have much to be grateful for. I appreciate my parents and the rest of my family for their demonstration of unconditional love, morality and generosity of spirit. I am thankful for my incredible son—who goes by the name Cody in this story—and that other smiley, beaming creature he hangs around with. You are a constant source of learning and joy for me. Thank you for your heart. I love you all. My brother's perseverance, courage and ultimate honesty were inspiring. I am grateful for the lessons I learned from his experiences.

I thank Pete for his "teachings" and gifts. I appreciate all the other real "teachers-in-disguise" in Babylon, particularly Walt, Kate, Nate and his family, Danielle, Roni, Jane, Roger, Tristan, and especially Sophie—still one of my dearest friends. I have grown because of my contact with each of you. My love to Miriam, Edith, Joel, Derek, Nan and the gang from "Emerson." You are some of the best folks in the world! I thank the community of "Babylon"—for providing a womb for my development. I am grateful not only for your compassion towards my family, but also for the lack of it, because I know sometimes it was out of your reach.

I acknowledge the members of my Babylon writer's group, particularly Jason (an absolutely incredible writer) and Mike (also a talented scribe). Your early input helped me to launch this story. Curt, your feedback and encouragement were critical in the revision of this book! You rock! Nancy, your patience and wisdom were wonderful. I'd also like to thank "Sophie," Kathryn, Jean, Dorthe, Elizabeth, Sally, Linda, Karen, Margaret, Deborah, Edna, Sara, Michelle, Teresa, Lynn, Mandell, Liz, Colorado Heidi, my aunt and dear friend Lisa, and my many students. Ananda, you are wise beyond your years. Thank you! I want to take this opportunity to thank PSI Seminars (particularly Denver!). I set many a goal in your classes, and the support/coaching was great! Two films that helped to validate my belief that people are ready for a shift in consciousness were *The Secret* and *What the Bleep Do We Know*. I am grateful for them, because it makes these things easier to talk about. I appreciate everyone from Denver PLD Teams 30 and 40 and Michelle Fournier, PSI 7 Class 401, WLS C-90 for their support, the folks from *A Celebration of Miracles*, and the Mile Hi Church community (particularly Dr. Roger & Rev. Cynthia) and my SOM classes for their friendship, encouragement and assistance in the writing process. Robert Moss, words cannot express my gratitude for everything you have given and shared! Author Dan Millman gave me some great advice on my query. Other teachers, friends and authors I honor are: Hank Wesselman, Roger Smith, Mark Shearon, Tim O'Kelley, Todd Campbell (who asked *when exactly*), Robert Fritz, Alex Haley, Kay Cordell Whitaker, Laurie Cabot, Peter Gabriel, Jean Houston, JZ Knight and the Ram. There were many others … Oprah … Maya … Joseph Campbell … Homer …

In addition, I am indebted to Elizabeth Bishop for her guidance in the publishing process. Without you I might still be looking for an agent and wondering when this book would be in the public's hands. Thank you for your friendship, wisdom and generosity.

Mark—you are a wonder man—I couldn't have done this without you! Thank you for the sacrifices you have made for this and me, and thank you for loving me as I am!

Gratefully,

Michele

Book One

Part One

1

New Year's Eve 1996
Lumen Home, Babylon, Maine

"Enlightenment consists not merely in the seeing of luminous shapes and visions, but in making the darkness visible."

~Carl Jung~

"I can't stand it any longer! We have got to do something about that stench!" Mare Lumen pleaded with her husband. "It is horrible. Cody and I are going to pass out from the fumes pretty soon. It can't be healthy for a person to breathe in this every day."

In late fall, Mare and Pete had heard rustling and squeaks in the living room chimney. Not long after, when the chill of early winter began to seep through the drafty nooks of their 1907 farmhouse, they noticed the odor.

Inactive and untouched for years, the fireplace chimney was now—apparently—the burial site for some animal. A squirrel, they suspected, trying to find a warm and safe winter haven, had made the shaft his home. Some days the smell was stronger and more offensive than others.

The couple tried to ignore it at first, hoping it would go away.

Pete thought for a moment and nodded. "You're right. Seth said he'd be here in an hour. I doubt this was his idea of a fun New Year's Eve, but we can't put this off any longer. We need to do something." He began clearing the area. "Seth'll help. That's what friends are for, right?"

"That's what family is for," Mare added.

The lower opening to the shaft was blocked and had been for years. Pete removed the television from the hearth, as they had been using the space for an entertainment center. He looked up into the chute. Grabbing his electric screwdriver, he took out the metal sheet used to close off the chimney, which kept the warm air in and unwelcome rascals out. By the time Seth arrived, Pete was ready with gloves, a garbage bag, and tools in hand.

"Do you want to get up there and pry it out, or do you want to shovel the squirrel into the bag?" Pete asked.

"Don't matter to me—I'll scrape it out, I guess," his brother-in-law said.

Seth reached up into the chimney and pried open the flue. It was rusted, so he had to bang it out, forcefully. When the damper gate opened, everything that had piled up onto it for years came pouring down in a shower of tree branches, fur and squirrel carcasses. A pungent cloud of dust scattered throughout the room and hung there heavily. Mare picked up one year-old Cody, coughing, and ran into the kitchen.

"Holy shit!" Pete sputtered. "I guess we didn't know what we were getting ourselves into."

The two men poked around and shoveled out the remains. Not one, but four squirrels had been dislodged. In various stages of decomposition, some had been there for at least five, maybe ten years, though one looked very recent. Pete lifted it between his two gloved fingers and examined its stiff frame. Its little claws were clenched into fists near its throat. The odor was strong. "MAN, that is GROSS!" he said, gagging.

"Anything else up there?"

"Let's see," Seth said, reaching his gloved arm up into the duct and rummaging around. Two more of the unfortunate creatures dropped down and lay at Seth's feet. Seth tried to grab one by the brittle tail but it came off in his hand. "God, do these reek!" He waved his hand in front of his nose. "Shovel away. I hope you've got something to drink, because I'm sure as hell going to need one after this."

Pete brushed the ashes and fur off the bricks into a dust pan, while Mare began vacuuming. Seth opened the sliding glass door to clear the air. A frigid wave swept through the room.

When they were finished cleaning, Pete and Seth eyed each other in disgust.

"That was nasty," Seth said. "I'm covered in shit. I need a shower."

"Go ahead, man, you first."

Seth pulled out the sides of his shirt and glanced down. "I don't think I'm going to want to put these back on. You got something I can change into?"

Mare opened the lid of the washer. Cody, always the helper, toddled over to his mother and mimicked her as she moved clothes from the washer to the dryer. She gave him a few small items and he dutifully threw them into the machine. "Thank you!" she praised him, and he grinned proudly. She pressed "Start," and the dryer began rumbling.

Mare carried Cody to Daddy for a kiss.

"Nigh, Daah."

"Night, Cody!" Pete tickled him and kissed him on the cheek. The child's face erupted into a giggling smile.

"Night, Code-ster," his uncle Seth said, as he came down the stairs. The child waddled over and hugged his uncle's legs. Seth scooped him up and gave him a hug.

As Cody walk-crawled up the steps, Mare followed closely behind the tyke—her arms outstretched, guiding and steadying him since he had only in the last month begun to amble upright on his own. She ran some water and plopped him into the bathtub. Holding onto his back so he wouldn't slide, she poured water gently over his head and scrubbed some shampoo into his hair. Meanwhile, Cody grabbed palmfuls of water and squeezed them. When he was finished swatting at clumps of bubbles, Mare carefully pulled him out, quickly wrapped him in a soft towel, and sat on the toilet lid with him on her lap. She enveloped him in her arms for a second layer of warmth and protection, and snuggled with him for a few minutes. It was part of their bath-time ritual.

Mare stood up and carried him to his room. Cody, clean and drowsy from the warm bath, reached his arms into the air so his mother could pull some pajamas over his head and tuck him into his crib. They sat in the rocking chair while Mare read to him, and then with the familiar sound of his mother's voice singing his favorite lullabies, the one-year-old drifted off peacefully. Mare tip-toed out of Cody's room and went down to stoke the fire in the wood-stove.

On the way, Mare peeked into the kitchen. Pete was pouring what appeared to be a second round of shots and the two men, each in their late twenties, were talking about computers, one of their favorite subjects.

"It's freezing in here. I'm closing the door," Mare told them and started walking. "It's got to be below zero." She slid the door shut and shivered.

Pete came up from behind and wrapped his arms around her. "I'll stoke the fire," he said.

"Thanks." Mare turned around, tucked her hands into her neck, and burrowed into her husband's chest.

A yawn escaped Mare's lips. She squinted to see the clock.

Pete stepped back from his wife. "You're not going to fall asleep on us, are you?"

"I don't know if I'm going to make it to midnight." She shuffled over to the sink and ran herself a cold glass of water.

"Aw, come on, Mare; it's only a couple hours!" her husband said, nudging into her playfully and wrapping his arms around her waist.

He planted a smooch on his wife's neck and added with a bit of a slur, "Drrink with us; it's New Year's Eve. Tell her, Seth!"

Her brother, Seth, was sitting on the island's countertop, feet dangling and kicking the drawers below. "Yeah, don't be a wuss! It's only New Year's once a year. Help us put this crappy year behind us."

Mare regarded her brother sympathetically. *You have had a difficult time of it, haven't you?* She thought to herself. "Okay, but I need to finish the laundry first."

She grabbed the laundry basket and moved into the living room. Mare Lumen's celebration was more casual than in previous years. While her husband and brother did shots in the kitchen, she sat on the sofa with the laundry basket and started folding, her mind drifting back to her brother's comment. For Seth, the last few years *had* been riddled by small and larger-scale catastrophes.

Earlier that year a fire had gutted his house—in which he lived alone. It had taken several months before he was able to move back into his little cabin on Waldo Road. Some local teenage friends had helped with the restoration, but it was a slow process. Fortunately, Seth was not at home when the fire sparked. He owned an outdoor adventure business and had taken a group of young people on a weekend ski trip to Sunday River. He arrived home to a closed road and firefighters trying to contain the blaze.

The items Seth missed most were hundreds of pictures and an antique sewing machine that his great grandmother had left for him when she died. He used it to repair much of his camping gear, which was constantly being abused by his enthusiastic campers. The physical evidence of the fire had all but vanished now, but there was a lingering sadness in Seth, who believed himself cursed by bad luck. Mare worried that it was a self-fulfilling prophecy.

Mare matched a few last socks from the bottom of the laundry basket. She hated pairing socks. In fact, she kept a small, but blossoming pile of mate-less socks in one corner of her bedroom, ready to be thrown away or matched as soon as *all* the laundry was done. Somehow it never happened; a new pile always sprouted like a field of dandelions as soon as she finished the last load each week.

When Mare had put the clean clothes away, she went back to the kitchen where the two men were trading high school football memories and laughing foolishly.

"You going to have a drink with us now?" Seth asked her.

"Yeah, I guess so. I'll stay up a while longer, but I don't want to stay up until midnight." *Hmmm?* She looked at the shot glasses. The thought of the liquor going down her throat sent a shudder down Mare's spine. She wrinkled her nose in hesitation.

"I'll have one glass with you, but then I'm hitting the sack. Cody'll be waking up at five or six—if not before—so I need to get some rest. No vodka for me." She reached for a bottle of Merlot.

"As I was saying …" Pete continued, "Ah … what was I going to say? Oh ya, Mare—you wouldn't believe what a hard hitter your brother was in high school! Whenever we would scrimmage during practice and they'd hand off the ball to me, I always ran like hell, in a direction away from him! I knew Seth would hit me with everything he had. He was fast too!"

She nodded and sipped her wine. She had to chuckle. They seemed to have transported back to an earlier, simpler period in their lives. Seth and Pete had been friends for a long time, since they were in elementary school. As a child, Pete lived only three houses from the Mahonia family, and the boys would get together almost daily to play baseball or to shoot slingshots in the field behind Pete's house.

Whenever Pete talked about his football days, his face would fill with light. She had always been fond of "little Petey," but it wasn't until both of them had graduated with bachelor's degrees that they had bumped into one another and started dating. Seth was surprised when his old buddy and his older sister got engaged; yet Mare could tell he *was* pleased about it.

She smiled and sent a silent New Year's wish to her husband—*I hope this year, your new business becomes all you've dreamed it will be!*

It was 10:30 when Mare gulped down the last few drops of wine. "Goodnight, guys! Happy New Year to you!" She leaned over to Pete, and he gave her a sloppy, heartfelt kiss. Then she headed upstairs.

Before she went to bed, Mare peeked in on Cody first. Leaning over the crib rail, she whispered, "I love you, son. Happy New Year to you, too." As she drew the blanket up around his neck, protectively, and placed a gentle hand upon his back, she marveled at his peacefulness. His features were so smooth, and light, and innocent. *I could sit here and watch him forever,* she thought. *He's so calm and beautiful.* Looking at her son, Mare felt peaceful too. *Perhaps this will be a good year,* she concluded, reassured. *If you remain well and happy, Cody, it won't be too bad, will it?*

2

A Loose Thread

"When one tugs at a single thing in Nature, he finds it hitched to the rest of the Universe."

~John Muir~

The first two weeks of January passed uneventfully.

Then the telephone rang.

It rang a second time.

Pete didn't look up from his desktop, but his brow wrinkled—as it often did when he was distracted or tense. "Mare—you gonna get that?" he shouted.

"I'm right in the middle of something," his wife yelled back as she dropped a diaper full of poop into the garbage pail next to the changing table. "There's a phone on your desk—can't you do it?"

He saved his work on the computer and picked up the phone, "Hello."

"Hi, Pete."

"Seth! How's it going, buddy?"

"Not so great," Seth managed to get out.

"Oh-oh. Now what?" Pete was somewhat accustomed to these sorts of announcements, but he wondered what new calamity Seth had gotten himself into.

"Remember New Year's? How we closed the door on the old year and looked forward to a better one; well, we should have just kept our friggin' mouths shut!"

"Why? What's going on?" Pete asked, with growing impatience.

Seth paused momentarily as if Pete wasn't going to believe it. "Someone broke into my house."

"What! … You're kidding!"

"I wish I was.… What is it with me? Just when things start to come together, something else goes wrong."

"What'd they take? How did they get in? Do you have any idea who did it?"

Having overheard bits and pieces of the conversation, Mare was now beside Pete, trying to figure out what the hell was going on. Whatever it was, it didn't sound good. "Peete?" she beseeched in a whisper. He held up his palm.

"It happened last night between seven and eight," Seth said. "I was running a Sportsmen's Club meeting. When I came home, the door going from my garage to my house had been opened—with a crow bar, by the looks of it. Man, my heart just took a plunge as soon as I saw that. I couldn't believe it. They took my video game system and some games, my camcorder, and they apparently tried to unhook my CD player, but Grandpa must have spooked them when he came to plow the driveway."

"Holy shit, Seth! That's terrible. Did they get your laptop?" Pete asked.

Mare began tugging on Pete's sleeve, "What's going on?" she demanded to know.

Pete covered the receiver and whispered, "Someone broke in."

"Oh, god," she said, squeezing her hand over her temples.

"What'dya say, Seth?" Pete interrupted.

"I said, no—they didn't get my computer. Fortunately, I took *that* to the meeting."

"So you think it was more than one person, huh?"

"I looked out back. There are two sets of footprints."

"Do you think it was Sammy?" Pete asked him.

"Most likely. But I haven't seen him since that incident last summer."

"Did you call the police yet?"

"Yah—last night. They sent a detective over to check it out and ask me questions. He was pretty cool about it. I gave him Sam Hazzard's name and some of the other kids who hang around here. I can't figure out who would've helped him though … He does hang around with Chris a lot." Seth pondered that possibility for a moment, but he didn't like where it led him. "Naw, Chris wouldn't do that to me."

Chris Gibb had been a good friend of Seth's in the past few years, but when he got into high school, he didn't come around as much.

Seth was all the more afraid that if he pulled on that strand too hard, it would direct him back to Chris's brother, Nate. He couldn't bear the thought of that. The eighth grader had helped Seth rebuild his house after the fire. The two were close friends. Seth often took the kid to football games and on skiing trips. Nate even begged Seth to buy him a snowboard and promised to work on the house to help pay for it.... Nate wouldn't help to steal from him. Would he?

"You gonna be okay?" Pete asked in concern.

"I guess so. I'll just be relieved when I get my stuff back and this is settled."

"Well, I'm sure once they track Hazzard down, they'll get the answers they need," Pete assured him. From his voice, it was clear that Seth felt betrayed, stabbed in the back by kids he had been trying to help.

Seth agreed, but was still worried. "He'll try to cause trouble. Sammy's made threats before."

"Let him try," Pete said. "He doesn't have much of a reputation around here. That little puke already has a criminal record, doesn't he?"

"I suppose you're right. The whole thing just sucks."

"Yep, it does that all right. Hang in there, Seth! How much worse could it get? Let us know if there is any news."

"I will. Thanks. Talk to you later."

"Bye, Seth."

Pete hung up the phone and leaned on the edge of his desk.

He looked over at Mare, who was sitting on the old, brown loveseat. She was hugging her knees loosely and watching him look at her, her light brown hair brushing over her pant-legs.

"Will it ever end?"

Pete sighed and shrugged. "Did you know about Sammy stealing Seth's credit card last summer?"

"He was one of his camp counselors, right? Stole his credit card and ordered a skateboard with it?" She was reaching back into her memory. "Didn't the company call Seth at work to tell him the item was out of stock?"

"Right. He didn't have a clue until then."

Though Seth had a steady job as a manager at the L.L. Bean catalogue center, he had also started an outdoor adventure camp for adolescent boys a few summers before. He used his home—a log cabin bordering the woods—as a base camp; one larger room had been furnished with several bunk beds. He had a big trampoline in his back yard. During the weeks Seth ran his camp, he would take the kids all over the state of Maine: canoeing, mountain biking, camping, and white water rafting. He taught them the life skills he thought would help them become confident and independent men, things like outdoor survival and how to cook in the wild. He read them Jack London stories around the campfire. He always chose activities he believed they would enjoy and benefit from, and he included them in the decision making process. The boys seemed to love the experience.

"Did he ever press charges against Sammy?" Mare asked her husband.

"He filed a police report, but I don't think they ever did much about it."

"So does he think it was Sammy who broke in this time?"

"Hard to say … he might be connected." Pete said as she shuffled through some papers on his desk.

As she listened to Pete fill in the details, she thought to herself—it doesn't sound so bad. Just a simple burglary, right? But, no matter how Mare looked at it, a lingering fear clung to her. She shivered and turned around to touch the glass of the bay window behind her. The cold was leaking in. Outside the sun was beginning to fade. She sighed and leaned her chin on the sofa back. Her eyes shut, she crossed her arms over them, and her vision went black.

She scanned the darkness, absent-mindedly noticing spots of colored light at first. Then she settled into the void and opened her eyes. She could hardly see at first.

As her vision adjusted, she could make out people. She was surrounded by them. They were so close she could have touched them with the slightest effort. She thought about tapping the one nearest to her, but then she realized that his eyes were closed. An artificial face had been painted over his cheeks and eyes like a doll's, and, though he was quite capable of opening them, he had not. She scanned the group. Each face was painted as though trying to hide the truth … and all eyes were closed. She touched her own face, wondering if she looked the same. One woman shivered and clutched herself as if cold or scared. Suddenly Mare could sense her loneliness, the penetrating loneliness that each person felt....

She heard Pete get up and go into the kitchen. She opened her eyes and blinked a few times in the diffused light of a pale winter day. A gray cat sat under the maple. His tail twitched and flicked against the ground. Then he gathered himself up tightly with hungry eyes directed at a tiny chickadee perched on a snowy limb.

3

Emerson District High School
(Population: 1200 students)

Remain always strong in your own song as the world appears to turn around you.

~Kay Cordell Whitaker, from The Reluctant Shaman~

The next morning Mare dropped off Cody across the street at Nana Margaret's and headed toward school. She passed through the quaint Main Street with its tiny specialized shops: a pharmacy, the gift shop, a men's clothing store, the chiropractor's office where Mare attempted to remedy her frequent headaches, and the hardware store. The women's clothing store had closed its doors after Wal-Mart moved in on Route 26. Many of the stores were empty, but locals involved in the economic development of Babylon had filled the barren windows with artwork to make the street seem livelier for those who walked or drove by. Mare squinted to look at some of these paintings as she waited for the car in front of her to move. As a teenager, she had cruised these same roads with friends, looking for something to do in this small town and waiting for someone else they knew to drive by.

When Mare arrived at her alma mater and current workplace, she turned into the driveway that led through an extensive parking area. The town of Babylon had about 6,000 residents; however, students were bussed in from up to a half-hour away. Eight towns in the county had banded together to pool their resources and provide the best education they could for their children.

She liked many things about this small town, even though she had never planned to return here after college.

At twenty-nine, Mare Lumen brought a diverse background to her students, many of whom had never been out of the state of Maine. "Seriously!?" They would ask in wide-eyed fascination, whenever she'd tell them she'd been a first lieutenant in the Army National Guard. "You don't look like an Army officer. I thought all women in the military had to be UGly," the guys would say, cracking up at themselves.

Mare would just grin and shake her head. "You boys have such a narrow view of women ... but ah—thank you ... for the compliment." Then she fired a benign smile at her—now blushing—students. "I got a full R.O.T.C. scholarship in college. I figured if we had to have a military, then we needed good leaders. I used to laugh when recruiters called in high school. I did not consider myself the military type, but later, it made sense."

In addition to the army, there had been the insurance sales job and finally grad school. She never imagined she would end up teaching at her old high school. Her former teachers and coaches were now her peers. If Mare and Pete hadn't discovered in their last month at grad school that Mare was pregnant, the two would probably be in Juneau, Alaska, now. But they decided they did not want to raise a baby so far from family. When the position opened at Emerson, it was fate.

Over the course of her time at Emerson, Mare developed a close bond with a core group of colleagues whose friendship and wisdom would help her in getting over some of the dark days that lay ahead. It was not age that linked them. It was a common intellectual curiosity and energy. Some of them were older, but seemed more spirited and interesting than some of the younger ones.

Mare and Kate Maguire were the two youngest teachers in the English Department at Emerson; both were in their second year of teaching, though Mare was older by about six years.

The two women had become quite close and usually spent their twenty-minute lunch together, talking about the ups and downs of teaching, the local gossip, literature, and, of course, relationships. On occasion, Walt, their department chair, would join them. He was much older, late fifties or early sixties, Mare guessed, based upon the white-hair and mostly bald head, though he never would tell his age or birthday. He was a real wit and always got them laughing with some snide remark. When Walt was around they always swore lavishly.

"How the hell are you, Mare?" Walt asked as he waltzed through the door to Mare's room.

"I'm pretty friggin' well, Walt, and you?" she volleyed back.

"Can't complain; well, I could but who the hell would listen! Ha. Hah! Where's Kate?"

"Dunno," Mare shrugged.

Just then Miss Maguire sauntered in carrying a bag of microwave popcorn and offering her hellos. With her long blond hair and blue eyes, she was a favorite among the single male teachers and hormones-raging male students. Male staffers used to joke with Walt about his unique talent for hiring the best looking teachers.

Mare tried to set Kate up with a couple of single male friends, but nothing ever seemed to work out beyond the first date or two. Mare could never figure out why Kate had gone so long without a boyfriend, as smart and pretty as she was.

Walt munched on his usual—baby carrots, yogurt, and a salad. He always claimed to be on a diet, but Mare could never understand why, since he was rather spindly-legged and scrawny in her opinion.

"Got to stay fit and lean to keep your wife happy, huh?" Mare ribbed him.

Walt simply glared flatly and smirked, digging around in his fruit salad. "Something like that."

Mare got the impression it was a topic Walt did not want to discuss, even in jest. How unusual, she thought—he never talks about her.

Time to change the subject, she sensed. "Someone broke into my brother's house yesterday."

"Really?" Kate asked. She had met Seth on a few occasions.

"It's always something with Seth," Mare said after filling her in on the details. "It's par for the course."

Aware that her colleague had been struggling through the publication process, Mare asked Kate how the school newspaper was coming.

"Not well! I'm frustrated. I spend so much time trying to get the whole thing laid out. None of the kids in my Journalism class know how to use the software, so I end up doing it all myself … and I am really just learning."

"Don't worry about it too much, Kate. It'll come together. It doesn't have to be perfect," Walt said.

"Sure. That's easy for you to say. When you were the advisor, everything was top-notch; I've seen copies of the *Eagle Journal* that you put out. That's tough to compete with. I'm under a lot of pressure here to produce a newspaper of quality," she grinned.

"Well, it helps when you've owned and operated a real newspaper."

"I didn't know you had your own paper, Walt!" Mare said. Kate just nodded.

He just sat there beaming. "I sure as hell had a lot of fun with that job," he reflected calmly.

"Tell us about it, Walt. I smell a story," Mare insisted.

"Oh, god, there are so many," he responded.

After reminiscing about some of his more colorful experiences, Mare said, "Wow, that's quite a tale."

"I've got a million of 'em." Walt crumbled up the remains of his lunch into the brown bag, and tossed it boldly across the table and into the trashcan. "Yes!"

"Have a good day, you two," Mare said, "See you tonight at T'ai Chi class, Kate. You're coming, right?"

"Yup, I'll be there. See you later, Walt."

The trio parted ways.

The smell of microwave popcorn lingered into third period.

*   *   *   *

"Before we start reading let's look at the book's cover, class. What can you speculate about the book by examining the front? Why do you think Maya Angelou chose *I Know Why the Caged Bird Sings* for a title?"

Mare Lumen waited. Gradually a few hands poked into the air.

"Is she talking literally about birds? Is this book about birds?" she teased.

"Of course not!" It was Aaron. "She means … umm … she's talking about people who feel trapped. Maybe they are looking for ways to get away from some type of confinement, find a reason to celebrate?"

"Okay, you may be on to something here. How many of you have ever felt trapped at some point in your life?" Mare gazed around at her students, whose desks were arranged in a circular pattern. Numerous hands rose.

Jamie said, "I don't think it's about celebrating so much as it is about being able to express yourself."

"Okaay. What do you mean *express* yourself? Don't we all express ourselves every day? People *talk* all the time," Mare mused.

"No, not that kind of expression," Stan said. "Not an ordinary sort of expression. Something more … important. Personal."

Mare probed further. "Are you trying to tell me that we don't *normally* express ourselves in this way, that most of our conversations are ordinary?" She gasped, playfully astonished.

A general nod undulated through the room.

"Let's just check something out. How many of you … feel that people in your life *really* know who you are?" she questioned them.

She waited.

Not one hand.

"Interesting," she said. "How can this be?"

Nikki, who didn't normally say much, quietly offered her conclusion. "Maybe because a lot of us don't really know who we are. So it's kind of hard to communicate it."

Mare put her finger to her lip and nodded, pleased. "Perfect, I hadn't really considered that aspect of it. So, we're on a journey of discovering our truth and expressing it? Great observation."

"Mrs. Lumen, look at the dedication page," Nikki continued. "It says, 'This book is dedicated to my son, Guy Johnson, and all the strong black birds of promise who defy the odds and gods and sing their songs.' That seems to connect in with the title."

"Yes! Very good. How many of you would like to discover—and sing—*your* song?"

All twenty-five fifteen-year-old hands reached skyward.

"Me, too," Mare told them.

4

Dualities

"There is balance in all things. If something is taken away, an equal amount will be returned to you. It is only the form in which it returns that is unknown."

~Thomas D. Willhite~

"You want to push hands, Mare?" Roger asked.

"Absolutely," she said.

Mare stood face to face with her T'ai Chi instructor, palms up and outstretched. The group spent the majority of the class polishing certain aspects of "the form" as far as they had learned, but when Roger shifted the focus to playing push hands, Mare always jumped at the chance. A guidance counselor at the high school, Roger was calm, peaceful, almost passive in some respects, but Mare had seen what he could do if someone approached him aggressively. Put the attacker on his butt! With just a subtle shift of his body, Roger could use the aggressor's force against him with powerful results. It looked so effortless. She wanted to learn.

The object was to get the other person off balance through pushing. But pushing was a misnomer really. It was more a game of absorbing and redirecting the opponent's energy. Roger, who had studied this ancient martial art for sixteen years, insisted they begin and follow through the process slowly and gently, so no one would get hurt. Mare, Pete, and Kate had been studying with Roger once a week for about two months now and were halfway through *the form*.

Mare waited patiently for Roger to initiate contact; he had encouraged her to pay attention to yielding, since she had a tendency towards aggressive movement and intent. Mare inhaled deeply and tried to focus totally on the movement of her arms and legs and on the nature of her breathing.

During the first months of her martial art study, Mare struggled constantly with the concept of non-resistance. Often, she would chuckle to herself how much her T'ai Chi practice mirrored her daily life. A proactive go-getter, Mare believed in creating the circumstances of life. She refused to wait passively for things to progress her way. In T'ai Chi, however, one needed balance and awareness of yin/yang principles.

"Ease up, Mare. Too heavy. Don't force your way in." Roger said calmly.

"Relax, but stay filled with energy. Don't fight it. Don't push." Over the months these simple instructions piled up in her consciousness. "Respond to the energy coming at you. Be aware of your energy and where it's going. Notice any tension and release it." The reminders dripped slowly into her mind like a warm April mist encouraging the residual winter ice to melt away and spring grasses to grow.

Yet even in these proddings to calm and prepare herself, there was an intensity and an urgency in the message. Mare was determined—and in her determination to influence the ways things were—she remained bound. She could not allow herself to be or appear weak. Frustration would mount in her when she observed Kate or some other classmate holding limp hands through the form. *Look alive,* she would think to herself. *Some of these people carry themselves like victims.*

"It's funny when I push hands with you and Pete," Roger said. "You are very different in your approaches. One's weakness is the other's strength."

He was right. In push hands, as in life, Mare and Pete were like yin and yang. Opposites. Mare made decisions quickly and then confidently plunged in. Pete hesitated trying to figure things out. He wanted to discover how to best approach the situation. Usually he would simply try to escape from Roger's attacks from a defensive standpoint. Pete even referred to himself as "a deer in headlights" when it came to pushing hands. Often he felt paralyzed. In the meantime, almost inevitably, Roger would work his way into Pete's space and topple him while he was still trying to decide how to respond.

Not Mare. She recognized this trap and resolved to keep her instructor from worming his way in and pushing her off balance. She would go on the offensive.

"Nice, Mare," Roger said. "You are well rooted and stable."

Their hands moved slowly, intertwining, and they would each shift their weight back and forth with any incoming force. Mare tried to work her way into Roger center of gravity.

She felt herself falling backwards.

"Unfortunately," Roger continued, "your grounding alone does not allow for flexibility and openness: essential ingredients in push hands," he smiled, "—and life."

Mare nodded in understanding, earnestly yearning to achieve that kind of fluid responsiveness.

"But you're doing much better," Roger continued, praising her on her progress. "Your shoulder has dropped significantly. You are learning to let go." He had noticed it during their first class together—one of Mare's shoulders was higher than the other. Roger expressed certainty that by focusing her awareness on her body, the spot would release and return to a natural state. Mare could not remember her shoulders ever being level with one another. She had two distinct memories of other people mentioning the phenomenon. Once was during her time as a cadet in the Army ROTC. A sergeant had come around the formation, while the soldiers were standing at attention, and instructed Mare to relax her shoulders. She was confused by the comment. He acted as if they were up around her ears. She felt relaxed enough—but she made an effort nonetheless. Unsatisfied, the sergeant circled behind her and forcibly pushed her shoulders down. They lowered a few inches. *Huh*, she thought. *Why couldn't I feel that?*

In recent months, Mare *had* become more conscious of her body. She wanted to grow in her understanding and awareness of herself. Walking down the halls at school, she'd intentionally drop her shoulders and, in the beginning, the forced relaxation ironically caused discomfort. The muscles, so long retracted, began to stretch and elongate. They ached, but Mare just let her shoulders hang there until they loosened. Her push hands technique was also becoming more supple and responsive.

T'ai Chi had attracted her with its graceful motions and power. It looked like a peaceful dance of life. But it was the idea of energy flow within a person that truly called to Mare. "Chi," Roger called it. When Mare glided through the form, she could sense this life current pulsing gently through her body. She left each class thirsting for more.

On the first day of class, Roger explained the history and basic principles of T'ai Chi Chuan to his class.

"According to legend," he had said, "a Taoist monk came across a crane attempting to snatch up a snake. The snake, due to its flexibility, was able to avoid and ward off the talons and beak of the larger, more powerful bird. Amazingly, the bird was also able to avoid the snake's counterattacks. Impressed with the interchange between the two creatures, the monk devised the original thirteen movements of T'ai Chi embodying the principle of yielding to and redirecting energy to overcome force. Some say he dreamed of the movements after observing the creatures."

The same image inspired Mare. She could picture the scene in her mind. The snake writhing … yielding in such a way that the bird can't get hold of it.

"Let me tell you another story," he began tonight. "A T'ai Chi master held a bird in his hand to demonstrate the principal of yielding to his students. The man's hand, ever aware and sensitive to the bird's slightest moments, would yield to the force of each attempt the bird made to lift off. Because the bird could not push off with his feet, he could not fly away. Power was hidden in the yielding."

On the way home, Mare quizzed Pete, "Kate doesn't seem to be getting as much out of the class. Is it just me, or does she drag herself through the moves? Sometimes I see the way she holds herself and I want to shake her. Like she's only partly there with us. Half alive."

"I don't know. That's just the way she is. Didn't you say she was really busy trying to juggle her master's program with teaching?" Pete said. "Maybe she's just tired."

"Yeah, I suppose," Mare mumbled. "I hope that's it. I'd be surprised if she stuck with it much longer."

"I have a question for ya," Pete said. "Do you think Roger is gay?"

"Why do you ask that?" said Mare, a little surprised.

"His voice is so … gentle. He's just kind of passive."

"He's married and he has a teenage daughter. I think that's just part of his T'ai Chi attitude."

When they arrived at the house, Cody was still awake and the little blond tyke hustled over to see them. "Mum-ma!" he called, arms outstretched. While Mother and son hugged hello, Dad thanked Grammie and Grandpa Mahonia for watching Cody.

"No problem," Mare's father said.

"Yup. It sure is tough to spend time with *that* kid," Joan added. She had waited a long time for a grandchild (or at least *she* thought so) and had quickly taken on the task of spoiling her one and only grandson. Both grandparents had a special bond with the little golden child. "Can Grammie have a hug goodbye?" she asked with an ear-to-ear grin spanning her round face. Cody returned her generous smile and threw his arms around her.

"Goodnight, Cody," Grandpa said, leading the toddler through a high five. "We luv ya."

"Night, Mom and Dad!" Mare smiled. "Thanks for watching Cody. See you at Sunday dinner."

After Mare's parents were gone, Pete took a deep breath in, and said thoughtfully, "Cody's pretty lucky to have all of his grandparents nearby. That kid's got a lot of love surrounding him!" He glanced over admiringly at his son who was sitting on the floor looking at a book. "I never really knew my grandparents. All I remember about them is when Dad's father would make us ice cream sundaes in Pennsylvania. I didn't get to see them very much. And my other grandmother was always in Florida, like your Grammie Lex. I think having that much family around with aunts and uncles and cousins is really going to be great for Cody."

Mare agreed. "We've got a pretty good thing going here."

"I'm glad we decided to move back, for his sake, if nothing else."

The two embraced somewhat sideways and looked over at Cody who was now getting riled up, because Daddy was hogging Mommy's attention.

Mare pulled away and stretching her arms up into the air, yawned, "Okay, little buddy—let's go read some books and hit the sack."

5

The Ties That Bind

"We cannot live for ourselves alone. Our lives are connected by a thousand invisible threads, and along these sympathetic fibers, our actions run as causes and return to us as results."

~Herman Melville~

Interwoven strands. Clumped together here, and loosely connected there. Winding and sliding through countless loops and twists. Red, bulbous sauce poured unsparingly over the top with clusters of hamburger meat filling in any gaps. Cody surveyed his meal hungrily, probably wondering about the best strategy for tackling such an entree.

How do you teach a one-year-old to eat spaghetti? His mother wondered. *You don't. Just give him a utensil and let him have at it.* Boldly, the child planted the fork in the middle of his pasta pile and then lifted the jumble of pasty cords to his mouth. Before reaching its destination, all but one noodle fell off. Undaunted, he tried again, but with similar success. On his third attempt, he abandoned courtesy altogether and dug in with his hands—much to his grandmother's delight.

"There you go, sweetie," she said. "That's the way to do it!"

Everybody laughed as they watched their son-grandson-nephew come up with new and creative ways to adorn himself in spaghetti. Joan initiated these ritual Sunday dinners when Cody was born so she would have one guaranteed visit per week by her grandson, her three grown children and her daughters' husbands.

"This is delicious, Mom," Pete said. He always called his mother-in-law *Mom.* "It sure hits the spot!"

"Good, glad you like it," she thanked him, her thin lips pursed together contentedly.

"The cinnamon rolls are over-cooked though," her husband said.

"You always have to find at least one thing wrong with every meal, don't you, Rick!" she complained.

"Well, if we're going to get picky, the green beans are a little too crunchy for my liking," Seth teased his mother.

Joan scowled silently, until her grandson drew her attention again; she couldn't stay irritated while she was watching him.

"So, what's the deal with the break-in? Have the police called you back yet?" Mare's younger sister Cassie asked.

"No! Not yet. It's been three days. You'd think they would have called with something by now," Seth said.

"It takes time for these things," her husband Rob added. "I'm sure you'll hear some news this week."

But Seth couldn't let it go. "They must have gone over to Sammy's house by now. I wonder what they found. They would have to get a search warrant, I imagine."

"They probably questioned some other people too, to see if Sammy is the one responsible. Did you call your insurance company to file a claim yet?" Seth's mother asked. "You really should let them know what happened and what was taken."

"Don't worry about it, Mom! I'll take care of it," her only son barked in mild annoyance. "I've got it under control!"

"You know, Seth, you ought to have that engraved on your forehead as your own personal slogan," Mare taunted her brother.

Joan Mahonia had a way of nosing herself into her children's business—all in the name of trying to help. She was excessively organized and kept track of all the things her children needed to be reminded of. Mare could hear her mother's voice. *Don't forget about that bill. Make sure you do that before this date.* Seth only lived around the corner from his parents and he was often over borrowing tools and whatnot. Since he tended to procrastinate and forget about things, Mare knew her mother felt she needed to remind him about the electric drill-set. She could understand her brother's resistance to their mother's controlling behavior; she had also haggled with her over different things, especially as a teenager, but not quite to the degree her brother had. She had a feeling that Seth *wanted* to be more loving towards his mother; he just couldn't overcome whatever barriers were between them.

Their father, Rick Mahonia, also found himself frustrated by his son's attitude. In the weeks following the fire, Seth stayed with his parents, and although his mother and father *wanted* to help him and be there for him in his time of need, they found his independent and bull-headed ways to be almost more than they could tolerate. Somehow, they all survived.

Seth got up from the table and headed for the living room to watch a football game. The other two men soon followed.

Cody wobbled into the living room, trailing after them.

Joan chuckled as she watched her grandson. "It's almost time to try for baby number two, isn't it, Mare?" her mother asked.

"Yes, Mom, we need another baby to relieve Cody from infinite spoilage. We need to spread the pampering around!"

"I'll say!" Cassie said.

"Seriously, though," Mare paused, "we would like to start later this year." She pushed a fork around in the remaining sauce. "I'd like to have a baby in the late winter or early spring of next year." She got up and walked to the sink with her plate. "Cody would be just over two and I could stay home for six or eight weeks and then go back to school for a few months." Mare handed Joan another plate to rinse off and then Joan passed it along to Cassie, who loaded it into the dishwasher. "By the time summer vacation rolls around, the baby will be a little older and mobile, so we can spend some time outside."

"It's just like you to have it all planned out," her mother said. "It doesn't always happen as planned."

"I know, but that's the way I would like it to happen."

"What do you want this next time? A boy or a girl?" her sister asked.

"I've always wanted a boy and a girl. So, it's time for a girl. A little girl would really balance out our family." Mare dabbed a paper towel over her lips, and sat back down at the kitchen table. Soon after, her mother and sister joined her. "You know, I've been reading this book that tells you how to have a boy or girl. It's called *How to Choose the Sex of Your Baby.*"

Pete, having overheard his wife's comments, yelled in from the living room—"Yah, to have a girl I have to put on a dress before we do it. Hah!" Everyone howled with laughter.

"Very funny, Pete—*that* I'd like to see!" she rebutted, as the snickering subsided. "That's not quite how it works. I thought you twerps were watching the game?" Then, turning back to her mother and sister, she continued, "Anyway … it's a matter of timing mostly, they say. My understanding is that male sperm swim pretty fast, but they don't have much endurance. Female sperm are slower getting to the egg, but they live longer." She tried to explain the basics to them. Somewhat dubiously and with amusement, the other women listened. "So if I want a girl then I can increase my chances by having sex a day or two *before* I'm supposed to ovulate, because mostly female sperm will be left over by the time the egg arrives."

Joan's eyes bugged out and rolled back in her head. "Well, I think you're going to have another boy. Let's see what my string says." Joan got up and opened the utility drawer. After rummaging around a bit, she came up with a needle and thread. "Okay, hold out your hand."

"Not this old wives' tale again, Mom. Haven't we done this before?" Mare sighed, as she stuck out her left palm.

"Yes, but I forget what it said last time." She brushed the needle three times along the side of Mare's hand and then let it dangle over her daughter's open palm. If the needle swung in a circular fashion, the first child was predicted to be a girl. The string swung in a straight line. Boy.

"That's a safe bet, since Cody *is* a boy," Mare said playfully.

Again, Joan placed the needle against the side of her daughter's hand and when it was brought above the palm, again the needle swung in a straight line. She tried it a third time, but it didn't swing much at all. "Well, there you go. Two boys."

"What if you *do* get another boy?" Cassie asked.

"It doesn't matter *that* much. It's just a preference. The most important thing to me is that Cody have a sibling. Male or female. I don't want him to be an only child."

Cassie flipped absent-mindedly through the pages of a recent issue of *Soap Opera Digest*. "What about Margaret? Is she willing to watch another child, or will you have to find daycare for the next one?"

"She says she's ready to watch the next one when the time comes." She swiped her bangs out of her eyes. "We're so lucky to have someone in the family taking care of Cody during the day!"

"Yeah, especially a family member who lives right across the street," Cassie said.

"True. She's good with the baby too … but he doesn't get to spend any time with other children really. When he does see other kids, he has a ball. I would never want to deny him a playmate to grow up with."

The women sat quietly around the kitchen table for a moment.

Mare continued slowly, "But I would still like to have a girl—to watch her walk down the aisle on her wedding day on her father's arm." She sniffed in some air and blinked.

"There are just certain rituals you want to see your children go through, you know? Boys go through their rites of passage, as do girls, but they are different." She stood up and went to the cupboard for a chocolate chip cookie. "Pete can't wait to take Cody to the lake so he can teach him how to fish. He claims he would be just as happy to take a daughter fishing or to train her to replace the brakes on her car, but I know—he was pretty ecstatic in the delivery room when he found out he had a son to carry on the Lumen name. I love Cody, and I'm happy we had a boy. But now, I'd like a girl. I want to pass on what I've learned about being a woman. I want to show her how to be strong and proud and independent."

"Well, good luck. I don't know if I can handle another grandchild," Joan grinned, "I'll have to get an extension on my credit card! So many toys, so little time."

The three women laughed.

"And we're running out of space already; we'll have to build an addition on the house."

"Try it on me," Seth interrupted, unexpectedly. He had come in to get a beverage and wanted to know what he would have for children.

"Oo-kaay." Joan pulled the string to him and went through the same scenario. This time, the needle swung in two circular paths. "Two girls, Seth," she said with eyebrows raised.

"I'll trade with you, Mare—I'd rather have sons that I can take hunting and fishing."

"Too bad, brother. It doesn't work that way. Besides, you've got to find the woman first."

"You've got a point there," he said and went back in to watch the game.

"I'm surprised he wanted me to do that on him," Joan said, quietly.

So were his sisters. "I didn't know he ever wanted to have kids," Mare added.

After a moment's reflection, Joan said, "Well, did I tell you that there's a woman he works with at Bean's who has been over to his house a couple of times? She seems very interested. Her name is Hope, I think. She is divorced, or going through a divorce. Seth talks as though he likes her too. Who knows? He's only twenty-eight. Maybe he will settle down one day."

6

House Under Siege

Experience is a hard teacher, because she gives the test first, the lesson afterwards.

~Vernon Saunders' Law~

Sitting on the tattered loveseat with the receiver against her cheek, Mare tried to collect herself so that she could tell Pete. A thousand thoughts swirled through her mind.

It was Thursday evening, January 30, 1997, the night the Mahonia family's world began to crumble, when Mare received the phone call from her Dad.

"Mare? It's your father."

"Yeah, hi, Dad—what's up?" She didn't like his heavy tone.

"You better come over."

"What's the matter? What's going on?"

He paused, as though considering whether he wanted to disclose such information over the telephone. "Tell me," she insisted.

Her father took a long breath and then explained, "They caught the kids who broke into Seth's house."

"That's great!" She waited a moment, "—Isn't it?"

Again, he hesitated. "They told the police they did it because Seth molested them."

Her reaction was slow, confused at first. Then it built into a surging, "WHAT?! No! … You can't be serious!"

He was barely able to get the words out.

She knew it was bad.

"Yup. I'm afraid so. Can you and Pete come over? Seth is here." Mare had never heard her father's voice sound so small and faint.

"Sure," she answered. "We'll be right there."

She stayed on the sofa, ear to receiver, listening to the dial tone.

Her heart was thudding thick and hard against her chest. She recognized the feeling of panic that was invading her body. She'd had a similar physical response five years earlier on Lake Pennebago, where some family friends owned a cabin. It was the one place in the world where she felt completely relaxed. Reclined on the giant hammock, hands behind her head, Mare had been reflecting on her life up to that point. *I have been so lucky. My parents have stayed together and were kind to us; I've done well in school; I've had many friends. We never had much money, but we always had what we needed. The only person in my family to die has been my great-great grandmother, and she was a hundred years old.*

It can't last, she thought to herself. *Everyone has his share of misery and heartache. Sure, I've been hurt physically and emotionally, but nothing too serious. People have to die eventually. Bad things happen to just about everyone, don't they? I'm no different.*

That same night, as the solitary occupant of the cottage, she had alarming dreams of people trying to get into the place and unsettling notions that she could not shake for days. Though she could not explain it or make sense of it at the time, she was apprehensive. Something was coming for her.

Strangely, she had asked for it. She had made a request to the universe ... for a story. And now, it was about to begin. While in college, Mare had taken a Hemingway seminar and joined the class on a trip to the JFK Library in Boston to explore the Hemingway Library. Family and friends had reportedly donated nearly all of the known Hemingway memorabilia: photos, safari remnants and many pages of early drafts of his works. Mare felt an unexplainable kinship with Papa Hemingway. Flipping through the pictures and reading the alternative endings to *A Farewell to Arms*, Mare thought to herself, *I must remember to save certain things. People may want them some day.* She paused. A second voice in Mare's head said, *What are you talking about? Where did that come from?* She wasn't consciously planning to write. But the first voice insisted ... she was supposed to write, to contribute somehow through her writing. That seed eventually grew into a compelling desire. Mare waited for a story idea to become clear. For years she combed through her own life looking for some scraps that she could pull together, but it was no use. There wasn't much to tell. Her early years had only been an uneventful preparation for something larger.

The day came when she looked towards the sky with outstretched arms and said, "Give me a story worth writing about!"

Be careful what you ask for.

Only now—five years later, and in the months and years following the phone call, would she begin to put the pieces together. Her life was going to change significantly and permanently.

Mare was about to be cast out of *the garden*, and her strange journey would not end until her initiation was complete.

She was not completely unprepared for it. Seth's choice to work with and help young people left him vulnerable to such attacks. In the beginning, Mare and her parents even questioned Seth's lifestyle. It was not within the *normal* range of adult existence. Each had interrogated Seth in his early to mid-twenties, to make sure that everything was on the up and up. "You have to be careful; some people will make assumptions about a situation like this," they would warn him.

"I don't give a crap what people think. These guys are my friends!" he said, with emphasis on *friends*. "Don't worry about it. It's my life," he assured them. "It doesn't affect you." He even appeared hurt by the insinuation. After that, the three backed off. Everything seemed okay. All of the kids appeared happy and healthy. In fact, it looked like they loved being over at Seth's place. Many parents had called or written to say what a positive impact Seth had had on their sons' lives. Recently, a mother of one of Mare's students had complimented her brother for the role model he was, and because her son could always count on Seth. *Maybe they had been watching too much Oprah,* as Seth suggested years before when his sister questioned him about his close friendship with a teenager.

After years of trying to analyze the situation, Mare had almost given up. He remained very private about his inner feelings, at least to members of his family. He dated a few women, but Seth was timid around strangers. Mare had even fixed Seth up with Kate, so the four could double date, and that went well, but her brother never followed up after their first meeting. Seth wanted to ask Kate to go fishing with him once—since they both were competent with fly rods. Kate never did get a call.

Mare believed that Seth felt less awkward around teenagers, because he was not yet ready to give up the adolescent way of life with football games, mountain biking, and practical jokes. He liked being able to help them out, enjoyed feeling needed and appreciated. He was like a big brother to them.

Those kids are saying Seth touched them so that they don't get in trouble for the robbery, Mare decided. *How could they do that to him after all that he's done for them? Greedy little bastards! They rob Seth and then try to destroy his life. I don't think they realize how serious an accusation like this is!*

"PEETE?" Mare yelled, trying to determine his location in the house.

"YEAH? I'm upstairs in the bedroom."

"Come 'ere, please; I need to tell you something."

On the way over to the Mahonia house, Mare and Pete sat in penetrating silence while their son jabbered nonsensically. "I'd love to be you, right now, Cody—oblivious to anything but what's going on in front of you," Pete said.

They pulled into the driveway. Pete opened his door. Mare willed herself to move, but she felt like she had swallowed an anchor that didn't want to budge.

She unclipped Cody from his car seat and carried him up the front steps. Pete followed. They walked through the mudroom and opened the door to the kitchen. No one greeted them. Mare scanned the living room from right to left, as she set Cody down on the carpet. Joan was planted in the rocking chair. Rick sat stiffly on the sofa. Seth was hunched over in the recliner; his eyes red and cheeks tear-stained. In fact, the couple could see that all three had been crying.

But Seth—he looked like a broken man, destroyed. If Mare hadn't recognized the room and its occupants, she could have mistaken the dense atmosphere for a memorial service.

She cleared her throat and searched for words, while removing Cody's hat, mittens and coat. Standing up straight and tall, she tried to inject some levity and confidence into her family's mood.

"The police have got to see through this little scheme of theirs. They admitted to breaking into the house, for cryin' out loud!" She was breathing hard, but quietly. "It was Sammy, right? Who was with him?" She waited for someone to respond. Seth could not. He just shook his head gravely.

Very upset, her mother said, "Apparently it was Sammy and Chris who stole the stuff. Then, the police found everything at Chris and Nate Gibb's house."

"So, Nate was in on the scheme as well?"

Tears poured down Seth's cheeks.

Pete questioned, "How did you find all this out?"

"Detective Potter came over to Seth's house with a search warrant."

"What?! They are taking these teenagers seriously? After all that's happened?" Mare just couldn't believe this was happening to her brother. "Exactly what did he say? Did he act like he believed Seth or the kids?" She looked at Seth.

He somehow composed himself enough to say, "I was in the backyard shoveling out a path when the detective came around back. I asked him what was up. I assumed he came over to tell me some news about the break in." He paused to try to steady his voice, and then continued with difficulty. "He showed me a search warrant. I asked him why he needed to search my house and he just glared at me and said, 'I think you know.' I assured him I had no idea." Seth began to cry again. She could not remember every seeing her brother cry. Not as an adult anyway.

"There's objectivity for you," Mare said, sarcastically. "Shouldn't he investigate the claims first before he makes assumptions like that?"

"Did they destroy the place?" Pete asked.

"Yes, but I didn't see that until I got back from the police station. They brought me in for questioning …"

Mare was fuming, "You met with them without a lawyer? They should have given you a chance to get a lawyer!"

"I know; they did—but I figured I didn't have anything to hide."

"Oh, god …" Mare rubbed her hands over her eyes, backing off, "This is a nightmare; this isn't happening."

Joan helped Cody get out his toys. She obviously wanted some distraction from this conversation. Pete got up and poured himself a glass of water. Cassie and Rob arrived.

"When I got home everything was turned upside down. A list was on the table of what they had taken."

Cassie asked, "Did they find anything?"

"No. They just took all the bedding and my mattress, a container of Vaseline, a book—*Getting Past No*—and pictures and videotapes. Also, my laptop computer."

"That book is mine," Pete hollered, "why the hell did they take that; it's for business sales?"

"I know, it's stupid," Seth sighed. "They found nothing concrete, so they are looking for anything."

"But everyone has those things," Mare said more gently.

"I know," said Seth. "As far as the bedding goes, I guess they're planning to run some tests."

Silence returned, while all this information sank in. Cody, who had been playing with some cars, began to bawl. His grandmother went over and hugged him. "He must think this tension is very strange."

Seth got up from the recliner and went to the bathroom sink to splash some cold water onto his burning eyes. He closed the door behind him. Afterwards, Pete and Rob talked in the kitchen, and Rick joined them.

Cassie quietly interrogated her mother about what she had missed. "Did anyone ask him if it was true?"

"Yes, we did," Joan said sadly. "He assures us it isn't. But we did find out something."

"What?" Mare asked with dread. She exchanged a worried glance with her younger sister.

Joan hesitated, but then plunged in. "The police chief asked Seth if he was gay—and he said yes." Then she began to cry again.

Mare's insides collapsed—her mother's words were a battering ram that had, with one strike, broken down the doors to her medieval fortress. Some unknown force had suddenly sucked all the air from the room. She couldn't breathe; she floundered internally like a drowning fish. *Focus*, she told herself. *Inhale slowly; you can get a little oxygen in those lungs.*

If Seth had made such a statement under different circumstances, it would have had a much less severe effect on Mare. It wasn't the simple mention that he was gay that skewered her senses. She had a number of friends—past and present—whose sexual preferences were as such. The problem was that Seth had chosen to tell the police BEFORE he had told anyone else that he had come to such a conclusion. An admitted gay man who is hanging out, almost exclusively, with teenage boys! A gay man who apparently has not had any homosexual relationships. What implications would this have? What would people think?

Yet an even more insistent question rang heavily in her thoughts—*if this is true—if he has kept this from us—what else might be true?*

"He told the police that he was gay?" Cassie repeated, herself gasping, uncertain if her ears were working properly. Unlike the rest of Mare's family, Cassie and Rob were Jehovah's Witnesses. Mare assumed that, like many Christian groups, Cassie's religion considered homosexuality an abomination.

"Yes," Joan said a second time. Then she continued with great difficulty, tears streaming from her eyes, "Chief Rolf asked him if he had ever had ..." Joan choked a bit on her words, "anal intercourse, and Seth said no. Then the chief asked, 'How do you know you are gay then,' 'I just know I am,' Seth said."

Their mother paused for a minute and composed herself as well as she could. "I don't care if he is gay," she burst out. "Some people are just born that way; that's what I believe. They can't help it. But why did he tell the police? He didn't have to tell Rolf that."

Mare weakly followed up, "Why did he?"

"He said he wanted to tell the truth. He didn't want them to think he was hiding anything." Her crying intensified, and Cassie went over and put her arms around her. She looked at Mare.

Mare shook off her own fears and the whirl of thoughts in her head and said, "Seth needs a lawyer! We'll have to find him one tomorrow. I guess it's stupid to ask if you are going to work, huh, Mom?"

"Are you kidding? What if this is in the paper tomorrow? Even if it isn't— I'm a wreck. I can't go into school like this." Joan was a teacher's aide in the Special Education department. "You're not going in, are you?" she asked Mare.

"I think so. Nothing is certain yet. I'm not going to hide my head in shame and let these kids win. I intend to work," Mare said.

The family talked and milled around bleakly for a while longer, until it was time for Cody to go to sleep. While Pete got their son ready to go, Mare went over to her brother. He was still red-eyed and sobbing silently. He thought his life was over.

"It'll be okay, Seth," she tried to assure him gently.

"Mare," he moaned in anguish, "even if we are able to prove that the accusations are untrue, NO ONE is going to let their child go on a camping trip with a man who's been accused of molesting children! All those years of building up a reputable business—they're gone. In one day, all my dreams are destroyed."

"You may still be able to keep your business. You don't know what the next few months and years will bring. You may come out of this okay," Mare said helplessly. She was one year older than Seth. This was her brother. They shared a bond despite their different paths in life. Mare couldn't help but experience his anguish.

Though they had been close as children, they had never been overly affectionate towards one another. Now she put her arms around him and hugged him. He squeezed her back and broke down again, his chest heaving, his body leaning heavily upon hers. "I know you are a good person, Seth," she told him. "I know that. Try to hang in there; the truth will set you free." She released him and they both swiped sleeves across watery eyes. "We'll call you tomorrow."

"I'm going to stay here with Mom and Dad tonight. I just can't stay alone," he spoke softly and unsteadily, like a frightened child.

More painful embraces were exchanged with other family members. Then Mare, Pete and Cody went home.

Mare did not sleep much that night. The handful of bees she had swallowed when her father called would not stop looping in somersaults and banging into the sides of her belly. Without the means to escape ... or was it the desire ... they would make the location their home for some time to come.

7

Day Breaks

The word "crisis" is from the Greek, meaning "a moment to decide." The recurrent moments of crisis and decision when understood, are growth junctures, points of initiation which mark a release from one state of being and a growth into the next.

~Jill Purce~

A dull throbbing woke up Mare. Was it in her head … her stomach … her heart … or was it external? The bell to the Universalist Church situated below Mare's house at the bottom of the hill began to toll—six times—about the same moment that Mare was trying to distinguish the physical and emotional sensations in her body. Usually the chiming comforted her; she had belonged to that congregation as a child—but today, rather than having a harmonious effect, it only added to the monstrous cacophony in her mind. *What was going to happen next? What should she do? What would people think? How would this affect her family? The community?*

The phone rang.

Pete rolled over, and Mare threw back the sheets quickly, so she could answer it before it woke Cody. It was usually not good when the phone rang early in the morning or in the middle of the night.

"Hello," she answered cautiously.

"Well, it's not in the newspaper—yet, at least."

"Good morning, Mother. That's a good thing."

She started in again. "You aren't seriously planning to go to work this morning, are you, Mare?"

"Mom, I told you yesterday. I'm going to try to—yes."

"Your father and I really don't think you should, Mare. This is going to be a difficult day for all of us; you can't expect to make it through a day of school on top of it. Don't do this to yourself."

"I know that you and Dad are concerned, but I'll be okay. Nothing is for certain. This whole thing might blow over in the next few days. I'm not going to hide out at home. What would I do with myself?" She swung the phone cord so that it hit the wall. "I'd rather stay busy. I'm not really prepared to have a sub in for me either. Besides, if this thing does blow, I'll want to take days off later. I need to save my personal days."

Her father took hold of the phone from his wife. "Come on, Mare. I really don't think it's a good idea for you to go in," his voice was firm but full of restrained emotion. Mare considered the idea for a moment; she was torn. However, the image of sitting around the house all day—stewing—was not something she felt she could handle now.

"I'll tell you what. I am going in—but, if I feel I can't continue … I'll get someone to cover my classes for me. Okay?"

"I still think it's a bad idea." He paused. "At least give us a call when you get back then, will you?"

"Sure, Dad. I'll call you or come over as soon as I get home. How's Seth holding up?"

"Not too well. He's still in his room, but I don't think he's slept much."

"Did any of us? All right. Well, say bye to Mom and try to stay positive."

"Yup," his voice cracked. "We'll try. Love ya. Bye."

"Bye. Love you, too." Her heart was heavy. *I can't stand to see my family like this*, Mare thought painfully.

"What was that about?" Pete yawned, Cody in his arms. The child looked at his mom and smiled, a bit cautiously, trying to read his mother's state of mind.

"Good morning, honey." She hugged her son and kissed him sentimentally on the check. "It's not in the paper this morning, and Mom and Dad don't think I should go in to school."

"I don't think you should either," Pete sympathized. "It's crazy."

"You're planning to work today. What's the difference?"

"For one, I work in a very small office. I don't have to interact with people in person all day like you do."

Mare sighed. "You may be right, but I feel like I have to try."

She did try. After she dropped Cody off across the street at Nana Margaret's, she headed into school. Mare imagined what it would be like. *No one knows yet, why should it be any different?*

But it was different. Very different. *She* knew what was going on—and that was all that mattered. She couldn't get it off her mind. Of primary concern was when and how it was going to come out in the papers. Should she wait until the story breaks or should she go to the newspaper and ask to give Seth's side? How would the community react? Mare took a deep breath and held it for a moment. She turned off the ignition and grabbed her laptop bag. Here goes, she whispered.

It was much harder than she expected. As she walked through the halls, she felt like everyone knew. That everyone was looking at her differently. Yet, rationally, Mare knew that was not possible. She headed towards the teachers' mailboxes, and up ahead she saw Walt approaching from the opposite direction. I need to talk to him, she thought; he used to own a newspaper. He'll know how this works and what we should do.

"Walt." She tried to keep it short, because she knew what would happen. But it was too late. Despite her efforts to the contrary, tears welled up in her eyes. The halls were crowded with teenagers so she fought them, but they rained down her face. "I need … to talk," Mare barely managed to get out.

His serious look of concern told her he understood the gravity of whatever was going on. "Sure. Let's go up to my office." He asked no questions.

The journey was not easy. Mare tried to maintain some composure, as Walt gently but quickly guided her by the elbow to his office. She did not look up or around, but kept her head low. Walt peeked in his classroom on the way and instructed his students to read silently until he returned. "Is your classroom all set for now?" he asked Mare. She nodded. "I have a planning period."

When the door closed behind them, her repressed emotions broke through her fragilely constructed barricade. She sat down and began weeping loudly. Walt rested his hand on her shoulder a moment, then pulled up a chair and waited for her to speak.

"Remember how I told you that my brother's house had been broken into?" Her voice was not steady.

He acknowledged that he did. When she told him about the allegations against Seth, his mouth dropped open, his face contorted empathetically, and he responded with, "Oh my God! Mare, I am so sorry." Walt bent down and tried to console her with a hug. Her body shook in agony.

"It gets worse too."

"What?"

"He told the police that he was gay," she began to cry again. "Not a very good time to reveal your sexual identity."

"Of all the things …" He grimaced and shook his head in frustration. "How can I help?"

"I don't know, Walt. I don't know what to do. I feel like I should DO something," she admitted, her voice rising in strength now that she'd had a chance to release at little. "I'm really worried about Seth. I've never seen him this low. I hope he doesn't do anything stupid."

"Do you think he might?"

"He feels like he's losing everything that ever mattered to him: his business, his friends … I'm afraid for him."

"Well, ask him about it. Sometimes I think that's the best thing to do. At any rate, you can't control what your brother does; you have to take care of yourself and the rest of your family."

"I know you're right. I just feel so powerless." She turned her watery brown eyes over at Walt.

He nodded in agreement. "Sometimes there is nothing you can do. Who knows how this'll play out?"

"What about the Press, Walt? It's going to come out in the papers. How long do you think it will be before they get hold of the story?"

"Jesus," he spouted, as if he had forgotten about that angle of it. "I don't know. It depends. They have access to the criminal logs. Has he been charged with anything yet?"

"No. They're investigating the case."

"Then, it probably won't be in there until they do that. Do you think they'll have enough to follow through with charges?"

"I don't know. I'm wondering if I should prepare a statement. I would like to be ready if and when this thing does blow. Wouldn't it be better if the press heard both sides of the story? … If people were aware that these accusations are a direct result of the break in? Well, won't the presentation make a difference? First impressions are important; you know that, Walt. If the papers take the angle of the thieves being caught … it doesn't take a brain surgeon to make the connection between the robbery and the allegations. They accused Seth so they could divert attention from their own actions."

"Hmmm …" Walt shook his head and pondered the implications.

"But on the other hand, I certainly don't want to alert them to a story if there's a possibility that there won't be one. You know what I mean?"

Walt nodded.

"What should I do, Walt? Out of anyone, I thought you would know."

"I seriously doubt it will be in the paper until he's officially charged. Then a reporter will find it in the logs. I wouldn't give the press *anything* until that happens. You might want to work on a statement in the meantime though, since you have no idea when he might be charged." He extended a box of tissues toward her.

"I just can't believe this is happening."

"It's awful, Mare. I know. But you'll come through this though, kid; I know you will." He looked at her with compassion, and then added, "Look, you can't stay here today."

"I know," Mare relented. "I'm sure I look a mess." There was a bathroom in the office and she went in to see how bad her eyes looked. They were red and puffy. "You're right. I look and feel terrible. I'm going to have to go home. I can't face my students right now."

"Go home. Work on a statement and make sure your brother gets a good lawyer. He's going to need a damn good one. Can your family afford to hire a decent lawyer?"

Mare rocked her head, and rolled her eyes in frustration. Her hands cupped her forehead. "Not really. I don't know how we're going to do that."

"Well, you need to find a way to hire a decent one. These are very serious charges."

"I know," Mare replied downheartedly. "I'll have to do some checking around about that. I guess I'd better get going. Can you make the arrangements for my classes to be covered?"

"Absolutely. Don't worry at all about it."

"Thanks, Walt. I appreciate it."

"Don't mention it. It's the least I can do." He embraced her again and added, "If there is anything I can do—anything at all—don't hesitate to ask."

"Thanks, I will."

"Take your time. Your family needs you now."

On the way out of the building, she passed the music teacher. The woman saw Mare's tears and asked with concern if she was okay. Mare shook her head no, but she couldn't stop and elaborate. She didn't even slow down. "But I will be," she added quietly. *Soon enough, you'll know. You'll all know.*

Driving aimlessly around town, Mare thought about what should happen next. She wondered how she could find her brother a good lawyer. Then she remembered Dan. *He specializes in business law, but he must know someone who can take a case like this.*

Once at home, Mare picked up the phone and dialed Dan's number. Although she was a little nervous about talking to him regarding the situation, when the desk clerk answered she confidently asked for him.

"Hello, Mare—what can I do for you," he asked pleasantly.

"Hi, Dan. I need your help with a personal problem."

"Sure. How can I be of assistance?"

"My brother is in trouble," her voice quivered and broke. "Some serious allegations have been raised against him—he's innocent, if that makes any difference to you." Was that *her* voice giggling awkwardly? "But he's going to need a good lawyer. He's already spoken to the police once without one." She was emotional and ran her words together quickly. Dan had to interrupt her.

"My partner, Hank, is the assistant DA—so I can't listen to any of the specifics of your brother's case; however, sounds like your brother needs a criminal attorney. I know of a few who are well respected in the area. Perhaps one of them can help Seth. Vance D'Angelo is one of the best around. I'd give him a call."

He gave her the number and other names, and she thanked him sincerely for his help.

"Good luck," Dan said in parting, and with genuine concern he added, "I hope everything works out for your family."

"Thank you. So do I."

The forces within Mare were mobilizing for battle. After she had taken care of the lawyer issue, she sat down at her desk to begin composing a statement to the newspaper. She looked at the blank screen, and then plopped her head down on the desk, tears flowing again. Her head hurt so much. She struggled to rally her troops. *The last thing I want to do now is write this, but they have to know the truth. Start moving, soldier! If Seth is charged they will need both perspectives.* She began typing.

Most of you are aware now of the accusations against my brother, Seth. My family and I would like you to know about the other side of his story. We know how difficult it is to believe that a young person would lie about something like this, but the allegations against him are false. The young people involved here have clear motives for fabricating this story.

You should know that a number of teenagers are being investigated on federal larceny charges. Seth's house was burglarized recently and over $2600 worth of property was stolen; this property has since been found in the possession of these teenagers. Their allegations are an attempt to create a smoke screen around the real issue. In addition, a credit card was stolen and used by one of these individuals last spring.

Seth has been a model member of our community and is being done a great injustice here. Eventually the truth will be known; in the meantime, he has the full support of his family.

Mare Lumen

When Mare was finished, she reread the draft and saved it. *Maybe I'll add more to it later or change some of it, but for now I have something.*

Friday morning was frigid. A gust of wind thrashed against Mare's cheek as she got out of her car and headed with difficulty back to work. She popped into the principal's office to apprise him of the situation. If her brother should be charged and she had to leave at a moment's notice, Todd needed to know. However, Principal Tyler was already aware of the investigation; the police had been pulling students into the station during school hours to question them about the case. The same thing was happening at the Middle School, he told her. Todd had not, though, been aware that Seth was Mare's brother, and expressed his sympathy and support to her.

Mare also stopped into Roger's cubbie and shared the news with him. He would be one to talk to troubled students about this. Perhaps having a more complete picture could help. She told him of her brother's announcement to the police chief, and Roger's calm reaction surprised her.

"Just because your brother is gay doesn't mean he's more likely to abuse children," he assured her.

Later in the week, during the middle of her last class, the Crisis Team Coordinator pulled her out of her classroom with a pained look. "Has my brother been arrested?" Mare asked hesitantly.

"No, but we wanted to talk about what might happen when or if he is." He placed a steady hand on her shoulder. "We have a list of teachers set up to cover for you in the event that you need to leave quickly or if you are feeling overwhelmed by it all and need someone to replace you for a period or two. We want to support you however we can."

"Wow, thank you." Trying to hold back her emotions, Mare was both relieved by the support structure and worried about the need to use it.

"Also, the staff really needs to be made aware of this case. Talk is already starting among students. Many are being pulled out of classes to speak to the police. Some are struggling emotionally with it. We need to inform faculty and make sure that the talk doesn't get out of control. Teachers will need to direct such students to guidance. We're having a faculty meeting today after school. We thought you should know. You may be more comfortable not attending. I recommend you head home right after school."

Mare nodded, swallowing. Now all ninety-eight of her colleagues would know, and then—her mind trailed ahead a few days—the people *they* know. Word spreads quickly in small towns, whether the word is true or false.

"Is there anything you want us to say, in particular, to the staff?"

Mare thought for a moment, and said with some effort, "Well, you might tell people I prefer not to talk about it right now. You might ask them not to bring up the issue during school, because I'm having a hard time holding it together as it is."

"Sure thing ... You okay?" he asked, when he saw her eyes try to harden against the water welling up in them again.

She shrugged sadly, nodded weakly, and headed towards the bathroom.

Minutes before the bell rang to mark the completion of the school day, Mare wrote down the reading assignment on the board. The intercom blared the afternoon announcements as students filed into corridors. "There will be an emergency faculty meeting in the conference room at 2:20. All staff, please attend." Mare shuddered as she bid her last few students farewell and began packing up some work to take home. An urgency drove her on. She wanted to leave quickly. She didn't want anyone to see her. Threading her arms through a warm parka, and pulling a composed expression over her face, she closed her classroom door behind her and locked it. *Just a little way to go*, she thought. The halls were crowded. She quickly moved through. "Hey, Mare." Two colleagues benignly joked as they passed her. "Where you goin'? We've got a faculty meeting. What, are ya skippin?"

"Oohh, I don't need to go to that one," she responded awkwardly, forcing a weak smile. "You'll find out when you get there." She didn't stop walking, nor did she slow down. She squinted as she went out the door, less on account of the bright February sun, than because she was trying to squeeze away the swelling moisture from her eyes.

That evening, the family gathered at Mare and Pete's, trying to find some collective comfort, to escape the waiting and the fearful dread, and to find some outlet for the anger. Pete's dad, Dr. John Lumen, stopped on his way back from the office to see how everyone was doing. Since he lived across the street, he noticed all the cars in the driveway. Hugging his daughter-in-law first, he made his rounds for Mare's family, expressing support. Something in his confident, professional, doctor-manner made them feel better. He could see that Joan and Rick Mahonia were in poor condition at the moment. Rick was quiet and withdrawn. Joan, feeling threatened, could not stop railing against the accusers. She was driven to protect her only son.

"Did Mare tell you yet?" she probed him. "One of Seth's summer campers heard about the break-in and called Seth with information to help him. Seth told his lawyer all this, and he checked it out. It should help Seth's case. Look, here's what Seth's lawyer sent to the DA."

The doctor perused the letter. The campers told the lawyer that Chris Gibb was thinking about stealing some stuff from Seth, knowing that the insurance company would reimburse him like they did after the fire.

Dr. Lumen nodded his head in agreement that this seemed important. He handled them almost as he would his worried patients, giving his personal prognosis of the situation and sharing a sense of personal strength. He took some time out especially to talk to Seth, since he had known him from the time his son and Seth were childhood friends. They had fished, hunted and skied together over the years.

Joan and Mare, who both worked in the school district, discussed the implications of the faculty meetings to notify staff. "I don't want to go in knowing everyone's going to be looking at me wondering if it's all true," Joan said. She worked at the middle school where some of the accusers attended. "People usually assume the worst."

"I know; it's going to be very strange. I just hope no one asks me about it, because I don't know what I'll say," Mare added.

Then she added, "I finished the press release. I wrote about the break-in and all that, so—if it comes out—people will have the whole story." She handed her mother a copy.

"Are you signing your name to it, Mare?" Joan asked as she scanned through its contents.

"Course, why not?"

"There is no reason to drag the Lumen name into it," Joan insisted.

Dr. John Lumen stepped into the conversation, clearing his throat. "It's okay with us. Go ahead, Mare. Sign off on it; we're behind you. We can handle it."

Mare smiled at her father-in-law gratefully. She thought for a moment about his position in the community. She also considered her young sister-in-law who was still in high school. "Thanks, Pop. I appreciate that."

Joan came around again. "The Mahonia name is already implicated. Why don't you let Dad or I sign it. They are our sentiments as well. Then you can keep the Lumens out of it for awhile."

"Well," John readied himself to head home—it was getting late. "It's up to you, dear; do what you need to do." He gave her another squeeze around the shoulders and bid his goodbye to the rest.

Pete walked his dad back out to his truck, and the two talked for a while longer in private.

Mare looked around the room. The remaining family was silent. All were looking into the glass window of the burning woodstove. Some eyes were filled with tears. She turned her gaze there as well, and watched the flames licking up from between the logs, spreading across the varying surfaces of the wood, turning everything in its path black.

8

Those First Contractions

… Life and death are one, even as the river and the sea are one.

~Khalil Gibran's The Prophet

Thirteen was Mare's favorite number. She had been born on the 13th, and considered it lucky. Without superstition she looked forward to Friday the 13th, too.

This day was not Friday, however; it was Thursday.

Exactly thirty years ago—on February 13th, 1967—her mother was pushing her out of the birth canal. According to Joan, Mare's delivery had been a fast and relatively easy one. It was on this day, precisely thirty years ago, Mare Elizabeth Mahonia, was evicted from that safe, warm womb, and thrust— blinking in confusion—as all babies are, into the bright light of her new world.

Mare's second delivery and birth would not be so smooth or uneventful. This one would take several years, and for it, she would have to act as her own midwife. In a sense, she would also be responsible for her own conception.

Before a soul can be born, it must experience death. That is the rule of the universe.

She did not know the journey that lay before her any more than that little babe whom the doctor had lifted away from her mother. All the babe could do was let out that hair-raising, but healthy cry of discomfort and confusion that signifies new life.

Like any other day she went to work on her birthday. As she was struggling to lead her students through an adequate, but brief discussion of Maya Angelou's rape in the book they were studying, her brother was being arrested for molesting adolescent boys.

Half of a chocolate birthday cake with vanilla icing remained on her desk at the end of class. One of her students had made it for her. Mare was wrapping it, when she was handed a little pink memo note. It read simpy, "Your mom says call home, as soon as possible."

Mare sat down at a student desk nearby, dropped her arms onto the surface, and lowered her forehead to her arms. She tightened her eyes shut, rubbed her head from side to side against her arms, and took a deep breath. When she opened her eyes, she was looking at the tiled floor, scuffed and smudged from winter wear. Her eyes followed the line of floor tiles laid out in an alternating black and white pattern. She didn't want to go any further. She didn't want to start what she knew was about to begin.

For a few moments today she had almost forgotten. But the heavy weight returned, like some invisible monkey hanging off her shoulders. A little wild, it didn't often sit still. It would swing back and forth, threatening to unbalance her. These last few weeks, it seemed a constant companion. It had started small, but it was growing. She could rarely shake it off for long.

Rather than go home, Mare decided to head straight for her parents' house before picking up Cody. She didn't have to be told the news. She knew.

"Your father is on his way home from work now. We have to raise bail. Between Seth's house and ours, we should be able to do it," she noted nervously, not looking at her daughter.

"What are the charges? Do you know what they're charging him with?"

"I'm not sure. Seth wasn't exactly sure. He said all the charges had names like—Class B sexual assault, unlawful sexual contact, etc. He wasn't sure what those meant exactly or which kids said what."

"Here's your father now," she added, gathering some paperwork and hustling to put her coat on. Mare walked out with her mother and greeted her dad who opened the car door and stood up on the inside of it.

"Hey, Mare. Happy 30th birthday, hon," he said softly, but with the unspoken, futile understanding that it would not be a pleasant one. He gave her shoulders a squeeze. She looked at him sorrowfully. *My poor gentle father*, she thought as she watched him in silent pain. *Tough on the outside, sensitive on the inside.* Mare heard an abrupt sniffle come from her mother. Both of them were suffering, but her mother was more proactive and verbal about it. *Mom is slightly better equipped to handle this.*

"We'll come over for cake after supper and after we get this straightened out," Joan said.

"Okay." It was difficult to look forward to a family gathering under the circumstances.

Mare stopped at the house to pick up two copies of the press release she had written and dropped them off at the local and regional newspaper offices. She had added the bit they had learned from the other young man. At least the public will know about the break-in, she figured. Her mother had already signed the document. Then she headed to the Lumen house to get Cody.

It couldn't have been a more depressing birthday party. A death in the family would not have been any more painful. Except for Cassie and Rob, who avoided birthdays because of their religion, all of the immediate family was there. Mare, Pete and Cody. Her parents, Joan and Rick. Her grandparents, Sylvia and Harold. Seth had also been released on bail—thanks to his parents—and he was there with his friend from work, Hope.

Mare greeted each of them at the door. They tried to smile at her and wish her a happy birthday. Each one hugged her as they entered her home. Or was it she who hugged them? She wasn't sure. Everyone was in need of some comfort. Mare didn't know how to provide it, though she wanted to.

For most of the evening, everyone sat in the living room, looking down at the floor. Faces were pink with tear-stains … men and women alike, old and young, except Cody. The one-year-old played with some blocks part of the time and then wandered from person to person, trying to get someone to smile at him.

"Tomorrow, for sure," Joan broke a period of silence. "It will be in the papers for sure now…. How are we ever going to walk down the streets again, even if he's found not guilty? How are we ever going to get through this," she choked and began sobbing.

Mare was searching in agony for words, trying to find a way to throw off the mood of oppression, when Pete broke the stillness.

"We will get through this," he said with determination and emphasis on the *will*. "I've lost a family once already, and I'm not about to lose this one." Mare gently reached out to cup Pete's bicep between her hands in subtle pride and reassurance, and hung on. His face spoke of his firm resolve. *Nobody's going to fuck with my family*, it said. Pete's parents had gone through a particularly ugly divorce when he was ten. His family had fallen apart in his mind, and it left him devastated.

The Lumen divorce was also hard on Seth. Pete had been like a brother to him in those early years, and then when Seth was twelve Pete had to move away with his mother to a neighboring town. To the Mahonias, Pete was family, beyond being a son-in-law. They had known him since he was a child. He was more like an actual son to Mare's parents than a son-in-law. Since before his marriage to their daughter he had called them "Mom" and "Dad." He was strong for them all now, and they leaned on his confidence gratefully. It was as if the family had become one, a single heavy being that had fallen over onto the floor. Pete stubbornly lifted the body back to standing. Somehow he reminded them of their need for dignity and unity.

It was a gift.

He swiped a sleeve across his swollen eyes. "We *will* get through this."

Several other nods followed Mare's. Then Joan got up and hugged Pete.

"It's somebody's birthday here, isn't it?" Pete reminded everyone. He grabbed Mare by the shoulders briskly and shook her a little.

She smiled at him, and Pete led everyone out to the kitchen.

"Your twenties are over, Mare. What'cha gonna wish for in your thirties?" her husband asked as she leaned toward the tiny flames. Her brow wrinkled together in slightly more light-hearted thought. She pressed her lips together, with more gather on the right side, while she paused to ponder. Her single dimple shone through the half grin. *What will my thirties bring?*

"I know," she turned and looked at Pete, who was waiting. "Can't tell though."

She filled her lungs with air, and forced it out over the thirty candles with one to grow on. She didn't miss a one.

"She's told no lies this year," her grandfather teased.

9

Headlines

"Sometimes humans beg for battles to be taken away from them, not realizing that only in struggling with shadows is the Light made manifest."

~W. Michael Gear~

"Mummaa!!" Cody jabbered from his crib. Mare snapped out of bed quickly—habitually, and hustled to Cody's room. She didn't like to let him cry out for long. He was standing against the rail with his arms reaching at her. His mother lifted him out over the edge and snuggled with him as she walked downstairs. After warming a bottle for her one-year-old son, Mare leaned her hand and weight for a moment on the counter-top. Placing Cody on his feet, she looked towards the front door. At some cellular level, semi-consciously, she hardened herself, and then marched tentatively to the door. She turned the handle and pulled, then pushed open the thin glass door on the outside, letting in a frosty surge of February air. The door pushed aside a bright blue, plastic bundle. Inside was *The Lewiston Daily Bugle*. It was delivered like this to thousands of homes in Western Maine. What would the front page have to say today? She braced herself.

Mare ripped open the plastic bag and started unrolling the newspaper. Pete came down the stairs rubbing his eyes, just as his wife's troubled face crumbled into tears.

"Oh my god!" she cried. "Oh my god."

"What does it say, Mare?"

Shaking her head in denial, she turned the paper around so her husband could read the headline. In large black letters at the top of the front page, he read ...

"Babylon Man Charged with Raping Boy." Below the headline was a close-up picture of her brother's face and just below that—in big, bold letters—was his name—Seth Mahonia.

Raping a boy!

Images aggressively transposed themselves onto her consciousness. She fought against them. She could not bear such visions. She could not believe them. Her brother. Forcing himself onto ... into ... some young child. It was horrific. All of her long-held assumptions crashed down onto her head. Rapist! Rapists are ... are ... monsters! Her eyes stung and her head became dizzy.

My brother is not a monster! Invisible teeth bit into her heart, stabbing, devouring.

Seth would never knowingly hurt anyone.

The paper was still clutched between her thumb and forefingers. She grabbed it and shook it. "A rapist? Nooo!" She sobbed loud and long.

Gradually, her voice softened which shifted the "no" into a mode of pleading. Her brain had a moment to look around. In that pause, her mind raced into the thousands of homes that would see this. She held her hands up like a crossing guard would to cars. Stop. Go no further. No, people! It isn't so. He's not a rapist. He didn't force some kid into having sex with him. He didn't. He couldn't.

But she couldn't go into each of those homes. She couldn't stop the story from spreading; the perceptions were already forming. She could not prevent the infection. People she had known nearly all of her life, and strangers she had never met, would now have that image carved into their brains. He had been sentenced publicly before he even understood what the charges were against him.

"I've got to call Seth."

She dialed her parents' phone number, assuming her brother would be there. Her mother was crying when she answered the phone. With caller ID, Joan knew it was Mare. After a few minutes, when Mare asked for Seth, Joan told her that he had slept at his own house last night. Rick, upon seeing the paper and reading the article, had only a moment ago rushed down to Seth's house to break the news to him. He was bringing the paper with him.

Mare quickly bid her mother goodbye and punched in Seth's number. He picked up the phone after two rings.

"Is Dad there yet?" Mare asked him.

"No. Why?" he asked fearfully. "Wait … He just pulled in. Here he is now."

"Have you seen the paper yet?"

"No, I haven't. What does it …? Hold on."

Seth carried his portable phone with him to open the door for his dad. Mare could visualize the scene in her head, even though she wasn't there. She heard them speak briefly. Then heard the sound of a ruffling newspaper.

In the next instant, just as her brother's eyes met with the headline, she heard a cry of the deepest anguish her ears had ever heard. "What! They think I raped a kid! What! No!" His voice screamed out in horror, shock and incredible pain. "They think I raped someone?! Oh my god. Oh my god. It's all over. My life is over," he sobbed again and again.

The extremity of his reaction and the obvious surprise of it gave her a few seconds of comfort. *I knew it! It isn't true*, she thought. *He wouldn't be reacting like this. It was too authentic, too raw.* Seth, too, was clearly appalled by the accusation.

It can't be true. Whatever else he may have done, Mare concluded, *he hadn't forced himself on anyone.* He hadn't physically injured anyone. She felt sure of that. That was something to be glad of. Whatever other people thought, she felt certain it stopped at least at that point. Seth was not a violent man. He wasn't, couldn't ever be, as bad as those *other* people.

But her brother's wailing snagged Mare's attention and brought it back to the phone. She was sure her father must be holding back his own tears. Her family was in such pain. She wanted to help them, to protect them all: her brother, her mother, her father … but there was little she could offer now, except her love and strength.

Mare began to grieve into the phone with them, though no ear was pressed against the other end to hear her. Seth had already dropped it.

"We'll get through this," she heard her dad try to console him. "Get up." She pictured her father, Rick, holding on to his only son by the arm, trying to pull him off the floor where he had slumped. He was trying to get Seth to stop crying. He hated to see people cry, especially a man.

Pete had his hand on Mare's back in an effort to bolster her also.

After a few moments, Seth got back on the phone and quietly told his sister that he had to go. "I'll talk to you later," he assured her.

She heard the dial-tone buzzing into her ear, leaned her elbows onto the counter, and with the phone still in her hand, pressed it against her forehead. Her eyelids dropped, but tears still found their way through the outlines. She rapped the receiver against her head slowly. One time. Two times. Then left it there. Her cheek was damp and the salty liquid was dripping across the curves and into the cracks of the telephone. When she abruptly opened her eyes again, they were facing that abominable headline. She let her gaze drift out of focus, so the sharp lettering of the newsprint faded into a haze of black and white formlessness. She did not want to open her sight again, but she was drawn to learn what the rest of the article said. For a moment, she was frozen—both pulled toward and repelled by her own questions.

"It isn't true," she told her husband. "He didn't do it." She explained.

"Well, maybe he didn't do that, but I have a feeling that some of the other stuff might be true, Mare." Mare turned her head the other way.

"My dad and I were talking about it the other night. You know when he came over and everyone was here. Out in the driveway, my dad said to me, 'He did it.' Why do you think so, Dad? I asked. He said, 'Because he's not denying it; because he's not fighting it. He's given up. If someone had accused me of that shit and I was innocent, I'd be standing tall and strong and declaring myself innocent. He isn't doing that, Pete. He's just sitting there and crying about how his life is over.' I have to agree, honey."

Mare considered his words. She pictured her father-in-law and the conversation.

She wished her brother had looked her in the eye and told her ... I didn't do it, Mare, but she hadn't asked. Only her parents had, and Seth had denied everything. That had been good enough for her. The truth was she had been too scared to ask.

"I know. I have thought of that too, Pete. But ... whether he's found innocent or guilty, everything HAS changed. He can never go back to running his camp business, no matter what happens. He loved that, Pete. None of the campers have accused him, just the local kids—a few that helped him with the camp and his house. Seth's dreams of running those trips are over. He has a right to be devastated, even if he is innocent, doesn't he?" She paused. "I can't consider what you are saying alone as an accurate gauge of guilt."

Pete looked at his wife. He could see her loyalty to her brother and her pain. She'll give him the benefit of the doubt until she has hard facts. He pulled her into his arms and held her softly. She wept quietly there.

After a time, when all the moisture in her body seemed drained and her whole being fatigued, Mare stopped crying. She said softly, "Guess I better call in sick today. Thank goodness we have February break next week. I dread going back to school now."

"Yeah, think I'll call in to work too; Dave can handle any network problems that come up today."

She felt a pull on her pant-leg. Cody wanted in on the family hug too. Mare composed herself, crouched down so she could look her son in the eyes—so he would know she could see him and that she cared—and said with effort, "Time for your breakfast, huh, big guy?"

10

A River in Egypt

Just being ourself is the biggest fear of humans.

~Don Miguel Ruiz, <u>The Four Agreements</u>~

Mare nervously made her way through the halls towards Kate's room for some sanctuary. School was over for the day. As Mare passed, most of the staff either smiled awkwardly or looked away. She began to roll the papers in her hands. *Everyone knows now,* Mare thought, and she kept her gaze lowered. Almost daily, the newspaper reported new information on her brother's case. It had also been featured regularly on all four of the local TV news stations. She doubted there was anyone at school, or in town, now, perhaps even in the state, who didn't know about Seth.

Mare looked up to search for the door to Kate's room, and her eyes met Matt's in the distance. He was coming towards her. His eyes were on her. He had been a friend to Seth and a student of Mare's. For show, she sensed … to send a message to her … he grabbed the neck of his buddy in front of him, shook it, and growled, "I'm coming after you, Man." Anyone watching would have taken the scene as harmless horseplay between the two, but Mare knew he wanted her to feel uncomfortable, to feel shame for what someone in her family had supposedly done. His eyes stayed on her as he went through these motions, but she looked away, and hurried into Kate's room trembling slightly from the mini-trek. Kate and Walt were both there. They abruptly stopped talking as she entered and looked Mare's way.

Mare had stepped into some heavier conversation, but she was not aware enough at the moment to notice consciously. Kate greeted her eagerly, and

Walt followed a moment later. He seemed a little put off, but quickly transitioned and questioned Mare with concern.

"How you doin', kiddo?"

"Umm, been better. Walking down the halls is very strange...."

"I'll bet," Walt said.

"Any more news?" Kate asked with a customary flip of her hand through her long, blond hair.

Mare took a seat in one of the student desks, and pulled it around to face her friends. Kate was already at her own desk, and Walt was sitting atop one of the student desks. They were positioned in a fairly even triangle.

"I don't know," Mare began. "A couple of Seth's younger friends called to talk to him just before his arrest last week. From what I gather, the police have been very suggestive in their questioning."

"In what way?" Walt wanted specifics.

"Well, some of Seth's friends have been telling him that, rather than asking about the nature of their relationship with Seth, or did anything ever happen with Seth that you would consider inappropriate—the police are asking things like.... Did he touch you here? Did he perform oral sex on you.... blah, blah, blah. According to these guys, all anybody has to say is yes. It's how they got the kid to say he was raped. He just kept answering yes. He rarely had to supply details; they set up whole stories for him."

"Also, when the police started questioning these kids, the cops made it sound like everyone else who had come in had already confirmed some abuse by Seth. The officers pretended they had all kinds of evidence, so that kids think they are just adding a little bit to the large pool of proof the police act like they already have. They are bluffing kids into confessions, whether they are true or not. Feels like a witch-hunt to me." Mare vaguely noticed a throbbing in her temples.

"Another thing that makes me wonder about their scruples is that, from what I understand, none of these kids had any parents or other adults with them. They got pulled out of classes and brought into the station—by themselves. That doesn't seem right to me."

"That does seem kind of odd," Walt agreed.

"Seth's lawyer listened to some of the recorded interviews, and was irritated by the unprofessional practices that went on. I think they asked this one kid what happened after the alleged rape; the kid told him he had locked himself in the bathroom so Seth couldn't get to him. Well, Seth doesn't even have a lock on his bathroom."

Mare's mind wandered to a thought about Seth's bathroom—the shower. After the fire, he'd replaced the damaged showerhead with a double shower-head, which had always bothered Mare. Why did a single man need a two-headed shower? But Mare mentioned nothing about it to her friends.

"That's too bad," Walt said.

"I really want to find out the truth," Mare told them, "whatever that is, but I would like to see them use fair and reliable methods. The police have been worse than the press about sensationalizing things." She leaned her head on her hand. "Well, what do I expect? The papers get most of their so-called facts from the cops anyway." She looked at her friends, and they saw the genuine emotion behind her words. "I get so angry whenever I read what the police have told the newspapers. They twist everything. You know, like with the whole bunkhouse thing. The man operated an outdoor adventure business! He kept a bunkroom in his house for the campers; it's not like that doesn't have a logical explanation. Everything doesn't have to have an ulterior, sexual motive. And when they talk about all the so-called *toys* he had for the teenagers, like the video games and the trampoline. It just makes me mad that they try to use everything to paint the worst possible picture before all the facts are in. The police chief would have him sentenced by the public before he's ever been tried."

Mare looked up at her friends. "I've written a letter to the editor about it. I was wondering … would you take a look at it?"

"Of course." Walt reached for the sheet Mare held out.

Letter to the Editor:

We would like to address the allegations made against Seth Mahonia. We feel it is important to remind readers that things are not always as they appear! In history, there have been many examples of individuals who were falsely accused or suspected, from the witch trials to Richard Jewell's assumed involvement in the Olympic bombing. Those of us who know and care about Seth are asking for only one thing: please, CONSIDER the POSSIBILITY that he is innocent. Remember, the law is designed so that every American citizen is regarded as innocent until proven guilty. Although a few responsible members of the media and law enforcement officials have attempted to keep this in mind and balance their investigations, many others have blatantly disregarded this basic right and chosen instead to sensationalize what they call "the facts" in order to relay the so-called truth. The facts and the truth can be misrepresented. What is a fact?

Fact:	the police have pictures/video footage of Seth and numerous teenagers.
Assumption:	that these pictures are in some way inappropriate or incriminating.
Truth:	Seth operated a legitimate and well-respected outdoor adventure camp and these are the same pictures that were sent home to parents to record their teenager's accomplishments. But readers don't know that, because the police don't bother to share that the photos are harmless.

Also at issue is the reliability of allegations made by individuals whose motives are, at the very least, suspect. Even official statements about the motivations of the teenagers involved in the break-in have been conflicting. Seth's lawyer and the district attorney have sworn statements from witnesses who heard these teenagers talk about the burglary plan prior to its implementation, as well as what they would do if they were to get caught. As details about the theft at Seth's house (just prior to these accusations) become public knowledge, readers may begin to question the veracity of statements made against Seth.

The conduct of the Babylon Police Department in this investigation has been extremely unprofessional and biased. Readers would be quite surprised to learn of some facts in this case, as well as the dishonest practices used in questioning possible witnesses. The rape charge is not only untrue; it's absurd. We have faith that when all is said and done, the individuals involved in this case will have the integrity to come forward honestly.

In the meantime, we would like to caution readers against believing everything they hear or read. So far, the public and news media have only been given one side of the story. Seth and his family would certainly like to give information to the media and speak out in his behalf even more; however, to respect the integrity of the case, such comments must naturally be limited. Make no mistake about it; we want the truth to be told. We care about the safety and welfare of all people, young and old. But Seth has been a model member of this community and he also has rights. Seth has earned the appreciation of many in this community, donating time and resources to local non-profit groups in projects benefiting residents and the environment. He operated a legitimate and well-respected outdoor adventure camp, which has earned raves from parents and campers alike. In addition, Seth has received notable awards at his place of employment for outstanding achievement and for being a positive role model. The evidence in his favor deserves to be heard.

Please beware of making judgments before the whole truth is known; a man's life is at stake here.

The Mahonia family and friends

Walt put down the page and paused with his index finger on his lip. "It's clear and effective, I think. Go for it." But Mare sensed some hesitation.

Kate nodded in agreement. "The example helps make your point too."

"Thanks, guys."

"How *is* your brother doing, Mare?" Walt wondered.

"He's alive. Pretty depressed. He's been staying with us for the last week or so. It's too hard for him to be around my parents, and it's hard for my parents to have him around also. There's a lot of stress there and sadness and fear. He asked if he could stay with us. I figured it would be easier for us to deal with it than my parents or grandparents. He's not the most pleasant presence right now. Most of the day he sits on the sofa and watches TV and cries. His employer has put him on leave until this is straightened out, so he can't work. All he can do is sit around the house and think about everything. My parents aren't much better either. The doctor has put them both on anti-depressants. But at least they are working again."

Mare started breathing deeply and slowly to fend off the emotions that were rising in her.

Her friends struggled to find something to say.

"Seth's been spending quite a bit of time with his coworker friend, Hope. Thank god for her. I don't know what he would do without her loving presence."

Walt and Kate nodded their heads slowly and thoughtfully in agreement.

"Well, I just pray for the truth." She was repeating herself. "All I ask is for an honest investigation. May the real truth, the whole truth and nothing but the truth be revealed. That is my wish."

The three chatted some more and then Mare got up as if she were getting ready to leave. "Tonight, Pete and I are taking Seth out to dinner and a movie to try to get all our minds off this mess. I'm going to pick up Cody and drop him off at Mom and Dad's. They're going to watch him overnight."

"That's good," Walt commented. "You need to get out. Try to have a decent time, will ya?"

When Mare arrived at her parents' home, she noticed her Uncle George's truck in the driveway. Inside, her aunt and uncle sat on the sofa looking solemn and forlorn. Her mother and father were in two other chairs in the living room. Mare got out a few toys for Cody, who went instead over to his grandmother to sit in her lap.

"What's up," Mare asked, feeling that something was awry.

Her mother brought her up to speed. "Uncle George knows the police chief, and went in to see him today to find out about the evidence they had on Seth, and how far this was really going to go. He was just about to tell us what he found out."

It was obvious by her uncle's face and her aunt's that the news was far from good. Mare braced herself again.

Joan piped in with obvious scorn for the officer, "So, what *did* he have to say?" She gave a little roll with her eyes, but her angry words could not belie the fear behind them. She spoke without her usual volume and assertiveness.

Uncle George spoke slowly and thoughtfully. His thick Maine accent curled around the pipe he had at his lips. He took a puff of his tobacco, and blew it out in a small o.

"Well, 'guess 'e's interviewed a lot of kids." He paused.

Mare stepped in, "Most of them connected with the break-in, right?"

"Well, one of the kids'et says something happened with Seth hasn't lived here for years. Has nothing to do whatsoever with the break-in. Lives in Texas, I guess, now. Rolf called him on the telephone. He says the kid—well, he's not a kid anymore; think he's married with a kid of his own on the way—anyway, he reluctantly told the chief that he did have a physical relationship with Seth when he was a teenager."

Mare's mind wandered while her uncle filled her in.

"The chief claims the man does not want to press charges. He doesn't want to hurt Seth. He said he seemed more embarrassed than anything else about the whole thing."

"Luke?" Mare asked. "Luke Matthews?"

"He wouldn't tell me his name."

"It has to be. I always had a feeling about the two of them. They spent so much time together." She felt a mixture of mortification and confirmation. Years earlier, during Seth's and Luke's friendship, Mare had confronted her brother about the nature of their relationship. She remembered back on how happy Seth was around Luke. That he was always smiling and bright, like a person in love. She had a funny feeling about it. With great difficulty, she finally asked him. He denied it, and emphasized that they were friends. Seth had been maybe 22 and Luke must have been about 16.

The reality of it all set in for those present. Everything was still and quiet. Droplets ran down her mother's nose.

"I don't understand," her uncle struggled. "How could this happen? How could he get into a relationship with him? It doesn't make any sense."

Mare was thinking, remembering … "I can understand how it happened," Mare mused. Her uncle looked at her in confusion. Part of her wanted to explain, but she couldn't. She knew the power of the human mind to rationalize. She had questioned Seth's psychology for many years. What motivated him? What he cared about and why. Why he behaved the way he did. There was not another family member closer to Seth, though there was much Mare didn't know. Being only a year apart, they had grown up side-by-side. She had seen changes in him. She had sensed things. Why hadn't she believed her own intuition? *Could I have done more*? She kept asking herself.

It was feeble, Mare knew, but she added, "I still think the kids who broke in are lying.…" But her thoughts turned next to Nate, who was an eighth grader. Seth and he had been similarly close. The bees in her stomach became more active and bounced again against the walls of their hive.

She returned home, pensive and uneasy, and ran upstairs to get ready for their night out. She wondered how she would handle this. Fortunately, Seth was in the spare bedroom with the door closed. She didn't have to face him yet. When she came back downstairs, Pete was pulling up their long, curved driveway. She went to the door to greet him. He motioned for her to come outside to the porch, so she threw on her coat. "What?" she asked him. His eyes were red and his expression flustered. Her eyes turned toward the cement porch floor for a moment trying to avoid what she feared might be coming next.

"My mother called me today," Pete started, placing his hand on his hips. "My step-brother, Tim, called Mom and Dale last night. The police working on Seth's case contacted him at his army barracks. They wanted to know if Seth had ever touched him."

Mare waited. Yet, her ears were trying to block out what came next. Her breathing intensified. No.

"Around the time when Tim was graduating from high school a few years back, Seth came over to help Tim work on a car. They got to wrestling, like guys do, but then Seth made a move on him. Tim was pretty surprised, and backed off, definitely not interested; fortunately Seth didn't push him about it. Another friend of Tim's recently called him and told him the same kind of thing. I guess the other kid told the police nothing happened, because he didn't want to get involved, but Tim told them the truth." As an afterthought, Pete added that his stepfather, Dale, was rip-shit angry about it.

"Tim was crying when he told them."

That was it. All of Mare's defenses came crashing down. Luke was one thing. An anomaly perhaps. A one-time thing, she had hoped. But with this double, reliable confirmation, she had nothing left with which she could defend her brother. He was a pedophile; she could no longer deny it.

Crushed, she turned her face to the porch wall and buried her face in her hands. She began to wail loudly. Then she felt her husband's body behind her, arms around her, either to comfort her or to hold himself up, she could not tell. It did not matter. They joined together in grief.

Mare could feel the cold, white siding of the house against her cheek. She could feel the salty moisture draining into the crease of her mouth. *How many young people had he touched?*

She wept for them.

How had this happened?

She was angry with her brother. For doing such things. For lying to the family.

She was angry at herself for not seeing it clearly and doing more.

Why didn't I trust my intuition? Why? I knew something was wrong. All the little signs. I should have believed the voice. I should have stopped it. I should have known.

She felt Pete's forehead lean into her shoulder blade and his arms tighten around her waist. Seth had been like a brother to him also, and now he had discovered that Seth had made a pass at his own stepbrother, the only brother he had.

"Oh, why didn't Tim tell us? We could have done something? Why didn't someone tell us?" Mare sobbed. Pete held her tighter.

What would I have done? She wondered.

"I would have done *something*," she cried out loud.

Mare stamped her foot and hammered the wall a few times with her palm. "I would have done something!"

She wanted to turn away from the world, to block it all out and go back to the way things were, but life and change came thundering in.

Once she had gathered her senses again, she realized that she was glad about one thing. If her brother was indeed a pedophile, then at least the line of victims would end here. Let no other young person be hurt by this. Let those involved get the help they may need. For this much alone, at this point, she was grateful.

Later, there would be other things.

It was a forty-five minute drive to Margarita's Restaurant in Lewiston. A light snow was wafting down onto the pavement in front of them. Mare had questions now. She thought she wanted answers. She had not directly confronted her brother in the last few weeks, but now she had to know more.

She sat in the front seat with her husband; her brother was in back behind Pete who was driving.

It was difficult to broach the topic. "Seth," she began cautiously. "Uncle George and Auntie came over to Mom and Dad's today. George spoke to Chief Rolf. Rolf claims Luke Matthews is among the people who have given statements. He says you and he had a physical relationship ... though Luke did not want to press any charges." She waited. "I want the truth, now."

Mare could see his eyes begin to well up with tears. He was quiet. His lip quivered, and he began to cry, discovered and defeated. His chin hung down to his chest and he bawled like a child.

Pete was silent. Mare looked out the window.

Mare took a deep swallow of air and continued, "You should also know, Seth, that Pete's Mom told us about the incident with Tim. Rolf has gotten a statement from him also."

Seth buried his hands in his face and moaned loudly. His shoulders shook from the shame of it all. "I'm sorry, guys. I'm so sorry. I never meant to hurt anyone." He moaned and leaned the side of his head against the window. "I tried to get help. I had nowhere to turn. I didn't know what to do. I can't tell you how many times I sat in my house with a shotgun in my mouth thinking I could not bear to live anymore."

Pete slowed his driving down a little and hesitated, unsure, but continued down the road.

Mare looked out the window at the darkness of the woods and the lightness of the snow. Two silent tears trickled down over her chin.

"Seth. Seth." She kept shaking her head in anguish.

"I called a hotline more than once. I tried to get counseling. In fact, I spoke to a counselor by phone. He told me he would be obligated to disclose the information to the police, if I came in. How could I do that to my family? ... I know it's happening now anyway, but I didn't know it would come to this. I knew I didn't like what was happening. I hated myself. I knew I needed help. But by getting help, I was guaranteeing jail time and damning my family publicly in the process. I just couldn't do it, Mare. I'm sorry. I didn't know what to do."

Now that his sister knew and he had started disclosing, he found it hard to stop, after so many years of silence and solitude with his burden. "I never really thought of myself as harming anyone. I never did hurt anyone physically, Mare; you've got to believe that! I never forced anyone to do anything. If they said no, I always stopped. Always."

Looking into the back seat, Mare retorted in frustration, "But these people were *too young* to make that kind of choice, to understand what was going on, to figure out the emotional mind-games that must have been played. Twelve. Thirteen. Fourteen-year-old boys, Seth! They're children. They never should have been put into a situation like that to begin with!"

"I know, I know. You're right." He ran a hand across his scalp. "Whenever something would happen, I would feel terrible—realizing—that it was wrong, and then I'd decide that it would never happen again. I could hold off for a long time. But then I would get so lonely for friendship again, for human contact. It always started out as friendship."

Mare lifted her head up and pressed both of her hands over her mouth. She looked out the window at the dense stands of trees that surrounded both sides of the road. The dark shapes of trees and houses kept whizzing through her view. "How did it start, Seth? When did it start?"

He flubbed some air out his mouth in discomfort. He thought back. "The first time it ever happened. I was thirteen. I was babysitting."

Mare was sure she did not want to hear this and moved her hands over her ears in a futile attempt to block out the next words. Oh, god, she thought. No.

"I was just curious. When he fell asleep, I touched him—gently."

Mare shuddered at the thought; her stomach churned and churned and churned.

"He was five. It was a hardly noticeable touch. He never woke up. That's when it started, but nothing else happened for many years."

Mare's hands moved to cover her water-soaked eyes. No, no, Seth. Not a five-year-old. Then her mind turned to Seth's age at the time. Same age as many of the kids he touched. Her mind was working; her body was reeling. She had trouble sorting out the many reactions she was having. She could see Pete shaking his head negatively, in disbelief. Seth was looking down and didn't notice.

Mare remembered a next-door neighbor child who had been about six. He and Seth were always hanging out when Seth was as adolescent. "What about Jeremy? Did anything ever happen with him?"

"No, nothing. That was a completely innocent friendship."

Mare was relieved.

She tried to reconcile somewhere in her brain the differences between her stereotyped beliefs about pedophiles and her brother. She could not get the two to match. Pedophile: monster ... greasy, nasty, violent, uncaring, dominating monster. Her brother: clean-cut, athletic, intelligent, sensitive, kind (albeit bull-headed). Her mind grabbed onto younger images of her brother. The young man who would bring home injured animals and nurse them back to health. She remembered the crow, which he'd rescued from a roadside after being hit by a car. He cared for it like a baby. It healed. He started to train it; he would talk to it. She recalled his tears when he found the cage with his dead crow in it. The cat had gotten to her. He always had a big heart. This is not man who touches children with an intent to harm. It can't be.

She knew these comparisons and stereotypes were ridiculous, but it had been programmed into her somehow.

The truth was a sex offender could be anyone.

Even your own damn brother.

She thought of her heartbroken parents. Even your own damn son. Anyone.

Then Mare's thoughts wandered into vast and overwhelmingly painful realms, where some children in the world couldn't even trust their own parents. She reflected back upon the students who had passed through her classroom doors. There were few stereotypes that held, she knew. She acquiesced to the knowledge and not just in theory this time. The face of victimizer takes many forms. *The children ... how do we protect them?*

Then Mare considered matters closer to home. *How can I protect my own son—in every moment—for his entire life? The poor parents of these victims!* Her heart went out to them. She felt helpless in that instant. Mare's lips trembled from sadness, from the pain of these thoughts.

All three passengers were in their own little world.

Finally Seth broke the silence again, "It usually happened at night. When things were quiet and I was lonely for companionship. I would initiate contact while they were sleeping."

Would it end? Just stop the car. I want to get off this ride, please, Mare thought to herself, but said nothing. She swallowed her anger and hurt for now and kept listening.

"Ironically, nothing ever happened with the campers. There were so many people around, having fun and learning, that I was never lonely. I felt important, and appreciated, even needed. I was never at risk for touching any of them. It was always when I felt more alone."

Seth cringed with embarrassment, never before having revealed so many of his vulnerabilities and shame.

Mixed in with disgust, Mare noticed that she wept not only for the children, but also for her brother. She could not condone his choices or behavior, but he was still her brother. She struggled, shifting between compassion and loathing.

"I want you to know also, that nothing ever happened with the kid who said I raped him. Nor did anything happen with Sammy either. They are lying. That's why this is so difficult. It's bad enough what I did do. To have people think I did even worse is almost impossible to bear. It's hard enough to admit the things I did. I can't confess to things I didn't do. That's why I'm trying to fight it."

Mare had to interject. "Just tell them the truth, Seth. Tell them what is true and what isn't."

"It's not that simple, Mare. It doesn't work like that. The charges get lumped together. My lawyer is trying to get them separated, so that the rape allegation and Sammy's accusation that I performed oral sex on him are tried on their own. I would certainly plead guilty to the stuff that is true, so those kids don't have to testify. I would hate to put them through that after everything else. But I can't plead guilty to offenses I did not commit, especially when they are the worst ones."

"Yeah, I agree you should fight those," Pete broke his silence.

"So do I," Mare acknowledged, but it was hard for her to picture the whole thing. Why couldn't he just go to the hearing and say—Yes, I am guilty of this. No, I'm not guilty of that. Why can't they just try him and sentence him on the charges he pleads guilty to and accept whatever punishment the judge decides—and then if they want to go after him for the other stuff, they could have a separate trial and present the evidence and testimonies?

There must be something she didn't understand about it all. She struggled to find logic in the legal process. She wanted to trust that it was a sensible and generally fair process.

As Mare climbed into bed later that night, her mind scanned through the day's events and conversations. Pete pulled off his pants and threw back the blankets on his side of the bed. Mare was facing his direction, but much of her face was buried in her pillow. The small bed lamp threw its yellow shadows across her cheek and Pete could see the skin was wet. He lay down next to her and pulled the covers up to his chest. They were facing each other, side by side, but her one exposed eye was closed. He watched her empathetically. Tears trickled down from their source and added themselves to the stream flowing down the side of her nose, dripping off her jaw onto her pillow. Every so often, formerly stifled sounds escaped.

"Oh, Mare," he sighed, and pulled her into him, wrapping his arms around her back, while she settled her face into his neck. In the warm confines of his embrace, her sobs found a greater release. He held her for some time until she was able to speak again.

"How could he, Pete?" Mare whispered, fully aware that her brother was only one room across from theirs. Cody's room was next to theirs, though he was staying over night at his grandparents' tonight. She was glad he was not there. Now that she knew more about her brother's problems, she knew she would never trust him around Cody.

"I don't know, honey." He spoke slowly, as if he were trying to figure it out too.

"Do you think we should continue to let Seth stay here with Cody around?"

Pete was a little surprised by the abrupt turn in the conversation. "Why? I don't think Seth would touch Cody. We never leave him alone with him anyway. What's the harm?"

"Yeah, but what about at night while we're all sleeping? Most of the stuff started while the kids were asleep."

Pete reconsidered that fact for a minute. "Mare, Cody would wake up if Seth ever went in there to try anything. He'd have to take his diaper off and everything. Cody would wake up and so would you. You know what a light sleeper you are." He drew his outside arm away from her, so he could see her better. "Besides, I don't think he would ever try anything. Cody's family, and he's too young."

"I guess you're right." She could not imagine where else Seth would live until this was settled. She did not want to burden the rest of the family. "We are best able to handle Seth's presence, and we are probably the best people for him to be around right now." Then she added, "But from now on—I'm going to close Cody's door, just to put up one additional barrier. It's noisy, and it sticks, and I would certainly hear it."

Her husband nodded in understanding and agreement.

A deep sigh pervaded the room, and then Mare added—still in a quiet voice, "My brother, Pete—my only brother—is a child molester. A child molester." Another outbreak of low sobs shook her. He placed a hand on his wife's shoulder to support her.

"I know. I know it's very hard, Mare."

"You have no idea, Pete. Seth is a male, sure, but he is the person in the world most like me. Cassie and I are more like him genetically than anyone else. And with regard to environment, we were all raised in the same home with the same parents, the same basic guidance, the same upbringing, and mostly the same kinds of experiences. In a way, I've got Cassie beat too, in terms of being the most like Seth, because she is five years younger and didn't hang out with us so much. I am only one year older than Seth. We spent a lot of time together growing up … throwing balls over the roof to each other, racing each other on our bikes, cracking up at each other during dinner. Sometimes when I laugh, it sounds like Seth's laugh. When I look in the mirror, sometimes I see Seth's expressions. I notice mannerisms of mine that are so like his." She paused painfully and rolled away from him.

"How can someone like me—do stuff like that?"

Pete could see her anguish, her sincere questioning for understanding, "Mare, you and Seth are not the same person." And almost as an afterthought, he added, "You aren't responsible for this."

He had hit it. She moaned, and began wailing again, as quietly as she could manage. Somehow she felt responsible. She wedged her hand underneath her cheek and swiped her finger over a tear duct.

Responsibility.

Pete, unaware of his wife's silent thought process, tried to lighten the mood a little. He continued, "Well, come to think of it, in terms of similarities, you both are pretty pig-headed and fond of being right." Then he chuckled. He gave her a somewhat playful shove against her shoulder.

"Stop it," she shook it off. A tiny elfin grin struggled to oust the frown she had worn so often these last weeks, but in a moment the traces of it vanished altogether.

11

Monkey Business

How else can humans come to find their own power but by dying to what they were and then to live anew?

~Kay Cordell Whitaker, <u>The Reluctant Shaman</u>~

Mare awoke at her usual time, even though it was Saturday morning and Cody was still at his grandmother's. She looked over at Pete who was sleeping soundly. He didn't stir at all when she rolled over onto her side, dropped her legs over the edge and stood up. Her fingers immediately found their way to her still sleepy eyes. She laid the tips of them gently over the lids. They felt warm and swollen still. Her eyes and temples ached from spilling so many tears, and she had slept fitfully, despite her exhaustion. She reached behind the closet door and pulled her robe from its hook, slid her toes into her soft slippers and descended the stairs to the first floor.

The stairway curved at the middle, and just after the turn, on her way down, Mare paused at the large rectangular window. She leaned in toward the glass. It was still dark, but the sun would be up shortly. She could, however, clearly see the whiteness that blanketed her sloping front lawn. Apparently, the snow had picked up after they returned from the movie. Everything was so calm. After the night's crying, she felt purged and empty, spent. However, her sensitivities now seemed heightened as a result.

Mare craved something warm. In the cupboard, she found some green tea and brought the box down to the counter. She grabbed her favorite mug and filled it with tap water. She liked to cup the warm round belly in her hands while she sipped her tea.

The microwave door popped open as she pushed the button, and she placed the mug inside. She hugged her arms to herself in a shiver and realized she'd better get another fire going in the woodstove to take off the chill.

The house was still and quiet, until the stove door creaked its opening and she began loading the cavity with kindling. Fortunately, a few hot coals remained after Pete had banked the fire the night before.

As she went to crumble up some newspaper from the pile, a calico cat double-squeaked her greeting like a little bird and arched her back against Mare's downy robe. "Hello, Choo Choo," Mare cooed affectionately and gave her a little rub under the chin. Within moments, her litter-mate Evinrude—his attention-radar triggered—was at her feet as well, talking in rolling chirp-purrs. Mare purr-chirped back in imitation and response. The little tigers had been her babies before Cody, especially the male—Evinrude—and he was obviously now thrilled to have Mare's full attention. With the door to the stove still open, and the first cracklings of a new fire coming from within, Mare sat down on the floor. As soon as she did, the orange and white male flopped his stocky body onto her lap and threw his neck back in clear invitation and instruction. Mare chuckled at him mildly and obliged. "Oh, Evinrude. You're so foolish," she said quietly. But her mood was still heavy, and the cat seemed to notice. After a moment in her lap, he got up and stretched his paws against her chest. He sniffed her chin and rolled his furry head against her cheek. His throat buzzing deeply. She put her arms around her cat, scooped him up, and hugged him like a baby. The cat gave no resistance.

The microwave signaled her water was ready, but Mare did not rush up to get it. She savored a few more moments with her feline companions and threw a few bigger logs onto the now flaming kindling.

The microwave beeped a second time. Mare retrieved her mug and plopped the teabag into its steaming waters. Carrying the cup by its handle, she walked back over to the stairs and climbed up a few steps. The house was so still. Pete and Seth had not wakened yet. She sat down on a higher stair and looked out through the big window onto the front yard. She wanted to surrender her confused mind and troubled heart to the serenity outside.

An orange and pink sun began to peek over the horizon, its rays breaking through the surrounding haze and streaking vividly through the barren trees, dispelling the darkness. Her mouth and eyes opened wide at the sight, and she inhaled sharply and deeply. Her eyes gazed briefly down and out across the hill she lived upon, and through big and small spaces in the leafless woods, she saw the hills to the east. As the sun started to rise from behind the hills, it cast a sublime glow upon the frosty landscape. The whiteness shimmered in shades of sunrise, and Mare's vision drank in the subtle, but growing luminosity of the snow-covered land. She cupped her drink in her hands and brought the warmth to her lips.

How frozen and beautiful everything looked. And peaceful. It touched her raw and seemingly delicate soul, like an infant drawing breath for the first time.

The spruce tree boughs hung heavily with the weight of the glistening snow, and the two maples who acted as gatekeepers to her driveway—to the right of her view—with their lovely, long limbs stretching high and wide—filled her with a calm she had forgotten existed. Her eyes followed the limbs, which were traced by a thick outline of white above the darker gray of the bark. The contrast was dramatic. The colorful sunrise was beginning to cast everything in a pastel pink-orange glow. The ice crystals, frozen within the snowy blanket, made everything sparkle and shine in the dim, early morning light. Mare took another sip of her tea, and began to forget about the darkness in her heart. The warm path of the liquid moved down through her body.

"Yes." She quickly set her cup on the wide ledge of the window and hustled quietly upstairs to dress. She hastened as noiselessly as possible, so she would not miss the stellar show and so Pete and her brother would not wake. She didn't want to share this pristine moment. She just wanted to melt into the scene and become part of it—in solitude.

Pete turned over once, restlessly, and Mare paused to see if his eyes would open. She pulled out her dresser drawers and collected a small pile of warm things to carry downstairs. She dressed there, threw on some boots and left the warming house through the side door.

The air was brisk, cold and fresh, and curls of white puffed from her mouth. The sides of her nose stuck together a little with each breath, but she sucked the air in deeply anyway. The porch roof was supported by a few white columns; the rest was open to the elements. A little of the snow had blown onto the edges of the porch's cement floor, and Mare could see by looking at the limbs of her favorite, two hundred-year-old maple, that they had gotten about six inches of snow during the night.

She smiled with pleasure at the wonderland surrounding her. Feeling like she was the first in the world to discover the treasure, Mare carefully placed a foot into the undisturbed whiteness. It was the first imprint to be made, and after that first careful step, she began to wade further in. It was cold, but she felt calmly enlivened. She walked around to the front of the house and climbed her way up the snowy stonework that led to the front door.

The sun was still very low and Mare savored the gentle, colorful rays that shone on everything. Light began to come to all areas that had formerly been in the shadow of darkness. She sat on the top step and swung her legs over the edge. She sliced a flat mitten into the snow beside her and brought the tip back up to her mouth. The cold she placed at the tip of her tongue, and then she broke into a child-like smile and turned to her left where the snow was unbroken. Taking off a mitten, she poked a naked finger into the crystalline carpet and wrote her name—M A R E. Then she pulled her neck back a little to examine it. Next, the 30-year-old wife and mother pointed her finger again and traced a round line around the letters. Spokes appeared, trailing out from the circle. As a child might, she had enclosed her name, her identity, within the safe and glowing center of the sun.

She looked up again and exhaled, enjoying her momentary escape from the heavy sadness in her heart. When the warmth of her breath and the cold air made contact, a white mist puffed away from her. A sudden, playful impulse struck her. She galloped back down the steps and bounded gracefully downhill through the snowy covering of her front yard, until at last she plowed through a deep drift, and dropped her warm and active body into the cold snow. She made a snow angel, and asked it to watch over her. Then, on one last whim— she slowly rolled in the fluffy moisture until she was covered with white from head to toe.

She rested there, content, eyes closed, until she felt she had sunk right into the Earth's nurturing embrace. Once she stopped moving—once her blood flow slowed again—she felt the chill press of the snow against her clothing, but she did not move. She simply noticed the cold contact, creeping closer, overtaking her.

Mare rolled onto her side facing the house and propped a snow-covered mitten under her hat-covered ear. *Nature can be so enlivening, so soothing*, she thought.

Something distracted her awareness and she looked up the hill to her house. Someone was tapping on the stairway window at her. She had a half-grin and was shaking her head from side to side. Then she lifted her palms in the air and shrugged her shoulders. Mare couldn't hear her voice, but she knew even without being able to read her lips that she was saying, "What in the world are you doing, foolish woman?" She squinted her eyes hard to see who was staring so wistfully down at her.

Pressing her nose against the window, Mare shivered and sighed. It *would* be a nice morning to play in the snow. Yet, she couldn't bring herself to get off the stair. Instead, she shook herself out of the vision. Only a child would do such a thing. It's too cold. The mug in her hands was getting cooler.

Hunger pulled at her insides and she felt a chill in her bones. Maybe she could talk Pete into making some hotcakes for breakfast.

"Feeling better this morning, Mare?" Pete watched his wife come into the kitchen after a warm shower.

A momentary pall crept over her face at the memory of their conversation the night before.

"A little … the sunrise was so gorgeous this morning, I forgot my heaviness … for a few minutes at least." She hesitated, trying to find the words to describe the experience and the temporary relief she felt. *The beauty of nature is always a comfort.* "The snow and sunrise were so magical. I lost myself and my worries … for a moment."

"Hey, Pete—you haven't met our new English teacher, Sophie, yet. She and her husband moved here this summer from out of state. His name is Tristan, and he teaches science. I've been working with them a lot on the Transition Team. They are really wonderful and interesting. Very outdoorsy, too. I'm going to see if Sophie wants to cross-country ski this week. I haven't gotten out on the snow in such a long time, it seems, and I'd really like to get to know her and Tristan better. I talk to them quite a bit at school, but I'd like to spend more time with them."

Pete nodded as he flipped a pancake over in the cast iron skillet and handed her a plate.

The pancakes filled the emptiness in her belly.

She began to clean up and load the dishwasher, while Pete sat down to enjoy his breakfast. "I figured you would sleep in, since Cody was at your mom's."

"I wasn't sleeping too well," she mumbled.

Mare covered and put the leftovers in the fridge for Seth.

Pete sat down at his desk and sighed. "I'm trying to figure out how to write up this business plan. I'm getting kind of tired of doing this stuff. I would like to find a way to stop working for this ISP and become more independent in my career."

With a graduate degree in economics and a skill with computers, Pete had been spending all his spare hours laying the groundwork for his own business. He still worked full-time for an Internet service provider, but he had *big* dreams.

"I'm going to be a millionaire before I'm forty," he would announce confidently to his wife.

"I know, honey. I certainly hope it is soon," she would respond. "We could use it." Since both had advanced degrees, they had huge student loan debts. Add these to the credit card and car payments, and you might have a few bucks left over to buy diapers and groceries. Pete was making decent money for living in rural Maine, but Mare was a high school teacher. Financially, they were barely making it. Yet both had high aspirations and plans, as well as the faith that they would be successful in all the ways that count.

"Well, what would you want to do?" Mare inquired. "I thought you wanted to take the business full-time."

"I'm thinking about going to med school."

Mare winced. *Not more student loans!* He had spoken of it before. She did not relish the idea of starting over again in such an initially costly career. She did not like the idea of never seeing her husband, because he was working too much, like doctors usually did. "Would you want to have your own practice, like your dad?" Mare asked with trepidation.

"No, Dad's hours are too long. I was thinking about radiology. They look at x-rays and stuff. They get to play with technologically cool programs. They work more regular hours, and they still make a pile of money."

"Well, I guess that would be better than being a general practitioner, but it takes so long and it requires a huge financial investment."

"Yeah, I know. I said I was just thinking about it. I'm just not happy doing what I'm doing."

Mare nodded and thought about the variety of jobs Pete had taken over the last several years. She didn't remember him happy with any of them. *I'm afraid you would spend the time, money and energy to switch careers, and then find you are still dissatisfied,* she thought but said nothing.

"The business is starting to pick up some too. I might be able to make a go of that. I'm already doing consulting, installing networks, etc. I could set my own hours then. People keep calling me to do work. I could take that on more full-time. I think I could swing it."

"Yup, that's a possibility too," Mare agreed cautiously, wanting to support him in being fulfilled, but afraid of the added financial risk during an already tight time. "But what about having a second child, Pete? Can we afford to go full with the business now, and have another baby? I would really like them to be close in age. I don't want to wait too long."

Pete's brow wrinkled in thought.

"And will we live on my income alone, then?" Mare asked. "How can we do that; we are barely managing with both."

"I am bringing in some money from the business part-time. It would go up if I were doing it full time."

A look of fear rolled across Mare's expression. "You work so much as it is; we hardly spend any time together anymore. Last night was the first night we'd been out in months, and then my brother was with us. It wasn't necessarily a relaxing or intimate evening."

"Well, that's not my fault. Ever since Cody was born you haven't had a lot of energy for me either. You're always at his beck and call. It's only gotten worse now that Seth is in this mess. Now all you do is cry and worry about your family," he retorted defensively.

Tears welled up in Mare's eyes, but she tried to fight them off. "I know things have changed since Cody was born, and even more so lately … with everything. I'm sorry."

Pete's features softened. "I'm not trying to blame you, but it hasn't been easy for me either. I just can't imagine working at this job forever, and I would like some support from you about it."

Mare nodded, and thought about the two options Pete was considering. She worried that Pete's workaholic tendencies would get even worse with the two career directions he was considering. She thought about Pete's dad, a doctor who always seemed to be working. She thought about Dr. Lumen's affair with a nurse during his first marriage. She added, almost with a wink, "If you were a doctor all of those nurses would be chasing after you."

Pete chuckled at the change in Mare's tone. "You could be right there."

"I want you to be happy, Pete, but aren't things a little too tight financially to consider going back to school. We both have pretty significant graduate loans already."

He sighed again, "Dad's on the admission board for the New England School of Osteopathic Medicine. He said a forty-year-old woman applied recently. It's not too late for me. I'm only 28. I'm still young enough."

"I'm not saying you are too old. I'm just afraid about the money at this time in our lives, Pete. We've got a child to think of. We are living on such a tight budget already."

"I know, I probably can't go. I was just thinking about it," he said in a huff. "We are too broke. I did send for an application from Sallie Mae to consolidate our student loans. We can because we're married." He shuffled through a stack of mail. "But once we consolidate them, we can't separate them again. If we were to divorce, we would still have a joint loan."

"Well, we don't have to worry about that. We threw our hats over the wall, remember."

In their wedding ceremony, they had asked the minister to recall the story of two Irish boys. They were walking in the woods and came to a high wall. The two tried to climb it, but could not. One of them gave up. The other boy asked him for his hat. He took off his own. Then he threw both over the wall. Now we'll HAVE to find a way over, he concluded. Mare and Pete had agreed to make such a commitment to one another. They knew that marriage wasn't always easy, but their intent was clear. Divorce would never be an option.

"Right," Pete agreed. "So consolidating our two loans will bring our monthly payment down. That should help us."

"Sounds good to me." She looked at her husband for a moment. "I want you to be happy, Pete. Whatever you decide you want to do with your life, I will support you. I just ask you to be sure. You some times get very excited about things, and then your enthusiasm wavers. I would hate to see that happen with something as important as this."

Pete nodded and surveyed his computer screen. He slapped his hands on the desk. "Forget it, I'm not working this morning. Let's sit down and watch TV for a while."

Seth was slumped on the sofa talking on the phone and watching *Geraldo Live*.

He looked over at them, "I just got off the phone with Hope."

"How's she doing?"

"She's okay, but her son got bit by a neighbor's dog. A shepherd. She took him to the hospital for stitches."

"Oh no, is he all right?"

"I spoke to him on the phone for a few minutes. He's pretty rattled, but I think he'll be fine."

"I thought you weren't allowed to have any contact with minors, except for family members when it was supervised?"

"It was just a phone call, Mare."

"I realize that; I was just asking. I don't really want to watch this. Can we turn it to something else?"

"Sure," he tossed the remote to his sister. "It's your TV."

As Mare began scanning the channels, she told her brother, "Some pancakes in the fridge for you."

"Thanks, but I'm not hungry," he mumbled and went upstairs.

Mare paused from her channel surfing on a nature program. The focus was the differences between chimps and bonobo monkeys, and their similarities to humans. According to the program, chimps and bonobos were around 98% genetically similar to humans. Mare expected it to be just another show on the animals, like many she had seen in the past. She was wrong.

As part of the introduction, the narrator compared the two related primates in terms of their social behavior. Chimp society was male dominated, competitive, and at times violent. Bonobo society, on the other hand, placed greater emphasis on female leadership. Their interactions were much more peaceful.

Bonobos? Mare had never heard of them before. She was curious when the researchers began to explore the sexual habits of the creatures. Unlike their genetic and geographic neighbors—the chimps—these primates' environment changed millions of years ago in such a way as to eliminate their former food competitors. The bonobos had a reliable and abundant food source, and no species to fight with over it. Bonobo society became more cooperative and relaxed. This circumstance over the long run affected the evolution of their sexual behaviors. The program went on to show how these bonobos engaged in sexual behaviors—all kinds of behaviors—and even used sex as a means of defusing tension in the group or for solving disputes that could become violent. The whole "make love, not war" idea seemed to apply well to these creatures. At first, Mare kind of chuckled at the animals' sexual habits … mounting each other at a seemingly extreme frequency. Then the program explored less-acceptable sexual practices, at least by typical human standards. At this Mare began to experience some discomfort.

On her television screen, she saw younger bonobos touching each other; she saw bonobos—male and female—masturbating; she watched same-sex contact in both genders, and even—much to her concern—adult bonobos touching younger members of their community in clearly sexual—and, apparently mutually enjoyable—ways. One voice in Mare's head encouraged her to shut off the TV. She shifted in the recliner uncomfortably, and yet she was curious.

It was one thing to judge human behavior and complex human psychology, but here was something in the natural world. Mare wanted to condemn some of what she saw; she didn't like it … but these are monkeys, a part of nature … how could she judge an animal?

Her mind wandered. *We are animals also, aren't we? Perhaps it is somewhat natural for primates, like us, to have some strange sexual urges. Yet, even the bonobos had taboos. Incest was not common.*

Mare struggled to make some sense. *It is one thing to have impulses. It's another thing to act on them. Primate or not, our brains are still bigger.*

Children touch themselves, or touch each other sometimes. Such behavior is usually either overlooked, discouraged, or even outright scolded.

When does a person really become an adult, and do we reach maturity at different times? She knew this was the case. But what determines adult status? Legally, it was clear. The law says we are adults at eighteen.

Perhaps the bonobos would touch the young sexually, but it was not okay for humans.

The whole thing troubled her throughout that day, and stayed with her. She was left thinking about all the sexual impulses that people were afraid of and too embarrassed to speak about. Mare thought of her own early experiences of arousal, and cringed.

A scene flashed across her brain. It was not the first time in the last few weeks, but this one was vivid. It embarrassed her terribly. She tried to rationalize it … *all children explore their bodies, experience sensations they don't understand. Don't most children play doctor?*

12

Media Appearances

"Your reputation is in the hands of others. That's what a reputation is. You can't control that. The only thing you can control is your character."

~Dr. Wayne W. Dyer~

"Seth has been arrested again, Mare."

"What?!" she hissed back into the phone to her mother.

"He violated bail conditions. He was not allowed to be around children who were not family, but he went over to Hope's to visit her and Tommy. I guess they were playing with walkie-talkies outside—all three of them, and a neighbor recognized Seth. She called the police."

"Is he just plain stupid or what?"

"I know.... I know."

*   *   *   *

Mare looked across the aisle where several members of her immediate and extended family sat on hard wooden benches. A few minutes later, her brother and a bailiff entered through the back of the courtroom. Seth was dressed in the orange jail suit. He had been handcuffed. Mare swallowed her discomfort. His expression was glum. The bailiff led Seth to the front row, a few rows in front of his family. Both sat down.

It was the first time Mare would see her brother in prisoner's garb. It would not be the last.

That night, Mare reluctantly turned on the local evening news. Her brother's arrest was—again—the leading story. Mare watched footage of her brother exiting the jail with the bailiff and walking the short distance to the courthouse. In the brief clip the station showed, her brother was smiling; he seemed to be chuckling. The announcer droned on about the details of the case and what had happened. Mare barely heard the words. She was watching the clips of her brother move across the screen. *Why was he amused,* she wondered? *That looks awful. It makes him look like he doesn't care about what's going on. What could he be laughing about?*

"The alleged abuse happened on 77 Waldo Road in Babylon. The log home had a bunkroom where police say Mahonia entertained young boys. The property was also filled with things children love: a trampoline, video games, mountain bikes ..." The reporter read the information off the teleprompter. On the television Mare saw the footage all the stations had of the front of Seth's house.

"Police say that the alleged abuser bribed the boys with gifts—snowboards and other items—so that they would return to his home. Authorities are referring to the situation as one of the worst sex abuse cases in Maine history." Again, they showed Mare's brother walking through the courthouse parking lot and grinning. The grin looked evil when joined to the reporter's words.

"Turn it off, Pete," Mare asked quietly.

"I just want to see if the other stations have it." He pressed the remote to another Maine television station. Pete listened to the tail end of their report on Seth.

Mare's fingers stretched out across her tense scalp and reached into the fine hair. She grabbed a chunk of the roots in each hand and squeezed the clump tightly on both sides pulling out a little, as if she were trying to release herself from some attachment. She sat back up against the couch and the moisture streamed down her cheeks.

A few minutes later, Pete turned off the set, and sat sullen in the recliner.

Fourteen-month-old Cody was sitting with his back towards the television playing with some wooden blocks. He had the corner of one in his mouth, and he ambled over to his mother's legs. He jabbered a bit and pulled on her hand. He wanted her to come ... sit on the floor with him and play.

His mother leaned forward with effort and rubbed her eyes with the palm of her hand. She tried to smile at her son. "Yes, Cody, sweet heart ... I will sit with you."

She slipped down to the carpet and wrapped her arms around him. "I love you so much, Cody. Do you know that? Your mommy loves you a whole bunch." Pete dropped down to his knees and encircled his wife and son in his own protective embrace.

Mare leaned her right ear and cheek on her husband's chest. With her exposed ear, Mare could hear the pit-pit-pit of sleet colliding with the windows, with the other the bum-bum-bump of her husband's heart.

The next morning, it was in all the papers again. All sorts of insinuations and distortions of fact. Mare went to school, talked about short stories, and showed students how to use commas properly. In the last few minutes of class, when students were working quietly and Mare was finished answering questions one on one, one of her freshman students came up behind her. While Mare was recording some grades in her book at the front table, the young woman, whose name was Shauna, circled her arms around her teacher's neck, leaned her head against the back of Mare's and squeezed gently. She held Mare in that way for a few moments. Mare sensed the girl's concern for her—her English teacher—her desire to offer some comfort. Mare choked back tears. The bell rang sounding the end of class. Shauna let go and rested a hand on Mare's shoulder, while Mare's other students emptied the classroom. Then she left, never having said a word.

When the door closed automatically behind the last student, Mare burst into tears. *How kind*, she thought. *How very kind of her. It takes courage to reach out in that way.*

Then a fear entered the teacher's mind. *I can't let my personal business interfere with my class. I can't let my students see how much I'm struggling personally. It isn't fair to them. I've got to pull myself together and snap out of this, so it doesn't interfere with their education. They shouldn't have to worry about me.*

*   *   *   *

Mare and Walt ate lunch alone this day. Kate was rehearsing a play with students in the auditorium. Mare told Walt what was true about Seth's allegations. She hardly noticed that he did not seem surprised. He just continued to offer his support, and Mare was grateful for his friendship.

*   *   *   *

Mare led her family to the lower door of the jailhouse. She had never visited anyone in jail before. She had never before had a reason to come to the County Jail. A red button stood out next to the door; she pushed it.

"Yes," she heard after a moment.

"We're here to visit Seth Mahonia," Mare responded awkwardly.

"Come up the stairs and beep again when you get to the second door," a man's voice said.

She heard a buzz and the snap of the latch lifting. She tried the door, and it swung open like a great jaw.

Mare stepped through the opening with a little hesitation. Her mother, father, husband and sister followed her.

At the second barrier, she followed the instructions the guard had given her.

Mare stepped up to the counter and spoke with the man behind the glass. After the family had given proper identification and signed in, the five were asked to wait in front of a third gateway.

While she stood, Mare wondered what to expect? Would her brother be behind glass? She had only seen such visits in the movies. She wasn't sure how these things worked.

Another guard appeared from behind the last door and led the group through and around into a room where a handful of other visitors waited for prisoners to arrive. They were instructed to sit on one side of three, long folding tables that had been linked together in an L shape. Five minutes later, four prisoners were led into the room. Guards stood at the doorway, while the inmates filed in and reached across the tables to hug their loved ones standing or sitting on the other side.

Seth's mother reached across to her son first and gave him a hug. Each member of the family followed. When Mare's arms went around her only brother, he felt more frail than usual.

Seth settled uncomfortably into his chair, as did each of his visitors. Mare looked at his eyes. Dark circles underlined them, and they revealed a feeling of embarrassment that his family had to see him under these conditions. It was certainly not a proud moment.

Mare could see in her peripheral vision that her mother had lifted her glasses a little and was swiping her eyes. Her father, on the other side of her mother, sat stiffly, trying to hold it together. Pete broke the awkwardness. "So, how are you holding up, Seth?"

Seth shrugged, and sniffed a breath quickly through his nose. "Been better."

"You being treated okay," his father asked with a hint of vulnerability showing from behind his stern tone.

"One of the guards is pretty nice. And I share a cell with two other guys. They've been decent to me, so far. I'm not sure how much they know. I haven't told them much. The cell is small, and it has one open toilet."

"You mean, you have to go to the bathroom in front of the other guys?" Cassie asked, mortified.

Seth nodded quietly.

"They let you go outside at all?" Mare wanted to know. *Do you get any fresh air* she was wondering.

"Yeah, a little. We get to go in the courtyard for about twenty minutes after lunch."

"Kind of cold out now, though, isn't it,"

"It's cold, but—it's better'n bein' cooped up in here all day."

The Mahonia family became silent, but the other visitors and prisoners voices echoed through the room.

Mare had a question. "Saw the news last night. It was awful, as always." She wasn't sure how to ask this. "They showed a clip of you walking to the court-house with the guard. You were laughing. It looked really strange, given the circumstances …"

Seth thought for a moment, then a slow grin came to his face. "Oh! I was walking with the guard, and the camera man for the TV station was right in front of us, trying to get everything set up in time to get a shot of me. Well, I mentioned to the guard how awful the media had been about reporting my case. The cameraman was walking backward with his big camera, and the reporter was beside him. I told the guard, "Geez, it would be just awful if the vulture fell on his ass." As I was thinking about him taking a tumble trying to squeeze in a shot of me during my moment of shame, I couldn't help chuckling about it."

"Ahhh," Mare mouthed as she was trying to visualize the scene in her mind. *I'm afraid I can't blame him. I'm not too happy with the press either at this point.*

"Well, it looked pretty bad on screen. It looked like you didn't give a shit about it all. Like it was some big joke. No doubt that was their intent. It was only a second or two of their filming, but they made sure that clip made it to the air."

Seth frowned and added, "I didn't even think about that while it was happening. I was uncomfortable and frustrated by the way they always twist my story. It gave me a little bit of entertainment that he might trip while he was trying to film me."

Their mother spoke up. "Grammie Lexi gets the paper mailed to her in Florida. Plus, she calls every couple of days, asking for an update. She's talked to Uncle George and Auntie too. She's really peeved at the television stations. She was ready to call them and tell them off, but I talked her out of it."

"She called me too," Mare admitted and chuckled thinking of her feisty, opinionated grandmother. "She was pissed alright—ready to knock some heads together. I told her it wasn't wise to call the station about it, right now." Mare bit her lip. "You know, maybe we should tell her that some of the stuff is true."

She felt her parents and her brother squirm when she said it.

"I would," her mother said, "but I'm not sure if it would help or make it worse for her. I just don't know what to do, or even how I would tell her. She's so far away. It's hard to talk about it over the phone."

"I know," Mare reassured her, "it's not an easy thing to say, but I think we need to break the news to some of the family."

"We will," her mother assured, "when the time is right and things are clearer."

The next day, Mare received a phone called from her father's mother, Lexi, in Florida.

"I called channel four," she announced boldly.

"You did WHAT? What did you say?"

"I told the newsperson, 'Someone is going to pay for what they're doing to my grandson, and it JOLLY WELL might be you!'"

"What?!" Mare sputtered, both shocked by the inappropriateness of the comment and amused by her grandmother's audacity. She found the phrasing of the sentiment to be particularly entertaining. "Gram, you can't go doing stuff like that! They are probably afraid you are going to come down to the station with a gun or something. You're going to hurt Seth's case more than help it." Her tone was harsh, but by the end, it had softened.

"I just can't sit here and do nothin' while my family is suffering so far away." Mare heard the determination in her voice, but also the pain. Lexi was very much like Mare's father. She was a tough old bird—don't show your weaknesses—but she had a tender heart, just like her son.

"I know it isn't easy, Gram, but … try to control yourself. You get another urge like that one, you call me, okay? Get it off your chest to one of us. The last thing we need is for the station to report that Mahonia's seventy-three-year-old grandmother is threatening them. God help us. It's bad enough already."

"I'm sorry," the elder woman acquiesced. "I probably shouldn't have done it. They just make me so mad!" Her voice rose in emphasis.

"It's okay, Gram. I'll call them and handle it. I'll explain that you're far away and feeling helpless, but that you're harmless. And that it won't happen again. Right?! You just can't go doing that anymore. Do you understand?"

"Yes, I'll do my best."

"Call me next time."

"All right."

A soundless moment crossed over the wires.

"I can't believe you said that to him. If it wasn't so serious, it'd be pretty darn hilarious.... *Someone's going to pay ... and it jolly well might be you ...* where'd you get that anyway?"

13

The Dirt

"We don't see things as they are, we see them as we are."

~Anais Nin ~

When a older cousin, Rosie, called and told Mare, "My sister and I really need to talk to you about Seth. We've got some information we think you should know about," Mare's heart skipped a beat. She stopped her cousin before she could go into it over the telephone. The police had been driving by the house a lot since Seth moved in, had tried to access his internet account, and the family had begun to speculate that perhaps they might also tap the phone line or something. Such talk generally caused Mare's eyes to roll back in her skull. This is a small-town Maine police department, people, not the FBI, for goodness sake, she would tell them. Get real. I seriously doubt they can do that. But the talk had caused a degree of paranoia in Mare about it. If the distant cousins had discovered some of the allegations against Seth were true, she didn't want to take any chances on the phone.

"Can you come over?" Rosie asked.

With some hesitation, Mare agreed and got directions. She had only seen her cousins at weddings and other family gatherings or at the grocery store.

Mare hung up the phone and started to wonder what they had uncovered. She wanted to tell everyone the truth, but this was a small town. It could hurt her brother to announce the facts to everyone before a trial. *What will I do*, she tried to prepare herself, *if they try to break the news to me that the charges are true? Will I act surprised?* No, Mare knew she was a terrible liar and couldn't bring herself to do it, even if the rationale for it were good. Lying feels awful.

Rosie's son, Ben, was friends with Seth, even after Seth admitted to him that he was gay. Ben and another teenage friend, Jimmy, stood by Seth and believed in his innocence. Mare did not want to be the one to destroy that, and yet she would not lie. If they asked her whether Seth was guilty, she decided she would tell them the truth, as she knew it. Beyond that, she would play it by ear, and just follow her intuition as she went. She was still nervous when she knocked on the door.

As soon as she stepped through the door, Mare tried to read the women's moods. Were they angry, suspicious? No. They greeted her warmly.

"How are you, Rosie? How have you been feeling?" Mare asked, aware that the woman's health had been touch and go.

"Still waiting for a new kidney. I'm on the list. Dialysis isn't much fun. I have good days and bad days."

Mare nodded and smiled sympathetically. Rosie's sister, Kitty, said hello and led Mare into the living room where the three sat down.

"We are so angry about what they are doing to Seth!" Rosie started. "He's been so good to Ben—it just drives me crazy to think what they are putting him through!"

Mare sighed with some relief, though she did not like the idea of deceiving the women. She wondered why they called her there to talk.

"Whenever I read what they write in the paper, I just want to call up Chief Rolf and give him a piece of my mind. That man is a snake and everyone in town knows it."

Her sister, Kitty, agreed and added, "Did you know that everyone in town's been talking about how he got some teenage girl pregnant?"

Mare nodded, many locals had come to her with the same information, though Mare could never get beyond the sketchy details. No one could provide her with a name or further contact information. It was always vague. Had she gotten more concrete information, Mare would certainly follow-up on it; she was no fan of Rolf.

"Do you know anything about the girl—who she is or how I could reach her?"

The two older women looked at each other, searching, but could not provide specific details.

"But Rolf's a hypocrite, if I ever saw one. He's no angel. Did you know he smokes dope?"

"Nope, I hadn't heard that one. How do you know this?" Mare wanted to be responsible about her own investigation. She understood hearsay and rumor, not that the women meant any harm; they sincerely wanted to help Seth. They clearly respected her brother.

"Rolf has a son who's in his twenties now. When he was a teenager, my friend's son used to hang out with him. We all got to talking the other day, and the son said that he and Rolf's son used to tap into Rolf's private stash of drugs and use them."

Mare raised an eyebrow. "Really?" However, she didn't know what she could do with the information, even if it was accurate.

Kitty continued, "Yup, and he also had some pornography that the boys would pull from hiding and watch when Rolf wasn't around."

Mare took a deep breath.

"There must be some way that you can expose Rolf for the scumbag he is," Rosie urged her, clutching a hand to her side, which seemed to be experiencing some pain.

"Are you okay, Rosie?" Mare asked in concern.

Rosie put a hand up in reassurance. "I'm okay. Do you think this will help Seth at all? He's just done so much for Ben, we want to support him."

Mare's heart was breaking. Ben was a student of Mare's this year also. She remembered her brother helping Ben on some of the homework she had assigned. She knew that the whole family wanted to rally 'round her brother. She wanted to gently break the news to them, before they would find out some other way, but it wasn't time. She couldn't just yet. It had to go through the legal process. Now was not the time.

Mare struggled. "I don't know, to be honest. I agree that there are some skeletons in the man's closet from everything I've heard, but I don't have much to go on, unless someone directly involved wants to come forward. I don't trust rumors in this town. I promise I will keep my ears open, though, and if I find an opportunity to uncover illegal behavior on his part that I can prove, I'll be right on it!"

She hesitated and then offered her thanks to the women. "I really appreciate your concern and support. Our whole family does. It means a lot. Thank you." She hugged each of her older cousins gently.

"You know, Ben has really enjoyed having you as a teacher this year. Thank you for all your help to him."

"My pleasure, Rosie. He's a great kid. Very genuine. I like him a lot."

She beamed with motherly pride. "Yes, he's a good boy."

On the way home, Mare stopped at the Lumen's to pick up Cody. Nana Margaret watched Cody during the week, but Dr. Lumen worked crazy doctor hours, and didn't get to spend as much time with his only grandson, the one who would carry on the Lumen name.

Mare walked into the kitchen where the old, wood cooking stove was lit. Margaret rarely cooked with it, but it provided warmth and that wood-burning smell that was so pleasant. Cody hustled over to his mother, and Mare scooped him up in her arms and covered his smooth baby face in kisses. The child giggled gleefully. Margaret, a petite woman who was John's second wife, smiled in her reserved sort of way, and checked on a roast that she had in the oven.

Pete's half sister, Victoria, was sitting at the table finishing a homework assignment. When Dr. John heard Mare's voice, he put down the paper and went to say hello to his favorite—and only—daughter-in-law.

"Hey, Mare," he embraced her in a side-arm bear hug. He was a doctor, but his personality was generally very informal. His patients appeared to like his down-to-earth style.

"Hi," she returned his affectionate greeting.

After exchanging some small talk, Mare admitted that she wanted to let them know about something more serious—regarding her brother. "We have learned recently," Mare revealed, "that some of the charges against Seth are true."

Dr. Lumen nodded and put a strong hand on Mare's shoulders. He gave a squeeze to the tightness there.

"The worst charge—the rape—is not true and a few of the others. And he never forced anyone … but he definitely has a problem."

"I'm sorry, Mare," he said. The four talked for a few minutes about it.

As Mare was getting Cody ready to leave, Mare said softly, "I just ask that you keep this quiet until the trial. I don't want this to get spread around until it's time."

John responded forcefully and with certainty, "Don't worry about that, Mare. This is family. If we get called to the stand, we'll lie. Always protect the family …"

A stunned Mare blinked a few times. Mare was thinking while he was talking. Mare put a hand out to interrupt him, "No, no, I'm not asking you to do that." *That's against the law."* I would never ask you to lie on the stand." *Hell, I wouldn't lie on the stand, brother or not, Mare thought to herself,* but she didn't want to offend her father-in-law. "I'm just saying, until a trial, let's keep this to ourselves."

"Of course, you can count on us."

"Thank you, Pop." Then she turned to her sister-in-law. "Same thing goes for school, too, Vicky. Please don't tell anybody else about this yet, not even your friends. Rumors are already rampant there. I just don't want to do any further damage to things right now. It's between us, okay?"

She nodded, and the look in her big, brown eyes convinced Mare that she would try to keep her word.

"Thank you—thank you all," Mare said.

Pete greeted Mare at the door when she arrived, kissed her quickly and took Cody from her arms. "Your father called. He said that in addition to Seth's and their house, your Great Uncle Dan is going to post his home as bail this time. Seth will be out of jail and back here before the end of the night."

"Wow, that's really generous of Uncle Dan. He's Grammie Lexi's brother, you know. I just met with his daughters tonight."

"Oh yeah, how'd that go?"

"It went fine," and she went on to fill in the details while she started to fix dinner.

Mare sat Cody in his high chair and heated up a mixture of peas and carrots. She placed a few crackers on Cody's tray.

"I forgot to tell you, Mare. Hope called and got the update on Seth. She would like you to call her when he gets here, so she can come over and visit."

"Thanks. That's easy enough."

"What's the deal with those two anyway."

"What'ya mean?"

"You know, is there something going on? I know she likes Seth, even after learning the truth. But what about Seth?"

"Last time they were over here, I saw them hold hands a little. I talked to Seth about it and he says that they are close. He likes her, but he's not sure if he will be able to ... you know ... have that kind of relationship."

"She's going through a divorce, right?"

"Right."

"Does she worry about Tommy at all, well, with Seth's history?"

"I asked her that the other day when she came over to ask about Seth. We talked for quite a while. She's really nice. She said she talked to Seth about Tommy, and Seth said that Tommy wasn't his type."

"What?" Pete gasped, his nose wrinkled.

"Apparently, Seth pointed to pictures in magazines and stuff of the type of ... males he's attracted to."

"Oh, god!"

"I know. I asked her about it, and I guess there's a particular body type and hair color—blond, he says, that he gets drawn to. Tommy doesn't fit that. Not that she's taking any chances. She's never left them alone. Plus, Tommy knows the deal and he's old enough to tell Hope if he were to try anything."

"Great. How encouraging." Pete moaned.

Mare had a similar reaction. Yet, she felt Hope was a solid person and would at the very least keep Tommy out of harm's way. She did wonder, however, what Hope saw in her brother that made her care about him so much. They had worked together for quite some time before this all came out. He's a pretty good looking guy, athletic, funny, but Mare still found it difficult to imagine that anyone who wasn't related to a pedophile could love one.

14

First Kisses

It seems to me we can never give up longing and wishing while we are alive. There are certain things we feel to be beautiful and good, and we must hunger for them.

~George Eliot~

The waitress brought ice water and took the women's hot sandwich orders.

"So how's everything with Seth," Kate inquired, aware of recent news reports.

"Well, we visited him in jail the other day," Mare followed filling her in on some of the details. "I've also recently made some discoveries regarding what is true and what isn't about my brother's case."

Kate listened as Mare elaborated. She did not seem entirely surprised that Seth was guilty of many of the allegations, but she did offer her sympathy.

"You know," Mare started out loud, then hesitated and stopped.

"What?" Kate encouraged her to continue.

Mare looked at her friend for a moment to see whether she would be able to broach the topic that was on her mind.

"I just keep thinking about when Seth and I were kids." She ran a nervous hand through her shoulder length, light brown hair. "I mean, there must be a time in a child's development when they start getting sexually curious, and their bodies begin to fill with strange sensations."

She remembered the bonobos.

Kate said nothing, but her eyes gave silent assent to continue. Mare looked around. They were in the back of the restaurant, and no one else was around. She lowered her voice anyway.

"It's really been bothering me lately, and I need to talk to someone about it.... You know how kids play doctor and touch each other and stuff ...?" She waited, hoping Kate was familiar and able to talk about the idea. It was a very private topic.

She nodded. "Yeah, sure."

With embarrassment, Mare continued. "Well, I can remember a very specific time in my grandmother's house when my brother and I did something like that." Her face was flushed in shameful remembering. We were upstairs by ourselves in a room. We touched each other and rubbed ourselves against each other." Her eyes immediately shot to the floor. "I know it's pretty common for kids—we must have been about eight—I don't even remember exactly—to have such experiences, but later on when I thought of it, I sensed it was wrong. I put the lid on my sexuality. I knew I needed to keep it in check. I sometimes wonder if that messed my brother up somehow. Because I was a year older, I've always felt ashamed and guilty about that. Other older children touched me a couple of times and vice-versa. Not in any way that ever hurt. It was enjoyable. But as I got older, I just felt it was bad. I've always wondered if it caused Seth's shyness around women, and now ... now that this has all come out. I wonder sometimes if I'm not partially responsible for some of the problems."

"Mare!" Kate piped in firmly and yet compassionately, "that is ridiculous! You are in no way responsible! You were a child. I think all kids have some experiences like that. I know I did. My childhood next-door neighbor used to come over and play, and the same kind of thing happened between her and me. It's perfectly natural, even though few people talk about it."

"Is it? I had some same-sex contact, too. The first time I remember, was an older female friend of mine in New Jersey. She must have been about ten. I think I was about five or six; she wanted to pretend we were dating. She made me put a sock in my pants and pretend I was a guy." Kate started giggling, and Mare couldn't help but join her. "I know, it's silly, isn't it. I remember I always wanted a turn being the girl, but I was also fascinated by breasts." Kate nodded, and Mare sighed deeply. "Pete and I have talked about this also. He had some childhood experiences as well. I've got to believe it isn't uncommon. If so many kids explore in that way, why is it I feel such incredible guilt over it?"

The two friends spoke of it for a while, but Mare seemed tired of focusing on her brother and related issues.

Kate decided to redirect the conversation a little. "So, how are you really, Mare? You've had a lot to deal with these last couple of months."

"I'm tired and stressed, and I feel like I'm a big whiner when I talk about it."

Kate waved off the thought.

"Well, I don't want to become a burden to you or any of my other friends. I feel like all we talk about is me."

"Mare, you are in the middle of a huge family crisis. It takes time to get through stuff like this. Besides, I'd rather talk about your life than mine anyway."

"I know it's natural to feel overwhelmed, but I feel bad for Pete, especially. I don't feel like I'm been much use to him lately. So bummed out about my brother and all." She paused.

"Things are okay, I guess. Our sex life has been a little stalled. I worry that Pete is going to lose patience with me. I wouldn't blame him. He hasn't said much yet, but I can sense it. I haven't exactly been a barrel of fun. I know he wants things to be normal again, like they were before we had the baby and before all this mess. His way of releasing stress and forgetting the chaos is to be sexual, and I'm just not that interested in being intimate in that way right now. I feel like I need to take a few steps back almost. I want things to be simple again."

Kate nodded and sipped her water through the straw.

"Sometimes I look at the high school students around me, and I'm envious."

Kate looked puzzled. "In what way?"

"Their lives seem so much freer than mine. I know that isn't always the case. I guess I just long for simpler days when I didn't have so much responsibility or weight on my shoulders. I miss just playing. Having fun. Not worrying. Being lighthearted."

Again, Kate nodded in affirmation, understanding now, a little light of sympathy in her eyes.

"You know what I miss most about my younger years," Mare shared, a gleam starting to peek out of his eyes. "I miss the excitement and passion of first kisses. You remember those? The newness of getting to know someone. The little bit of risk associated with it. The way your heart flutters because you are excited to be near someone. I used to have that in my relationship with Pete. It's been missing for a while. You know, first it was the changes that came with the baby. He needs me constantly. I get virtually no sleep. I'm in demand constantly. Work all day at school, then take care of him. By the time Cody's down, and the house is cleaned up a little, I'm so exhausted, all I can do is collapse onto my mattress." She took a sip of her water. "But Pete needs me, too. I know that. Then this whole thing with my brother happens, and an additional whirlwind of confusion and stress is added to our lives. We need some respite."

"That's perfectly normal, Mare. I suspect every marriage goes through such trials; you just got it all at once. You two will recover."

"I think so. I hope so. It feels like we are friends living in the same house right now. I love and respect him, and he often makes me laugh … I want to trust that it's just a phase, but I often catch myself fantasizing about first kisses. Even the first kiss with Pete. *I* kissed him. He was shocked, me being the sister of his best friend and all. But as soon as he got over that part it was very passionate and flirtatious. I still remember our first dinner date. I was chewing on the ice from my glass. He gave me a mischievous look and said that was a sign that the person eating the ice needed some sexual attention, or some such thing. I laughed. He was very attentive, very flirtatious. He worked hard to keep me interested. That was fun. If I got to relive high school again, I would approach it completely differently. I would have enjoyed it more. I would've expressed myself more." Then she thought about it again. "Then again, who would be crazy enough to want to relive high school?!"

A steak and cheese sandwich arrived, accompanied by a hot turkey. The two began eating.

"Speaking of sparks, I have sensed some affectionate vibes between you and another staff member this year," Kate teased, picking up a French fry and twirling it between her teeth.

Mare put her head back, surprised. "Really, who?" She had to think for a minute to whom she might be referring, then realized it must be everyone's favorite history teacher.

Kate interjected before Mare had a chance to say anything. "You know, Scott. He's handsome, intelligent, charming." She raised her eyebrows at Mare and contracted them.

"Uh-huh, and married."

"Well, that doesn't stop a chemical reaction."

"He is a great guy; there's no question there." For the first time, Mare consciously considered the warm feelings she had around the man. "We do share something. A mutual respect. I admire his spirit. If we had met each other before we had gotten married, we might have been very compatible." The woman exited the momentary fantasy and sighed, "But I'm married for life— by choice, and even if I wasn't—I would NEVER get into a relationship with a married man. It's not cool to do that to a sister," Mare asserted, then sighed playfully, "The timing was not ours, but I do appreciate his presence at school. He's a good soul. I like him…. Who doesn't?"

"Yes," Kate shifted in her seat and looked up at the wall décor. "Well, he is adorable," she concluded quietly.

"What about you, Kate? Any wonderful men in your sights?"

"Well," she hesitated. "There's this really good looking guy in my graduate class. I have talked to him a few times. I think he's interested."

"What's he like? Tell me more. I need to live vicariously through you until passion and intimacy re-enter my own life. So you gonna ask him out?" Mare urged her.

Kate humored her for a few minutes, and then suddenly pulled back. "I don't know. I don't know if I want to date right now. I was burned pretty badly in my last relationship." The two reminisced about Kate's college sweetheart.

"Well, you've got to take a chance on love again sometime, friend. You can't sit home grading papers your whole life."

Just then, they saw Walt's white head emerge from behind a corner. Kate turned her head to the side and rolled her eyes quickly. Walt scanned the room and spotted his two younger colleagues, then sat down in an empty chair at their table. "Hello, ladies!"

"Hey Walt!" Mare slapped a hand on his shoulder. "What's up?"

"Just saw your cars in the lot and thought I'd come in." He fingered a gold chain hanging in the V of his open collar. "Did I interrupt anything?" He looked from Mare to Kate. Kate said nothing, simply shook her head and smiled slightly.

"Just talking about men and relationships," Mare offered, giggling.

"Oh, really," Walt shot Kate a quick look to see what she might say. Still, she only nodded and smiled.

"You hungry, Walt? Don't think I can finish all this."

"No, thank you. I might get something to drink though."

He waved to the server.

Walt said, "Say, Kate, you need me to water your plants while you are up at your parents' house this weekend? I'd be glad to."

"Yes, thank you."

"What 'choo going to do this weekend, Walt, besides water Kate's plants?"

The waitress brought a cup of coffee over to Walt. He thanked her, took a sip, then said, "I've got a giant stack of essays to work on."

"Oh yeah," Mare echoed. "Me, too. It's like the laundry, always accumulating, no matter how often you tend to it."

"Well, I've really got to get going," Kate insisted. "I've got parents coming in for conferences in five minutes, and I've also got to get everything ready, so I can take off this weekend."

"I've got to go too. See you both later," Mare waved.

Walt wiped a coffee droplet from the edge of his mouth with a napkin, waved the napkin in goodbye, and watched the two women leave.

15

Pairs

Nobody believes a rumor here in Washington until it's officially denied.

~Edward Cheyfitz~

A plum-sized, blue dot compressed as it made contact with the wall, then expanded outward again at an angle with slightly less force than it arrived carrying. Kate stepped back and to her left a few, quick shuffles to hit the ball as it approached her. It wasn't a tough shot, but she missed. Mare jogged into the corner to retrieve the ball and paced back to the center of the court. "Nine serving 3," she announced; then tossing the ball into the air, she slammed her racket onto it. It ricocheted off the front wall, to the sidewall, then to Kate. "How was your weekend at your parents?"

The two colleagues volleyed back and forth a few rounds, but when Mare won the game and Kate leaned with annoyance against the wall, Mare asked her, "What's up, girl?"

The young woman, her behind now resting on the surface, with knees bent, was breathing hard. She pulled her shoulders up into her neck, propped her hands upon her knees, and dropped her head. Mare noticed her own thumping heart rate and felt a trickle of sweat slide down between her breasts. After a few moments, Kate looked up at her friend.

"Something's on your mind," Mare insisted. "Spill it."

Kate sighed hugely, and started to speak, but hesitated.

"Spill it."

"You're not going to believe this."

"Try me."

"Rumors are circling around school about Walt and me."

"What kind of rumors?" Mare asked, surprised, but calm.

"That we are having an affair."

"An affair?" Mare's eyebrows raised, then her mouth curled into a smile. "You've got to be kidding." She tried to imagine the picture in her mind. She laughed. The virtually bald, married man in his late fifties, and the pretty, twenty-three-year-old girl who could practically be his granddaughter. She thought about the friendship between the two teachers, and how much time she had spent in their presence. It was preposterous. Mare chuckled, "The three of us are together so much, they must think we are having a threesome then." She slapped her thigh and rolled her eyes. *Mare and Walt, oh THAT'S a good one*, she thought. "Oh well, you know how rumors go. Don't pay any attention to them." She popped the ball against the floor a few times.

"Yeah, I know, but there's more." Mare looked up from her bouncing. "Debby Swenson, the head secretary, called Walt's wife, Ginny, and told her we were sleeping together."

"What!" Mare bellowed, holding the ball still in her palm. "You can't be serious. Why would she do that? I don't understand."

"She did."

"This is crazy! *As if* you two are an item. Where are people getting these ideas? Just because you spend time together? 'Cause you are old friends? It doesn't make sense."

"I know. It's ridiculous," Kate said, raising her arms behind her head and tightening her ponytail loop.

"What are you going to do?"

"I don't know. I called Ginny and told her it was just foolish gossip. I think she believed me. Walt told her the same thing. I think I'll go see Debby and tell her to keep her trap shut and mind her own business."

"Wow," Mare murmured. "It's just so unreal.... Well, you ought to be lambasting those balls. You certainly have reason to be angry."

"Don't I though? You'd think I would be kicking your butt here."

"Shall we play another game?" Mare held up the little blue ball and rolled it between her thumb and index finger. "If what you say about Debby is true, just pretend this is her and get your frustration out." Mare bounced it another time and shrugged. Kate nodded.

"Let's play."

Later that night, Mare told her husband about the conversation with Kate. "Well, is she sleeping with him?" he asked.

"What do you think?" Mare responded with some sarcasm.

Pete looked as if he was trying to envision the two together. The age-span between them was too large. He couldn't do it. "I guess you're right. I can't see it. Hey, did you ask her about going out with Howie? I think the two of them would be great together."

"Yes, I did. Told her we wanted to introduce her to a friend. Thought we would bring him to the dance. I asked her if it was okay that we give him her number. She said, sure."

"Awesome," Pete yipped, pulling his shirt over his head. "I think those two should hook up."

Mare's head bobbed in silent agreement. Pete sat on the opposite side of the bed and began pulling off his pants. Mare turned her back to Pete and got undressed. Pete climbed into bed naked, while Mare pulled a green pajama top over her head. Her husband watched her, and though her back was turned, she could sense him smiling. She turned off the small light on her bed stand, but instead of climbing into bed, she headed off to the bathroom.

Mare closed the bathroom door behind her and looked at herself in the mirror while she brushed her teeth. Dark circles shadowed her eyes. *I am tired*, she thought. But there was more. She spit out the toothpaste and rinsed her mouth. Her mouth tingled from the peppermint. She pulled a towel off the hand rack and patted her lips softly. Again, she met her own eyes in the mirror. *The eyes … they can speak volumes.* They looked so sad. Mare tried to look away. The reflection seemed trapped in some other dimension, begging for release, hoping to be noticed and embraced. The towel paused on Mare's bottom lip. She closed her eyes and sighed, pushing the thought away.

She was in no hurry, rather she was intentionally delaying, hoping her husband would fall asleep waiting for her to return. She placed the towel on the counter, ran a brush through her light brown hair and walked into the hallway. She quietly entered Cody's room and peeked over the rail into his crib. He was sleeping peacefully. Mare reached her fingertips to his forehead and stroked his brow gently as she had done so many times. The child's head rolled to the right and his body followed. She turned to leave and grabbed the door handle. The hinges creaked as she pulled it shut. She was glad for this noise, so that she could wake if it were opened during the night by her brother. She didn't think he would ever touch Cody, but she wasn't going to take any chances.

The door to her brother's room—closed tightly—was just a little further down.

She wondered if Seth was sleeping. He spent many miserable hours in the room by himself, often avoiding the family, partly to spare them his melancholy presence, partly because he felt the need to be alone.

Mare tiptoed quietly into her dark bedroom. She slid between the sheets and rolled her body so she was facing the alarm clock beside her. Immediately, she felt her husband's body moving closer to hers. His arms came around her waist. She placed her hands on his and hugged them to her, trying to keep them there. It did feel good to be close. *Let's just stay like this*, she thought. It was almost a prayer, a plea. *Let's snuggle.* She closed her eyes, and settled into him comfortably. Pete's body wrapped completely around hers. His chin rested on the top of her head. She felt safe and sheltered.

But soon there grew a hardness against her lower back. She could feel it. Pete's hands moved upwards from her waist and cupped her breasts. The more he squeezed her, the more his urgency grew. However, Mare's her own body tensed unpleasantly. Her shoulders rose to her ears and she shook them a little, to get rid of the feeling. She tried to relax, but she kept thinking of her brother across the hall and why he was there. Pete used his hands to try to roll his wife to face him. Mare complied, and as soon as he was close enough, he began kissing her passionately and reaching his hand between her legs. Mare kissed him back, but could not equal his passion. Instead, she turned her head into his neck and tried to hug him, to slow him down, to maybe talk a little.

Pete slid his arms behind his wife and with his hands on her behind, tried to pull her body into his. Mare tried to think of something to say. Pete was kissing her neck and unbuttoning her top. *Wait a minute, wait a minute*, she thought—but said nothing.

Her breasts wanted to go into hiding, but he was coming for them. They sent a message to Mare's brain. *Do something.* "Pe-Pete. Pete, please," she asked weakly.

His mouth reached her nipples and clamped on. A nervous jolt hit Mare. "Pete, stop!"

He let go abruptly and stared at her. She sat bolt upright, and pulled the two sides of her nightshirt together.

"What, Mare? What's going on?" He was not happy.

"I just feel … I mean, I'm … I'm not ready."

"What do you mean you're not ready?"

"I just … want … to cuddle. Can we not have sex tonight?"

"I guess so," he responded, indignant and clearly disappointed, "Why?"

"I don't know how to explain it. Seth is in the next room. I'm afraid he'll hear. I don't know. Maybe it's not that. I just … I mean … this whole thing has been very hard, and I'm still struggling to make sense of it." She began to cry. "I'm just so preoccupied with it. I'm still hurting. When I think about sex, I keep thinking about Seth and those boys …"

Pete tried to understand, but his patience with this business was waning. "Mare, there was nothing you could have done. We didn't know. It's not your fault." The words were becoming automatic and harder to say than the previous times he had spoken them.

"I realize that, Pete, but … the last thing on my mind right now is sex. I just don't feel very sexual right now. I need some time. I need to take it slow. Until I get myself together again. I'm so tired. I don't want to just go through the motions. Can we work on building a different kind of intimacy until then?" She grabbed a tissue and wiped her eyes and nose.

"I guess so, but I don't understand why you are still having so much trouble with it. I mean, there comes a time when you just need to let go and get on with living."

In trying to express herself to him, Mare began crying harder. "I know. I want to shake it. It's just so hard knowing your own brother is a pedophile, Pete." She tried to keep her voice down. This had been going on for weeks now, she realized—her dark mood and physical aloofness, but she couldn't step out of it. She needed to fix something in herself. She needed to figure things out before she could think about being very sexual again. She was trapped in a particular state of questioning, and had not found the way out of the labyrinth she had stumbled into.

Mare found herself stepping into Seth's shoes and trying to understand him: his motivation, his pain and loss, his feelings of remorse. Plus, she didn't know what to do with her own embarrassment, anger and sadness regarding it. Somehow the two perspectives were interconnected. She could not figure out how to disentangle herself from her brother's sticky situation. Unlike Pete, she needed time to process it. Her worldview was being rocked, her previous beliefs being challenged, and the compost of her old thoughts had not yet transformed into the rich humus from which expanded consciousness grows.

It would take many months before she would begin to free herself from darker thoughts. "Pedophiles are monsters, Pete. Is my own brother a monster? How can a person like me in so many ways do that? How could it happen?" she sobbed. "I just can't stop thinking about it all."

Pete's demeanor was getting angrier. He was obviously not going to be able to enjoy any real physical contact with his wife tonight. "You can't keep crying forever, Mare. Let it go, for Christ's sake! Enough, already." He rolled away from her, and was silent.

16

Home

Fear always springs from ignorance.

~Ralph Waldo Emerson~

"Hi, I'd like to order a pepperoni pizza and a hamburger, green pepper and mushroom pizza…. Yes, the name's Mahonia."

Mare fired a shocked look at her mother, though the woman wasn't looking. Joan hung up the phone.

"Mom, what'ya doing?"

"Huh? What?" She turned to her daughter, looking confused.

"Why are you leaving the name Mahonia? Why don't you just leave your first name or … invent a name … or something?"

"Oh—right," she said, realizing her mistake. "I don't know why I did that. I usually leave just my first name, but I forgot this time. Sorry." Mare didn't have to tell her mother what she was thinking.

Since her brother's charges had been plastered across the tops of Maine newspapers and his story had stuffed the guts of each, and his face and name lingered like a phantom on television screens across the state, Mare had been careful not to leave her last name for things like pizza orders. Babylon was a rural hub of about 6,000. Everyone knew about Seth. The name—Mahonia—had become more than notorious in the last few months. To many, it was nearly as despicable a label as *Nazi* was to Jews. Homosexual pedophile. Mare could only imagine what employees of the pizza chain might do to their pizza in silent retaliation and punishment for what Seth had done and what he represented, even if it was not Seth who would ever eat the thing.

"I'd rather not have my pizza spit on, or dropped on the floor, or lord knows what else!"

The current stigma on the family name bothered Mare a great deal. Yet despite her desire to distance herself from the association with her brother and his acts, Mare would catch herself accidentally signing checks with her maiden name again nearly four years after she had given it up. At first it confused her.

Though now married, she was born Mahonia. She had been Mahonia. Many in the area still remembered her as Mare Mahonia. It would always be a part of her, like it or not. Something about reclaiming—even inadvertently—the family name felt like solidarity to her.

Mare looked around her own kitchen for a diversion. An old, 70s style brown and orange patterned wallpaper covered the walls. *I've got to paint over that stuff,* she thought to herself. *It's so ugly. I need to cover the walls with something brighter, more cheerful. I want my home to be comforting and light! It's too old and drab.*

The Lumens had moved into the 1907 farmhouse on the hill the summer before. They had a rent-to-own deal with their landlord. Two years of rent would ultimately become their down payment. The property included four acres and a large, two-story barn—situated across the driveway from the house. Next to it, closer to the house, but still disconnected from it, was another storage building, much smaller, that looked like a greenhouse from the front. Pete said the place had probably housed cows in its farm days. In the summer, its front edge was covered with dozens of thick orange tiger lilies. Within it were three rooms. Pete had recently finished putting in a wooden floor in the front room, which they referred to as *the greenhouse.* The new floor covered the dirt floor that had always been there. Tonight, after dinner, their small T'ai Chi class was to meet there for the first time. Pete had a space heater out there to get the room warmed for their guests.

Beside the greenhouse and behind the main house was a tall, vine-covered stone hearth, where family and friends would often gather in warmer months.

Mare's favorite thing about her home was the land, particularly the little path and clearing that trailed behind the pond. It was a beautiful, peaceful place. Mare's spirit would wander back there, even when the snow was too deep to trudge through easily.

Dr. John Lumen and his wife, Margaret, lived right across the street, in a lovely and spacious white-columned home. From Pete's barn, you could see his father's palatial structure. Dr. Lumen was happy to store some of his bigger toys in Pete and Mare's enormous garage. He wanted family nearby, so he had initiated the arrangements with the owner. Mare wasn't exactly sure how they were going to swing it financially—in a little over a year now—but Dr. Lumen had said not to worry about it. He would help out, if necessary.

Even though the house, its outbuildings and property were somewhat beyond the Lumen's modest budget, thus causing some financial stress for the couple, Mare was grateful to live there. She was happy outside, and it was a great outdoor location for parties. Mare loved to throw parties, inviting her friends and colleagues into her home.

*   *   *   *

After a few minutes of warm up movements, Roger Beaumont announced to his class, "We are going to try something a little different." He briefly looked at Mare. "Tonight, when we go through the form, I want you to move through each motion with a particular emotion in mind. I'll start with one and then we'll shift into the next."

Pete and Mare glanced at each other.

"We'll begin with sadness."

Mare swallowed hard.

"Whatever comes up for you with regard to your own sadness, let the feeling sweep through the movement. Each step, each glide of your arm, each turn of your body … let sadness fill it and be expressed into it. If tears come, let them flow. Let the energy of sadness flow through your expression of the form."

"Okay, wu chi stance." He readied himself slowly.

Mare got herself into preparation with her hands at her sides.

Then Roger signaled them to begin. His arms and hands lowered with a gentle arch. His students followed his unhurried and deliberate pace, and each tried to get in touch with the emotion of sadness.

At first, Mare resisted the prompt. She did not want to go to sadness again. Her limbs felt stiff, her movements forced. She wanted Roger to pick up the pace; she was impatient.

Then Mare heard a voice from her mind say, *Let it go. You can't deny what's there. It's okay. Allow what's there to arise naturally. Yield to it. You don't need to hide it or change it, Mare. You don't need to do anything with it. Just notice it.*

So she took a deep breath, and allowed her sadness to be.

Each beautiful curl of her arm gave dignity to the emotion. Each gentle sweep of her arms in ward off motion, spoke the sad language of her body. She listened to her body, as a busy mother might to her mildly neglected child. Hearing its pain pushed tears up into her eyes and down her cheeks in silent release. Mare tried to practice the Taoist principles behind this art. She tried to empty herself of thoughts and be present. She let them drift by, and kept notic-ing her body express its sadness. It began to pulsate with warmth, rising from her center up through her neck, until her whole face gave off a rosy glow of peace. Tension began to melt with each circular sweep of movement. Suppleness returned. All the way down her arms and out her fingers, Mare felt her energy flow. The space around and within her became charged with the honest flow of sadness. She could actually feel the radiation of her life force expand outward from every part of her body like an isolated glowing ember in a fire.

About a third of the way through the form, yet without stopping his own movement, Roger asked them to shift. "This time, feel the emotion of anger. Let your body speak its anger. Fill each movement with anger."

Mare struggled, but followed the direction. Anger. She thought of Seth. *How could he?* She angrily moved through Embrace Tiger, Return to Mountain. The strange names of each movement snagged her attention. Then she remem-bered her task. She let the anger flow for a change. Fire filled her veins, and pumped out her fingertips into the walls like gunfire. More fire sank down through her feet and out into the earth. She stomped a foot down as she began Repulse Monkey. Flames whipped out from elbows to her hands and out at the imaginary monkey being repulsed. She felt her power. With each backward step and forward push of energy out with her arms, the energetic fire shot out in front of her. Her hands came together, one over the other, palms facing each other. Mare imagined the ball of energy that Roger always emphasized. She could feel this ball that her hands fueled and her arms encircled. She held on to it an instant longer than Roger held his movement. She felt strong, and wanted to preserve this surging sphere in her possession ... but Roger moved on to the next posture. Diagonal flying ... Wave Hands Like Clouds ... left ... right ... Snake Creeps up ...

After some time with anger, Roger invited them to move into a place of peace and serenity for the last handful of movements, suggesting even the pos-sibility of joy. Let your body feel its joy. A lightness and freedom found their way into the gathering.

When the class finished with the form, Roger looked at Mare to see how she was. He could see a tear stain down her cheek, but she was glowing. She smiled at him peacefully. He nodded, and continued with class.

Mare turned off the lights, and began walking back the short distance to the house. She looked up at the stars, which were brilliant. She felt well and jogged up the porch steps, but stopped before getting to her front door. She turned to her right and looked at the giant Maple. Stepping down into the snow-covered grass, she walked up to it and her fingers traced an outline in the bark. Its trunk was so wide that it would take three people with arms outspread to reach around it. Of all the trees on the property, this was Mare's favorite. She considered it the treasure of the property. "Teach me to have your strength, will you?" she asked the old tree.

The weight of Pete's arm across Mare's belly woke her up. It felt heavy and stifling. His leg was also draped over her legs. She was pinned. The close contact produced a furnace of uncomfortable heat, and Mare was sweating. "Uggh," she moaned quietly. *Too hot, too smothering.* Lifting his arm off from her, and turning so his leg fell away, Mare rolled off the side of the bed and headed towards the bathroom. She was groggy and barely opened her eyes as she tiptoed down the hall. She turned her back to the toilet and sat down, but making no contact with the seat cover, fell down into the chilly bowl. She felt the cold wetness splash around her bare behind. "Dammit, Pete!" she snapped, though he could not hear her. Quickly, she stretched her legs out across the opening to lift herself up, finished her business, and cleaned and dried her rear end. She was fully awake then. "I wish you would put the stinking seat down when you're done," she said to no one.

17

Slavery and Innocence

"If you think you are free, You are free. If you think you are bound, You are bound. For the saying is true: You are what you think."

~Ashtavakra Gita 1:11~

"**Rationalize**," Tara Jones said as she wrote down the day's vocabulary word on the overhead. Her classmates glanced up at the screen and then scribbled down what Tara was writing on their own identical sheets. Her dry erase marker etched in looping arcs a definition, which got magnified onto the screen.

Rationalize: To explain or justify one's actions to oneself or others so it seems okay.

The juniors continued to follow their classmate as she jotted down the words. "It's a verb," Tara informed them. "There are some other definitions, but Ms. Lumen said this one worked for our purposes. Can anyone tell me any synonyms for this word?" Hands went up. *Give excuses for. Cop out. Justify. Get free from blame. Defend.* "Good," Tara said as she awkwardly added them to her transparency. Next, she added ones she had found that they had not come up with. *Attempt to make acceptable. Make logical. Simplify.* "Now antonyms?" Students struggled to think of words that represented the opposite of rationalize. Tara recorded hers. *Blame. Prosecute. Assign or accept responsibility for. Complicate.* One student yelled out, *"face the facts."* Tara decided, "Yah, I think that fits."

Then she asked them if they could think of another form of the word. They were silent.

"How about a noun?" Mare asked. Then she gave them a sample sentence where a noun might be used. "The student offered a flimsy _blank_ why his homework wasn't done."

"Rationalization?" someone offered.

"Yes."

Then Tara and Mare suggested some examples of how to use the word and finally some non-examples. It was the same process at the beginning of each class; only Mare chose a different word for each day. Mare was thinking to herself, _I wish I could use Seth as an example. He has a rationalization for almost everything that has happened. Come to think of it, so do I. In trying to make sense of it, I try to find reasons to make myself feel better. Maybe it's just human nature._ Mare twisted her pencil between her fingers, while her students used the word in a written sentence for their note-sheets.

When the class was finished with the word of the day, Mare moved on to the next activity.

"In the last few weeks, we've been spending time watching the film _Roots._ Now that we're finished, I'd like to hear some of your reactions."

A palm went up. "It would have really sucked to be a slave," one said. "I mean, before he was taken from Africa, Kunta Kinte was initiated into manhood … with those … ritual things. It was wicked hard, but he stuck with it." A few students giggled uncomfortably, thinking about the circumcision scene. "He could hold his head high. He had proven he was a man. He tried to be that man after he was taken, but everything got turned upside down."

"Yeah, all the honor was gone; he was treated like an animal then," another student added.

Mare nodded, and one of her other students said, "Slaves could hardly do anything they wanted. Which was a bummer, especially for the women." Students quieted for a moment while they mentally reviewed the images of brutal and inhumane treatment. Mare remained silent as well, letting them stir around the soup of their minds.

"And they got beat for all kinds of things. I can't believe they weren't even allowed to read and write," another voice echoed.

"Why _did_ their "masters" not want them to learn to read and write?" Mare questioned them.

The teenagers had to think about that for a few minutes. Mare waited.

"Well, they were able to do more things when they could write … like Kizzy … she wrote that note, so her boyfriend could get away. Didn't work in the end, but it could have!"

"Right. By denying slaves that form of communication, expression or knowledge—slave-owners could keep them sheltered. They could maintain a higher degree of control over their slaves if slaves remained illiterate. Slaves who could read or write could become more aware, articulate, and more powerful. Some ultimately used their literacy to help, to put an end to slavery and other forms of mistreatment of their people. Frederick Douglas was a great example of that, but there were others. Literacy is often a powerful advantage. That is why cultures or regimes around the world often try to keep certain groups—particularly women or the poor—from getting an education. Education equals power in many respects. Keep your people in the dark and you have more power over them. All kinds of worlds open up to those who can read well and write. You've probably heard the phrase *the pen is mightier than the sword …*"

"Why couldn't slaves just learn to read secretively, Mrs. Lumen?"

"Well, you saw the consequences. Slaves would be punished severely, if caught. Plus, these people came from Africa. The first slaves didn't know how to communicate in our language when they arrived here. Who was going to teach them to read? Unless a white person took the initiative to educate slaves in the written word, and a few did, there was no one to learn from. They learned or were born into oral English language, but it usually stopped there. Also, those who somehow knew how to read were taking an enormous personal risk if they showed others how to read or write. Now, aren't you glad that you are not only allowed, but also *able* to read and write? You are very lucky, you know." She grinned playfully.

Mare noticed a few of her junior boys having a side conversation and decided to intervene. "Very lucky, aren't you, Mr. Bean?"

Austin Bean immediately sat up straight and cleared his throat. "Well, yes Ma'am, of course we are VERY lucky that we have *you* to teach us how to read and write well," Austin drawled in a soft, slight Southern accent. The young man had moved to Maine at the beginning of the year to live with his father. He flashed a charming smile at her. He was a blond-haired football player, taller and brawnier than many of his classmates.

It was unusual that a student in the Northeast would address a teacher as Ma'am or Sir.

"Yes, Ma'am?" she repeated with amusement, tickled by the uncommon phrase and not-at-all disguised flattery. "Did you hear that folks? ... Yes, Ma'am," she tried to imitate his Dixie accent. "In't that cute?"

Before she knew it, she heard some hoots from a few of her male students. "Oooh, she think's he's cuute. She likes him."

"Oh, cut it out, people!" Mare retorted, rolling her eyes and chuckling. "What are we in kindergarten? I said the accent was cute. I think all of you should start calling me Ma'am as a show of respect. And a little insincere praise from time to time wouldn't hurt either. Maybe that's what's wrong with our society. Each day you should come in and bow to your teacher, like they do in Eastern cultures, and tell her how appreciative you are." She dipped down with her hands at her side as a model of respect. "Then when the teacher asks you questions, you should say 'yes Ma'am'.... I like that idea," Mare's mind drifted off into fantasy mode.

Her students laughed. "Oh sure, Mrs. L—keep dreaming!"

"But I was sincere, Miz Lumen," Austin protested.

"Sure, Austin." She nodded, smiled and winked mischievously, and continued on with the lesson.

"Anyway, now that we're finished watching *Roots*, I want to do some writing with it."

"Ohhh, Mrs. Lumen, no!"

She stretched her fingers into the air to silence them. "This'll be fun. I've never done it before. You'll be my guinea pigs. You're going to do a puzzle."

"I thought you said we were writing."

"You are, but not in any way you ever have before. I'm going to give you pieces of an essay I wrote about *Roots*, and you are going to put the pieces together into a final product."

"What?"

"That's right. We're going to get in groups of three. I'm going to give you an envelope with sentences cut out. You are going to lay them out into an essay."

The slightest hint of enthusiasm began to grow in the room. They liked the idea that they didn't actually have to *write* an essay. This *could* possibly be fun.

The teens got into groups and Mare handed each team leader a packet. They started pulling out clipped sentences.

"Now." Mare had them pause. "Let's talk strategy here. How are you going to go about constructing this essay?"

"Ummm ... we need to group ideas first."

"That's not a bad idea. First you've got to read the slips and figure out what?"

"What this essay's about?"

"Right. Then what's the first sentence you should find?"

"The thesis?"

"Bingo! Find the thesis, then what?"

"Tell us!"

"You've got brains—think! Remember the writing process? You've got to do this in reverse. How would you outline an essay?"

"Oh, oh ... the focus of each supporting paragraph, the topic sentences?"

"Yes, very good! Read through the sentences together, and see if you can agree about the focus of this essay in front of you. Consult with your group members, and let me know when you find the thesis and topics of this essay."

The noise level in the room immediately rose as students began reading the sentences on each clip of paper.

Mare went from group to group to see how each was doing. She heard a cacophony of voices reading sentences. "Although many slaves accepted their positions either because they feared the punishments or desired the rewards, other slaves refused to accept their confinement."

After each had read through all the slips and discussed topics with their groups for a few minutes, Mare asked for their attention again.

"I'd like to hear votes about what the thesis statement is."

"We may not be able to change all that is wrong in the world or in our lives; however, we may change the way we operate within those situations?"

"Okay, well, do you think the entire essay is about how we operate in the world?"

"No, it's about *Roots*," another student shouted out. "Oooh, we've got it, I think."

Mare nodded for her to go.

"Every slave in *Roots* had to face the choice of whether to accept his or her bondage or whether to resist it."

"Let's see, folks—are most of the sentences in front of you relating to this issue of choice ... of whether the characters accepted or resisted the circumstances in front of them?"

She got an affirmative response from the whole.

"Do you really think slaves had a choice, Mrs. Lumen? I mean, they seemed pretty powerless to me."

"Let me tell you this one thing, folks, and I want you to listen carefully, because this goes far beyond this classroom.... We *all* have a choice in *every* moment. No matter what is going on in life—remember this—you *always* have *at least* one choice," she poked her index finger to emphasize one, "even if it seems like you have none. The choice is this: you can either accept the way things are and be at peace with that, or you can resist your situation—either physically or emotionally. No one can ever take that away from you, my friends. You are never a victim in that sense."

Her students were quiet for a moment, considering her words.

"How about this sentence, Mrs. Lumen, 'Kunta Kinte and his family learned that there is a time to fight and a time to accept things as they are.'"

"Yes, knowing when to choose one or the other is the real challenge for each of us. If you don't realize that you have choices, in effect you are a slave to life's circumstances, no matter what they are. Even a slave can achieve some degree of freedom, though it might not be the physical kind.... And even a so-called free human being is *enslaved* if she abdicates—or gives up—her own power of choice.

When the school day was over, Mare walked over to Kate's classroom to visit and unwind from the day. Walt was there already, and both greeted her.

Mare asked, "what do you think it'd be like if we raised our children to say 'yes, ma'am or no, sir' to their teachers? I think it might increase their attitude of respect, don't you?"

"They do in the South," Walt said.

"I know. I have a student who just moved from there, and it is refreshing." The three joked around for a few minutes.

"Speaking of respect and lacks thereof ... I can't get the kids in my third period class to quiet down; all they want to do is socialize. One kid threw an eraser at me today. I've tried everything; I don't know what to do next."

"It's all in your presence, Kate; you've got to show them who's the boss. I never have any problems with behavior; you know why? I just don't fucking tolerate it. Kids know I mean business; they don't mess with me," Walt insisted.

Kate's eyes rolled back, as if she'd heard it all before.

Indeed, the young teachers had both seen the killer looks he could shoot, as if you had just walked onto a land mine and heard the click; you dared not take another step. Walt was not a person you wanted to anger. As good a guy as he was, he'd had a sometimes troubling past and a low tolerance for opposition.

After fifteen minutes of wandering conversation, Walt asked Mare for an update on her brother's status.

"He's been trying to get the charges separated, so that he can plead guilty to those which are true and fight the bogus allegations. His lawyer has filed the paperwork. Seth doesn't want the kids who are telling the truth to have to go through a difficult trial, but he also doesn't want to plead guilty to false rape charges. It's bad enough what did happen."

Kate took a bite out of an apple she'd been eating and nodded, absentmindedly. Walt sat on the edge of her desk and crossed his arms, listening closely.

Mare looked at the floor, somewhat helplessly and added, "I asked Seth to just admit what he's done … to tell them what was true and what wasn't." It was that same rut of thinking that she couldn't seem to climb out of. She looked for agreement from her friends. "I mean, why can't he? What does he have to lose? He's going to go to jail anyway. There is no avoiding that. He's broken the law and he's ready to take responsibility for that. I think he needs to. He's hurt young people—emotionally at the very least. There have to be consequences. He's made mistakes. I know that, and he knows that. If he admits to the charges that are true, they can sentence him on those, and then have a trial for those that aren't true. Does that make sense?" Mare paused. "But Seth says it can't work that way. I guess he's talked to his lawyer about it. I don't know. I just don't understand. Why can't he just tell them the truth and go from there?"

Walt looked at Kate, and Kate looked at him. Then they both turned to Mare. Kate shrugged and Walt shook his head negatively.

"I guess it would be nice if it all worked that way, but it usually doesn't," Walt insisted. "Best to leave it up to the lawyers, I think."

Mare searched their expressions. It seemed like they thought her naïve for such a conclusion.

All she could do was sigh.

Why can't the truth just be told? She wondered. *He's willing to accept the consequences of his actions now that it's coming out in the open …* It seemed sensible to her. *Lies and secrecy … they only breed trouble.*

Mare mind wandered into the past. She remembered lying to her mother once as a child. She had asked to bike over to a friend's house. Her mother had said no. Because she really wanted to go, instead, she told her mother that she was going to play at a closer neighbor's home; then went with her original plan. When her mother later probed her about her travels, Mare caved and admitted that she had lied. Her mother was furious. She remembered feeling shitty about herself afterwards. She had decided lying was bad for you, and tried to never do it again. She wanted to be able to feel good about herself. Lying didn't just get people angry with you; it violated something inside.

Apparently, however, not everyone had reached that same conclusion, and Mare had trouble seeing the other side. She recalled her father-in-law's words when she told him about Seth. "We'll lie if we are called." *Is it unnatural for me to want the truth to be told? For his own well being, Seth needs to be honest,* she thought. *Lying for him wouldn't be doing him any favors really. I could not lie for him on the stand. I could not do that to myself. I could not do that to my society, family or not.*

On Sunday of the same week, Kate called Mare from her parents' house.

"Hi, Kate, I didn't know you were heading home this weekend."

"It was an unexpected trip.... I've got something I need to tell you, Mare. I'm sorry I haven't told you sooner. My parents think it's very important I tell you now." Her voice was shaky, but also a little hard.

"What is it, Kate?" Mare asked with sincere concern, sensing the importance of what was to come, but with no clue about what she would say.

"You remember the rumors I told you about—about Walt and me?"

Mare gulped hard and answered with trepidation, "Yes."

"Well ... they are true."

WHAT? was the word echoing through Mare's brain, but only silence filled the line between the two women, while one braced herself for the worst, and the other tried to catch her breath and make sense of what her friend was telling her.

"You ... and ... and Walt ... have been having an affair?" Mare blinked hard, and sat down on her old sofa. "You and Walt?"

"Yes, I'm afraid so."

Mare was speechless. She tried to envision the two. *He's so much older. I mean, Walt's a great guy and all, but he could be Kate's grandfather!*

She sucked in a few breaths.

Kate couldn't wait any longer to end the quiet, "It's been going on for over a year. I know what you're thinking, and I can't understand it myself."

Over a year? Mare's confusion intensified. *How could I have been so blind? This can't be.*

Then she pulled herself together realizing it was a difficult admission for Kate.

"I can't say I'm not shocked. I never saw it.... I guess I was too close to it all. But ... thank you for telling me. I'm sure it wasn't easy.... Wow.... Ummm ... so what's going on now?"

"Walt's wife, Ginny, called my parents. That's why I'm up here. You know they used to all be neighbors ... and friends." Kate had to pause. Mare had a moment to think and still could hardly believe it, even though Kate was saying the words. "I have to end it. I have ended it with him. We are just going to be friends now."

Friends, Mare thought. *My god, Kate and Walt have been together sexually.* She felt a tremor of discomfort rattle down her bones, but eventually brushed it aside and said, "Kate, you and Walt are grown people. It's not for me to judge. I will support you both however I can." She meant it.

"Thank you. I *would* like to ask a favor."

"Go ahead."

"I've already talked to Walt. I told him I was going to tell you, and I asked for my spare apartment key back. Could he drop it off at your place?"

"Ahhh, sure."

"Thank you. Again, I am sorry."

"You're welcome. Ahh, okay, I'll see you back in school, I guess."

"Bye, Mare." Then she heard a dial-tone.

Later on, Walt called. "Mare, I'm so sorry we didn't tell you."

"Well, you two are big enough to make your own decisions, Walt. It's not my place to interfere with it."

He drove the few miles over to Mare's house, and placed the key on the coffee table. He looked a little uncomfortable. His face was whiter than usual.

Mare rotated the toe of her shoe on the rug. "I'm sure this has got to be pretty tough right about now."

"Yes. I'm not sure what you're thinking, Mare, but I want you to know that I love her. She's very important to me."

Mare hesitated and looked at the sincerity in his eyes. "I'm sure you do love her, Walt," Mare got out with some discomfort.

He hesitated, obviously uncomfortable himself.

"She needs your friendship now. Be *her* friend, Mare."

"Well, I hope I can still be a friend to both of you." Images started to pop into Mare's mind about how strange department meetings were going to be now.

"Yes, well, we'll see. Thank you for your support, Mare."

"It's the least I can do. You've always been there for me." She reached out to hug him. She wanted him to know she still considered him a friend, that the admission hadn't changed that.

That evening, Kate called to ask Mare if she could meet her at her apartment. She didn't want to re-enter it alone.

A white stairway angled its way up to the second floor. Mare followed behind Kate up to her apartment. Kate turned the key in the lock and opened it.

Mare wasn't sure what Kate expected to find, but as they went into each room, Kate pointed out little alterations that Walt had made over the weekend, while she was gone. He had left a card and some unusual gifts for her. Kate handed the envelope to Mare and motioned her to open it. It was a lewd, cartooned image denoting oral sex and it had some personalized comments written on the bottom about Kate. Mare glanced at it quickly, disgusted. It was supposed to be a humorous card between intimate partners, but it creeped her out. Kate was very unsettled too.

Spurned lovers do strange things to hang on, Mare thought. He had moved some of Kate's belongings around, and altered a gift he had given her slightly, so only Kate would notice and understand. Kate tried to explain a few things about them, but Mare was anxious to leave and not terribly interested in learning any more of the details of Walt's disturbing visit.

After helping Kate rearrange and get rid of some things, and after Kate filled Mare in on more details of their relationship, Mare hugged her friend goodnight. "Call me if you need anything," she said firmly.

"I will. Thank you for coming over."

Mare snuggled up in her husband's arms that night after informing him of the new information on Walt and Mare. He was shocked, but quickly laughed about it. Long after she heard Pete's quiet snores, she was awake. Her eyes open. Every time she would close them, she would see images of the mismatched couple—her friends who were colleagues, her boss and one of his subordinates. *How would this change things at school?* Mare wondered.

She twisted her neck around a few times, trying to loosen the muscles, and wiggled herself from her husband's grasp. First her brother, now this. Two sets of images she did not want to examine. A young man with younger boys. An old man with a much younger, pretty woman. Her eyes scanned the darkness, studying the moon-shadowed shapes in her room, the glow of a beam reflecting off her bureau mirror, the white ceiling. In time, she heard Cody fussing and went to his door. She shoved it hard to unwedge it. It noisily gave way. She scooped up her son since he was already standing with arms outstretched. She cuddled him against her neck and eased herself down onto the rocking chair. She wrapped the little bundle against her chest and rocked him back and forth until he fell asleep.

18

Fallout

A lie has speed, but truth has endurance.

~Edgar J. Mohn~

Now that Mare's eyes had been opened to the private side of Walt and Kate's relationship, she discovered quickly just how widespread the rumors had become. Everyone knew about it. *How could I have missed it,* Mare asked herself with frustration. With her brother, she had at least been suspicious enough to ask him about things in the years before.

Her brain traveled back over memories of the year and a half the three had worked together.

Oddly enough, Mare, Walt and Kate continued to eat lunch together even after the disclosure ... for a while. Kate and Walt wanted to remain friends, though Mare, often sitting between them, found the tension to be challenging. While the other two were talking casually, Mare watched Kate drinking some milk through a straw, which triggered a recollection of another time Mare saw Kate with a straw. A couple of students had been working in Walt's room after school when Mare entered. Walt and Kate were joking around quietly. Mare joined their conversation, and while they were talking Kate wrapped her tongue around the straw in an absentmindedly seductive way. Mare noticed Walt's smiling reaction. It was a small thing, but why hadn't she noticed the intimacy? Her attention came back to the present, and Mare shifted in her seat.

"I've moved out of the house," Walt announced. "Got an apartment in town."

Mare nodded rhythmically, chewing her sandwich. Kate just kept spooning out her yogurt.

Mare didn't know what to say. She struggled to find some way to respond. *Obviously, things were not going so well with his wife. I wonder if she kicked him out.*

"Oh yeah," Mare said. "Where is it? Do you like the place?"

While Walt began to ramble about the interior of the place, Mare remembered that Kate and Walt had gone to the Bill Clinton speech together in Portland. Mare had always wondered why she hadn't been invited, but figured they assumed she couldn't go because of Cody. The thought never occurred to her, until now, that they were an item and wanted to go alone. Despite the rampant rumors around school, none had ever reached Mare's ears. *Probably because people knew we were all close friends. Well, I thought we all were close friends, but even people who are supposed to be close keep things from each other, I guess. I suppose they had a right to their privacy. I just feel like such a fool.* Mare was confronted by all the little inklings of intuition she had ignored—all because the idea was so preposterous that her psyche wouldn't acknowledge the clues.

*   *   *   *

Later, Mare stopped by Sophie's classroom and invited her to go cross-country skiing that weekend. Mare noticed a quiet dignity and wisdom in the new department member that she always wanted to learn more about. Sophie had gotten her master's degree at Harvard, but it wasn't the book smarts that Mare admired about the woman. It was her gentle strength and the way she listened closely without interrupting. Unlike Mare, she was not aggressive, but she exuded a strength and confidence that was so natural and peaceful. The two teachers had spent some time together, but not as much as Mare wanted. Her brother's legal and personal problems, full-time teaching and motherhood had made it more challenging to socialize.

The afternoon of their ski date was glorious. The two friends said little when they started out on the trail. They simply enjoyed the rays of sun flickering through the trees warming their necks, the sometimes icy glide of their skis across the groomed trail, and the fresh, cool March air.

After reaching the top of a hill or a scenic spot, they would stop regularly and chat.

Nothing was forced, just an easy, comfortable conversation about how Sophie and her husband Tristan had met in the White Mountains one summer. How they had gone trekking through the Northeast and spent some time in a Buddhist monastery in Canada, volunteering their time and energy while there in exchange for temporary room and board. Ultimately, how they decided to move to Maine. Mare chuckled when Sophie recalled how they had narrowed their choices down to a handful of places.

Though Sophie had chosen to teach English, she also was strong in the sciences, a unique trait for an English teacher, Mare thought. Tristan taught science at Emerson High, so all three were colleagues. Mare thought the two a well-matched, playful and respectful couple, and she was happy to know them.

Mare intentionally steered the conversation into areas she found easy and fun to talk about.

"Do you think you guys will start a family anytime soon?" Mare asked Sophie.

"We're not in any hurry. I would like a family, but not right away. Tristan is much more hesitant about children. I think it will take him a little longer to get there," she puffed a few dark brown hairs out of her mouth and adjusted her hat. "Tristan's dad left his mum when he was a baby. Having the responsibility for children sort of scares him, I think." The two looked out across a frozen stream, and Sophie remarked how beautiful it was.

"How about you, Mare? Are you going to give Cody a sibling soon?"

"Yes. We would really like two children. We were hoping to have them be about two years apart, and Cody is getting close to a year and a half, so we'd better get started!" *But I have to get my act together, if that's going to happen. I need to jump start my sex drive again pretty darn soon!* Then she continued, "having a child is such an incredible experience. I've been happy before—many times in my life—but I never knew joy—until I had my son. To hold him against me, to hear him giggle, to see his twinkling eyes … it's pure joy."

"Really?" Sophie asked, clearly moved by the thought.

"Nothing compares to it," Mare added. She wiggled her fingers in her gloves to get them warm. "You want to start skiing again?" she asked.

Sophie nodded, in way that indicated she was still thinking about what Mare had said.

Blue skies surrounded the women as they planted poles and slid through the winding trails among the trees and over small bridges.

Back at Sophie and Tristan's home, the women peeled off their outer garments to reveal glowing, flushed skin. Sophie twisted off her red scarf and Tristan came by and planted his hands on her shoulders.

"How was the skiing?" he asked with his English accent.

"Amaazing!" Sophie murmured, contentedly.

"Yah, it was a little icy on the trails, but it sure was pretty," Mare added. "What 'choo been doing, Tris?"

He pointed to the stack of papers on the table. "Scoring some lab reports," he said, groaning slightly.

"It never ends, does it?" Mare commiserated, hanging her parka on a hook and moving near the woodstove. She leaned her behind closer to the heat and stuck her hands behind her.

"No, I suppose it doesn't," he said. "You want some tea, ladies?"

Both women nodded, as he got the teapot and mugs ready.

"I don't know how you and Sophie do it, I tell you," he continued. "I don't have nearly as much writing to evaluate as you do, and it's still really hard."

Mare nodded. "It's the thing I least like about teaching. It's hard to keep on it with so many students."

"My brother's a teacher in New Jersey and he has even more students than we do. I think he averages about 35 students a class," Sophie told her.

"You're kidding!" Mare said. She could not imagine juggling much higher numbers.

"Nope, I think Emerson has pretty reasonable numbers compared to many places in the country."

"Maybe so, but it still keeps you busy."

While they were waiting for the water to boil, Tristan came over to Mare and pretended to spar with her. "Come on T'ai chi, girl. Show me what you've got!" He swiped a few pretend blows at her and the two wrestled harmlessly. Tristan had been studying a different martial art—Muay Tai Boxing—for several years.

Sophie laughed at them. "Okay, okay … the water's boiling."

A few minutes later, Tristan poured them each a mug.

Mare sipped hers greedily. "So, I have to ask you guys…. Did you know about Walt and Kate? I just found out this week, but it appears I was the last to know."

The couple looked to one another, and Sophie, not normally one to gossip, reluctantly told her, "Yes, we did hear about it."

Tristan took over, "I didn't really see that much, but a lot of people were talking about how much Walt changed once Kate came on staff. I understand he became much more animated." The Brit broke out a box of cookies for them to eat with their tea. "I mean, we weren't here then, so it was harder for us to see a change, and I guess the same was true for you. Weren't you and Kate hired together?"

Mare nodded.

"Well, apparently Walt never used to wear his shirts all buttoned down and his gold chains dangling."

"That would explain part of why I had trouble seeing it, I guess."

Sophie said softly, "I just know that it seemed like whenever I went to one or the other's room, they were always together."

"I know. I just thought it was because Kate grew up next door to Walt. That they had been longtime friends. Shows you what I know …"

Trying to console Mare a bit, Sophie said, "It was not THAT obvious. It's understandable that you didn't know. They tried to keep it secret. It's just hard to hide feelings from others sometimes. It seems to shine through whether you intend it or not. You were just so close to it, you didn't suspect."

"Blind to the truth," Mare moaned, teasing herself.

"Trusting. That's a good quality," Sophie insisted.

"Thanks. You have a knack for saying just the right thing, Soph."

"Speaking of feeling better," Tristan interrupted, "how is everything with your brother?"

"Legally, about the same. But his company has put him on paid leave until this is settled, so he sits around my house most of the day, either in his room or watching the television. Before they did that, he had come clean with many of his friends there, telling them he was gay. He felt liberated about not having to hide that part of himself." Then she paused, and considered whether she wanted to make her new friends privy to the extra information. Aside from Walt and Kate, few people dared to ask. Most avoided Mare, unsure of what to say.

She wanted the two to be part of her life. She wanted their friendship to grow deeper and stronger. She looked at them and knew their integrity. She decided to entrust them with the knowledge she had. "Since the initial stuff came out, I have discovered more about what's true and what isn't." She sighed. They listened. Then she launched in on what was becoming more and more of a routine disclosure for her. "Some of the charges are true. My brother has a problem." With some emotion, she shared more of the details with them.

Sophie leaned over in her chair and hugged Mare. "I'm sorry, Mare," she said.

"That's got to be incredibly hard," Tristan added, more gently than she had ever heard him speak.

"Thanks, guys," she uttered gratefully and swiped a few tears on her sleeve. "Just something my family has to deal with and get over, I suppose." Changing the subject, she started fake punching Tristan again. "You know, on a more positive note, T'ai chi's coming along. Before you know it, I'm going to be able to put you on your ass!" The five-foot-four and a half-inch woman grinned up at the much taller man. "I'll just grab that ponytail of yours and flip you over, pal!"

"Oh, sure, Mare—that'll be the day." He rolled his eyes teasingly, and proudly flipped his shoulder-length, strawberry blonde mane.

The next time Mare saw Kate, Mare's intuition told her something was up with Walt. She asked Kate about it.

"He came over last night, wanting to reconcile," she admitted. "He had been drinking. He's been drinking a lot lately."

"Did you ask him to leave, I hope?"

"I did, but he stayed, and we talked and" she braced herself for Mare's reaction, "we ended up sleeping together again."

Mare's stomach turned over. "What! Ohh, Kate, why? I thought you wanted to end things."

"I do, but it's hard. I have trouble saying no. The thought of it totally disgusts me now. I don't know how it happened. I don't know how I can be with him. The thought just grosses me out."

"Do you want to continue dating him? Is that what you want?"

She shook her head no. "But I don't know how to break it off. I'm not that strong. He keeps pressing me, and I give in."

"You are plenty strong enough."

"I guess so, but he just seems to have some power over me."

"Only if you give it to him. You need to figure out what it is you really want."

"It's not a healthy relationship for me. I want it to be over."

"Then tell him so, set your boundaries and stick to them!"

"I will try, Mare. I will."

Mare wished Kate could make that commitment with more certainty in her voice.

Driving home one day that week, Mare passed Kate's apartment building. She could see Walt in Kate's driveway. He seemed to be yelling at her. Mare was behind someone trying to parallel-park on the street, so she had a moment to consider what she should do. Walt was clearly angry, but Kate seemed to be safe. At least they were outside and not in her apartment. Traffic began to move again. *It isn't my place to interfere with this.* Mare continued driving, deciding to call Kate when she got home to make sure she was okay. The woman was crying when she answered, but thankfully Walt had left.

"Joel saw us and stopped. He asked if everything was okay. Walt said it was and then left. I don't know what to do, Mare. Maybe I should file a restraining order. He just won't leave me alone."

"It's up to you, Kate. I don't have the answer. If you have asked him to leave you alone, and he will not do that, you have a right to take action. Do what you feel you need to. I'll support you however I can."

"I'll have to sleep on it."

"Okay, well, you call if you need to. Don't open the door or talk to him on the phone. Keep your boundaries. Okay?"

"I will. Goodnight."

Mare ran up to Joel's room after school the following day. He also taught English, and was a friend of Mare's. A department meeting was scheduled for that afternoon, and Mare was nervous about it. She also wanted to get his reaction on the driveway scene. If Joel was seeing the same things Mare was, perhaps he would have some thoughts about what to do.

"I know. It's getting weird," Joel said in his quirky, New Yorker style. "I was driving by Kate's house last night on the way home and I saw them in Kate's driveway."

"Me too. It was crazy, wasn't it? I didn't know what to do. I decided to call when I got home, but I'm glad you stopped."

"It's bizarre. I've talked to her and she says one thing. He says something different. I don't know who to believe."

Mare nodded. "Most of the time I feel like both are lying to me." She watched Joel erase his whiteboard. "Today's meeting is going to be tense," Mare said.

All twelve department members knew what was going on, yet there was no public acknowledgement to the group about the affair. Sure, Walt could talk about money to buy books or curriculum issues or whom to give English awards to, but everyone would know about the big pink elephant in the room, even if no one talked about it.

Sweat beaded up on Walt's age-spotted skin as he led them through several items on the agenda. His voice did not falter from nervousness; in fact, it was harder than usual. Obviously, he was toughening himself to get through this, overcompensating for his fear of being in the hot seat. Kate sat near the door and kept her head directed towards the stack of papers in front of her.

Mare felt awful for her friends. *This has got to be so difficult. It's a struggle for me, and I'm not even the one who had the affair.*

Walt's words traveled through the air, but Mare's thoughts were on the future. Walt was their chairperson, their supervisor—how would this work? Both Kate and Mare had to go through Walt for book requests and issues regarding students. *Would he be fair to Kate now?* She had to wonder. Then a new idea occurred to her. *Had he shown preference to Kate or Mare in the past because of his closeness to them?* Mare was beginning to get more and more uncomfortable with this line of thought and her head began to ache. *How can we continue to have department meetings like this?*

Later that day, Kate went to the police station to fill out the paperwork for a restraining order, but in the end Mare discovered that she never filed it.

A few days later, Walt entered Mare's room, looking upset.

"What can I do for you, Walt?" Mare asked him.

"You know Kate has threatened to put the restraining order on me, right?"

"Yes, she told me."

"I've been trying to stay away from her, Mare; I really have. But the other night about 10 o'clock she starts knocking on my apartment door and crying to me that she doesn't know what to do and that she misses me. Has she told you this? What am I supposed to do?"

Mare looked at him with disbelief and then confusion. *I can't believe she would do such a thing.... Wait a minute, yes, I can.* Confusion gave way to empathy. *What should he do? She's a beautiful, smart young woman. Of course, he would be attracted to her. I don't blame the poor man. She sets boundaries and then violates them herself.*

"Honestly, Walt, I don't know. She tells me one thing, and then she goes and does something different. Both of you have lied to me, and I don't know what to believe anymore. I have trouble trusting both of you these days."

When Mare approached Kate about her visit to Walt's place the night before, Kate started crying.

"Yes, I went there."

"Why, Kate? I just don't understand. You were about to file a restraining order on him. How is he supposed to deal with these mixed messages?" Mare's voice was frustrated and angrier than she usually allowed it to be.

Kate sniffed, and pulled her long blond hair out of her eyes. "I'm sorry. I don't understand it myself. I don't know why I went there."

"You *can't* do this anymore. You need to make up your mind for everyone's sake. Do you want him or don't you?" Mare looked at the woman. Her body was held together tensely, and her shoulders were hunched slightly. Mare remembered T'ai Chi class, when Kate would go through the motions so limply.

Kate nodded, "I know. I know. We can't be in a relationship! I just wish we could still be friends, but we don't seem able to be friends and not be romantically involved. I don't know how we are going to manage teaching together."

"I don't know either, Kate."

19

Spring Buds Break Through

April showers bring May flowers? What do Mayflowers bring?

~Unknown~

Mare remembered her favorite childhood riddle as she flipped the page of her calendar from April to May. She always liked the play on words. In Maine, snow often covered the ground in April, but in May—May was a time of reliable spring. New, fresh greens were bursting from every spot covered in soil. Mare moved to her classroom window and scanned the campus lawn, swathed in colors of spring.

It was a time of romance and fertility. Mare and Pete had tried to put the stress surrounding them aside to start trying for a second child. Mare's freshman honors class was studying *Romeo and Juliet*. She always reserved it for the end of the year because it was a time of hope for lovers, and spirits were high in anticipation of the end of the school year. Prom was around the corner. Students were busily picking out dresses, describing them in full detail to Mare between classes, and discussing who was going with whom to the grand event.

Feeling unusually light and refreshed today because of the beautiful weather, Mare swung her lunch bag widely as she walked down the hall towards the picnic area. Like one of the new red bulbs, swollen with ripe readiness and about to burst from the tree limbs she had seen that morning, Mare glowed with the possibility of renewed life. She was smiling, calm and radiant as she ambled by the Prom ticket table, where a couple of students sat and others were milling around, handling money and passing tickets across the table.

"Hey, Miz Lumen!" she heard her name called from the back of the table.

Mare squinted to see who called her. "Oh, hey Austin! How's it going?" Mare responded kindly, but kept on walking.

"You wanna go to Prom with me?" he invited with a handsome grin and a quick raise of his eyebrows.

Mare laughed warmly and blushed at the foolishness of the suggestion. He was 17; she was 30 and married, and she was his teacher, no less.

"Very funny, Austin. What's the matter? You don't have a date yet?" she inquired, slowing down her steps slightly to find out.

"Oh, I have a date. I'd just rather not go with her…. It's my ex-girlfriend."

"Oh, I see," she acknowledged with mock gravity.

"We're going as friends."

Mare nodded, and quickened her pace a little. "Oh, I'm sure you'll have a great time, Mr. Bean!"

"At least save me a dance!" he shouted after her.

She chuckled for a few moments after she passed by the group.

"I just got asked to go to Prom!" Mare laughed as she swung her leg over the bench. Sophie, Tristan, Kate and Joel were seated already.

"Oh really," Sophie asked.

"Yup, he's supposed to go with his ex, but doesn't really want to. Hmm … I haven't been asked to Prom for … ohhh …" she counted back in her mind, "… twelve years."

"So, did you turn him down gently?" Kate asked.

"Oh, sure, I did. Speaking of prom," Mare directed her comments to Kate, "Do you remember our friend, Howie? The one we told you about before, Kate?"

"Yes, I remember."

"Pete thinks you and he should chaperone the Prom together. Get your mind off everything. Have some fun."

"I don't know …"

"It can be totally light and carefree, no strings. Just go have a good time. Pete can tell him that you've just come out of a difficult relationship, and aren't looking for anything romantic."

"Sounds like a great idea to me," Joel said. "Besides, we're all going. You should be there too."

"Well, I would like to see some of my students all dressed up. Does Howie dance?"

"Sure does!"

"Okay then."

*   *   *   *

Mare slid on her silk stockings and slipped on her heels. She glanced in the mirror and cleaned a slight mascara smudge off her eyelid. She swept a hand into her light brown hair and spritzed a little hairspray to give it more fullness and lift. She struck a playful pose. "You look fabulous, sistah," she said out loud.

"Wow!" Pete said as she alighted on the bottom step. "You look good, Mare." He nuzzled into her. "You sure we've got to go to this?"

She slapped him playfully on his lapel.

"I dropped Cody off at your parents', so we can sleep in tomorrow morning," he said seductively.

"Come on, they'll be here any minute!" Mare said, pulling his wandering hands off her.

"Hey, guys—you look good." Seth murmured as he walked through the kitchen, but he hardly looked at them.

"Thanks, bro," Mare said, watching him fly by.

"We'll be back around 1-1:30," she told him.

"K," he answered as he jogged up the stairs.

Mare shook her head negatively, but remained upbeat.

When Howie and Kate arrived they all headed up to the Sunday River Resort to help chaperone the Prom.

After dining together, the chaperones were assigned task rotations and ultimately greeted bedecked students as they arrived.

Kate and Howie flirted mildly all night, and Pete was pleased with himself that he had fixed them up. "Maybe she'll get this whole Walt business out of her system if she hangs around Howie for awhile," he hummed to his wife, and ambled over to speak to his buddy.

Mare crossed the room to get to the punch and snack table, and Austin greeted her.

"You look good, Miz Lumen," he told her. She could hardly hear him over the thumping bass coming from the speakers.

"Thanks," she beamed.

They chatted for a minute, until his date ran up and grabbed his hand and started dragging him off to the dance floor. "Have fun!" he breathed to her on the way by, but he did not dare invite her to dance.

Mare grinned at them with amusement. They were shaking their booties on the dance floor, spinning around and singing with the music. *I'm gonna miss him next year when he's a senior,* she thought. *He's a sweetheart.*

Pete's arms coiling around her waist interrupted the thought. His legs were bobbing and his dancing almost spilled her punch.

She set it down and pulled him onto the dance floor. "Hey Mrs.Lumen— alright!" she heard her students say as she danced near each of them. Mare loved to dance, although she was a little more inhibited around her students than she might have been out on the town in Portland. Still, it was only the younger teachers who danced to the faster music, so students were always thrilled to see a teacher out there. Sophie danced too, and impressed Mare with the free-flowing movement of her arms. She looked like a graceful bird, spreading her wings. Nobody else danced quite like Sophie, but Sophie wasn't wondering about the reactions of others; she simply listened to the music and let her body do what it wanted. Mare admired that freedom.

Kate and Howie managed to get out on the floor for a few of the slower songs, and by the end of the night seemed to be quite comfortable together. Prom was a success. The music was loud, the food was good, and the students were gorgeous. And the last marker of success: Mare discovered in the morning—that all had arrived home safely.

Later in the week, Howie confided to Pete that when he took Kate home, things had gotten rather passionate. They made plans to see each other again, but Kate had backed out abruptly when he called her a few days later.

Just when Mare began to think that things between Walt and Kate had tamed, trouble started to brew again. It escalated gradually. More difficult department meetings followed. Snappy conversations. Walt barking at co-workers. Kate becoming more and more distant. Small reports from coworkers or Kate herself that Walt was following Kate around town like a stalker. Mare witnessed many of these moments herself. The problem came to a head one day when Mare was walking up to Kate's classroom after school. Down the hallway from Kate's room, even with the door closed, Mare could hear Walt's raised voice shouting angrily at Kate—about what Mare did not know. She only caught the tail end as she walked through the door, ignoring the intended barrier. "Why don't you ever listen to me?" he was yelling, but stopped abruptly when he saw Mare enter. Without question, he was irritated that Mare had interrupted them.

Kate stood with her head down and her arms stretched protectively across her chest.

Mare didn't acknowledge the argument. Instead, she said, "I need to talk to Kate about something. Could I borrow her?" Of course, she knew it wasn't a good time from Walt's point of view, but he left. Kate was shaking a little. Mare just looked at her, and a desire to protect this woman slid its way into her psyche.

"Look, Kate, I don't know what is going on with you two, or who's at fault, but this can't continue! How can either of you get any work done? It isn't fair to anyone. Have you talked to your parents about this?"

"Yes, they want me to go to the principal."

"Have you considered it?" The idea was beginning to hold some appeal to Mare as well.

"I have, but Todd pulled me into his office earlier this year and asked me if there was something going on between Walt and me. If I go to him now and tell him differently, he'll know I lied."

"Yes, he will, but he will have more respect for you if you go and tell him yourself at least." Mare's arms crossed her own chest, and she shook her head. "I can understand how it would be hard, and it's your decision, but I can't imagine working under these circumstances. I mean, Walt is your supervisor! You can't keep worrying about him getting in your face while you are trying to do your job. It's one thing if the conflict stays out of the building for the most part, but this has gone too far! It's not helping you OR Walt to be working under these conditions. Maybe Todd can help to alleviate some of the problems, if he knows about it."

Kate slouched down into her chair. "You may be right. I'll think about it."

"I just don't know what to do anymore, Kate. It's wearing me down to be in the middle like this. I don't want to interfere, and yet I'm trying to be a friend. I promised Walt in the beginning that I would be your friend."

"Thanks," Kate nodded glumly. "I'll talk to my parents tonight."

That night, Mare's phone rang. "Mare?"

"Yes, this is she."

"This is Janet Maguire, Kate's mother."

"Oh, hello, Mrs. Maguire."

"We've been trying to get Kate through this. We are just sick about the whole thing. I can't understand it all, but we're trying to make sure that Kate does the right thing ... the best thing for her."

"I understand."

"We strongly feel she should go to the principal, and she told us today that you agreed with that. Is that true?"

"Things are getting worse, not better. I don't know what else to do. She can't keep teaching under these conditions. It's far too stressful and unpredictable."

"We agree. We are hoping you will help her speak with Principal Tyler tomorrow after school. It's a difficult thing for her to do, and we are afraid she will change her mind if she doesn't have your support."

Mare hesitated and squirmed a little, then straightened. "If she has made that decision, I will help her to talk to Todd."

"Thank you so much. This situation is simply causing incredible stress for us at home. For so long our two families have been friends … for ages!"

"I know, Mrs. Maguire. Kate told me. I'm very sorry."

"Well, we do appreciate all the friendship you have shown Kate. We are so far away; it's hard for us to do very much. It's nice to know she has an ally at Emerson."

Mare thanked her and said goodbye. She had wanted to avoid taking sides, but she was sure now that Walt was not going to be happy about the course of action they were about to take. *I wish I could see some other way to resolve this, but I'm afraid for everyone if something is not done soon. I hope this is the right thing.*

Pete was even less certain about it. "Are you sure you want to get involved with this? It might be better if you just stayed out of it."

"I know how people can get kind of crazy over lost relationships, and I understand how hard this has been for Walt, but it just can't go on, Pete. It isn't a healthy work environment for any of us. I don't know what else to do."

"It's your choice, Mare, but I guarantee you Walt is going to be pissed! He's going to get in trouble."

"Maybe, but maybe not. Maybe Todd will just pull them both into the office and tell them to have no contact with each other beyond professional necessity. I mean, what else would he do? I don't think he'll fire Walt. He's a good teacher. He might lose his department chair position, but—in all honesty—Pete, maybe he should. Sure, they seem to have entered into the relationship consensually and mutually, but they both had to know that it could cause departmental troubles. They had to know they were taking some risks. I'm not sure Walt should continue as department chair. I feel uncomfortable now, having him as my superior. Their choices have altered the professional climate. I hesitate to go to him like I used to about department issues. How can he supervise Kate now? I mean, no one in the department is feeling good about this situation. It might be the best thing for everyone, Walt included, if he were no longer chair. I don't know! At least the power dynamics would be even again."

"Like I said, it's up to you. He's just going to be pissed, and you're going to be the scapegoat for helping her."

"You are probably right." Mare flopped onto the sofa. She spread out her hands and looked at her palms. "If they could have kept it out of school, everything would have been fine. It was their business. I was hoping they could take care of it, and get past it. But it's not working, and they seem unable to find a way to make it work. They both made it my business—the school's business—when they let the problem seep into the workplace. Now the problem has gone beyond them. It's affecting a greater number of people, including students." Whatever hesitation she was feeling started to dissipate. "No, I need to do something. I can't live like this anymore. The tension at school is almost unbearable."

Pete's head bobbed, "I suppose you're right. If it's gotten that bad...."

"I have to tell Walt first though," Mare concluded, leaning her head back on the pillow. "I don't want to do this behind his back. I owe him that much."

The orange sun dipped below the horizon, circled the globe, and, at dawn, climbed again spreading its rose-pink fingers, like it had every other morning across time.

Mare waited until school was over, went upstairs, shut the door behind her, and told Walt she had to talk to him privately.

"Walt, Kate's parents called me last night. They are very concerned about Kate's well being. They feel things have gotten out of hand and have encouraged Kate to go to the principal."

Walt started to interrupt, but Mare asked him to let her finish first.

"Kate intends to go see Todd and tell him the truth. The Maguires have asked me to help her do this, and I've agreed."

"What! Mare! You can't do this; I'll lose my job!"

"I don't think so, Walt." Mare tried to be consoling and look on the positive side. "Maybe Todd can help."

He looked at her with disgust and superiority, "Don't be naïve, Mare. He's going to nail my ass to the wall."

Mare cringed uncomfortably. "Walt, things can't keep going as they have been. Yesterday, you were screaming at her in the classroom! You're her department chair! You can't be doing that! It's harassment. It's just not right."

He sidestepped her point, and started pleading with her. "Mare, she's been lying to you all along. She hasn't always told you the truth."

Mare nodded in agreement. "That may be, Walt, but I have still witnessed very unprofessional behavior. Behavior that makes me uncomfortable as a department member."

She could see the blood rising upward to his face. He looked about ready to burst.

Mare scrambled to defend her position. "What am I supposed to do, Walt? When you two first confessed to me this whole thing, you asked me to be Kate's friend. You asked me! I have wanted to preserve my friendships with both of you, but you have put me in a very tough position. This mess has degraded so much that it's unhealthy for all of us. I know that you don't agree with or understand what I've decided to do, but I'm making the best decision I know how. I'm hoping that it will ultimately make things better for everyone."

"You're right, Mare." He said coldly. "I do disagree. Very strongly. This is a mistake. You're screwing me over."

Mare winced, and added with a note of finality, "I'm sorry you feel that way, Walt—I really am—I'm sorry it has come to this—but I need to act according to what I feel is right. I've thought a lot about it. We are going to the principal."

Walt's lips pressed together in rage and helplessness, and Mare walked out of the room, breathing heavily and trembling slightly. She did not like confrontation at all. She didn't like the idea of possibly hurting Walt, but she could see no other way.

Kate and she had arranged to meet in Kate's room, so Mare headed to it next.

"I just told Walt what we were going to do."

"Oh, god—let's find a different room before he comes here."

When they had arrived at an empty and dark home economics room, Mare asked Kate if she was sure this was what she wanted to do. With some hesitation and obvious fear, Kate nodded.

"But I don't think I can talk to Todd myself first. I can't bear to see his reaction. Would you go and tell him, and then have him meet me in here?"

Mare sighed at the request. She would have preferred Kate do it, but she understood the woman's concerns and she wanted the conflict to end, so she answered, "I guess so."

They discussed briefly what Mare should say, then Mare made the short, but difficult trek down to Todd's office.

"Todd, may I speak to you about something important?"

"Sure, Mare, let's go into the conference room." He placed his arm gently on her back to guide her in the direction he intended. Mare and Principal Todd Tyler had worked together on the *transition team*, a committee designed to envision a philosophical remodeling of the school in conjunction with some physical redesign that had been happening the last few years. Emerson had been divided the year before into sub-schools, and Mare was one of two leaders from her particular school. She and Todd had spent many meetings with the group hashing out ideological and logistical issues. Occasionally, Mare would openly, though respectfully, challenge some of Todd's political answers. He seemed to respect her for the way she interacted in the group, as well as for her teaching abilities. He was additionally sympathetic to her regarding her brother's situation.

"What can I do for you, Mare?" he asked with full attention. They each took a chair at an oval table that was just long enough and wide enough to fit it. The conference room hugged the main hallway outside, where only a few students were lingering and passing by. Mare could see them in the glass partition that separated the room from the hall.

She took a deep breath and replied. "Todd, Kate has asked me to come down and talk to you. She is nervous about doing it herself, so I told her I would help her. You remember earlier this year when you asked her about Walt and her?" Mare's eyes reached to his.

"Yes, I do." She could see the glimmer of recognition and expectation in his expression. Then behind Todd, at precisely that moment, Mare saw Walt through the glass windows. He noticed Mare with Todd, got an angry look on his face, and kept walking. "Oh, god, there he is. Walt. He's pissed at me. I told him I was going to tell you."

Todd's head stretched behind him to look. "Oh, don't worry about him. What were you going to say?"

Mare shook off the threatening look she'd been given, "Well, you were right. They had a relationship."

He inhaled slowly and pressed his hands together flatly.

Mare added, "I had NO idea, Todd—I want you to know—until a few weeks ago when they told me.... Anyway, Kate and her parents felt it was important to be honest with you now. Things have been getting out of hand. I am very concerned at this point, and I'm hoping that you can do something to remedy the problem it has become."

Mare filled Todd in on a few of the details, but wanted to reserve the majority of the conversation for Kate. Mare led Todd up to where she was waiting.

Todd sat down across from her and offered a greeting. "Mare tells me that you want to talk about Walt?"

Kate nodded, and told him she was sorry for lying. She appeared very frail and timid in that moment.

Mare excused herself, so they could talk privately. She did not want to be involved any further.

At least it was done. *Let the cards fall where they may. It's out of my hands now.*

That week, Kate spent a fair amount of time at the superintendent's office with Todd and the superintendent, Dr. Elaine Bailey.

Mare got reports from Kate after each. The two administrators were trying to get her to sign sexual harassment papers against Walt. They wanted her to press charges.

That Walt's behavior was illegal in the eyes of the law was not a surprise to Mare. She was not comfortable, however, with the idea of Kate pressing charges against Walt. Fortunately, Kate spoke with a legal rep from the teacher's association and, in the end, resisted the pressure to sign.

This relieved Mare. Though it may have been professionally inappropriate and perhaps technically illegal for Walt to engage in a sexual relationship with Kate—as her superior—it didn't fit that he should be prosecuted for it. Somehow, Mare couldn't believe that Kate might have felt pressure to sleep with Walt or lose her job or be discriminated against if she didn't. It didn't seem to fit with what Mare had witnessed. It didn't feel right that he should be charged with a crime for entering into a romance with her.

However, it did feel like sexual harassment after they broke up.

Shortly after Kate finalized her decision, only a few days before the school year ended, Mare got an unexpected call from Walt's wife, Ginny. She had never spoken to or met the woman before in her life.

"Is this Mare Lumen?"

"Yes, it is."

The woman identified herself and immediately began railing against Mare's involvement in the situation with Kate.

"Do you know my husband lost his department chair position?" she yelled into the phone.

"No, I hadn't heard that." The woman barely let Mare get the words out.

"Well! He did and you are to blame for it! Do you know it's going to cost us $3,000 a year? That stipend makes a big difference in our income, young lady. It's no small loss."

Mare was feeling like a scolded grandchild.

"I'm sorry to hear that, Mrs. Douglas."

"Why did you have to go and tell the principal? It isn't right that he should lose that position. Now what are we going to do?"

While her rants continued, Mare wondered why Ginny was defending the husband who had betrayed her with a twenty-something-year-old woman and then left her.

"Now that Walt's moved out, and we still haven't sold our old home, I'm going to have to go out and get a job. I haven't had a job in all the time I've been married. I've raised my children and then taken care of our home. I'm sixty-two years old. What am I supposed to do now? Why did you do it, Mare?"

Hmmm … maybe I have miscalculated Walt's age, Mare wondered.

Mare tried to respond and explain, but Ginny would not accept her thinking. Finally, Mare began to cry. "Ginny, I really am sorry. I never set out to hurt Walt or you. I was just trying to do the best thing I knew to do. If I made a mistake, I am truly sorry, but I can't change the past. I did what I thought best at the moment. That is all I can do. I meant no malice in it. Walt was very good to me when my brother got into trouble."

Ginny's anger softened a little when she heard Mare express these thoughts. Her voice reflected this. "Well, yes, I know about your brother. Walt and I felt very sorry for you and your family. We've been through our own crises in the past." The woman cleared her throat. "Maybe you *were* doing what you thought was best, but Kate is two-faced. She's been stringing you along right along. You should always question what she tells you. She can't be trusted, that sly thing. I'll never forgive her for seducing my husband." Ginny couldn't stop defending him. "I mean, how is he supposed to resist when she throws herself at him?"

Oh no, Mare was thinking. *I really don't think I want to go here, even if it's true.*

"I just want my husband back, and now he's lost his chair position. I've already started looking for a job."

"I'm sorry, Ginny. I wish I knew what to tell you. I only did what I thought best."

"Well, I understand, dear, this hasn't been an easy time for you either."

Five minutes after Ginny had hung up, the phone rang again. It was Walt.

"I just got off the phone with my wife."

Mare's heart thudded in her chest. She didn't think she could take an assault from him right now.

"Mare, I know you think that Kate is your friend," he began with coldness, but without shouting, "but are you aware how much she's lied to you? She's not a real friend. Do you want to hear the stuff she told me in the last few months?"

"Well, I ... I ..."

Then he reeled off a list of things, one right after the other. "She said your brother was guilty, and you should just get over it." Mare reacted silently, but with growing pain to each statement. "She said she can't believe that you are trying to have another baby when your marriage is hanging by a thread ... and she also told me that you are in love with Scott Wallace!"

"What?" Mare was left flabbergast. "She said what? She said those things? I'm not in love with Scott; I never told her that. I just said he was a great guy and I liked him. *She* insinuated that we had chemistry. And my marriage is not on the brink of divorce! Sure, we are struggling, but we've been under a great deal of stress. It's understandable. We are fully committed to each other ... and ... I—I can't believe she said those things to you."

Anything I mentioned to Kate in private was skewed and passed on to Walt, my department chair! I'm glad he's no longer department chair now that I know this. I had no idea that she was telling him such things ...

"I'm just telling you what she's said. Now do you think she's such a good friend?" he hissed with sarcasm.

"Perhaps not, Walt. I'm going to have to talk to her about these."

"I should think so."

A short while later, Mare arrived unannounced at Kate's doorstep, fuming and ready to make a verbal knockout, if what Walt said was true. She pressed the doorbell button. Quick footsteps rattled their way down the stairs. Kate peeped out the window to see who was there. She was surprised to find Mare standing stiffly, but opened the door. Thick, coke-bottle glasses covered Kate's pretty blue eyes. The sight startled Mare, who had only seen her friend with contacts. She couldn't help but stare at this new picture of Kate for a moment. The glasses somehow conflicted with her everyday public persona. The image shaved twelve years off Kate's age. It took Mare a moment to reconcile the two versions of her friend's appearance.

More calmly than she had arrived feeling, she said, "I need to talk to you, Kate."

Kate nodded and led her upstairs to her apartment. They both sat down on the living room futon. Kate looked at Mare, and waited.

"I've never seen you with glasses before."

Kate pulled on the rim. "I have terrible vision. I don't like to wear them, ah, obviously," she admitted uncomfortably. "I didn't realize you were coming over."

Kate looked so meek and small. The anger started to melt away as Mare studied the face of her colleague. She was seeing her in a new light. Kate could have been ten years old in Mare's eyes. The public presentation Kate flaunted was one of an intelligent, pretty, confident woman. As Mare watched her now, that exterior illusion faded. She gazed into the face of a little girl, insecure, feeling ugly, embarrassed, weak. Mare blinked a couple of times, but could not erase or alter the impression. This was a scared and fragile child, bumbling her way through life. She barely realized what she was doing.

The edge was gone. She did not feel like strangling this strange girl. An almost-motherly sympathy took over. *This person has made mistakes, but she is not wicked.* Mare's voice was firm. She wanted Kate to know this was serious, but Mare no longer wanted to hurt her with her words as Kate had done to Mare. She stated the facts. "Walt and Ginny called. They are very angry. Walt will not be department chair next year."

Kate's head dropped and nodded quietly.

"He also told me some things that he claims you said to him that trouble me greatly."

Kate's head stayed low, like a dog about to be scolded. Mare studied her reactions, squinting.

She listed off the things Walt said.

Kate was silent, so Mare continued firmly. "I am angry that you shared personal information with him without my knowledge or permission. I am furious that you said I was in love with Scott. That is not what we talked about! How dare you say these things, particularly so skewed, to Walt? And my marriage is not on the rocks! Even if it were, it was not your place to tell my supervisor so! Those were your own conclusions. They were not based on fact, though they were presented as fact, and they were not especially kind to me. I don't appreciate that, Kate. I thought we were friends."

Kate had managed to look up while Mare was going through each item. She nodded her head in acceptance to each, and tears came swelling out from below the wide wedges over her eyes. It was hard to see sharply the blue orbs below the layers of magnification. Mare could not stop gaping at them. Something. Something was there.

Has Kate been abused along the way? By an older man?

Kate could say little in her own defense. She groveled and apologized.

Mare felt pity for the child buried not so deeply in Kate. Though she condemned the behavior of the adult, Mare saw through to something more complex that she was not yet prepared to judge. *Human beings,* she thought to herself. *What are we all about?*

"Well, what's done is done. Can't change the past—BUT—I would like to be able to trust you, Kate. You have not been honest with me, and that makes it very hard."

"I know, Mare. I've been messed up since I started working here. This isn't me. Things will be different from here, I promise. I'm sorry."

Mare went home, but began to worry that Walt might tell Pete the erroneous information out of spite that she was in love with Scott. She decided she would have to talk to him before that happened. It was better he hear the truth from her.

20

The River and Mare

The great Tao flows everywhere.
All things are born from it,
But it doesn't create them....
Since all things vanish into it
And it alone endures,
It can be called great.

~Tao Te Ching (verse 34)/Stephen Mitchell translation~

Mare's hands were on the steering wheel as the forests of central Maine passed by her windshield. The Lumens had decided to spend a long weekend alone together at Pete's father's cabin, now that school was out for the summer. They needed some time alone to begin to rebuild some long lost intimacy.

But Mare had something on her mind. She had to tell Pete about the Scott thing before Walt might mention it to him, trying to cause conflict for Mare. She wanted to get it out of the way so she could enjoy the trip. She tried to think of the best way to initiate the conversation. Mare flipped on her blinker to turn onto the interstate ramp.

After an hour of struggling with it, she finally jumped in. "Pete, can I ask you a question?"

"Shoot."

"Do you think ... that once you get married, you stop being attracted to other people? I mean, do you still look at some women and think, *Man, she's pretty?*"

"Well, of course. I don't think you stop being human just because you're married."

"I'm glad to hear you say that because I need to tell you something … Kate and I had a conversation once about Scott Wallace. She suggested that Scott was a really great guy and intimated there was some attraction between us."

"Yah?"

"I admitted to her that I found him attractive. He's a wonderful man, but that was it. Nothing would ever happen there, but then crazy Kate told Walt that I was in love with Scott. It isn't true, but I wanted to let you know about it, in case Walt tried to get back at me for losing his stipend position. I didn't want you to hear something like that out of the blue. Otherwise, it wouldn't even be worth mentioning."

He thought about it for a minute, which made Mare nervous.

"Scott is a great guy. I can see how you'd be attracted to him."

Mare smiled over at her husband. "Thanks for understanding."

"But touch him and I'll kill ya," he ribbed her.

"Not to worry about that. I promise you," she put her palm up as if making a solemn pledge, "I will never sleep with another man while we are married, and since we're going to be married forever, I guess it's a pretty safe bet."

He grabbed her hand and smiled.

"Hey, speaking about relationships," Mare chimed in, "Let's listen to that audiotape on *Soulmates* by Thomas Moore."

Pete smirked momentarily, but then seeing his wife's enthusiasm and knowing they had a long ride ahead, he agreed. "Okay."

Mare clapped her hands in child-like enthusiasm. "Cool."

The content was a little different than Mare and Pete had expected. Among other things, Moore talked about what happens when a spouse has an affair, what causes it and how a couple can rebuild something after an affair.

When the tape was finished, Mare acknowledged, "Kind of strange, don't you think, that he spent so much time talking about adultery when we were just talking about attraction in marriage. Plus, given the whole situation with Walt and Kate?"

"Yeah," Pete told her, "it was an interesting coincidence, but surprisingly, I like it. He made some great points. I never really thought about it much from that point of view. I mean, my father had an affair on my mother when I was nine or so. I always figured that if my spouse fooled around on me that would be the end of it. But I'm not so sure it would have to go that way after listening to him talk about it."

"I liked it too, but you aren't going to have to worry about me. If things ever got that bad, I would talk to you first. I wouldn't jump into bed with someone else. That's not my style."

"I know, honey," he tapped her hand again. "Me neither."

*   *   *   *

Mare stood on the enormous boulder overlooking the 15-foot waterfall and the surging power of Grand Lake Stream. The rush and hum of the swirling rapids caused a swell of energy to build within her chest. Her breathing intensified, and her eyes gaped widely. The water. Something about it was so enlivening and comforting. It was such a contrast to the way she felt after these many draining months: spent, low, stagnant, tamed. All of this flittered on her psyche like a dream; she was not quite aware of her longing to reclaim her wild nature, her passion, her fluidity. She looked back down to the riverside where her husband was sitting on a downed tree in the river squeezing into his shorty wet suit. Climbing down to join him, she was careful to place her steps wisely, so as not to slip and fall. When both were outfitted in full snorkeling gear, she looked around at the water that lay below the falls. The area right in front of the waterfall was gushing forcefully. Pete paused to give her some instructions.

"The river is moving really fast today. You are going to have to swim very fast through the rapids until you get to that eddy on the opposite side." He pointed across the river. "That's the best place to start from. It's shallow, and there's no current there." He put his hand upon her shoulder and looked at her. "All set?"

"All set," she assured him. Mare used to be a lifeguard and swim instructor, so she was a strong swimmer, yet the speed and power of the water scared her a little.

Pete walked into the river and, just before hitting the foamy center rush, lunged forward, mask in water and fins kicking with strength and speed. When he reached the eddy, he stood up and motioned for her to go.

It was a good thirty to forty feet to the other side of the river. Mare stood in her own eddy, the water moving and splashing across her knees. She took a few steps toward the center, until she was in up to her thighs. The cold wet against her bare legs sent a shiver up her spine, and she could feel her heart pumping with fear and excitement. Her balance wavered in the flow. She steadied herself and pulled the goggles over her eyes, adjusting the straps to fit her head. She moved the mouthpiece of the snorkel between her lips and teeth. Quick, shallow breaths blew out the top of the snorkel, rhythmically. Mare tried to take a few deep, calm breaths. Then she leapt—arms outstretched—into the blasting current. Her limbs were moving before she hit. Her face was in the water, but even if her eyes had been open, she couldn't have seen anything save for a flurry of white bubbles. Her legs kicked furiously to propel her across the river before being carried too far downstream. Her arms stroked down to her sides to streamline her journey, and she used cues from her body to tell her when she began to near the opposite eddy. Mare then lifted her eyes out of the water to better direct her movement, once she had passed through the surging rapids.

She continued to kick until she could feel her knees barely brush against the solid shore. Then she pushed her hands against the sand and rock-covered bottom, arched her back and flattened her fins on the ground, and walked herself to a standing position beside Pete.

Her breaths came out in short, tired pants—almost more from the intensity of feeling from crossing than from the exertion itself.

"Great job!" her husband patted her on the back.

"Thanks," she returned, somewhat breathless. "That was a rush!"

He nodded. "We're much closer to the falls on this side. Let's check it out."

The couple walked close to the torrent again, and when they were near, crouched down and dove forward, careful to keep their snorkels above water for now. Mare could see from the edge of the rapids that the river was clear and deep. She had never snorkeled in a river before; the flow of adrenaline from it was strong. Mare paddled around the slower sections of the river, stretching her neck up and down and rotated it to the side to see everything around her. A hand motioned her to follow, and she kicked a few strokes to join Pete below the waterfall. He pointed in to the center, and then swam forward.

Where the water fell in a rich cascade over the rocks, the turbulence chopped the water in a giant arch around its front. Below the surface, Mare could see a thick curtain of bubbles, as the force of the falling water hit the lower level. Pete wanted her to see behind that curtain of white bubbles, so Mare poked her head through. She had to keep her feet kicking so she would not get pulled backward, but when she peered through the bubbling wall, she could see fish swimming behind and through the bubbles. It was hard to gauge their size exactly; the water distorted perception. They seemed about six inches long, had dark green backs and wavy black lines along their topsides. Mare was most impressed by the spots along their sides: light green and orange. Pretty fish, flitting about in the calm behind the turbulence. Mare needed to resurface to take a breath. She blew the water out through the snorkel spout, and then sucked in a breath of air through it. Within seconds, Pete bobbed up beside her.

"D'ja see those brookies?"

Mare spit out her snorkel bit. "Yes, that was awesome!"

"I never realized that they hide behind there. I'm going to have to remember that next time I go fishing."

"They were beautiful."

"I'm going to snorkel in the current now. Come on!"

Each replaced their mouthpiece and slid back into the water.

Mare followed her husband who went up to the edge of the waterfall again, then spun around and dove down under the surface. Mare followed, but did not dive below. She chose instead to drift on the surface and breathe through her snorkel. The rapids pushed her downstream quickly. She watched Pete ahead of her, flipping his legs and steering his body slightly to check out the big boulders and contours of the river as he zoomed past. Then Mare stopped watching Pete and dropped her vision down closer to her own body. She did little, except let the river push her along. She was surprised how quickly she moved downstream. The river was clean and clear, and Mare watched the waterscape pass by with fascination. It might have been 25 feet deep in the center of the river, perhaps more. Some huge gray boulders speckled the river bottom. Sand filled in the empty spaces. Because the rocks that zipped by her were all different sizes, it left the impression of multi-dimensionality. The river floor was textured by dark, round surfaces, jagged edges and nooks on the rock faces. Spaces between rocks brought to mind an image of otters, flickering around and between the structures, using the stones as a playground. She observed from a distance all that filled the river. Within a few minutes, Mare realized that Pete had pulled off to the right into the eddy, so they could return to the waterfall again. She stroked her arms to do the same. They trudged carefully to the shallow water and made their way upstream on foot, walking backwards with their fins on. They reentered the water. This time, Mare decided to dive under, instead of simply scanning from the surface. It was thrilling to move with the river and glide so near to the rocks that were scattered on the bottom. Each time she made one of these runs, she relaxed more and more.

Gradually, something happened. Her own self-awareness began to fade; her thoughts drifted off. She felt not only the strength, but also the suppleness of the river. The flow. At first she moved with it, trying to ride the force. But with each dive through the center of the current, her sense of being separate from it diminished. She hardly noticed this shift in perception. At first, she simply felt the contrast between herself and the river. It moved. It undulated. The rocks in its path did not stop its movement; rather, it slid with ease around them. In fact, the giant boulders drifting below her vision seemed like the ruins of some ancient underwater temple that only she could enter, untouched for ages unknown.

The river flowed freely and fully. In comparison to the river, Mare felt stiff, weighted, awkward and sad. Oh, to be more like the river! She dove down into the cool depths of the water, and released everything she could in her body. She let the river take her, without resistance. Her head and neck bobbed weightlessly in the flow; her arms waved fluidly behind her—the way seaweed floats and waves in the tide; her legs trailed gently, moving to whatever degree the river coaxed them. Mare let the pure energy of the river wash through her. Every cell in her body seemed aligned with the water gliding around her. It almost felt like she was flying, though she didn't need to expend any effort to soar in this realm.

An extraordinary event then occurred, though Mare didn't *think* about it until it was over. She surrendered to the river, joined with it. She let go of herself, and in that trust and release, felt a nurturing, protective embrace accept her. In that prolonged moment, when she was not just a swimmer in the river, but one with it, the river took away her pain and waved a lightness, a vitality, through her whole being. She had never felt so natural and at peace. She just closed her eyes and merged with the fluidity that surrounded her, and the River tenderly salved her wounds. Mare experienced liberation and healing like she had never felt before.

Then the instant passed almost as quickly as it had come. She resurfaced, blew water out of her snorkel, and began breathing fresh air again. Her whole being tingled. She swam to the riverside and sat in the eddy. She put her head in her hands briefly, then swiped a tear from the corner of her eye. She laid back in eight inches of water and let it support her weight. Her flippers touched the bottom, but the water supported the rest of her body. She wanted to prolong the feeling. She simply laid back and let the waves nudge against her cheek. The wind brushed across her exposed skin; the water felt warmer than the air. She could hear a woodpecker tapping against a tree trunk. She sunk into it all.

A pair of lips touched hers, and she responded. "Sneaking up on me, huh?"

"What'cha doin', Mare?"

She waited before answering. She looked up into his face, which was framed by a cloudless blue sky and pine trees. How could she describe what she had just felt? She smiled instead, and mildly offered, "I was just relaxing. What a great day." She inhaled fully, and sighed breathily on the exhale. Her husband kissed her again, and she wrapped her arms around his neck. Then they released each other, and Pete laid back beside his wife.

The gentle rise and fall of their bodies in response to the waves soothed them. Mare reached a hand over to Pete, so they could stay connected, like two boats drifting on the ocean. She sent a silent thank-you to spirit of the River.

After they packed up their gear and stripped off their wetsuits, Mare and Pete began walking back to the car. Pete unlocked the truck and tossed in their belongings. Then he shut the trunk and grabbed his wife's hand. Both were still in damp swimsuits and sandals. Mare wondered briefly where Pete was taking her, and then realized his intent. He walked her into the forest a ways from the picnic area, behind a large boulder. He began to undo the clip on her swimsuit, and as he did he kissed her passionately. The surface of the stone was angled, and Pete carefully leaned his wife back onto it. She met his kisses and began to reach for his trunks, so as to pull them down.

It appeared they were alone, and the trees and rocks protected them from view. Once their bodies were free of the restriction of clothing, Mare lifted her right knee and leaned the sole of her sandal against the rock, so as to allow her husband to approach more intimately. Pete stood back and surveyed his wife's beautiful body. A ray of sun, slicing through the leaves and startling the shadows, shone across Mare's ear and down at an angle upon her chest. A few water droplets still glistened on her breasts. He noticed the line the sunlight had drawn between the white and tan of the upper curves. Cold-water contact had left her nipples firm. He leaned one hand against the rock and cupped the other over her breast. It more than filled his palm. He pinched the nipple in his fingers and brought his mouth to it.

Mare felt his cool, moist body press against hers, as a warm breeze blew.

In this remote and natural setting, they made love, semi-standing, under the canopy of evergreens and birch trees that encircled them.

21

Spirals

*Energy is interacting to form a gigantic, dynamic pattern of rhyth-
mically repeating energy interactions. In other words, a dance of
energy. We are all part of a gigantic dance of energy.*

~Robert Burney~ <u>Twin Souls, Souls Mates, and Kindred Spirits</u>

Mare reached for the head of Romaine lettuce, stuffed it into the bag, then
leaned over to hug and kiss Cody, who was sitting in the front of the cart.

"Mare, dear! How ARE you?" A kind voice boomed out of the blue.

Mare turned around to see another English colleague, Miriam Chamberlin,
walking towards her. Miriam was about twenty years older than Mare, a warm,
intelligent and powerful personality.

"Hi, Miriam! How are you? How's your summer?"

"Oh, Mare, it's just wonderful. I've been gardening and reading and doing a
little traveling. It's just great!" Her eyes twinkled with clarity and presence. "Hi,
Cody!" She clasped her hands together and leaned towards him.

"That's super," Mare said.

"I take it you've heard about Walt losing the department chair position?"
Miriam placed a hand on Mare's cart.

"Yes, I have." Mare responded quietly.

"Well, have you considered applying for it, Mare? I think you'd be great."

"Ohh, thank you … very much, Miriam. I appreciate you saying so. Todd
asked me the same question. He has been encouraging me to apply as well."

"That's great," her colleague placed a hand on her arm. "So, are you going to
do it?"

"I don't think so." Mare grimaced a little. "Walt and Kate were my friends. I wouldn't feel right about personally benefiting from Walt's loss, even if I agree with his removal."

"Oh Mare, that wasn't your fault. Don't you even worry about that."

"It may not have been my fault, but I do worry about it. Plus, I've got Cody. I'm just afraid that I would have trouble juggling any more."

"I understand," Miriam frowned, "but I wish you'd reconsider. You'd make a wonderful chairwoman!" She waved goodbye, and continued with her shopping.

*   *   *   *

Mare studied the 3x5-curled photo in her hand. Just look at him. The soft blond hair, the bright eyes, the cute little button nose, the innocent smile. She compared the image to what she knew now. No one would ever suspect that this beautiful five-year-old child, so full of light and wonder, would become a child molester. Anyone who ever saw this bright, good child could never think he was lecherous. The two could not go together. He was not born a pedophile. The child only wanted to give and receive love, as every child does.

She picked up a second picture taken when Seth was about fifteen. Something had changed. She shuffled through other family photos. Seth with his two puppies when he was about twenty-five. There was a darkness around him. A sadness. Mare placed this older picture next to the picture of the child and studied the two side by side. She brought one closer to her nose and looked into the child's big brown eyes. "What happened? What happened to that light, Seth? I know it is still in there, but it got clouded by darkness somewhere along the way," she spoke to him, half hoping that he could tell her the things she did not know. Then she placed the photo down and rummaged through the rest of her pile. She picked up another, taken a little earlier than the first. Brother and sister were smiling radiantly for the camera, holding hands. Mare and Seth, at three and four, holding hands and smiling. Her hands dropped, but she was still clutching the photos. She found a picture of herself alone in a pink dance costume. Long blond hair flowing. A smile that was serene and bright. "I used to shine too. How did I get duller?" She packed away the pictures, but kept the one in her costume and placed it on her dresser mirror as a reminder. "I want to get all of that glow back!"

*   *   *   *

Pete wedged open the can of off-white paint, and handed brushes to Seth, Hope and Mare.

The couple had agreed to help the Lumens paint the kitchen and stairway walls.

"How come you're not going to strip the wallpaper first?" Hope asked.

"Because we have old horsehair plaster underneath, and we can't afford to do that huge of an overhaul. Removing it also makes a giant mess, so we just figured it'd be simpler and cheaper this way."

"Ah," she nodded, her thick, dark hair bobbing.

The four got to work on the walls, and even managed to have a good time doing it. Hope was fun, and it was easy to see the friendship that had developed between her and Seth. They joked around, painted each other's noses, and talked non-stop. Mare even saw them kiss a few times. She was reminded of the other times she'd seen her brother date. They were few and far between, but he had gone out with a handful of women. She recalled what her mother had recently told her, that Seth admitted to her after being with Hope sexually, that he was beginning to wonder if he really was gay or whether he could be happy with a woman, too.

Mare flipped her brush back and forth over what she considered to be hideous wallpaper. It felt good to cover up the ugliness with something calmer, brighter and cleaner. While her brush stroked across the pictures in front of her, she thought about her brother again. *How had this happened? Had he been abused himself?* She tried to think of potential abusers. *Maybe when we lived in New Jersey and were very young ... maybe we had a babysitter who touched Seth while he was asleep. I mean, he usually started touching kids when they were asleep at his house.* She felt that was a strange fact—well, all of it was strange. *Perhaps someone touched him when he was asleep and he didn't realize it consciously.* She thought back to New Jersey. *That older kid that I didn't care for ... the one that I didn't trust who was kind of a bully ... Justin. He babysat us once, Mom said, I think. Then he ended up committing suicide several years after we left. Oh, I don't know. I'll have to ask him. I want to make sure Cody isn't at risk from anyone we know. It just seems like this couldn't have come out of nowhere.*

Pete had the roller and was covering larger areas of the wall, particularly places none of them could reach on the stairway.

"Hey guys, I have a question for you," Seth paused in his painting. "Actually a favor to ask.... My lawyer tried to arrange a lie-detector test. They won't separate the charges, so I figured if I could take a lie-detector test about the stuff that isn't true, then maybe I could get them to change their mind. The court won't approve a partial test. The DA won't go for it."

"Well, why not," Mare asked.

"They've got nothing to lose by keeping things as they are."

"So, anyway, I want to hire someone to run the test on me, but it costs $1,000. I don't have a thousand dollars, so I need to figure out a way to get the money for it."

"Yes, so what can we do? We don't have the money either."

"I know, but your washer and dryer are pretty old and don't work so great. I thought you might be able to save up some money and buy mine, since they are practically brand-new and I could take yours. You know, maybe you could roll the cost into your loan when you buy your house or something."

"Maybe," Pete answered.

"We could certainly use a new set," Mare admitted. "We'll have to see."

"Okay," Seth resumed his painting. "Just thought I'd check. I just can't accept the rape charges that Eugene Grover is putting on me, or the oral sex claims that Sammy is accusing me of. I can't plead guilty to those. I just can't."

"So, if you have to go to trial—couldn't you just get on the stand and say these five charges are true, and these two charges are not true. Or whatever the numbers are … Don't bother to waste your time or the witnesses' time on those. I accept whatever punishment you feel is fair on those. However, I would like to contest these other two?" Mare attempted to persuade him again.

"I can't do that. The lawyer says I can't do that. It doesn't work that way."

I still don't understand why not. Mare continued with the painting of her walls in silence. *That's what I would do,* Mare moaned in her head. *I don't care what the lawyer said I could or couldn't do.*

*   *   *   *

Mare and Roger arranged a private T'ai Chi session, since class had taken a hiatus for their summer break. They found a quiet spot behind the pond in the circular clearing that Mare loved. They did *the form*, played some push hands and then sat down on the grass to enjoy their surroundings.

"I had this dream last night," Mare started telling him.

"Oh, I love dreams. Tell me about it."

"I don't remember much, but I was climbing up a wooden spiral staircase. The place reminded me of my in-laws house across the street, only it was much higher. I kept climbing up and around, until I came to the top. I had to stop at the ceiling. I could go no further."

"How'd you feel during the dream?"

"Good, like I was making progress, like I was getting somewhere, but then I had to stop."

"Hmmmm … I had a similar dream, not too long ago, except in this one I was flying."

"Oh, I've had a few flying dreams in my life. I wish I could have more. I remember a couple of great flying dreams from when I was a kid," Mare gushed.

"Yes, well, the awesome thing about this dream was that I kept flying higher and higher. I realized I was dreaming, so I wanted to see how far I could go. I hit a kind of ceiling, so I knocked on it, to see if I could get in."

"Wow, really, what happened?"

"I heard a booming voice say, 'You're not ready yet,' then I started falling down. I woke up."

The two laughed.

Mare pulled at a blade of grass and slowly eased one out of its place in the earth. She began to separate the pieces. "I would like to wake up in my dreams more. I would like to fly in my dreams again. Flying is so incredible. When I was a kid I remember flying near my junior high. I flapped my arms like they were wings." She grinned.

"Yes, I wish I could control it better too. You eventually learn that you don't have to flap. Your intention to fly is enough to get you flying." He leaned back into the lawn. "Well, if you ever have a lucid dream, come get me and we can go traveling together."

Mare laughed again, *as if.* "Okay, if I ever wake up in a dream, I'll try to come find you in dream space." Her mind wandered. "I've been reading a little about lucid dreaming. I've been trying some techniques to wake up in dreams. Some of them talk about out-of-body experiences. I find it very curious and interesting."

"Those skills can be developed with practice. There are strategies to help you wake up in the dream."

Mare nodded. "I've tried some, but I haven't had much luck yet."

"It will come. The more you focus your attention on it, the easier it will get."

Mare's thoughts wandered. "Roger, have you seen the movie *Contact*? Pete and I went to see it the other day. It's based on the book by Carl Sagan."

Roger nodded and smiled in understanding.

"It was so good. I loved the whole science vs. faith issue. Matthew McConahey was gorgeous, too, of course, but I thought Jody Foster did an absolutely amazing job playing Dr. Arroway!"

Roger agreed.

"The best scene of them all was when Ellie was in the machine going through the wormhole. When she was being hurled through those tunnels in space, I had a visceral recognition of the feelings she went through, like I had been tossed around in tunnels like that before. It felt so familiar to me, for some reason.... And the awe that she demonstrated, looking at the wonders that surrounded her! It was profound. I felt like I had taken the ride with her. I was trembling when I left the theater, it impacted me so." Mare neglected to mention to him that she had also shed a tear or two during the wormhole journey and then again when Ellie was speaking to the commission at the end. She didn't want him to think her silly for being so affected by a movie, even though he might have understood better than most.

"It was a great film. I, too, felt those last few scenes were powerful. Since we were just talking about dreaming, I will say also that it reminds me of dreaming."

"Yes, in dreaming ... but I can't recall a specific memory of it."

"You've got a child, Mare. Have you ever watched or read the *Hoober-Bloob Highway* by Dr. Seuss? ... Maybe it was a flashback to when you were rushing out the birth canal and the flood of energy that came with it."

Mare laughed out loud. "Maybe!" She continued to smile at the image, and pulled out another blade of grass.

"Speaking of energy, I've been so interested in the work we are doing with T'ai Chi. I've read a little about the chakras."

"Oh yeah? Roger hummed.

"There are seven major ones that correspond to places in the body, right?"

"Yes, these are energy centers. In Hindu texts, they are often represented as spinning wheels or lotus blossoms. The energy of your spirit flows through these centers and reflects your state of consciousness. If you are spiritually well, there is a natural flow within the chakras. You are healthy. However, if there is an issue your psyche is grappling with—whether you are consciously aware of the conflict or not—and you do not become aware and act to remedy the issue, these energy centers may become blocked or the energy flow restricted. In this way, your body is given a physical message that something is out of balance, and you can become ill. Once you acknowledge the truth of the matter and shift your way of being, the symptom can then be released."

"I've always believed that there is a connection between the mind and the body. Since I've started doing T'ai Chi, I've noticed my own energy flow so much more. I used to have this little wart here on my index finger." She pointed to the spot on her hand. "I'd had it for several years. It wouldn't go away. I was thinking about having it removed. But once I started doing T'ai Chi and using *beautiful lady's hands* like you instructed and creating balls of energy with my hands, it disappeared. Nothing else changed. It had to be T'ai Chi. I can feel the energy flowing through my fingers, hands, and arms … everywhere … every time we do it. It's incredible!"

He sat up again, and his eyebrows raised in agreement.

Mare nodded. I had one big experience when I was in the Army that made me realize the power of energy flow. Before that, I had never really thought about it."

"What was that?"

"I was at my R.O.T.C. Advanced Camp—that's like basic training, only for officers-to-be—at Fort Bragg. I was one of five women in a platoon of 44. I noticed this one male cadet in another platoon of our company who kept looking at me with these beautiful, steamy eyes. It unsettled me every time he looked at me like that…. Like he was looking deep inside me. I just figured he was attracted to me, but there was something different about him." She looked up with slight embarrassment.

"So, one day I'm standing in this long line. Maybe a hundred people in it. I'm up near the front, and the line winds around behind me back and forth and around the building, like a giant camouflaged snake. I'm just standing in this line facing the front and I feel something on my back, like something is touching me, only I know no one is. I squirm my shoulders around and try to shrug it off a little, but it's still there. Without thinking, I turn around and, like a detective, intuitively follow the trail of energy quickly back to this one guy. I didn't see any faces before his, despite the fact that we were surround by so many. I didn't look at anyone else along the way. It was like I followed a string … one I couldn't technically see, but that I could feel. I traced the energy line back to its source and as soon as I did, I found this one guy looking directly at me. Our eyes met instantly from probably fifty feet apart. A ton of people sur-rounded us, but it was an isolated moment between the two of us."

Mare looked over to Roger with emphasis. "He was staring right at me and I felt it! I actually felt it before I saw it, Roger. I didn't scan the group to find out what was going on. I had no idea he was behind me. I followed the energy. To me, that proved the existence of energy streams in that moment, without any doubt. It gave me chills. We had a powerful attraction to each other, and there was something special about him. He would often pop up in my dreams while I was there too."

Roger was nodding the entire time. "Yes, I believe you. That can happen. Have you ever actually seen with your eyes the energy around people … or yourself?"

"Well, after I read *The Celestine Prophecy* a few years ago, I did. I tried the same experiment that the main character did. I managed to see a little glow around my hands in certain lighting. And in class sometimes in the mirror, I think I can see a shiny layer around me, if the light in the room is low."

"As your awareness increases, you will be able to see more, I bet. Some people can see full color auras around people, though I can't. I have read about it."

"Well, everything is filled with energy. Matter is energy at varying levels of compression, right?" she smiled.

"Western science is catching up with Eastern Philosophy. They can even photograph energy now. Have you heard of Kirlian photography?"

"Yes, I've seen some of the pictures; it's pretty amazing." Mare rolled over onto her belly on the grass.

Roger continued, "Keeping the energy flowing in your body is critical to health. Keeping your energy full and flowing, like a river, is the way to good health and mental clarity. T'ai chi is all about fluidity—both at a physical and energetic level. That's why we move in circular, natural postures. Rigidity and force are not where true power lies. To be rooted in the Earth, balanced, and yet soft and responsive to the world … that is the source of strength and success."

Roger stood up, and indicated that he needed to leave soon.

"My wife and I are renewing our vows this weekend. I need to get some things ready."

They began walking towards the house.

"The reason why I began studying T'ai Chi sixteen years ago was that I noticed how different it was from other martial arts I had practiced and witnessed. In most others, students are taught to block and punch. They use stiff, hard movements and linear strikes. You need to be physically strong to overcome your opponents. Unlike these, T'ai Chi focuses on relaxation and yielding, circular movements and inner awareness of subtle energy dynamics. T'ai Chi Chuan's soft approach absorbs energy and redirects it. Very little physical strength is necessary for masters of this art. It takes years to gain such skills though. I'm still a novice myself. But it's a worthy pursuit." He grinned, showing his straight, white teeth. His face was bright.

Mare returned the smile and nodded. "I think so."

He put a hand on her shoulder. "And you are doing well, Mare. You are becoming suppler in push hands. You still try to push and force your way in sometimes, but you are developing a higher awareness of yourself and the way you use your energy. You have the understanding. You just have some old patterns to overcome, as we all do."

22

The Start of School— September 1997

If you judge people, you have no time to love them.

~Mother Teresa~

The world mourned the deaths of Princess Diana and Mother Teresa.

When she was a young teenager, Mare had watched the royal wedding. Some of her current students had not even been born. Since that time, Mare had admired the honest beauty and grace of Diana. She respected both Diana and Mother Teresa for their giant hearts. Whatever else may have been going on in their lives, they were role models for compassion. During the first few weeks of class, students wanted to talk about the women. Mare allowed them to explore their thoughts and feelings.

Because some of them were so young during the early years of the Aids crisis, Mare shared the story of how Diana had hugged a patient with HIV. So many misconceptions and stereotypes had existed. Diana blew folks away. The world was stunned and inspired by her gesture of kindness and love. She told them about Diana's work with land mine victims, among them children who had lost limbs.

"She cared," Mare told them with sadness in her voice. "And Mother Teresa helped people in the poorest communities. People with diseased bodies and heartbroken spirits. She had few possessions of her own. She just kept giving from her heart, and somehow that filled her up. Both of these people were larger than life, and yet they still seemed so human. What was it about these two women who could embrace humankind in ways few others could?" She paused, after thinking out loud.

"We know a little about what these two human beings did to make a difference in the world, but you don't have to be famous to give of yourself. What legacy would you like to leave the world?" she asked her class.

*   *   *   *

"Bernard, there is no way I can keep this student in my class this year," Mare said as she handed her friend and new department chair her class list. She pointed to a name.

"Sammy Hazzard is one of the boys who is accusing my brother. He's been in trouble with the law before and is a compulsive liar. If he stays in my American Studies class, I know there will be problems."

"I hear you, Mare. Let's go downstairs and see if Roger can pull up his schedule for us."

"The only other English class that will fit with Sammy's schedule," Roger said, "is Ted's honors English." He looked up at Mare with sympathy. "There's no way he can handle a college prep class. He doesn't have the skills or motivation to succeed in that class."

"I'm telling you guys, if he stays in my class, I know what will happen. He will do nothing, and he will fail. Then when he fails, he will say I failed him because he accused my brother and that I am getting back at him. It won't work. I'm not going to put myself in that position."

"Have you talked to him about it?"

"Yes. In fact, this morning I asked him—'don't you feel uncomfortable being in my class after everything that's going on with my brother? You do know I'm Seth's sister, right?' He said, 'Yah, I knew that. I don't have a problem with it,' he said, 'Do you?' And I told him, 'Well, yes, I do, Sammy.' I mean of course I do! I don't care if he's in over his head in Ted's class. I can't have him in mine."

"Well," Bernard said, "check with Ted and explain the situation to him. Maybe we can find a solution." In the end, Mare won. He was removed from her class, much to her relief.

*   *   *   *

"What's up with that?" Emily asked her friend Shauna, just loud enough in the quiet, but not silent study hall, that Mare could hear.

"I don't know; maybe she likes him." She responded matter-of-factly.

Mare coughed a bit out of surprise at the comment, but continued nodding her head as Austin told her about his eventful summer. On his way to lunch, he had seen Mrs. Lumen sitting at her desk. He had poked his head in the door to say hi.

"How are you, Miz Lumen?"

"Hi, Austin! Mare waved him in, and he sat down. They chatted casually for a few minutes.

Mare was aware of Emily's interest in Austin. She wondered if perhaps Emily might be the reason he was visiting so enthusiastically with her, knowing that Emily was in the room. But then again, probably Emily expected him to come and visit with HER and not Mare.

Anyway, that's nonsense. Of course I like Austin. I enjoy seeing him. I like being around him. But not in the way Shauna's insinuating. Mare said nothing to Emily and Shauna, and just let the moment pass, since the girls did not seem aware that their teacher had heard. They must know that the thought is ridiculous.

Austin, now a senior, sat tall in the chair and looked around, grinning at the girls that he recognized and giving a wave. Then he turned back to Mare. "I've got a job now."

"Oh, really? What are you doing?" Mare asked.

"I'm working down at the telemarketing center. I get to call people up and sell them stuff. Not a lot of fun, but I'm trying to save up for a new stereo for my truck. Dad says he'll pay half for my 18th birthday next month if I pay the other half."

"Cool," Mare nodded.

Austin's head bobbed, too, and he looked around again.

"So whatcha been doing for fun, Miz Lumen?"

"Oh, not too much. I'm still doing some T'ai Chi," she told him about the class. "I've just been taking care of my son and trying to get ready for school again … writing up lesson plans and all that."

"You know, when I'm twenty-one, I'm going to have a big keg party. You'll have to come then and drink with us. What do ya say?"

"Maybe." Then she imagined the picture for a minute. "As long as there are no under-age drinkers there." Her eyes went wide.

"Cool. Cool. Well, I should probably head to lunch before it's over. Been nice talking to you. Later."

"Bye, Austin."

*   *   *   *

"Kate, I think a former student of mine has the hots for me."

"Oh, yeah, who's that?"

"Austin Bean, the one who asked me to Prom last year."

"Oh, he's a cutie-pie."

"He came by to visit me today."

"Ohhh, wow," she said teasingly.

"Yeah, you're one to talk, I've seen the way that Trevor looks at you. I saw it at the play last spring. I'm sure you have a bunch of 'em panting after you."

"A few maybe. Trevor did a great job in that play last spring. I was very impressed. He's so intelligent for a 17-year-old. Not your ordinary high school senior."

"He does seems pretty mature for his age."

"Yeah, he often gets annoyed with his classmates and their behavior. He's anxious to graduate in the spring."

"What senior isn't? Last year, I had a freshman student that really impressed me. Christian McKay. Do you know him?"

Kate indicated that she did not.

"We were writing essays last year on *I Know Why the Caged Bird Sings*, and I was walking around the class. I checked to see how he was doing. He was frustrated working on his thesis, because he thought that Maya did a lot of stupid things when she was a kid. I told him—I never said that the thesis had to be flattering to the author. You don't have to pick an argument that you think pleases me. Choose an opinion you feel strongly about. If you think she made a lot of dumb moves and you can prove it, then go for it, man! He went on to write a fantastic essay. He's got a lot going on in that brain, that one. I like him. I invited him to come back and take my new elective class. He'll be great in Creative Expressions this year, along with a few of my former freshmen girls. Sometimes I can't believe he's only a sophomore."

"Yeah, certain students you really connect with."

"Considering we have a hundred or more every year, I guess there's bound to be a few who find a special place in your heart. One of the things I appreciate about this Christian kid is that he's always challenging things intellectually, me included. He gets me going, and that makes class more fun. He's got a sharp wit."

"Trevor, too. Christian McKay, huh? Well, I'll have to keep my eyes open for him."

*   *   *   *

Mare introduced Roger to her freshman class. "Mr. Beaumont is a guidance counselor. Some of you will be working with him when you apply for colleges or when you need to change your schedule. Mr. Beaumont is also an instructor of T'ai Chi. I told you last class that he might be coming in. In Esvlin's *Heroes, Gods and Monsters of the Greek Myths,* Esvlin retells the story of how Theseus defeated the bandits on the road to Athens. In this version of the myth, he uses those same energy principles as we do in T'ai Chi to defeat creatures like the beastly Minotaur—the half man, half bull creature that lives in the labyrinth. Mr. Beaumont is going to talk to you a little bit about how it might be possible to overcome a force larger or stronger than yourself."

Roger stepped up. "Hello, gang. Before we start with the physical principles, I'd like to talk a little about the philosophy behind T'ai Chi." He grabbed a marker and stood in front of the white board. "How many of you are familiar with the yin/yang symbol?" He scrawled a circle on the board.

Almost every hand in the room went up.

"This is actually the T'ai Chi symbol. It represents the world of opposites." He finished drawing the interior of the circle.

"Tell me what you know about this symbol."

"It's associated with male and female," one kid shouted, "hard and soft. Any set of opposites."

"Okay, yes, yin is passive and yang is dominant and so on. Right. This symbol reflects the nature of the universe. Harmony comes from a balance of yin-yang principles." He started creating a T-chart on the board. "The universe works in cycles, always changing like the seasons. This is why the image is in a circle. The two shapes within also suggest movement. I'll explain in a minute."

Yin		Yang
female		male
Moon/night		Sun/day
passive		active
dark/black		light/white
empty		full
absorbing		penetrating
receptive		assertive
Earth		Heaven
Soft		Hard
internal		external
cool		hot
water		fire
downward		upward
expanding		contracting
emotion		thought
intuitive		analytical
flowing		staccato
winter		summer
destruction/disintegration		creation
death		life

"If you look at these paired sets you will see that they compliment each other as well as oppose. The interlocking spirals can never exist without some part of the other. This is why you see the opposite colored dots in the middle. There is never destruction without some creation; nothing is ever all active or all passive."

A student raised her hand. "On the list it says upward and downward. What does that have to do with?"

"Good question. Well, you can see these are opposites, but they also relate to the symbol. You can get a sense of the direction of movement in this circle. Change is the only constant in the universe. If you look at the black, as it gets bigger, the white gets smaller. As the white gets bigger, the black gets smaller. It can go round and round and round, just like a heavenly body in the sky. In a similar way, you never have all good or all bad. If you are female, you have some qualities that are more masculine. Males have some qualities that are more feminine."

He demonstrated a posture from the form. "This leg is *yang* right now. My weight is on it; it is full and strong. As I shift in movement, the yang leg empties and becomes receptive, while the *yin* leg transitions into strength. It's an interchange. Harmony and equilibrium are the goals, following the natural rhythm of life … In our culture we tend to value one over the other side, like with good and bad. The idea of wholeness is valued by most eastern religions. When something is out of balance, disharmony follows. That is the way of all life. Taoism and T'ai Chi seek a flowing balance of these dualities so as to create a natural *oneness* as represented by the circle as a whole. One side is not better or worse than the other. Both are essential for completion. We must embrace the whole and seek a balance."

"That's pretty cool," one young man said. Roger nodded.

"Now, let's see how this interchange of energy can be put to practical use. Getting back to the original question. How do you defeat something bigger than you? Any ideas?" Roger queried.

"Use your brains."

"That's one way, but there is another also."

He paused. "I need a volunteer." He picked the biggest boy he could find.

"Now, I want you to come at me in slow motion as if you are going to punch me. Slow motion now! Okay? I don't want you to get hurt."

The group laughed. The boy nodded with a grin.

The rest of the class gathered around the two in the wide area below the hall stairway. A two—story window stretched over them, providing light.

Billy bunched his fist into a ball and began slowly arcing his way towards Roger.

Roger spoke as he went through the motions. "Instead of blocking this punch, like most people would try to do, T'ai Chi absorbs the energy of it and goes *with* the flow."

He placed a hand on top of the fist as it was moving towards him and pulled the boy's arm in the direction the blow was going. At the same time, he stepped aside. The force of Roger's pulling, added to the boy's own force, caused the boy to tumble forward at an increased speed. Then Roger placed his left hand on the boy's elbow and brought the burly young man down to the floor. Since the demonstration happened in slow motion, he was not at all hurt.

"The bigger the opponent, the more powerful the force coming at you—the more control you have—IF—you yield to the force, absorb its energy, and then redirect it as you wish."

Wowed expressions spouted from Mare's students. A buzzing murmur flushed the open hallway.

"Go ahead. Find a partner and try it. Only do it slowly."

After students had experimented with it, Roger asked them to quiet down for another exercise. "Okay, stay with your partner. One of you grab the other person's arm. Now, people with your arm being held—without injuring the other person—get him to let go."

Students struggled to try to forcefully remove the grip of their classmate. Having given them a chance to see how difficult a process it was using force, Roger asked them, "Is there another way to handle this that's easier?" He looked at Mare. "Mrs. Lumen, would you please grab my arm."

Mare did as he requested.

"Mrs. Lumen, would you please let go of my arm?"

Mare complied with a smile.

Recognizing the trick, students moaned. Mare could see a few light bulbs going off, however.

"How many of you even consider asking? You don't always have to push your way through things. What if you didn't have to bully another or force them to submit to your wishes? Sometimes a softer approach is the best strategy. Try it sometime."

                    *   *   *   *

That evening, as Mare and Pete were exiting the karate studio where their T'ai Chi class was held, Mare asked her husband, "Are you going to write out a check for Roger or do you want me to?"

"I guess so, but I'm running kind of low; I need to send Charlene the rent payment," he responded.

"I paid the bills you gave me. I thought you sent the others around the same time, Pete. Why did you wait until now to do it?"

"I didn't have the funds, Mare!" he groaned in annoyance. "If you think it's so easy, why don't you just manage the bills yourself?" He squeezed his shoulders into his neck as if he were trying to loosen the muscles, inhaled slowly and deeply, and rubbed his eyes.

"Well, I just don't see how we can be so behind all the time."

"Dammit, Mare, why don't you just get off my back!" he roared and started running away from her.

"Where are you going?" she yelled after him.

He did not respond.

She got into the car quickly to follow him, but could not spot him once she was on the road. After driving back and forth on the road for a while without any luck, she drove home.

"Where's Pete?" her father asked when she arrived alone.

"I don't know. He got pissed off after class and just took off. He didn't say where he was going. He just ran off in a huff—literally." She shrugged. "It was very strange."

Joan and Rick put on their jackets and, getting Cody to blow kisses as they left, closed the door behind them.

About fifteen minutes later, Pete entered, panting wildly.

"Where did you go?" his wife questioned him.

His mood had changed. He chuckled. "I was so angry, I just crossed the street, then ran through the woods."

"All the way home, Pete? That's a couple of miles, isn't it."

He nodded. "I know."

"You ran all the way across the hill—through the woods—without a trail?

"Yup."

"Why?"

"I was mad.… But now I'm okay. I got it out of my system."

*   *   *   *

Several dawns came and went. Mare returned home one day from work with Cody and found Seth crying on the couch.

"What's the matter, Seth?"

"I told Hope it wasn't going to work for us romantically. She was pretty upset. I tried and it just won't work. It doesn't feel right for me. I love her, but I'm not attracted to her." His crying intensified. In between sniffs, he added, "I'm so tired. I'm so tired of all this. I just want it to be resolved. I've got nothing left. I've got no life. I can't work right now. My business is gone. I have no friends."

"You have us," Mare offered futilely.

"Yes, and I appreciate that, but it's not the same. My entire life has changed, Mare. All my friends are gone. Not only am I forbidden to see them by the court, but most of them don't want to see me anymore either. My whole life revolved around those guys, and now it's all gone." His head plopped into his hands. He mumbled on. "I know it's my own fault, but that doesn't change the fact that I've lost everything. My job, my dreams, the respect of my community, my friends."

Though Cody wasn't aware enough to understand what his uncle had just said, he knew that Uncle Seth was sad. He walked over to him, put a hand on his knee and looked up. "You're a good boy, Code!" he said to him, patting him on the head. Then he turned away from the child into the sofa back and began to cry again, though he tried to muffle the noises for the Cody's sake.

Mare scooped Cody up and brought him into another room to play with some toys.

She returned to the living room after a moment and tried to console her brother.

"Seth, I know it's hard, but once this is all settled, you will be able to rebuild your life again, and make new friends—friends closer to your own age who share your interests."

It seemed so far away to him it wasn't real.

"Imagine, Mare, that you put all of your friends into a room. Then an explosion goes off and BOOM everyone you care about is dead! GONE! In an instant, everything changes. It's like that for me. All my friends are gone from me. It was a lot more than sex, you know. Most of them I never touched. I cared about all of them. We had a lot of fun times together … skiing and hiking and mountain biking and going to games and playing football and rock climbing. They were my friends, my companions. I have lost *all* of them. I have nothing now. I am still grieving. The hurt just won't go away." He looked up at his sister. "And then knowing what I have put some of them through … It kills me." He sniffled and sat up.

"My life is shit. If it weren't for you guys and Mom and Dad and the rest of the family—if I hadn't put you through so much already—I would just … just …" he searched for the words. "Quit!" He stood, and made his way up the stairs to his room. Mare knew that he was talking about suicide.

"Seth," Mare called after him. "You've got a few friends still … Ben and Jimmy are still behind you. They still care about you, even after you told them you were gay."

He yelled back down, almost to the second floor. "Yes, but I'm not allowed to see them, and when they learn the whole story, I will lose them too."

She heard his door close.

*   *   *   *

"Mare, we think you should see a doctor. You aren't yourself these days. You are depressed; can't you see that?" Her mother put a hand on her shoulder. "You've had a lot to deal with this year. Maybe you should go see a doctor and get on medication. We worry about you when we see you so down-hearted for so long. It's not like you."

"I'm not depressed!" Mare contested vehemently. "Mom, I know you and dad are only trying to help. I appreciate your concern; I really do." She turned to her father. "But I'm alright. I'm sad, yes, and I'm working some stuff out, but I will come out of it. I just need time and space to process it all. I don't want to take some antidepressant to feel better." She squirmed in her chair. "I've got stuff to figure out. I can't ignore the feelings, and I don't want to push them away with chemicals. I need to do the work. I'm glad the antidepressants are working for you guys. I am. But it's not for me. I want to get through this naturally and in my own way."

*   *   *   *

"My parents think I'm depressed and should see a doctor for meds."
Sophie just looked at her and listened.
"What do *you* think?" she asked, never one to push her opinion on another.
Mare paused to consider that. "I know that I'm in a dark place. I know that I'm still hurting, and I'm not sure how to come out of it. It's affecting my marriage, and that concerns me. But I REALLY don't want to go on any drugs. I don't want to just escape it! Well, sometimes I do, just for a little relief, but I know in the long run that won't help me. I have never done drugs in all my thirty years … well, not illegal drugs anyway. It is rare that someone my age can say that. I made an agreement with myself a long time ago that I wouldn't give up control of my life to a mood-altering substance. I want to make good choices. I also like being able to tell my students that it is possible for a person to go through life without doing drugs. It always amazes most of them. Some of them don't believe me, but I think others are inspired by it. I just always imagined it was like putting poison into your body. I've seen too many people get trapped into a lifestyle and personality that wasn't them. I know that antidepressants are legal, but I have tried to avoid drugs my whole life. I want to heal naturally. I want to face it fully and get rid of it for good. If I don't, I'm afraid I *will* get sick down the road. There is a connection between the health of the mind or spirit and the well being of the body. I'm trying to heal for real, not pretend I'm okay and forget about it all the things that hurt and confuse me."
"I agree, and I support you in that. You talk a lot about energy and the mind-body connection. You know, Mare, I'm thinking you would like my landlord, Jane. She lives upstairs. She's a psychotherapist, an energy worker and dance instructor. You should make an appointment with her. Maybe she can help you find your way through this darkness."

*   *   *   *

Mare opened the dishwasher and found baby bottles strewn around the bottom and wedged into the mechanism.

"PEete!" she yelled.

"He's upstairs," Seth told her, while he sipped a cup of coffee.

"What?" Pete asked as he came through the kitchen door.

"Can you please NOT stick the baby bottles on this rack over here? They always end up on the bottom."

"It really doesn't matter, Mare."

Mare looked at him in confusion. "Sure, it does. Sometimes the plastic lids melt down there. If you could just wedge them onto these pieces here, they stay in place and get clean."

"It's just dishes. What's the big deal? Back off."

Both were getting angrier and angrier. "Pete, it's just a simple request. Just put them over here." She pointed.

"No, I'll put them wherever I want to, because it makes NO difference."

"It does make a difference though. Why won't you …?"

"Be happy I'm even loading the dishwasher!"

"Guys, guys!" Seth interrupted. "There are a lot bigger problems in the world than bickering about how to load the damn dishwasher. Chill out!"

Mare took a deep breath and collected herself. She put her hands on her hips.

"Seth, maybe this ISN'T about the dishwasher. Maybe we are all just under a lot of stress. It hasn't been easy for you to deal with this, but how do you think it's been for us? Every one of us is under a lot of strain."

He put his hands up in the air, in a gesture of truce. "Okay, okay. You're right. I know it's been stressful. I know. I'm sorry. I'm more sorry than I can express." He picked up his mug slowly and went upstairs. She knew that he was beginning to cry.

Mare sat down at the table and dropped her head in her hands. She felt so drained. She wanted to fly away.

23

Hearing the Music

You cannot separate the just from the unjust and the good from the wicked, for they stand together before the face of the sun as the black thread and the white are woven together. And when the black thread breaks, the weaver shall look into the whole cloth, and he shall examine the loom also.

~Kahlil Gibran, *The Prophet*~

The Eagles won their Homecoming game against the Portland Vipers. Mare and Sophie chaperoned the Homecoming dance. Their husbands stayed at home.

"The girls' dresses are getting more and more formal for these things. Almost looks like they are going to prom," Mare confided to Sophie as spaghetti-strapped teenage girls giggled past them. One young lady passed them wearing a bright blue dress, which was held up by only one thick shoulder strap. The other shoulder was bare.

"Aren't they wearing less and less, too?" Sophie asked her.

"Ooh yeah."

"Hi, Mrs. Lumen! Hi, Ms. Tucker!"

They greeted Emily who was pretty in strapless aquamarine.

"You look fabulous," Mrs. Lumen complimented her.

"Thanks. You guys look nice, too."

Mare wore an autumn-colored tank dress hovering just above the knees and a brown sweater over it. Sophie's broomstick skirt brushed the floor.

"Thanks," they nodded as Emily flittered away towards the dance floor. Mare watched her glide across the gymnasium floor and put her arms around her date.

"Ahh, she came with Austin.... Good for her. They *are* adorable together."

Mare continued to watch as the two teenagers shook their bodies to a fast song. Austin leaned his face into Emily's, and Mare could see him singing loud and unabashedly while looking into her eyes. Mare smiled. When he got close enough to touch his nose to hers, he playfully rubbed his nose back and forth against hers.

Mare cupped her chin between her thumb and index finger and chuckled.

"Come on, Sophie, let's go dance."

Before long, Austin's tie was off, his white, pressed shirt was untucked and unbuttoned down to his chest. He was hot and moist from dancing so much.

When the dance was over and Emily had stepped away to the ladies' room, Austin grabbed Mare's hand and pulled her out the school doors into the parking lot. They rushed to his car where he leaned over and kissed her slowly. Pulling out his key he unlocked the door, and opened it for her. Mare got into the car and waited for Austin to join her. He climbed in, wrapped his arms around her and held her. She melted into his embrace, though she was afraid that someone might see them. She looked around the darkened parking lot. Austin put a hand to her face and guided it to his lips. She pulled some of his blond hair out of his eyes, and slid her hand down to his cheek. He kissed her with increasing passion, and Mare responded in full. They made out in the parked car.

Whoa! Mare sat bolt upright in bed. She put her hand to her heart, still feeling the exhilaration and affection of the dream. Her heart rate was high, and her breathing was rapid. She turned her head and saw her husband's sleeping body in the shadows beside her.

Oh thank god! It was just a dream. I didn't do anything wrong. It wasn't real.

She settled back down into bed and rolled onto her side facing the wall. She let her mind wander back into the images and feelings from the dream. They were comfortable and pleasant. She mentally scolded herself for dreaming about an eighteen-year-old student. But her mind was in conflict. It had been a long time since she had felt as alive and vibrant as she did in the dream.

But it was just a dream.

*   *   *   *

In October, as Mare was driving to work, she listened to a horrific radio report. "A kidnapped ten-year-old boy from Massachusetts has been killed and his body dumped in a river. Police say that Jeffrey Curley's abductors covered his mouth with a gasoline-soaked rag, which killed him. Then his body was molested and dumped in a Maine river."

"What!" Mare said out loud, though she was alone. Appalled, she covered a hand over her throat and thought of the boy who was only ten. Her throat ached. She had trouble swallowing. *Ten! How could anyone do such a horrible thing?*

For the remainder of the week, she looked at newspaper reports of the case. She saw a picture of him. A sweet little child wearing a blue baseball cap. So young. *I just can't understand.*

*   *   *   *

Mare was relieved to meet Jane, Sophie's landlord. The woman had a kind face and grizzled gray-black hair down to her shoulders. She was just a little shorter than Mare. She reached for Mare's hand with both of hers. "Sophie and Tristan have told me wonderful things about you."

Jane led her up a stairway into a loft workshop. It had a lovely, natural feel to it. Unstained wood covered the walls. A large, multi-paned window on the slanted roof faced south, letting in lots of diffused sunlight. A ficus tree filled one corner. Full green spider plants hung from the rafters. Purple African violets lined a smaller windowsill. The air was warm, and the space felt safe and comfortable.

Jane invited Mare to sit. Then she took a chair. "So, what can I do for you?"

Mare struggled, "I'm not really sure."

Jane waited and continued to listen.

Mare took a deep breath. So much was there; she didn't know where to begin. She'd been holding it together for so long.

"Jane, I've been having a tough time," she started hesitantly. "Have you heard about my brother, Seth Mahonia?"

Jane tried to place him.

"He's been in all the newspapers this year, and in the news."

"Well, that explains why I don't know him. I try not to pay attention to that stuff. It's bad for my health. I get the important news in other ways."

"Ahh, well, I can sympathize with that. You never know if what you are getting is the truth. My brother … my brother has been charged with molesting adolescent boys."

She looked to Jane to gauge her response. She saw no judgment, and the woman did nothing but listen respectfully.

Mare relaxed, and filled Jane in on the essentials of the situation. "I'm having a difficult time making sense of it all." Opening herself to a stranger made it easier for Mare to let go of the strong woman persona she had grown up with. She cried a little.

"That's a very difficult thing to assimilate, Mare. No wonder you have been out of sorts. Why don't you come over to table here and we'll see what your body has to say. Have you ever had Reiki done on you before?"

"No."

Mare laid on her back on the table. Jane started with the head. She held her hand out over Mare's crown. Do you have a head injury earlier in your life?"

"Yes, how did you know that? When I was about eight, the tailgate of my grandfather's truck came down flat on my head."

"Ouch," Jane winced.

"It knocked me to the ground. Mom says I had a concussion. I can't remember it myself. But I have endured headaches for as long as I can remember."

"You have a lot of compacted energy here. Let me see if I can help you release some of that."

Mare couldn't see what the woman was doing, but she felt a tingling in her scalp. Next, Jane massaged Mare's head and face for a few minutes, and gradually put her hands on her shoulders.

Jane was feeling for the energy. As a doctor might, she said, "Your right side is much more contracted than your left side. Did you know that the right side is the outside world? You are carrying other people's burdens. It is weighing you down." She said these things rather matter-of-factly, but the simple truth of it pierced the barriers Mare had built up to keep her emotions in check. She began to sob.

"I try not to worry about things I can't change, but I want to change things. I want to do something about what I see going on around me, but I feel so powerless sometimes."

She took Mare's hand gently. "Let it all out, dear. Go ahead and cry it out. It will help. You will feel better after." Mare responded to the permission by not only letting the tears run, but out of her throat came great sobs that rocked her whole body. Jane simply stayed with Mare, listening and holding her hand. Mare sensed her compassion, but she also appreciated that Jane didn't treat her as though she was fragile and that crying would break her.

"I have already cried so much. You'd think I'd be empty by now." Mare's body shook as she faced the pain inside. But she was not alone. She was safe.

She felt her temperature rise, and the blood pumping through her body. She let go of all she could—wanting to free herself from its hold, but there was more.

"In addition to worrying about my brother, I have heard a few things that have really troubled me recently."

"And what would those be," she asked, still working her way around Mare's body, trying to see what was off.

"It's pretty awful," Mare said.

Jane nodded her okay.

"A ten-year-old boy was kidnapped in Massachusetts. Two men tried to bribe him with money and a bike. They, or at least one of the men, had been stalking him for some time. When the child refused to do what they wanted, one of the men placed a rag soaked with gasoline over his mouth and killed him. Then the boy's dead body was molested." Her body ached and tears were streaming down her face as she told the story about the child she did not know, but felt connected to. "They finally dumped him in a river."

"Oh, how terrible."

"Yes, and it is killing me. I can't shake the thought. I have a son. I work with young people. I worry about children. I feel so badly for this ten-year-old boy and his family." She paused. "Then I start thinking about the killers, and I want to do something."

A look of astonishment and discomfort passed over Jane's face. "What do you mean: do something?"

Mare sighed and said, "I can't imagine how anyone could harm a child like that so violently and thoughtlessly. Only a person who feels almost entirely disconnected from the human race could do that.... And when I think of the degree of isolation and pain such people feel, I feel pain for them as well. I want to help somehow. I want to help people feel connected. I want to help them feel compassion for one another, so that they don't hurt each other in these ways. I can't bear to think of the hurting on both sides."

Jane's face melted with understanding and affection. "I see."

"I think of my brother. He didn't physically hurt anyone, and he didn't realize the degree of emotional damage he was doing. I don't want to minimize what he did, because I think it was wrong, but I want to help people like my brother, too. How can I help them? Isolation and loneliness were big parts of the problem for Seth. He had feelings that he couldn't express to anyone. He thought he was gay, but he didn't feel he would be accepted, so he kept quiet. Isn't that part of the problem?" Mare was processing her thoughts out loud. "What if people could be honest about their longings and desires and their true selves, and really get help—without the threat of persecution or ridicule?

What if people could embrace their humanity, instead of hiding it—flawed as it may be?"

Jane nodded in agreement and shook Mare's arm to release some blocked energy.

After a few quiet moments, Jane asked, "Do you remember a change in your brother?"

Mare's memory traced its way through the pathways of time. "Yes." She vaguely recalled a shift. Her brother seemed to have become darker over time, quieter, more sullen, less himself. "In junior high, I noticed a change, but I don't think I noticed it consciously at the time."

"You probably didn't. It may have been an intuitive impression."

"Something must have happened along the way. Everywhere you look in the newspapers and on local TV, you hear these kinds of stories. I think I may not look at another newspaper or watch another local news program in my whole life. It sickens and depresses me. I read a story in Time magazine too. I'm sorry for talking about this stuff, but if I don't get some of it out, I think I might burst…. A teenage boy in New Jersey met a 43-year-old man over the Internet in a gay chat room. They entered into a relationship. The teenager later went on to sexually assault and then murder an 11-year-old who was going door-to-door trying to sell something for a school fundraiser. A fifteen-year-old. The article said that the teenager had a website where he wrote about how much he really wanted true friends. My brother has said the same things. He wanted closeness. He wanted friends. The sexuality was only a small part of it for him. How do we help these people? The headline of this article talked about how a victim had turned victimizer. I don't know if my brother was a victim at any point, but I sure as heck don't want his victims to continue the cycle of destructive relationships. Then whenever stuff like this happens, people start bashing gays again." Mare looked up at Jane with pain in her eyes. "Surely, that is not the answer," Mare said, looking to Jane as if to find a solution in her eyes. "It kills me to think that if my brother had experienced more acceptance and safety in questioning his sexuality, his relationships might have followed a healthier path and the young people would have been spared their experiences."

Mare stopped for a second, and then asked, "Why are people so lonely when we are surrounded by a population of billions?"

Jane examined Mare's serious expression with kindness. She put a hand on her shoulder. "You do have a lot on your mind, don't you? Dear, Mare—you are asking some big questions, and I think that's wonderful. You have a big commitment and a big heart. You will find your way and your own answers."

"I'm going to give you a writing assignment for when you get home. Is that okay? You are an English teacher, right?"

Mare nodded and said sure. "I like to write."

"Your assignment is to notice what you are feeling in your body when you get home and then write about it. In particular, I want you to talk to your shoulder and find out what it has to say."

Mare grinned. Then Jane added, "I would love for you to join my light-workers group sometime."

It was nearly dusk when Mare tried to find a quiet, peaceful spot. She went up to Cody's room, the most calm and quiet room in the house, and sat in a rocker near the window facing the backyard. Her son was taking a nap. The wind was blowing fiercely. Mare opened the window to let a little of the brisk October air in. She had a notebook in her lap as she leaned back against the padded seat. The wind rattled the window casing. It blew against her cheek and swirled around her outstretched legs. It was powerful and cool, and she felt her own spirit lift and spiral along with the rushing, whirling air.

She picked up her pen and began writing. She let her mind wander and whip like the wind outside, and she didn't let the pen drop or stop. She just rolled on, exploring the residual sensations she was feeling.

When her shoulder told her that she was carrying too many *shoulds*, Mare noticed that the word shoulder contained *should* in it. *I do operate from should a lot. Why do I feel so responsible? Why do I feel I need to stand on my own and prove that I am good?* Mare began to explore the four significant memories that came to her from childhood.

She journeyed back to second grade where she got caught cheating on a math test and was publicly humiliated by the teacher. She had been too shy and embarrassed to ask for help. The teacher seemed to suggest that she was not a good girl.

And then there was the Philadelphia Zoo when her mother turned her back on Mare and Seth to buy some monkeys on a stick, and despite Mare's warnings, Seth had wandered through the turnstile out of the park. Mare followed to look after him. On the way back into the park, their mother berated them fiercely and publicly. Mare was five or six. They never got the monkeys.

Mare leaned back in the chair and closed her eyes. Two more memories came to her that she knew had been pivotal in her development and decisions.

At age ten, Mare hadn't been invited to a neighbor's party, and she watched the girls play through her bedroom window. They were older, yes, but it still hurt to be excluded. *I won't be a puppy-dog and follow people around. I'm not going to be that needy. I'm fine on my own.*

But all these were small potatoes compared to the last memory. Henry. Why had she lost it and kicked him so violently?

She had seen him get picked on so many times on that bus. Yeah, he could be obnoxious. She remembered how her friends had goaded her on. Something snapped. She let loose. When she emerged from her daze, she looked back at a Henry's outstretched hands, trying to cover his face, then she looked over to her friends whose jaws were on the floor. Was that Mare … quiet, kind, little Mare? She sat down and said nothing. Henry avoided her after that. Naturally.

The incident pained her still. How could she do such a thing? He was just a poor, needy kid who didn't get a lot of positive attention. She kept putting herself in Henry's shoes. What was his life like? Did he get beaten at home? Did he get enough to eat? Did he have any friends?

The ugly incident would shape her future in unexpected ways. She decided that day, somewhere in her subconscious, that she had to be careful of her power. She had to keep a lid on it, tightly controlled. Yet, it was also the birthplace of a deeper compassion.

Mare put her pen down and looked out the window again. The pale orange glow of sunset filled the spaces between the tree trunks at the edge of her property. But something closer to the house caught her eye. To the left of the stone fireplace, she saw the giant elm. Dutch Elm disease had killed most elms in Maine earlier in the century. Somehow, this beauty in its solitude had survived. Its limbs stretched skyward in a graceful "Y." Mare studied the elm meditatively as it flipped back and forth and rolled around in circles in the wind.

She became entranced by the way the tree moved in response to the charged airflow around it. Its roots were firmly in the ground, but the top was flexible enough to bend gracefully with each sweeping gust. Piles of loose yellow leaves were scooped up and spun in spirals. On this particular day, the wind was chaotic and choppy. It tossed the treetop in all directions. Yet, it seemed like the tree almost enjoyed the opportunity to dance. The top-most limbs spread outward, like a fountain, loosely rolling with each draft of air.

Mare visualized a woman in its place, her arms over her head, rhythmically dancing to some slow tune. If she were the tree, she could release her tension and feel the undulations of the energy around her. Mare's mind, without thinking, placed her consciousness in the trunk and limbs of the tree.

Her roots delved deeper into the earth. She felt supple, relaxed and lithe … her head and her arms drifting in wave-like motions. She did not resist the gusts; she was free flowing. Nor did she blow away like a fragile leaf would. She was rooted. Mare closed her eyes and felt the wind toss her, this way and that. She felt light and peaceful, and savored the moment of simply being a flexible and strong tree bending in the wind.

24

Polygraph

But it's no use going back to yesterday, because I was a different person then.

~Alice in Lewis Carroll's Alice's Adventures in Wonderland~

"I failed the polygraph," Seth bewailed when he arrived home after the test.

"What? How could that happen?" Mare asked.

"I don't know," Seth said, clearly dejected from the results.

"He asked me a bunch of sexual questions and I got all nervous, and apparently he got a physiological response that matched lying."

"He only asked you questions about Sammy and Eugene, right?"

"Right. But I'm a private person and talking about any sex, especially sexual relations with boys, is very uncomfortable for me. I was sweating the whole time."

"I'm sorry," Mare told him.

"I believed those tests were irrefutable. Now I've lost $1,000 AND my chance to separate the charges. The only options now are to go to trial for the whole thing and put the kids who are telling the truth through the ordeal of testifying, or take a plea agreement and say yes to complete guilt." Tears streamed down his face.

Mare frowned in sympathy. "What will you do?"

"I think there is only one choice, really."

"Will you take the plea bargain?"

"Plea agreement." He corrected her language, despondently. "It's hardly a bargain."

On a frigid evening some weeks later, Mare entered her guest bedroom, Seth's room, to find a flashlight she had stashed in the bedside table drawer. Seth was not home at the time. She opened the drawer and found a few sheets of folded paper. She opened them and perused a few lines of writing.

It began … "I used to know who I was. It's hard to believe how one minute I saw myself as someone who has devoted his life to kids, who loved and cared about them; who tried to keep them safe and help them get through the difficult times in their lives."

"I shouldn't read this," Mare thought to herself, beginning to fold it again. But another voice urged her on. She continued. It was the letter he wanted to read to the judge when his time in court came.

In it, he wrote about his perception of himself, how he wanted to help kids, how he now realized that he has a problem. He talked about the evolution of his struggles. And then, Mare's eyes stopped. She sat down on the cushy twin bed. Her eyes wide.

"When I was 13, I too was the victim of sexual abuse …" So there it was. All those times Mare had asked her brother to tell her if Cody might one day be at risk from someone they knew. He had said that he didn't know of anyone in the family or connected to the family who might abuse children. Now she knew, at least in part, what had happened to her brother.

She read the paragraph over again. "When I was 13, I too was the victim of sexual abuse by a college student outside of our family. At the time I didn't feel like I was a victim. I could have said no but I didn't. I could have stopped coming back but I craved the attention of someone that made me feel important. What I thought didn't hurt me when I was 13 ended up leading me down a path that destroyed my life, destroyed my dreams but most importantly of all it destroyed my friendships. I know this young man didn't want to do me any harm. I believe he wanted the same thing that I wanted, to feel love and a connection to someone. To feel O.K. and accepted. To me it was never about sex. I don't think either one of us realized the consequences of what was happening. From that summer on my life was changed forever."

Mare let her hands and the letter fall into her lap. So that's what happened … in junior high. *That's when I sensed a change. About the same age as most of the young people he touched.*

Most of the statement was very good. Honest. Raw. Mare did wince a little when she read a paragraph attacking the police, because she wasn't convinced that stance would serve him. "Much of what the public has heard is untrue. Including false rumors of videos and pictures. I did not have anal sex with 12-year-old Eugene Grover or anyone else. Sammy Hazzard did not wake up to me performing oral sex and neither did anyone else, because those things did not happen. Many other facts have been grossly distorted. Despite the fact that Eugene and Sammy's stories are total fabrications, the others are telling some version of the truth. Some more true than others. I can't blame the kids considering the way in which Daryl Rolf questioned many of them. Saying things like, 'Don't you want to help us put this guy away?' and 'Let me guess what happened.' I can't forget that he lied and misled kids and parents about the facts, to get them to say something. Not to mention that he yelled at kids who said nothing ever happened, accusing them of lying. Did I mention that he took kids out of school without their parents' permission, questioned kids over and over to the point of harassing them, when they said nothing happened? Shame on you, Daryl. With those tactics it's no wonder that you produced two more victims than there really were."

Mare read on and on, until she got to the last paragraph, which started, "This last year has been hell, living with the fact that I hurt the people that I loved more than life itself. The unimaginable loss and guilt that I feel every day is nearly unbearable. The words 'I'm sorry' just simply aren't enough." Even so, the paragraph ended with his apologies.

Inhaling, Mare reflected on her brother's words. Some of it was not new, but it was eye opening to read his thoughts in one piece like this. She was glad to know of the abuser. She wanted to ask him more about it. She was glad he was accepting responsibility for his actions. It seemed the first step to recovery for everyone.

When her brother returned home, she told him with some difficulty, "I was looking for something of mine in your room, and I accidentally found the letter you've been working on. The one to the court."

He thought about it for a moment. She thought she saw a hint of anger at first, but it faded. "So now you know."

"Yes, were you ever going to tell us?"

Seth shrugged. "I didn't want you all to go after him. I don't think he meant me any harm."

"Perhaps not, Seth, but what if he is continuing this behavior with more young people. If so, then he needs to be stopped."

"I don't think he is, but … I don't know. I don't know where he is anymore."

"I don't suppose you will give me his name?"

He shook his head no.

"Where? How did this happen?"

"At the lake."

"At the lake?" *Lake Pennebago,* Mare thought. *Where swimming made us strong and lithe, and the sun made us brown? We went there virtually every day all day every summer we were old enough. I suppose that is the most likely place. Lots of woods surrounded the beaches.* All three Mahonia children had taken swim lessons there every year. Mare knew many of the teachers. Had he been a teacher? Had she known the man? She could not pinpoint anyone from her memory.

"I wish you could have told me. I wish I had known."

Seth was silent.

She sighed, "Well, I recommend that you temper that stuff about the chief, even though it is true."

"Yeah, I know. It's only a first draft. I'll probably change it some. I was mostly getting it all off my chest. I will make final decisions when the time comes."

*   *   *   *

At Cody's second birthday, Mare decided it was time to move the toddler from his crib to a double bed. The child was excited. One cold December night, Mare read Cody a book as she did every night. "Goodnight moon, goodnight air, goodnight noises everywhere." Then she sang to him one of her favorite Kenny Loggins' songs "The House at Pooh Corner." She snuggled with her son after the song, to help him get used to the new double bed. Exhausted and comfortable, Mare fell asleep beside him.

"Mom!" Cody let out a cry. She circled her arms around him, and reassured him she was there.

"What's wrong, honey?" she asked. His eyes seemed partially open.

He pointed his finger in the air to the right of the bed. She could see nothing.

"See that orange dot," he questioned her, but he seemed only partially awake.

Mare tried to see what he was pointing at.

"That orange light there," he kept pointing.

"I don't see it, Cody."

He laid back down and went to sleep instantly. Mare looked back at the location he had indicated. Although she had not seen what her son had seen, she knew that, in his altered state of consciousness, it was possible he had indeed seen something. In the morning, Cody remembered nothing of it.

A few days later, Mare was again sleeping next to Cody. She was having a dream about being chased by people who needed her blood. They were asking her to slice her wrists, so they could drink her life force. Their need frightened her. They didn't seem evil, and yet she couldn't bring herself to do as they asked. She wanted to get away. She realized she was dreaming and quickly fought her way to consciousness. She opened her eyes almost instantly, and when she did she saw a small ball of orange light exit from her head.

She watched it float away—across the room—slowly. She didn't feel frightened anymore. She sensed a benevolence associated with the small point of colored energy as it moved away through an exterior wall. *How could that be?* Unlike some other "clouds" of energy that she had sensed, seen or dreamed of in the house, this one did not trouble her. *Was it a guide figure who had visited her in the dream? Are we visited in this way by spirits through our dreams? Was it trying to teach me something?*

*   *   *   *

As the winter holidays approached, Babylon streets were decked out in Christmas cheer. Evergreen wreaths with red bows hung from the lampposts. Silver and gold dangled from storefront windows. Mare wanted to feel the joy of the season, but something was in the way. She spoke to Pete.

"It's been ... what ... nine months now that Seth's been staying with us." She counted on her fingers. "February, March, April, May, June, July, August, September, October, November, December." She held them up. "Eleven ... ten or eleven months. I am realizing that his constant presence at the house is getting to be too much for us. I think I'm going to ask him to stay with Gram and Gramp at the farm now that the worst seems to be over. I just can't carry it any more."

Pete looked at her with a mixture of emotions. "Are you sure? I thought you didn't want to burden the rest of your family with this ... that we were the strongest and that he should stay with us?"

"Yes, that *was* how I felt. But now I feel like I can't give any more. Look at us, Pete. We are washed out from it all, and having his constant and depressing presence around is not helping us to get on with our lives. It's taken a toll on us.... Gram and Grandpa are aware of the truth now. Mom talked to them. Grandpa said that there were people who had done a lot worse things in the world. Now that they know the truth, I don't feel I have to worry about them so much. They will take him. Seth could even help with the horses and other animals. It'll give him something to do while he waits for resolution. I just can't do it anymore. I need a little distance."

"Okay, it's up to you." He hugged her.

As soon as she made the decision, she felt lighter. Feeling more comfortable with the written word and being afraid of her brother's reaction, she wrote him a letter and left it on his bed. She let him know she still cared, but that she was tired.

Later that evening, Pete found a note from Seth on the kitchen table.

Mare and Pete,

Thanks for allowing me to stay with you the last several months. I realize I'm not the most cheerful person to be around and I'm sorry I've outstayed my welcome. It's been a difficult year for everyone and I'm sorry you guys were hurt by everything that happened. I know it hasn't been easy for you or anyone else for that matter. I wish I could change the past, but I can't. Thanks for everything.

Love,
Seth

P.S. I would like to use your computer once in a while to do some writing if it's okay.

"His stuff is all out of his room," Pete said.

Mare felt badly for her brother, but her relief was even greater.

*   *   *   *

Mare and her friend, Derek, sat down at a conference room table to catch up with each other.

Derek told her, "I know the young man who has accused Seth of rape. He comes from a troubled family. The sister accused the stepfather of rape, and I've heard that somebody found some of the kids in bed together. I think he's struggling with some things at home. I have him as a student. He hasn't said anything to me about it, but I wonder."

"That's sad. I wish someone would talk to him and get him to tell the truth. I really don't think anything happened between him and Seth. Seth swears it, and he's been honest now about the other stuff. I don't think he would lie now. If Eugene's charges were dropped, things would be a lot easier for my brother. It's the only rape charge. Do you think … you might be close enough to say something to him, Derek? I know it's a lot to ask."

"I don't know, Mare. That's a tough one."

"I understand." They sat for a moment in silence.

"I would like to talk to you about something else, something I've been wanting to tell you."

Mare listened.

"I've been thinking about telling you for awhile, and now seems a good time." He hesitated, then admitted, "Mare, I'm gay."

She nodded and smiled. "Thanks for trusting me enough to share that. I hope you know it makes no difference to me."

"Thanks. I haven't told that many people around here. It's a pretty conservative community."

"You think?" Mare asked, sarcastically. You know, I had a college roommate once who told me she was bi-sexual. I didn't know how to respond. It didn't matter to me, but she moved out shortly thereafter, because she assumed it bothered me. I just wasn't mature enough to know what to say. I was speechless for a few moments, then she changed the subject before I found the words to reply."

"Todd knows. A female student of mine had a crush on me once. She accused me of hitting on her. I figured I would tell him. He was very cool about it."

"I'm glad he was supportive. It's scary to think that a student can just come out and accuse a teacher of something like that. I know that students sometimes become attracted to teachers. How do you know that one isn't going to come pointing the finger at you?" She picked up a pen and tapped it on the table a few times.

"How is your brother doing?"

"Not wonderfully, but better now that he's decided to take a plea agreement. I just wish he had more friends his age that he could lean on. All he's got is family pretty much."

"I should talk with him sometime. It isn't always easy being gay, that I know."

"I'm sure he would appreciate a conversation."

Derek sighed. "I sometimes feel isolated myself. I guess we all do. I understand his situation, probably better than some folks, I had some relationships with older men during my earlier years that were probably borderline acceptable. I'm still trying to figure those out."

"Do you know, since everything with my brother has come out, I've had several people make some very private disclosures to me. One person told me he was molested as a child. Another told me that a family friend raped her. It's difficult to hear, but I think it's healthy for people to have an outlet to talk about it."

*   *   *   *

"Hey, Pete? Sophie, Tristan, Derek and I are going to climb Quarry Mountain tomorrow for the Winter Solstice. We're going to start celebrating the sun annually. You wanna come? Mom and Dad'll watch Cody. I already asked."

"Nah, I've got work to do. You go.

"Oh, come on," she pleaded good-naturedly. "I'd like you to be with us. Tristan has asked us each to bring something to represent the sun. Should be fun."

"No, really. I don't want to."

"It's your choice, I guess," Mare said, disappointed.

Before Mare was to go on the hike, she sat down at her home computer. She logged into the school bulletin board system and began writing an email. They had not spoken for some time.

From: Mare Lumen
Subject: Good Tidings
To: Walt Douglas

I hope you are able to find some solace this holiday season. I know we have both been quite angry with one another at times during these past several months, and that we have both disagreed with choices that were made. However, every once in a while I am almost able to forget that, and I am reminded of the times when we were able to make each other laugh. I still remember when we were friends. Despite what you may believe, I would like you to be able to find some peace and contentment, and I hope this Christmas gives you an opportunity to have that.

Sincerely,
Mare

As Tristan's car slugged its way up the paved road to Quarry Mountain, the four friends chatted. Abruptly, Tristan slammed on his brakes. A scraggly coyote was crossing in front of them. It turned up the road.

"Look at that thing. God, it's mangy."

"Doesn't look like it's in too good a shape." Mare whipped out her camera and took a picture of the ragged creature.

The animal galloped in front of the vehicle for over a mile before it whipped off into the forest.

The route to the top of Quarry was slippery, but the four friends laughed and talked all the way up the mountain. The temperature hovered around 24 degrees, though the day was sunny. Much of the rocky trail was covered with thick layers of ice. Snow was scattered in thin clumps between the pines and spruces that dotted the slope. When the four arrived at the top, they got out a Frisbee and slid along the open areas to catch it. Derek did a little acrobatic flip, and Mare laughed creating a place of deep contentment in her belly.

Derek pulled out four Clementine oranges and laid them in a circle. "Let's give thanks to the sun for giving life to all that we see. I brought these because they look like mini-suns … and I figured we might need a snack."

Sophie then launched into a little song she knew about the sun. The others caught on and they began playfully running circles around the oranges as they sang. When they finished the song and were warm from jogging, the four plopped down into the light layer of crusty snow and began pulling open the oranges.

"Let's take a picture," Mare insisted, and set up her camera for an automatic, timed shot. Each held up their sun item, standing shoulder to shoulder, and smiled.

As Mare sat, eating orange slices and the sun-shaped cookies that Sophie had made, she reflected back upon the long year. Its end was near. She remembered the previous New Year's when her brother had come over and helped dig out the squirrels from the chimney. *Little did I know then what was on the horizon. So much has happened this year … but I'm okay. I'm getting stronger every day.*

I wonder what this next year will bring? A gust of wind swirled around her as she looked across the horizon towards the West and the tall White Mountains of neighboring New Hampshire.

25

Disasters: Natural and Otherwise

January 1998

We must learn to live together as brothers or perish together as fools.

~Dr. Martin Luther King, Jr.~

"The tree which moves some to tears of joy is, in the eyes of others, only a green thing which stands in their way."

~William Blake~

Mare and Pete sat next to each other in the crowded movie theater. Leonardo DiCaprio and Kate Winslet were attempting to escape the sinking Titanic. Kate's character, Rose, valiantly strove to save her man from a watery death, while the gallant band played on to keep passengers calm. Mare marveled at the selflessness portrayed. She felt uplifted by Rose and Jack's fictional heroism. She rooted for Molly Brown's strength and clear thinking. Her heart ached for the mother who, unable to escape to the upper decks, coaxed her unknowing children to sleep while the ship was gradually going down. Mare thought of her own child, and her own love caught in her throat. She watched both the bravery and the cowardice of a group of people in crisis and considered the choices each made. She admired Rose's perseverance. She saw Jack sink to the bottom of the sea. She was captivated by the whole story.

Mare fluttered out of the theater like a filmy ghost, slipped into the passenger seat and rode to her parent's home in silence. Her heart was beating, and her eyes were red. *Bravo. What a movie. What an event. Fifteen hundred people died, and it was not a pleasant way to go. Children lost fathers. Wives lost husbands. So many suffered. Imagine what it would have been like to truly watch the mammoth ship go down and have to see all those people dying. What an enormous tragedy!* The scale of it haunted her and dwarfed her own puny struggles.

When they got to the Mahonia house, Mare quietly dropped down in the recliner. Her parents looked at her, then Joan asked Pete, "What's with her?"

As if he were accustomed to such behavior and because he was aware of his wife's idiosyncrasies, Pete blurted out—laughing, "Oh, don't worry about Mare. She's still floundering out in the cold Atlantic with dead bodies floating around her. She'll come back soon."

Mare's parents joined in Pete's amusement.

"I can't help it. Leave me alone," she insisted, smiling awkwardly. "It was sad. Can't I be affected by a movie?"

But Pete was right, and Mare knew it. She *was* still drifting in the ocean with those involved in the Titanic disaster. From years of literature study, Mare had become accustomed to putting herself in other characters' shoes. She could easily slip into a vicarious or imaginary experience and feel as if it were her own. No, Mare thought, it started long before that. It started with Henry. The kid on the bus in 6th grade. Feeling Henry's pain and embarrassment after she had attacked him had left an indelible mark on her.

Her mother's voice interrupted her historic train of thought. "Seth is going to take a plea agreement, but he has to plead guilty to all the charges. There's a hearing in a few weeks on it."

"Well, it stinks that he can't deny the false charges, but at least everyone will have some resolution when it's done," Mare said.

"The lawyer also said that we will all have opportunities to make statements on Seth's behalf before the judge passes sentence on him."

"But the other side gets to say what they want as well," Rick added.

Pete added his two cents with a sarcastic, "Oh, THAT sounds like it's going to be a lot of fun."

"Yeah, I'm going to have to take a valium that day for sure," Joan groaned with the slight hint of a grin.

"You better not, Mom. When you took one during the last hearing, you couldn't stop giggling and smiling. It was a little unnerving considering the circumstances."

"Yeah, you may be right."

*   *   *   *

"Will this dreary rain ever end? It's not supposed to rain in January." Mare shook off her hair and pulled Cody's hood back. "It's just cold enough to freeze when it hits the road." She put him down and then crouched to his eye level. "It's pretty slippery out there isn't it, Code?"

Cody nodded his head in agreement. "Slippy," he said.

Mare smiled at his innocence and took off his jacket.

In the wee hours of the morn, Mare was awakened by what sounded like an explosion. It came from the back of the house. She got up from bed and rushed to Cody's room, so she could look out his window. In a moment, she heard another splintering and then a crash. Giant limbs were falling.

The sound startled Cody and he awoke, crying. His mother picked him up and cuddled him.

"Holy moly! Pete—check this out!"

Pete stumbled in and strained to see through the glass into the dark night. "Wow, that ice is getting pretty heavy, isn't it? Looks like some big limbs are coming down. Bet'cha we don't have power tomorrow."

Mare thought about her favorite old trees. She glanced outside again. The giant elm seemed to be okay. "Is there anything we can do protect our big trees from damage?"

Pete was quiet for a moment. "I don't think so. We're just going to have to ride out this ice storm and hope for the best. I'll go downstairs and stoke the fire, in case we don't have power in the morning."

The clamor of branches collapsing and wires breaking continued through the night. In the morning, Mare noticed her alarm clock light was not working. "No power."

She ran to Cody's window again, and, since they had recently moved Cody out of the crib and into his own double bed, her son was at her knee.

"Oh my god!" she gasped when she saw the degree of destruction. In the dim light of morning, she could see debris scattered everywhere; trees were down; limbs were piled around their former roots; a layer of ice nearly two inches thick engulfed all that could be seen. "Oh no! The elm!"

Pete came scurrying to his wife's side.

Two of its giant limbs were fractured like matchsticks, as if a giant had strolled by and pulled two arms out of the tree's sockets. With that extent of damage, the tree could not be saved. The weight of the ice had been too much. Mare had so hoped her elm would be spared from the crackling crashes that echoed over the hillside, as it had been spared from Dutch Elm Disease, but it's luck had run out. She felt disheartened.

Then another thought occurred to her, "My Maple!" her eyes gaped wide. She ran downstairs, threw on her coat and boots and exited to the porch. Strewn about the base and along the porch and driveway were many branches, but the bulk of the tree was intact and seemed solid. "Thank goodness," Mare acknowledged, clasping her gloved hands together. "Look at the ice," she murmured to herself, as her eyes trailed down the glassy driveway. Everything was coated in solid water, still and unmoving. She walked to the edge of the porch and onto the driveway, very carefully, so she wouldn't fall. It was breathtaking and horrifying at the same time. Mare slid down the driveway and attempted to descend to the littered pavement. Another maple closer to the front of the house seemed okay, as well as the two great gatekeeper maples at the bottom of the driveway. But everywhere she looked, devastation had arrived first. A crystallized war zone unfolded before her, a wasteland of natural and man-made rubble, glazed in a beautiful, translucent coating of ice. The enormous silence that surrounded Mare was only occasionally broken by a deafening gasp and rip of limbs that were still fighting an ongoing battle with Mother Nature. Many would succumb to her power in the next few days as the rain from a warmer level of the atmosphere continued to fall, and ground temperatures stayed below freezing.

Mare made her way back up the obstacle course that her sloping driveway had become. Pete and a bundled Cody met her at the top. All three walked to the backyard. Mare stood in front of the elm she had danced in the wind with earlier that fall. From ground level, it looked like a natural, wooden cross. The top limb traveled straight up and spread out into smaller branches. The roots went into the earth. But the now horizontal limbs to the right and left of Mare's vision leaned groundward. They would never again point to the sky. The whole tree had been sacrificed to the storm, along with many of its companions.

"Look at the birches," Pete pointed, as they made their way further back into their property. A big white birch that marked the entry to the circular clearing was bowing down to the ground.

"How interesting," Mare commented. Pete looked at her, confused.

"Think of T'ai Chi … the birches are *yielding* to the weight. Their strength is in yielding, unlike the other trees which were holding firm to one position."

"Ah, I see what you're saying."

"I wonder if they will survive the ice storm. We'll have to check it out in the spring."

The family surveyed the rest of the damage to their property, and then started back for the house. "I don't think we're going to be having school for a while. Guess we're going to have a cold breakfast. That is, unless we want to heat something up on top of the woodstove."

"Yeah, we're not going to be able to flush the toilets either, until I can switch our water over from the uphill well. I wouldn't drink it; it hasn't been tested, but we'll be able to flush at least."

Later that day, Pete's father came over with his chain saw. "Let's go clear some of this debris out of the road, so that we can eventually get mobile again. You can't get anywhere in this stuff. The roads are covered with whole trees, big limbs and power lines. You both steer clear of those lines, you hear?"

Mare nodded. Pete put on his jacket and joined his father outside.

"Do you have everything you need, for now, hon?" John Lumen asked his daughter-in-law.

"Yes, I think so, for now."

"Good, cause you won't be going anywhere for a day or two. Keep the fire going."

"I will," she assured him.

The sky was overcast and everything was dark without the light of the sun or electricity. Mare pulled out all the flashlights she could find, candles and kerosene lamps. She brought in a couple of loads of wood and dropped them with a loud rumble next to the stove. She put an extra sweater on Cody and took a peek in the fridge. No computer, no phone, no television, no electricity. The damage outside looked pretty bad. *I wonder how long the power will be out.* She turned on the weather radio and listened to a report. El Nino was blamed for the extreme weather patterns. It was indeed a serious storm, stretching from New York State all the way up into Canada. Maine seemed to be one of the worst hit. Schools were closed; in fact, Emerson was in the process of being turned into an emergency shelter by the Red Cross. The electric company had restored power to the center of town, so the school, hospital and a handful of businesses were now connected. At least families could go to Mare's school to stay warm and get a hot meal ... maybe a cot to sleep on—that is, if they could make it to the sanctuary. Travel was still limited.

The next day, Pete stayed home to watch Cody, while Mare slowly inched the car down the hill and out to the grocery store. Since she was just a few streets up from Main St, she could get out. Folks in outlying areas on back roads would be forced to wait longer. A line of about forty people had already formed by the time Mare arrived. Without a full staff and access to resupply lines, store employees would only allow twenty people at a time into the store. Customers were limited to fifteen items. They could purchase no more until transportation opened up again and the store could receive more shipments. Mare waited in the frosty air, trying to figure out what items she would purchase. A generator kept the minimal lights functioning when she entered. Browsing the aisles, she was glad that Cody was no longer on formula. It would be very hard for mothers who no longer had a milk supply to keep their babies fed with this rationing. *Better to keep some backup supplies on hand for such emergencies,* Mare resolved.

Next, she went to the local department store. Inside the store was darkness, and Mare could see that employees were leading customers through the aisles only a few at a time—by flashlight—to get what they needed. When it was Mare's turn, she asked to be taken to the battery section, where she grabbed a few of each.

When she returned home, Pete had reconnected their phone line, which had snapped and separated from the house. Mare called her parents and a few friends to make sure everyone was okay. She invited one family of friends to stay overnight, since they did not have a woodstove and were not expected to get power back for several days. Few went to work while the power was out. Even those who got power back sometimes lost it again. Tropical fish perished as the powerless days went by.

Mare began to realize how dependent her family was on electricity. *We are so interdependent upon each other. If the infrastructure of this country were to fail, how would we survive? Americans used to live on farms. They canned goods for the winter. They kept their own animals. They were more self-sufficient. Few families lived that way now. Could people work together again to survive?* Mare began to fantasize about creating an underground bunker to store food, supplies, and gear for such an event. *Someday I will have a house where I can go off the power grid. Why don't we develop alternative sources of power? How would I start a fire without a match? Could I construct a snare to trap food? Could I grow grains? I don't keep seeds here. Could I recognize edible wild plants? ... We are so spoiled and complacent; we don't realize how precarious our existence really is. How interconnected and dependent we are …*

It rained for three days straight. Fifteen counties in Maine were declared federal disaster areas. States of Emergency were issued all over the Northeast. The Ice Storm of 1998 was dubbed "the worst winter storm on record." At least 700,000 people were without power; some figures claimed it was closer to 130,000. All in the dead of a frigid Northeast winter. After the rain stopped, the temperature plummeted. The low temps, gusty winds and physical dangers threatened lives. Maine and many other parts of the Northeast were swallowed by a cavernous darkness.

But when folks crawled out of their dark holes, communities came together. Neighbors reached out to one another. The descendents of the Puritans, Irish, French, Scandinavian, German and British Isle immigrants, among others; gay and straight; dark-skinned and light-skinned; rich and poor—forgot their differences and helped each other to overcome nature's onslaught. Neighbors realized they needed each other, and some discovered it felt good to give. *Something about calamities brings people closer,* Mare observed. *Some heroic part of our characters is allowed to emerge. Our hearts mount the white horse in fearless anticipation.*

Encompassed by her dark and cold home, Mare began to write her letter to the judge. It felt strange to compose in a notebook again; she had gotten so used to writing with the computer. Being iced in for so long felt like camping indoors—now people had to read, eat and entertain themselves by the light of fires, lanterns or candles.

*   *   *   *

The Lumens were without power for a week. School closed for a week and a half. Some of Mare's students from more rural areas would still not have power when they returned to class. While holed up in her cave for that time, in addition to the court statement, Mare began to write about her experiences in the last year. They seemed worth sharing. She had always wanted to be a writer. Sitting in the darkness, with little else to do, she reflected back over 1997. She let the pen move with her mind. Two chapters were born out of the darkness, as was a plan, a dream … to share a piece of herself with the world, to reach out and touch others. Since her brother's story seemed to be coming to a close, she thought now was a good time to begin. Besides there was little else to do until the power returned. She could see the whole story, or so she thought. She did not perceive yet that her story would become so much larger than her original vision.

*   *   *   *

Seth's lawyer asked the Mahonias to travel to his office in Lewiston and meet with him about a week before the sentencing. Vance D'Angelo was a handsome man and a successful attorney. Mare noticed Native American paintings around his spacious office. She had met him a few times before, and felt, despite the fact that he defended criminals, that the man had integrity.

He outlined to the family what would happen at the hearing. He encouraged anyone who hadn't written to the judge to compose letters asking for leniency. He explained that the victims and their families would have an opportunity to speak, and he told them that Seth himself would have a say before sentencing. He answered their questions.

"I have read your letters to the judge, so far, and I would caution you in one respect. Seth must take responsibility for all charges. If the judge thinks that Seth is denying any part of the charges before sentencing, he may go for a more extreme judgment. That goes for attacking the police too. I agree that they bungled this investigation in many respects, but this is not the time and place to criticize them. The judge doesn't care about that and he won't want to hear about it, so leave it out, please."

Mare's head bowed. She would certainly have to revise. Hers was too defensive. She had criticized the police. She had talked about the charges that weren't true. She had also talked about the homophobia of the Babylon community.

Then he asked Mare if he could speak with her for a moment in private.

"Certainly," she replied, though she couldn't imagine what he might want to talk to her about separately.

The two stepped into a side office. He pointed to a chair and Mare sat down. Vance sat opposite her in his desk chair.

"Mare, I'm going to ask you something that may be a little uncomfortable, but I'm trying to look for angles to speak on Seth's behalf, so I'm looking into each lead that I have."

A puzzled look crossed Mare's face.

"Seth told me that when you and he were children, that you touched each other."

What? Why is this relevant? A defensive reaction was building, but she tried to remain calm. "When we were seven or eight, yes, but it was pretty innocent."

"What happened?"

Mare's face flushed with humiliation. She huffed out a quick breath through her nostrils. "We just touched each other and rubbed against each other," she looked away from the attractive man.

"There was no penetration?"

"No!" she gasped, mortified. "Never. And no oral contact either. Did he tell you there was?" *Does D'Angelo think we had an incestuous relationship?* The perceived ugliness of it killed her. She did not want to be implicated in his sexual problems. It brought back an uncomfortable dream memory for Mare. Before she consciously knew about her brother's problems, during a time of concern for him, she had dreamed they *had* joined together physically. Upon waking, she was so disturbed by the dream that she went to a friend who had majored in psychology and asked her to tell her what the dream meant.

The friend reassured her that it was okay, and had suggested possible meanings for the dream. "You are probably just worried about him, maybe you are connected with him at some spiritual level, or you could be trying to make that connection," she told her. Mare tried to forget the dream. She heard that some people bury early sexual experiences and don't remember them. Mare considered that possibility, but she had a clear memory of the time they had touched each other. It had never gone any further. She was certain she had never been abused either because she remembered having to break her hymen the first time she used a tampon. She tried to shake off all of the unpleasant thoughts.

D'Angelo's voice interrupted the train. "No, Seth never claimed that more happened. He just reported the same thing you did. When we were looking at reasons why this behavior might have happened—when I first took on the case, he relayed the experience with you. I thought I would follow up to make sure."

"Oh he did, did he?" Mare said with growing anger. "Didn't he tell you about the experience he had with the college guy?"

"No, I haven't heard about that."

"Yes, well, he's trying to protect him." She filled him in briefly on what she knew. "I would say that that experience had a much greater bearing on Seth's development and problems than the little incident between us. All kids are curious about their bodies. We were just exploring; we didn't know what we were doing. We just knew that we had sensations down there," Mare was blushing, sharing such private things with a man she hardly knew.

He nodded. "I'm sorry for asking. I know it's uncomfortable. I just needed to check. I'm sure this has been very difficult for you," he said kindly.

"Harder than you can imagine," she admitted. "I'm writing about it. Maybe there will be a book one day."

"I'd like to read that," he told her with sincerity in his eyes. "Thank you for your time and honesty."

Mare nodded and exited the room, still fuming that her brother had attempted to pass some of the blame for his behavior onto her. She twisted her shoulders uncomfortably, trying to free herself from the sticky mess that seemed to follow her brother and ooze onto her by virtue of proximity.

She accosted Seth about it the next time they were alone.

He claimed he never blamed Mare; he was just relaying sexual kinds of experiences that happened when he was young, because the lawyer asked about them.

"Yet, you never told him about the guy at the lake."

He was silent. "That was way back when I first went to my attorney. I hadn't told anyone then."

Mare nodded and tried to let the experience go. It was done with. In the past.

26

Punishment, Revenge or Justice

A man should not act as a judge either for someone he loves or for someone he hates. For no man can see the guilt of someone he loves or the good qualities in someone he hates.

~Babylonian Talmud, tractate Ketubbot~

The night before the hearing to sentence Seth, the extended family, Hope, and her son got together to spend one last evening with Seth. It was unlike any gathering Mare had ever experienced. It was not a birthday party or a Christmas celebration. It was not even a post-funeral get together. The purpose was a sort of bon voyage. *I suppose it is a kind of trip,* Mare thought. It was the closest definition she could come up with. *Gee, have a nice long visit to jail.*

All shared this last meal of freedom together and wished Seth well. Many teary hugs were exchanged. Seth's young cousin, Ashley, who was in 8th grade at the time, gave Seth a picture of her to bring to jail. She had written him a letter of encouragement also telling him not to forget her. She gave him a giant hug before she went home. She knew the truth, and yet she still loved him no matter what.

Mare sat on the floor next to her bed alone in a dark room that night, her hands in her lap. Pete was downstairs watching television. Her stomach was aching, nervous about the hearing. She was afraid to hear the victims and their parents speak about what a monster her brother was and how they should put him away for life. She was afraid of getting up in front of the courtroom and people who must now shun her family.

She wanted to get her attention off herself and off of her fears and onto her intent. She thought about praying.

Though she had been raised a protestant, her Universalist congregation was very liberal. What she remembered most about the minister of her youth was how he encouraged them to question, to find their own truth. The man had organized debates about creation and the bible with other youth groups, where Mare discovered that some people interpreted the text much more literally than she. They did not seem to question its content, even when it contradicted itself, which it seemed to often do. Mare respected the words and felt there was much truth and wisdom to them, but she also felt free to challenge it. After all, she thought, men wrote down the words, and men have their own fears and agendas. A healthy suspicion seemed in order to her.

For much of her adult life, Mare struggled to define her religious beliefs. Agnostic fit the best at this point. It was too soon to make a judgment. She couldn't see a divine power in human male form sticking his nose in every person's business. It didn't fit for her, yet she couldn't say she didn't believe in a higher power. The universe seemed too ... orderly ... for that.

God was such a charged term. People had fought and killed each other in the name of God. What was God?

Because she couldn't get a sense of the word, she avoided using it. She preferred to attribute the mysteries of life to *The Universe.*

However, on this eve of her brother's sentencing, Mare overcame her own uncertainties and decided to have a talk with this ... Great Spirit. This time, she chose to use *the word.* Using it was a form of surrender for her.

She put her hands together and spoke aloud. She did not know if anyone was listening or if she was somehow opening up a higher channel in herself. She did not know what she was going to say. Unlike other times, she didn't plan it all out. She just opened her mouth and tried to listen to what her heart wanted to express. She spoke aloud, because somehow she sensed it was more powerful.

"Dear God," she said, then paused to consider her direction.

"On this eve of Seth's sentencing I ask that you grant me strength. Allow me to express myself with clarity, wisdom and authenticity." Her voice choked with emotion.

"Help me to free myself from self-oriented concerns and to complete the task before me with composure and warmth." She stopped again until she felt a pull into the next thought. "Assist me in opening up a channel of compassion tomorrow ... so that people are able to see Seth's humanity. May everyone present in the courtroom experience a deep sense of cleansing and completion. May this be a solid step toward healing for all."

She sighed and reached inside herself for words. "Please give Seth the courage to speak with sincerity, so that people see who he is, where he's been and what his vision of a healthy future is. Wherever the court chooses to send him, PLEASE ..." her voice cracking with heartfelt fear, "please, keep him safe from harm there."

Mare sat in stillness and lucidity while her soul spoke. "Let him reenter society in a few years ... more wise, more humble and in sound mind and body."

"Grant my parents and the rest of our family the will to endure, and eventually thrive, in the face of these circumstances. Help them glean insight from their pain and direct them on the path to acceptance and peace of mind." She sniffled quietly and thought of the police chief and those who had lied. "Encourage ... *is that the right word?* Encourage those who have been deceitful in this process to become aware of their ... shortcomings ... and help them to take steps to make amends or redirect themselves onto a path of integrity."

"Let there be an experience of true connection among each of the people who attend the hearing tomorrow." She envisioned the sight in her mind's eye. She illustrated the outcome she wanted. People reaching past their differences and relating to one another. "From me to the judge, from the judge to Seth, to the lawyers, to our family and friends, to the young men who were involved and their families and friends. May there be such an exchange of energy and compassion that no person will remain unchanged. May each of us ultimately be improved by our involvement in this."

"I ask for a fair and just sentence. I ask for a miracle in that courtroom, if you should will it. Amen."

*   *   *   *

Mare got out of the car and looked up at the gold-domed roof of the courthouse. She collected her things and began walking into the building. Sophie and Kate followed Mare and her family into the courthouse, because Mare had asked for support. She didn't want to do it alone this time.

Before sitting, Mare found the reporter from the *Lewiston Daily Bugle* and handed her a printout entitled "Open Letter to the Community." She then passed another copy of the letter to the Babylon newspaperman. She hoped each paper would print what she had written.

Mare sat down several rows behind her brother and looked around the courtroom. On the other side of the room sat those who came to speak against

Seth. She saw the Gibb family with one of the sons that Seth had been close to. She saw others she recognized vaguely. The reporters sat on that side as well. The right side of the room was quite full. Mare's stomach fluttered.

Seth, his lawyer, his parents, Mare, Pete, Cassie, Uncle George, and Uncle Carl, Grandpa Franklin and several cousins and friends sat on the left side of the courtroom. One person that Mare did not know came in and sat down on the left side, then quickly realizing that she was sitting on the *wrong* side, she got up and sat in the right side of the room. Though the left side was clearly in the minority, it was not a small group.

The list of charges against Seth was read again, and Seth officially changed his plea to guilty. The judge addressed those in attendance. "I know that this is a very difficult case for all of you that are here today. I want you to know that I have read the letters sent to me from both sides and I appreciate your contributions. I will give you an opportunity to speak today, if you wish. All you have to do is come up to the microphone here." He pointed to the spot in front of the seats. "State your name and then say your piece. Let's start with those who would like to speak from the side representing the victims. Then, when those folks are finished, we will allow the Mahonia family and friends to say what they would like to say. Any questions?"

"Okay, then, we can begin. Whoever would like to start, feel free to step up."

Several people on the right side of the room looked around at each other, but eventually a parent of one of the victims rose. Mare took a deep breath to prepare herself.

"I'm Suzanne Gibb. Seth Mahonia abused both of my older sons. I can't even tell you how angry I am that my two babies, the sons that I gave birth to and have tried to nurture and protect all their lives have been molested by this man. I put my trust in Seth and he betrayed us. Before all this happened, my sons were healthy and happy children. Now, I see them struggling in school. They can't sleep at night. They used to feel hope about life. Now they are tortured by what happened to them. I have to witness their suffering, and there is little I can do but try to help them pick up the pieces and move on." The bailiff brought up a box of tissues and placed it on the podium. The mother nodded and thanked him. "The worst thing about this is that Seth knew how much I loved and protected my children, and yet he violated them anyway. My trust has been broken and my sons' emotional well being thrown to the wayside for his sexual pleasure. That man took away my children's childhood, not one child, but two!" Her voice was emotional, but strong. "Two of my babies!" she spurted out in anguish, and Mare's own eyes were full of tears. "It's every mother's worst nightmare, but it is one that my family cannot wake from. I would like to make sure that Seth is required to register as a sex offender in Maine. It rips my heart apart to think what pain Seth has caused the people I love; I want to make sure he never re-offends. Please require that he get counseling, because he is a sick, sick man."

Mrs. Gibb returned to her seat, and her husband took to the podium. Mare could see Seth's back slouched over and it was heaving with his silent sobs.

"Hello, your honor." He nodded. "I am Tom Gibb, that was my wife who just spoke." He took a deep breath and began to tell the story of his involvement with Seth. "Seth has been in our lives for several years now. My older son, Chris, spent time working for Seth's camp business, and more recently my middle son, Nate. They would go mountain biking with him, snowboarding or skiing. He took them camping and hiking. They each spent a lot of time with him, first Chris, until he stopped going over to Seth's, then Nate. They would play football together. In the beginning, I was a little distrustful, but the boys seemed fine with it. When they began to spend the night over there, I wanted to make sure everything was on the up and up, because it is unusual for a man his age to spend so much time with a younger crowd. I was suspicious, but I didn't really have anything to go on.... I had a talk with Seth anyway. He swore to me that he would never do anything to hurt my children. He said they were his friends. He promised me that they were safe with him. I believed him, but he just manipulated me. He lied, and that's what makes this even harder for me, because he looked me in the eye and told me that I could trust him with my sons. I even defended him when another parent asked me what I thought because she was concerned. I am devastated by what has happened to my children, and I am angry with Seth. He has put my family through a living hell. Seth's own family are just as much victims of his lies as we are and just as brokenhearted. I know that they were fooled by his act, and my heart aches for their suffering as well as my own." Tears rolled down Mare's checks, as did many around her.

"I ask that you recognize this is no ordinary crime. When the children tried to resist or confront him, he twisted it around so they thought they were at fault. My boys don't dare to go camping anymore. They have many sleepless nights. School and other activities that Seth was a part of are now all tainted for them. Their dreams of life have changed forever and can't be repaired. There is no punishment that will make up for the pain he has caused. So, I don't know what a fair sentence would be. I only know that he lied and manipulated the people who trusted him. He needs some serious counseling and hopefully he will get that where he's going. There's a part in my heart that still feels sorry for Seth that he's done these things. But there's so much anger there too." He looked up. "That's all I have to say, your honor."

"Thank you, Mr. Gibb," the judge said.

Mare listened as one after another mother, father, grandmother came forward to tell of the effect of Seth's actions on their family and children. How overwhelming the ordeal had been for each family.

"Our son's life will never be the same. He has given up on everything. He has given up on life."

"I hope someday you realize," one mother said, turning slightly to Seth, "just how bad you hurt these kids."

Seth was visibly shaken by every word and the emotions behind the words. He was forced to shoulder what he had created. A steady stream rained down his withered face.

Up to this point in the proceedings, no victim had spoken. Only one that Mare was acquainted with, Nate Gibb, was even in the room. The judge asked if anyone else would like to speak before moving to the other side of the room. The DA asked the judge to hold on for a moment and he went over to speak to Nate. Mare could not hear their whispers, but she saw Nate nod reluctantly. The 9th grader walked up to the podium and cleared his throat. His scruffy blond hair hung into his eyes, and his shoulders were hunched in as he spoke into the microphone.

"My name is Nate Gibb. I don't really like talking into the microphone, but since none of the other victims wanted to come today, I figured I should. They want to forget about all this, forget about Seth, but I am having a lot of trouble doing that. Seth was my friend for a few years. We did a lot of fun stuff together," his voice choked and cracked. The words came out almost as a rushed wheeze. "All of us kids trusted him, looked up to him. He shattered all that. No matter where I go, whatever I do, his name will always go with me." He tried to collect himself. "It is unbelievably impossible to live every day without thinking about what he did to me. I can't sleep. He's there. No matter what you try to do, you can't. He's always right there in your mind." He broke down.

"Take your time, son," the judge reassured him. "I know this is very hard. It's courageous of you to speak." Mare couldn't stop the tears that continuously strained down her cheeks, nor could her sister, Cassie, beside her. She noticed in the front row that Seth's face was in his hands and every once in a while you could hear a deep, muffled sob escape.

Nate continued. "I have a lot of trouble trusting people now. Everything has changed. I'm doing terribly in school. I just don't know what to do. All of us kids are having trouble. He shattered all of our hopes and dreams. He ruined my life. No matter how long I live I will never be able to understand why he did this. Never." He held his hand up, to indicate he could not continue and moved back to his seat.

"I want you to know that I appreciate all of the comments you have made and that I will give them the greatest consideration. Are there members of the Mahonia camp who would like to make a comment."

A hand went up. "I would, your honor." Joan's brother, Mare's Uncle Carl, took the podium. Mare always had a special affection for her Uncle Carl. In some ways, he and Mare had the most in common of any two members of the family. When his friends and family got together, they would stay up to the wee hours playing board games—men against the women. Mare's family was very competitive. But today was not a light, family get together. They had bonded together. Carl was their best voice. He could always be counted on.

"Your honor, I am Carl Franklin. I am here to plead for leniency in sentencing my nephew, Seth. I believe that Seth was raised in a loving and functional family environment. My sister's family and mine have spent many times together at birthdays, holidays, camping and other family functions. Because of this closeness, I have known Seth his entire life. Seth is an outstanding individual in many ways. He puts other's needs ahead of his own. He has been an excellent student, teacher, and worker in many endeavors of his life. Seth has always been somewhat shy and withdrawn, especially through his teen years. Finding out that he was sexually abused when he was thirteen, certainly sheds light on his personality traits. I can't begin to imagine what this must have done to his ego and self-esteem. I don't claim to be an expert at psychology, but I'm sure this incident must have had an effect of Seth's future behavior. This is not meant to excuse his guilt. What he did is wrong and he should receive punishment for his crime."

Carl swiped a tear from under his glasses, and tried to keep his normally strong voice steady. "We must also acknowledge the pain and suffering of the victims and their families. Seth is carrying a tremendous burden of guilt and responsibility … as he should be. What he needs is light, not darkness; hope, not despair; and help—not solitude!"

"I am asking for your compassion in his sentencing. I hope the environment you place him in is one of counseling, support and protection from the abuse of others. Seth is not a hardened criminal! I have worked with hundreds of employees in my twenty-five year career as a manager of people and I think I am a good judge of character. Seth's soul is good—he needs help! The amount of time in confinement and the amount of counseling he receives will have a direct impact upon his ability to return as a productive member of our society. Please do everything in your power to help Seth find the appropriate road to recovery. I know he is remorseful and I know he is ready, willing and capable of rehabilitation."

"Thank you for your consideration."

The judge nodded, as Carl stepped down. Mare's mother rose up onto wobbly legs and walked up to the microphone.

"I am Seth's mother, Joan," she said. "My husband wrote a letter that he has asked me to read. So I'd like to do that." She looked down at the paper and began with great difficulty. "I have three beautiful children and I would give my life to any one of them. I have always been very proud of them, and I have always thought of myself as having been a very fortunate father. They all did well in school. None of them ever did drugs or got into trouble, which is unusual for most kids now-a-days. The greatest moment of my life was when my son was born … The blackest was when I learned of these crimes."

A quick thought darted across Mare's mind. *What do you mean the greatest moment … what about my birth?* She brushed aside the silly thought.

"I weep for the victims' families. I weep for my own family. I weep for my son, because of his abuse at age 13."

It was almost more painful for Mare to listen to her father's heartbroken words than anyone else's.

"I know that Seth can't change the past, but I hope you will allow him to have a chance to set his future right. I don't understand how all this happened. I can hardly bring myself to acknowledge what he has done, but I love my son. I fear that a lengthy sentence will do more damage than anything else." Mare's mother read on with strength and relative composure, and she thanked the judge when she was finished.

Several other members of the family and some friends got up and shared their experiences about Seth. Mare was last to go.

"Thank you for letting me address the court, your honor," Mare looked up at the judge who nodded.

"I'm sure some people are wondering how I am able to get up here and defend someone who has admitted to sexual misconduct with minors. Let me tell you, it is not easy; I do so with a heavy heart." Something was gripping her throat tightly; the words were having trouble pressing through Mare's trembling lips. She swallowed hard and bolstered herself to get through this. She had to speak. The emotion had to wait.

"My personal upbringing has taught me that such actions are deplorable—and they are! Trust me when I say that we have our own hurt and anger to deal with towards my brother—but we also love him and we worry about him too."

"Our hearts go out to these teenagers and their families who were implicated in and affected by this case. This situation has had painful repercussions
throughout the community. We are truly sorry that a member of our family
has been the source of such upheaval."

"However, we know Seth. At his core, he has a good and loving heart."

"If we are able to suspend our judgments about him for just a moment, we
can see that Seth made a positive difference in the lives of many young people!
I'm not trying to excuse his grave errors—but I remember more than one
occasion in which Seth called me and asked for details about an assignment I
had given in class, because he was helping one of his friends with his homework. This was common. Not only did he assist with learning, but he was there
for them. He watched their sporting events, he encouraged them to avoid
drugs and other trouble, he took them places they might never have gone otherwise—to football games, hiking in the Mahoosics, rock climbing, canoeing.
Seth used to receive phone calls—even late at night—from kids who needed a
ride home from a game or some other event, or because their own vehicle had
broken down. These teenagers counted on Seth for so much, and he thrived on
being able to help them. Seth has gotten many letters and calls over the years—
from parents and grandparents alike telling him what a positive impact he had
made in their teenager's life. The last thing Seth wanted to do was hurt these
kids."

"But let's face it—his perception of reality was distorted, thanks to a childhood experience of his own. It may be hard to imagine, but Seth was a young
boy once too. He felt lonely as many kids do, and he was confused and needed
a friend. Seth trusted someone outside the family and was taken advantage of
sexually. We never knew this until recently. How does this affect a person's
development? These cycles must be broken. People like Seth need our help,
when problems are beginning to surface. Fortunately, the young people in this
case will be able to get psychological help now, if they should desire it. At thirteen, Seth was not so fortunate."

"I wish as a society, we could be there for someone with problems like Seth,
early on. I wish we could put aside our judgments about the longings—for a
moment—and do what needs to be done to help not only the offender, but—
in the process—his future victims."

"Seth has deep-seated issues stemming from his own abuse. I beg you; get
him the help he needs! Counseling—not a lengthy prison term!"

"No matter how desperately he would like to, Seth cannot change what has
been done. He can only begin anew—now. The first step in recreating his life
has been to acknowledge both to himself and the community what happened

and take responsibility for it. This he has done. In addition, the remorse he has felt this year has been profound. He lived with my husband and me almost this entire year; I've seen the steady tears and shame."

"You've heard people on both sides of this case now, either in letters or in person, and soon, you will hear Seth's side of the story. I don't envy your job. I'm sure this will be a difficult decision to make with all the emotional testimonies given. Please consider Seth's own abuse and his good deeds as you deliberate. You don't cure alcoholism by throwing the alcoholic in jail for several years. Please, arrange for Seth to get the treatment he needs. I know your judgment will be fair and just and in the best interest of the community, no matter what you decide. Thank you for the opportunity to speak, your honor, and I thank the rest of you for listening." Mare bowed ever so slightly and returned to her seat with tears streaming down her cheeks. She felt a few pats on her shoulders.

The judge shifted in his seat, trying to gather his thoughts. "Well, Mr. Mahonia, it's your turn. Would you like to step up?"

Seth blew his nose and struggled with his emotions. He leaned towards his lawyer.

"Your honor, this has been very overwhelming for my client. We ask for a brief recess."

"All right. We'll take a fifteen-minute recess, then we'll hear Mr. Mahonia speak."

The judge rose and when he exited the courtroom, people got up out of their seats and began to stretch and mill about.

Mare looked over to the right side of the room. To her sister she murmured, "I'm going to talk to some of the parents."

She nodded, "I'll come with you."

Her heart was beating, because she did not know how the other side would receive her, but she had to express what was in her heart. She approached the Gibbs. Nate was not there, but his parents and little brother were. "Mr. and Mrs. Gibb," Mare said gravely. "I am so sorry for what your family has gone through. I really am." Tears came to her eyes, and Tom Gibb opened wide his arms. Mare moved into them, and the virtual stranger held her like a protected daughter.

"I know you are," he said gently. "I know. And I feel for your family's sorrow."

Cassie and Suzanne also hugged in their mutual anguish. In those brief moments, a healing energy wrapped around the foursome. They were not enemies.

"Thank you," Mare whispered as she let go of Mr. Gibb and reached for his wife. She was grateful for the generosity of his spirit. No other words needed to be spoken. She placed a hand on the youngest son's shoulder, and then the sisters moved to speak to a few of the other parents of victims.

Just before the proceedings were about the start, Mare headed back to her seat, and gave her brother a squeeze on the shoulder as she passed his location.

He stood, walked to the podium and laid his prepared thoughts out on the surface. He took a deep breath. Mare knew this was about the most difficult thing he would ever have to do.

"I used to know who I was. It's hard to believe how one minute I saw myself as someone who has devoted his life to kids, who loved and cared about them; who tried to keep them safe and help them get through the difficult times in their lives. The next minute I was feeling the guilt of committing crimes against them. I knew I wasn't this monster that the press made me out to be. I'm not some kind of heartless person that would take from those that I cared the most about. The facts hadn't changed, yet there was a point in which my own perception went from one extreme to another.

Here I was, a man with my own home, my own summer camp, a good job, I was the president of the local Sportsman's Club, popular amongst my co-workers. I had received numerous awards for being a role model and leader. I received many letters from parents saying that I was a positive influence and that they have seen positive changes in their sons. I received a letter from a teenager saying that I was more of a father to him than his own father was. A grandmother even called to say what a difference I made in her grandson's life. On my birthday I received the gift of a five dollar bill and written on it said, "Thanks for being there for us, Seth." This is the person that I thought I was. I started my summer camp wanting to continue this positive aspect of my life, the part where I felt important to these kids. The part where I felt I could make a positive difference. I have always felt that I had some sort of gift with kids, maybe even god-given.

I am a generous, loving, caring, moral person who gave a crap when many others didn't. I was there watching these kids participating in sports. Often, I was there when no one else was. There is nothing greater than to hear a young person say thanks, or you're the best. There is nothing more satisfying than to see a kid accomplish something that they thought they couldn't accomplish, all because of your encouragement. Nothing makes you more proud than to see your friend win a wrestling match, pitch a strike out or to get a trophy for most improved. There were dozens of kids that I considered my friends. They were my whole world. They were my family. I would give my life for any of them. How could I hurt the ones I loved the most? The truth is, at the time, I didn't think I was hurting anyone.

Obviously I was wrong. I was wrong about a lot of things and I compromised everything that was truly important in my life.

If someone would have come to me in the beginning and told me straight out what I have come to realize since, I would have told them they were wrong. Through searching for the truth about my own life, I finally began to realize how things that happened years earlier influenced the direction of my life.

Each one of us feels a certain way about certain things because of our past experiences. I didn't understand why my happiness was so dependent on having kids around. I was so dependent that I became depressed after only a few days without them in my life. I had no idea why. Many people will be surprised to hear that I was often suicidal and constantly lapsing in and out of depression. All my life I just assumed that it was just who I was. What was it about them that seemed so necessary for my happiness? Despite most people's presumptions it wasn't sexual. It was that close friendship, that connection that I needed most.

When I was 13, I too was the victim of sexual abuse by a college student outside of our family. At the time I didn't feel like I was a victim. I could have said no but I didn't. I could have stopped coming back but I craved the attention of someone that made me feel important. What I thought didn't hurt me when I was 13 ended up leading me down a path that destroyed my life, destroyed my dreams, but most importantly of all it destroyed my friendships. I know this young man didn't want to do me any harm. I believe he wanted the same thing that I wanted, to feel love and a connection to someone. To feel okay and accepted. To me it was never about sex. I don't think either one of us realized the consequences of what was happening. From that summer on my life was changed forever.

Serious thoughts of suicide in my early 20s made me seek help, only to find out I couldn't talk about the abuse because of mandatory reporting laws. That aspect of my life, which so desperately needed correcting, went without the help that I sought. In order to get help I would lose all of my friends and the respect of the community. I would be risking the support of my family and I would be guaranteed public humiliation. So instead of having the courage to do the right thing and go into counseling and the legal system, I was a coward and did not go forward with the treatment program that I desperately wanted. Despite many promises to myself that I would never let this happen again, things didn't change. It was clear that this was a problem that I could not handle on my own. The law that was made to protect kids was the law that kept me from getting the help I needed and have always wanted. Because of this law I went on to abuse 6 more innocent teenagers instead of getting professional help at a time when I needed it most. These laws need to be revised and I intend to do everything in my powers to make that happen. They are only reactive when they should be proactive to prevent future abuse. Don't get me wrong, I don't blame the law for what I have done, but for these cycles of abuse to stop, we must stop creating deterrents that discourage people like me from getting help, especially for those who seek it. The alternative is keeping up the barriers and allowing this type of problem to go untreated until the abuse gets discovered.

Through reading several books I began to realize how others with similar childhood experiences had fallen down the same path. I did not make it up. Someone had traveled this path before me. I didn't wake up one day and say I think I'll be a pedophile. It was something that evolved from my own abuse. Something that I hated being yet without help I felt I couldn't escape becoming.

Because I didn't feel (at the time) what had happened to me had done me any harm, I thought others would take it the same as I had. Somehow in my twisted perception of reality I thought as long as I wasn't forcing anyone it was O.K. Somehow I felt I was different than those people we all hear about on the evening news. Most of these kids had been my friends for many years and continued to be, even after things happened. It didn't seem to affect our friendships and none of these kids had ever stopped being my friends. I honestly never expected that I was harming anyone. I cared so much for these kids. Their involvement in my life was never about my sexual gratification. I hope they understand that.

For every kid that I actually had sexual contact with, there were dozens and dozens of kids that I didn't. We spent thousands and thousands of hours and hundreds of days filled with only good and positive interaction. I realize now that means very little to most people. The truth is, it takes just a few bad moments to ruin all the good that was done. They were my friends, first and foremost. It was only when I felt most alone that I would revert back to my childhood experiences. This is no doubt why I never felt any sexual need during my camp sessions and why none of my campers were ever involved. My camp sessions were some of the happiest and most satisfying days of my life. Now that is gone forever and it's all my fault and no one else's.

I'm not angry with these kids. I don't hate them. The truth is I have no one to blame but myself. I'm proud of these kids. I'm proud because they stood up and did what was right. It took courage to change the way things were … and things needed to change. They faced ridicule and embarrassment to do the right thing. Because of what they have done I can finally get the help that I needed so long ago, to begin dealing with my own sexual abuse and the abuse of others. I only wish I could have been more of the person that I thought I was and less of the person that I came to realize had hurt so many people. I'm sorry guys," he was crying fully now, "sorry that this was so difficult. I'm sorry that I hurt you. I can only hope that someday you can understand how this could happen and maybe someday you can find it in your heart to forgive me. I know that's a lot to ask. I love you guys, believe it or not. Please remember the good times. We had so many of them. Years from now, if I see you walking down the street, I'll nod and remember the good times we shared. I only hope you can do the same. Anyone that knows me knows that my friends were my whole life. I miss them terribly. I just want them to be O.K.

I realize now how painful this must be for the kids. Not just the kids doing the accusing, but also to the kids who looked up to me and considered me to be their friend. For those teenagers that were not involved, I'm also sorry. I'm sorry you were in a position to stick up for me only to find out the truth. Sorry I couldn't have been more honest with you. Sorry that I hurt you too. I wanted to tell you the truth. To try and help you understand my problem. I guess I didn't really understand it myself. I hope you can someday forgive me.

I've thought about how painful it must be for the parents, who trusted me and told other parents that they could trust me. How you must feel betrayed and angry that I could do this to your families. I'm sure I can't begin to imagine the hatred you must feel toward me. I had no right to do the things I did. I am truly sorry to have put your families through this hell. I deceived you, you were not alone, and it is not your fault. I hope you aren't putting any blame on yourself. The only one at fault here is Seth Mahonia. You believed in me, you trusted me, and you had no reason to believe things weren't O.K. I'm so sorry that I betrayed you.

I've thought about my parents and other relatives who have to carry with them the burden that I have placed on our family. I've thought about those who put their houses up for my bail, only to be named in the newspaper the next day. I cried for my parents who had to face their friends and coworkers. I cried for my young cousins and my nephew, who have to live with knowing that someone they believed in had done such a thing. I cried for them. I don't care that I lost my job, my camp, and my home. I care only how this has affected the kids, my family and my friends. I cried not because I was afraid to go to prison, but because I hurt the people that meant the most to me. All this pain caused by the acts that at one time I truly believed weren't hurting anyone, yet deep down I knew something was terribly wrong.

After being arrested I was experiencing an avalanche of guilt for hurting my friends. I was literally in a fog, unable to get off the couch, unable to think about anything but how the kids were getting through this. I missed them terribly. It was as if an atomic bomb went off and I was the only one remaining. But it was worse than that, it was worse than death. Many days I sat at my house, alone and in the dark, with a loaded pistol in my mouth. Not trying to think of reasons why I should die, but why I should live. I just couldn't do it because of my parents, my friends and those kids that I know still care. This ordeal has been hell, living with the fact that I hurt the people that I loved more than life itself. The unimaginable loss and guilt that I feel every day is nearly unbearable. The words "I'm sorry" just simply are not enough. Words cannot begin to convey how bad I feel about the effects of what I have done. My entire life was devoted to these kids. I wanted nothing but the best for them. I wanted to protect them, but instead it was me they needed protection from. It's been a year since this all began and I've cried every single day. I am truly sorry. Please forgive me."

The courtroom was silent as Seth returned to his seat. It took a few minutes before the judge himself spoke, clearly taking a moment, like the rest of the audience, to process what this man had just said. Though Seth's voice had broken and his cheeks were washed with tears, Mare felt her brother looked cleaner somehow. His public acknowledgment and apology for his crimes had done him some good. *And at least they have heard his side now. They can see there was no malice intended. Hopefully, that will give them some small degree of comfort, though it can't change or erase what did happen. I'm glad he had a chance to face them all.*

Finally, the judge moved on, "Mr. Hawkins, would you like to address the court before I pass sentence?"

"Yes, your honor; I would." He moved to the front. Assistant DA Hawkins acknowledged that Seth sounded sincere in his remorse. He agreed that Seth had owned up to his mistakes and had not attempted to blame the victims at all. However, he reminded the court of the number and ages of the victims, and he urged the court to consider these aggravating circumstances when ruling on an appropriate sentence for Seth. Seth had, after all, touched many of the children while they were asleep. He recalled Seth's practice of buying gifts for them in exchange for spending time at his home. He summarized the manipulations and the deceit. "A lesser sentence would diminish the gravity of the victims' experiences," he told the judge.

Vance D'Angelo also presented his closing arguments, attempting to highlight the mitigating elements in the case, such as Seth's desire to spare the victims the "spectacle of a public trial." D'Angelo outlined the many losses Seth had already experienced: the lost friends, the lost job and recreational guide business, the likely loss of his home through bankruptcy and the lost respect of the community. "Any sentence the court imposes would be in addition to these other important losses. Mr. Mahonia has admitted what he has done, and has begun the first step in the recovery process by doing so. The maximum sentence may feel best to victims, their families and an angry public, but several years in jail will only delay Seth's treatment and rehabilitation. The State of Maine does not provide official treatment in correctional facilities for people with Seth's problem. Even though the Mahonia's have offered to pay for counseling while Seth is in one of these facilities, there is no guarantee that he will have the access." Seth's attorney argued for a lighter sentence, and when he was finished, he took his seat next to his client.

The judge pondered for a moment. "There has been a lot of passion and compassion here today. I need to collect my thoughts before passing sentence. The court will take another recess while I consider your words."

Mare and her family gathered around Seth and told him that he had done well, and that hopefully the judge would be fair. Seth thanked everyone for being there. "It means a lot," he told them. Mare noticed the couple of bags at Seth's feet. Soon, her brother would be handcuffed and led away to jail. She would have to visit him in one of the correctional facilities. Seth's lawyer had told them that it would be a few weeks before they would be able to see him after today. She bit her lip as her family continued trying to chat lightly while they waited for the judge to pass sentence.

During this time, one of the young people from the other side tentatively came over to Seth. It was not one of the victims, but a young man close to the victims, a teenager who had spent a lot of time at Seth's and had originally considered him a friend. The teen extended a hand to Seth. Mare put a hand to her mouth. They embraced. Seth was crying with happiness that the other had reached out to him in kindness. "I never touched Eugene," he whispered to the boy. You've got to know that, man."

When the judge reentered the room, he recounted the primary issues in the case. The way the judge spoke, Mare at first thought that he would be more lenient on her brother, but later on in his comments, she knew it was not going to go his way.

"Mr. Gibb's testimony was particularly helpful to me," he said, "because it showed that Seth had been confronted with the crime long before the police got involved. He denied it."

"I regret that Maine does not provide treatment for offenders, but I can't condone a shorter sentence given the age of the victims and the number of victims involved."

At some point, Seth was required to stand. Mare heard the words, "Twelve years in prison with all but five suspended, followed by six years of probation with the conditions that you have no contact with children under age 16. You must undergo treatment for sex offenders to the satisfaction of the Department of Corrections probation officers."

Five years in jail, Mare thought. *Five years!* It was exactly what the DA had asked for. *No contact with children, so Cody cannot see his uncle. Not that I want him to while he's in jail. What am I going to tell Cody? Perhaps the lawyer could file for a family exception, like he had for the earlier rulings.* As long as there was supervision, when Seth got out maybe he would be able to attend family events. Would he be able to join the family for Christmas and birthday and for barbecues and the like? Mare had more questions than answers, but five years was a certainty. Would her brother be able to make it through five years in prison?

The bailiff let them say goodbye to Seth and give him a hug before they took him away. As Mare watched him being led out of the courtroom to a temporary cell at the county jail, she wondered, *What is our ultimate goal with the justice system: to protect victims and reform perpetrators, or simply to punish? What is justice and has it been done?*

That evening, Mare dragged herself to bed, a fatigued soldier having fought a long, hard battle, who was now hoping that the war was almost over. Her temples were pounding from all the bombs that had exploded around her in the last year, especially today's.... Her eyes were weary from crying. Finally, she could rest. A cease-fire had been called, at least for this night. She closed her eyes and gave herself up to her dreams.

Mare was in her kitchen when Sophie entered. Her dear friend walked up to Mare and gave her some instructions. Mare could not remember the specific words spoken. Sophie placed her index finger in the center spot of her forehead just above her eyes, at the spot where the third eye chakra is supposed to be. The contact seemed to open up a secret panel in Mare's head. As soon as the finger touched her, a forceful beam of white light poured in and flushed out all the heaviness and pain that had been stashed within. The finger slid across to the left and then over to the right, and as it did, charged energy came pouring through the floodgate, sweeping out the debris and replacing it with a tingling, radiant sensation of peace and power.

Upon awakening, Mare felt incredibly energized and relieved. The dream felt so real and so healing that Mare could not shake the experience. She felt lighter; her headache was gone. Something happened in that dream that Mare could not explain, something too significant and too moving to deny. It felt like a source greater than she had deposited something new and wonderful inside her. The pressure in her skull had been released and in its place was pure electric light. She decided she would ask Jane about it.

Why was Sophie a central figure in the dream?

"The dream you experienced is a very ancient one," Jane told her later that week, smiling graciously. "In Hinduism, it's called *Shaktipat*. It's the experience students have when their divine master touches them. It's an infusion or transfer of energy that signifies a spiritual awakening, essentially an initiation. It represents enlightenment, Mare." She looked into the young woman's eyes. "I would say this is only the beginning of an interesting journey, rather than an end, my friend."

Jane shared some information about Shakti/Kali—the Hindu mother goddess who represents the natural process of creation and destruction. A multi-armed warrior goddess of awesome power, she demonstrates the relationship between birth and death. Mare considered the interplay of the two forces within her own life.

"Are you familiar with Joseph Campbell's work, Mare?"

"Yes, some. I really like mythology. I always sensed there was more behind the stories."

"Well, Campbell identified a classic *Monomyth* pattern that recurs through the stories of most cultures across time. The lead character in each myth is cast out of familiar territory into the world of the unknown. He or she passes through a gateway and crosses into a fantastic, difficult, and evolutionary realm."

She placed a hand on Mare's shoulder. "This new realm represents our inner world, our psyche, our consciousness. During this internal or metaphysical journey, the traveler meets hideous monsters and many strange beings, has to solve riddles and face many trials, receives guidance from supernatural powers, and often travels to the Underworld—a frightening place." She looked at Mare. "And, along the way, the hero is being transformed. His or her consciousness is undergoing a profound change. We can each be the hero of our own life story, if we don't get trapped in one of the many challenges of life's labyrinth." She paused. "It sounds like you are just beginning your adventures into unfamiliar seas and lands unknown, young Skywalker," she grinned. "Enjoy the ride."

Part Two

Crossing the
Threshold

27

From the Soil, Seeds Sprout

*"If you want to make your dreams come true,
the first thing you have to do is wake up."*

~J.M. Power~

The morning after Seth's sentencing and Mare's powerful dream, Mare opened
the Lewiston paper and couldn't avoid the front page headline:

"Pedophile sentenced: Mahonia faces five years for sexual acts with boys."

Mare noticed that within the front page account of the hearing was a box
that read in smaller, bold-faced lettering, "**Mahonia's sister addresses community. Page A6.**"

Pete brought over the Babylon paper and exposed its headline.

"Passion and compassion dot testimony before sentencing of confessed child molester."

Mare looked at the word *compassion*. She liked that headline better. *I wonder if newspapers and journalists realize their words have the power to shape a reader or listener's experience so strongly.* She read both articles and related
commentaries. They were fair for the most part, this time, and accurate. She
turned to the open letter she had written to the community and read her own

words in newspaper print. A few parts were the same as she had said in court, but she had tailored it to a wider public audience. She needed to say something to them.

Dear Neighbors,

My family has been deeply saddened by the events as they have unfolded to us in the last year. As many of you know, my brother, Seth, has accepted a plea agreement in the case against him. Since most of the Mahonias and related family members have lived here all or much of their lives, I thought it important to express some of the emotions we are experiencing. Although other relatives touched by this case will share some of my sentiments here, I can really only speak for myself.

We know this has impacted the entire community, and we are truly sorry that a member of our family has been the cause of so much pain. Many of you, friends and extended family, have been immensely supportive through the duration of this process, and we can only imagine how troubling this must be for you. We, ourselves, learned of the truth only in bits and pieces over the course of the last year, and were crushed to discover what in fact did happen between my brother and some of the young people who accused him.

Seth has admitted he has a problem and needs counseling. Let me assure you that I'm not in denial about what my brother HAS done. Since Seth pleaded guilty to all the charges, most people are assuming he is guilty of all charges. Not so. Seth was told that he needed to plead guilty to all eight of the charges if he was going to go through with a plea bargain. Seth is not a rapist. The facts have been gravely distorted here. We feel certain based on evidence in Seth's favor that this could have been proven at trial. However, since most of the other charges contain the truth, Seth took the plea arrangement, so that the teens telling the truth would not have to suffer through a trial.

I don't want to diminish the effect this has had on the families of Seth's victims at all, but this past year has also been excruciating for the people closest to Seth, as well as Seth himself. The shame and remorse he has felt this year have been profound.

Yet, my purpose here is not to garner sympathy for my brother. He must face and is accepting the consequences of his actions and will have to atone for them as best he can. The people I'm most concerned about now are my parents and other Mahonia relatives who, despite their total innocence in this situation, must find a way to cope and live in this community. A number of Mahonia families reside locally, and they have long held a respectable standing. Family members have done their best to maintain high standards for themselves and to contribute to the Babylon community. Some of the youngest who carry the Mahonia name are still in grade school. I worry about how this stigma will affect them. It is not fair that they should suffer for the mistakes of someone related to them. I beg you to treat them with kindness.

My parents, especially, have taken this very hard! They keep looking back to see where they went wrong and what they could have done differently. I'm here to tell you that my mother and father were caring, ethical and committed role models! I grew up to believe that sex offenders were despised monsters, so I would not blame any of you if you were to draw such conclusions. However, knowing my brother, who at his core has a good and loving heart, has now forced me to open myself compassionately. Seth did make a positive difference in the lives of many young people. It is possible for someone who has a problem like this to be a good person who came from a loving and moral family. Many victimizers like my brother want help, but don't know how to get it.

As a community, we cannot simply throw Seth behind bars and pretend the issue will go quietly away. Silence is what manifested this problem in the first place. We need to confront the fact that child sexual abuse exists. Let's take the conversation out from behind closed doors, or else we may never be able to help young victims. We must find a way to open up communication with people like Seth, people who otherwise might be decent human beings, and find out what we can do to prevent this cycle. This is not only Seth's problem, but a societal issue that mustn't be ignored.

Thank you for taking the time to hear me out.

Mare Lumen

"It's a good letter, Mare," Pete told her. "Looks like they printed the whole thing, huh?"

"Yes, they did." *Seth said his piece to the court. I said mine to the community. Evaluate us as they will. We have said what we had to say. Now they'll take it as they will.*

When Derek saw Mare first thing that morning at school, he embraced her. "I just read your letter. It was perfect," he said. "Just perfect."

Later that day she found cards and notes in her school mailbox, as well as in her email box. The letters would keep pouring in over the next few weeks. Some of the people she knew well; others were only acquaintances.

Dear Mare,

I just read your eloquent and courageous letter to the community and want to express my sympathy to you and your family in your long ordeal. I hope the worst is now in the past, so you and Seth can now begin the healing.

With all best wishes,
Abby Wallace

Mare,

In times of stress and confusion, you and your family need to be reassured that all of you are in our thoughts and prayers. If you need anything beyond a cheery smile and a kind word, don't hesitate to ask.

Sincerely,
The Lowrys

Dear Mare,

This is just a note to let you know I am thinking about you. I will be glad to support you in any way that will be helpful—just listening, just sitting quietly with you …

Miriam

Mare,

Remember I'm your friend and am here for you.

Edith

Mare,

Your courtroom comments were very much appreciated and beautifully conceived. I'd think that your perspective is widely shared. May the healing proceed for all of the community, especially your dear brother and family.

Sincerely,
Michael

One letter was from Mare's high school guidance counselor—now a colleague—that she had gotten close to when she was a student at Emerson....

What a courageous family statement you made at the trial. Your parents must be very proud of you, Mare. It would have been so easy for your love for your brother to turn to hate because of all the pain your family has suffered. I admire you and your family for being willing to express your compassion publicly for your brother and all the families affected.

Dear old friend, you are one in a million!

One of the tech teachers wrote ...

I read your article in the paper, and I agree with you that because a person may have done some bad things in there life doesn't necessarily make them a bad person for life. Unfortunately our society is filled with hypocrites, and uninformed. These people will close their eyes and ears to the problems of our world in hopes that the problem will go away. I feel for you and your family, and if there is anything I can do to help just ask.

Joe

The biggest surprise was an email from Walt that really touched her heart.

Mare,

I read today's paper. My heart aches for you and your family. It may help you to remember that everything happens for a purpose, although frequently we do not discover that purpose until much later when we are ready to discover it. If I can do anything to help you through this difficult time, please let me know.

Austin also passed her in the hall and gave her a squeeze on the shoulder, checking to see how she was. He said little. She could just see in his eyes that he was concerned for her.

Within a few days, Joan and Rick got a letter from Seth. Joan handed it to Mare.

Dear Mom and Dad,

It's finally over. I'm so sorry I put you through this. At least now you and I can move on. I'm okay, I really am. Don't worry about me. No one has given me any trouble and I don't expect them to. Didn't get to see the paper or the news but I can only guess what they had to say. A funny thing happened though. After all that was said and done, it didn't really matter what I didn't do (to me anyway). Especially since Toby came up to me after my statement and shook my hand. All those lies mean nothing now. Seeing Nate cry has haunted me all night. I didn't really hear the words he used but the emotions crushed me. I can honestly say that I could never ever do those things to another child. The parents' statements were powerful, but hearing it from him was devastating … but necessary. I love you, Mom and Dad. I'm so sorry all this has happened. I let a lot of people down, but it's all over now. You have stood behind me and supported me even after all the pain I brought to the family. The words "unconditional love" is something I feel from you. I want you to know how much that has meant to me. I can't make it up to you. All I can do is ensure that it never happens again and with help I know I can reach that goal. I know that sometimes I overreact to your attempts to help me, but I want you to know that I will always need your support, and after all that has happened in the last year or more, I'm pretty sure I'll never lose it. Thank you!

I've enclosed an application to visit. Keep a blank copy and make copies for anyone who wants to visit. Takes about six weeks, so I won't see you for a while. I should be able to call you sometime next week, but if I don't, don't be worried. They have to give me an ID # and a bunch of junk. I could use some money for stamps. Sunday I can mail two letters. If you can send a check for $30, I would be grateful. Tell everyone I love them and that I am okay. Tell Ashley thanks for the picture, I'll keep it with me always. She's such a great kid. Here's my address. Hope everyone is doing okay. Tell Hope I love her, and I hope she's doing okay.

I love you,
Seth

Mare showed her mother a letter she had received from Pat Riley, a stranger who had befriended the family when Seth's charges first came out. She had been a great support and comfort to Joan especially. Pat's own son had been charged with raping a woman several years earlier. He was still in jail. It had been devastating to Pat and her family. She had come to the courtroom the day of Seth's sentencing, just to add support to the family. She wrote ...

Dear Pete and Mare,

I don't know either of you only to know who you are. Just wanted to tell you how well you both did at the trial. It was a real tough time for all of you. I was so impressed with your letter, Mare. It was written with such compassion and from the heart. Your brother must feel so loved by his family. He is a fine young man, and he will be okay. With the family he has to back him and love him and his friends and others, he will make it.

People are people and until you go through a crisis yourself it is easy to look down on others, but by the Grace of God it could happen to them.

Our son's situation was similar and he will be out later this year, after twelve long years. We have learned much through all the tears and sleepless nights, but I want you to know it does change your life, yet there are friends and family that will stand by all of you and Seth, and those are real friends.

God Bless you both, you are both very strong, mature people with much to give. Knowing your family and just being able to help a bit and to support you all has helped me so much with all of my emotions and feelings.

We love Seth as we love our son and will keep in touch with him and your mom. We'll be praying for all of you.

Lovingly,
Pat Riley

Mare read over the real friends part. She had been wishing that her best high school friends would contact her. She had not heard from any of the three. One was in grad school. Mare knew she was busy, but she hadn't heard from her since before the time her brother's mess had begun a year earlier. Another friend was married, with a child Cody's age and a hectic job. Both women's parents lived in the community still. The third was in Jersey, and she had a child and the excuse of distance. *I wish they would call me.* Pete urged her to call them, but her pride interfered. *If they loved me, they would call,* she told herself. *I do not want to be a needy puppy. Perhaps they don't want to be friends anymore.* It was still hard, after that childhood rejection, to go after those she loved if she wasn't sure they wanted her.

Around that time, Mare attended a play at school. She coincidentally sat next to the second friend's mother.

"I haven't heard from Rachel for so long," Mare admitted. "How is she?"

"Not so great, Mare. She has left her husband. He started doing cocaine behind her back, and she couldn't take it. I've been worried about her."

"Oh, no," Mare kicked herself. *I was so busy feeling sorry for myself, I didn't consider that she might be going through a crisis too.* "Is she okay?"

"She's been doing better lately. She's found a place for her son and her in Portland. I think it's getting better now."

"I should call her. I haven't talked to her or Jody for so long. I miss her and Jody."

*   *   *   *

The phone rang later that week. It was Jody.

"I've been thinking about you a lot lately, girl. Where you been?" Mare wanted to know.

"Just busy with classes. My boyfriend and I broke up as well. It's been tough. I know you've been going through stuff too. I'm sorry I've been out of touch."

"Did Pete call you? He did, didn't he?"

"Yes, he's concerned about you, and he thinks you're too stubborn to call."

Mare grinned. "He's right. I should've probably called you too. I've just been preoccupied with my own nonsense."

"Well, it's time for you, Rachel, and I to get together and have some Margaritas."

"Count me in. Have you been in touch with her? You must know about her impending divorce?"

"I have spoken with her, but not as much as I would like. Drive up to Portland this Friday, and let's all have dinner at my place."

"I'd love to."

That Friday, the three friends ate by candlelight, spilled their guts about each of their struggles and reaffirmed their friendship. They sang and hugged and drank, and part of the hole in Mare began to fill.

*   *   *   *

A few weeks later, Joan got another card from a second cousin and handed it to Mare. She opened the note.

Joan and Rick—

I have had this card for a few weeks now and I have been wanting to write you. I can't even begin to imagine what hell your life has been for the last year. My heart goes out to your whole family and to Seth.

Mare's article in the paper was a great help to me. I'm sure it was a comfort for all extended family. You and Rick have every right to be proud of your children and for the example you have always set for them.

Every family has its ups and downs, and I want you to know you have all our support. My wish is that you can get on with life and enjoying your family again. My wish for Seth is that he gets all the help he needs to resume a healthy life. I truly believe Seth is a good person.

I have too much respect for you people to let this go unsaid.

Love, Gail

P.S. On a lighter note, I saw a picture of your grandson! Don't we just have the cutest grandchildren?

After all the reports and articles about the sentencing hearing many letters poured in. There was even one from the owner of a local pizza place, saying that she thought Seth was a good person and wishing the family well.

Mare heard mostly from supportive people, though she knew others were still angry.

One of the math teachers at Emerson was one. He bumped into Mare after the hearing and told her, "Your brother got off easy. He should've gotten more."

Though it stabbed at Mare, all she said was, "I'm sure some people think so." Then she walked off. It wasn't worth fighting about. It was his choice to feel that way.

Her brother's mailbox had been demolished one night, even though he hadn't lived there for many months. The anger and the fear behind it were not gone, but Mare and her family appreciated all the compassion that came their way.

Perhaps the most surprising email that winter was from one of the victims, Nate Gibb. The freshman had contacted her via the school's email system, but

Mare had difficulty decoding the message. It made no sense. Mare decided to send a brief email in response. She was worried about Nate. One of the biggest problems her brother faced after his own abuse was that he didn't see it as abuse, because it was consensual. Mare wondered if Nate was experiencing any guilt or other confused emotions with regard to his own participation in the incidents, so she wrote,

To: Nate

If you ever want to talk, I'm here to listen. I realize it was probably a joke attempt to contact me; however, I know some things about this situation that others don't. So, if you need someone to talk to, I think you know where to find me. Even it it's via email (just don't attack me, please). I am worried about you. I do want you to be able to live a healthy life.

He replied back …

i really fell bad for you and your family I know that it is just as hard on you as it is on me. i really feel for you and Pete i know how nice and caring you both are I know that allot of the kids will have hard feelings against your whole family but I have a very forgiving hart. i know that it is going to be hard to know that his uncle was a pedifile.

nate gibb

"His uncle was a pedophile?" Mare said out loud. "What does that mean?"

Mare's mind scrambled through her family? Does he mean one of Seth's uncles was a pedophile? It was hard to read the young man's barely literate email. Then Mare calmed down. *He must be talking about Cody … that it will be difficult to find out that HIS uncle Seth was a pedophile?*

Nate wrote again and asked her to get some games that he had left over at Seth's. By phone Seth agreed that there was a box of stuff at his house he wanted her to give to Nate, including the games. Mare left it in the main office for Nate and sent him a message. Later Mare discovered that Nate had lied about the games being his, and that he was just trying to get some free stuff from Seth. Mare sent out another email telling Nate that he could have just asked for the items, rather than lie, because Seth would have just given them to him anyway. She got back a surprising reaction.

i don'y care if seth wrote you a letter and told you that the only reason he gave that gave to me was because he owed it to me and i don't care if it bothers you that i lied to you i was skrewed over and so weren't you so i think that you should save you bitching for someone who cares.

love,
nate gibb

Mare's stomach turned over with a sick feeling. She realized she could not be the one to help Nate, even if she wanted to. She learned—too late—to just stay out of it. Hopefully his family could arrange some support and counseling for him. *He could certainly use an English tutor, that's for sure.*

*   *   *   *

Mare pulled her vision away from her stack of exams on *The Odyssey*, stretched to loosen her muscles and slumped backward into her chair. She had been hunched over for an hour and her eyes were beginning to blur. Since childhood, Mare had loved mythology. The more she taught the myths, the more she began to see truths from her own life echoed in the stories. *The Odyssey* was one of her favorites. Man fights some terrible battles at Troy, faces enormous obstacles and endures great suffering and many losses, and finds his way home to his kingdom in Ithaca … He arrives an altered human being. *Will I ever find my Ithaca,* Mare wondered. *How far along am I on my journey? Will Athena, goddess of wisdom, guide me, too?*

As part of their final test on *The Odyssey*, Mare had asked her students to imagine they were the Greek hero, Odysseus.

> *Now, you are finally reunited with your beloved family and home. At a celebratory banquet, you—Odysseus—feel moved to give a speech. For what or whom are you grateful now that you are back in Ithaca? Write as if you are Odysseus delivering this speech.*

Mare picked up another test and began reading the written portion.

Dear friends and family,

I would like to thank my family who were faithful to me for twenty years and for believing in me when I didn't even believe in myself. Without Athena and her protective eye, I never would've gotten home to Ithaca. She has been a shining teacher. I am indebted to my ship-mates and I offer my apologies to them. I learned many lessons in my adventure, but I'm afraid my experiences cost you your lives. I faced many temptations along the way, and if not for you, my crew, I never would've escaped them. I would have given up. It may seem like I am a lone hero, but that is not the case. Many heroes were born from this journey. The other goddesses who assisted me also deserve thanks. Without Circe's guidance and support, I couldn't have completed the trip to the Underworld. Calypso, too, offered my refuge and instruction. Finally, I would like to thank the great god, Poseidon, who unintentionally taught me the biggest lessons of my life. The trials He put me through taught me things that every worthy man must know. After I poked out the Cyclop's eye, I let my rash pride run rampant. I have since learned that humility is important, and that a man must stay in control of himself. I have learned not to let emotions and pride lead me through my life, but rather to be led by the wisdom that Athena represents. It is this ability to control my emotional reactions that allowed me to overcome the reckless suitors who had overtaken my home and pursued my faithful wife, Penelope. So, thank you, Poseidon—Earth-Shaker, it is to you I owe my life.

Mare's eyes widened and she grabbed a pen.

Dear Amy,

Your speech was beautifully written and passionate! Virtually everyone thanks the hero's family and his crewmen (even though they all died) and his obvious helpers along the way. But you are the first in my experience to acknowledge the antagonist of the story—Poseidon, the God of the Sea, who ravaged and plagued Odysseus and his crew at every turn. Yet, in the end, your Odysseus is grateful to his persecutor. That is a mature insight, one that most do not understand! Odysseus has gone on an incredible journey. His painful experiences have allowed him to learn life-altering lessons. Without his antagonist, he would still be in the dark ... a cocky warrior, reacting quickly and foolishly to outside challenges. Brava, Ames, for having the insight to acknowledge the unlikely source of his new knowledge—his so-called enemy—the God of the Sea! What would happen if all people learned this ... that we need to view our own antagonists ... the people, circumstances and ordeals that test us ... as allies in the sense that they TEACH us and force us to grow beyond our former selves? Conflicts in our lives can make us stronger and smarter, and ultimately are responsible for helping us arrive home with gratitude in our hearts.

Nice work, kiddo! 20/20

*   *   *   *

That night, Mare decided she would go on a fast. The third eye dream had jump-started something in her. She wanted to continue to purge anything heavy from her system. She decided to stop eating for a few days, and survive on fluids alone. It was hard to explain to her family why she was doing this. They thought she would starve.

"The body can go weeks, even months, without food," she would try to tell them, but they thought she was weird. "A fast removes toxins from the body. People have been doing it for thousands of years, even Jesus did it, for goodness sakes. Some people even do it for spiritual clarity."

Mare did not tell them she was pursuing the fast primarily for this reason. She wanted to cleanse herself—in body, mind and spirit.

Her college boyfriend, Don, had introduced her to the idea of fasting, particularly juice fasting. He would mix lemon juice, real maple syrup and cayenne pepper with warm water, and drink it throughout the day. *The master cleanse*, he called it, and gave her strict instructions about how to do it all. Supposedly, the hunger passed after two or three days. Mare had never gotten beyond the first two days when she was living with Don, but she was only 19 at the time and not as self-disciplined.

Pete thought the fast was kind of strange too, but he did not interfere with Mare's plan.

On the third night of the fast, Mare dreamed she was in the shower. Water was pouring down and splashing over her head and down her shoulders. Steam rose. Someone handed Mare a special container of shampoo. When she poured the shampoo into her hand and began rubbing it onto her scalp, she felt an enormous tingling sensation, unlike any "real" shampoo could ever provoke. *It was like a chemical reaction,* she would later write in her dream journal, *as if bubbles formed and fizzled inside my skull on my brain. The tingling penetrated my skin and my skull. It went deep. It felt so invigorating! It literally washed my mind! I felt cleansed, open and energized.* It was the second healing dream in a week. Had the fast caused this? The dream was amazing and unforgettable. Stunned by the power of these two recent healing visions, Mare resolved to do some research on dreaming as soon as possible.

*   *   *   *

Mare wandered into the metaphysics section of the giant book store in Portland—one of her favorite places, and began browsing for titles on dreaming. One title popped out at her. *Conscious Dreaming* by Robert Moss. She thumbed through the table of contents and skimmed some pages. She turned to the back and read the author bit. The white-haired picture of the author caught her eye. He looked familiar, a little mischievous and mysterious. She bought it and a few others.

*   *   *   *

"Did you know that there are several different types of dreaming?" Mare asked her husband later.

"Nope," he nodded, still typing away at his computer.

She wanted him to share in the discoveries with her. She wanted him to understand what she was feeling. To journey with her. She began to outline what she had read. "Yeah, the healing dream is one type of dream that this guy writes about. He gives a bunch of examples of people's healing dreams. I'm sure my two dreams were healing dreams. I think I might write to him about them and see what he thinks."

Absent-mindedly, he said, "That sounds good."

"He also says that we should make personal dream dictionaries where we take a look at people in our lives who pop up in dreams and see what associations we have with that person. He says that dream characters can represent parts of ourselves." She stepped around to Pete's side to get his attention. "Pete?" He looked up from the screen. "For example, you know the dream where Sophie touches my forehead? I think she represents the spiritual part of myself, because Sophie is such an honest and spiritual person. I see her as representing goodness, purity and intelligence. I admire her. I'm not surprised now that she showed up in that dream, given how much I respect her integrity."

"That's great, Mare," he offered weakly, then turned back to his work.

His wife sighed.

*   *   *   *

Mare took Cody to one of the Eagles' basketball games. She met Sophie and Tristan there, and sat behind them. Sophie and the couple's dance instructor, Veronica Ford, sat on either side of Tristan. The dancer preferred to be called *Roni*. Mare listened to Tristan and Roni joke around, and Mare recalled the times when she and Roni—who was a few years older—were in dance classes together. Roni was an incredible dancer, and Mare always admired the way Roni used her body so gracefully and confidently. In fact, all of the younger dancers looked up to her. Now she ran her own dance studio and taught many different styles. She had always been a beautiful woman: lean, yet powerful.

Roni had taught Sophie and Tristan and several other couples a folk dance that they recently performed. Roni and her husband, Sophie and Tristan and a third teacher and his wife had since become close friends.

Above the murmur and cheers coming from the stands and the whistles of the referees, Mare could hear Roni giggling like a schoolgirl. Whatever Tristan had said must have been very funny. *She is flirting with him,* Mare observed.

*   *   *   *

Jane's studio was warm and relaxing. Burning wood was crackling in the stove.

"Jane, we have been trying for a year now," Mare said. "I had no trouble getting pregnant with Cody. I wasn't even trying then, but I wasn't trying hard not to have a child either, since we had been married two years already. I really want a second baby. I don't want them to be too far apart."

"Well, sometimes trying is not a helpful thing."

"Things have been up and down for Pete and me, too. It's like we lost something, and I don't know how to get it back. His idea of intimacy is grabbing my crotch on the way down the stairs, or giving my breasts a squeeze while I'm doing the dishes. There's nothing wrong with that, if there is a foundation that has something more, but I don't feel like we have that anymore. I feel disconnected from him, like we don't know each other really. I want him to know me. I want to talk about things. I've tried to talk to him about it. I've tried to offer some suggestions, but he keeps reverting back to the same old way of relating, and it's not working for me."

"You have both been under a lot of stress in the last year. You do need to take some time to rebuild and recreate yourselves. Keep sharing these thoughts with him. Let's take a look at what's going on in your body; it may not be ready to have another baby. It may need more time to gather energy and for you to heal your emotional wounds."

Mare climbed onto the table and closed her eyes.

Jane started at Mare's head like she always did. They talked little. Jane touched some pressure points in Mare's shoulders and arms. "Let go of anything that's weighing you down, particularly anything from Seth's sentencing. It's not your fault. You bear no responsibility."

"Where in your body do you feel incomplete?"

"My throat and my jaw."

"Your center of expression. I read your letter from the last session. It is understandable that you would feel stalled there. Let go of all the pain. Let yourself feel and speak your truth. When you look, what is there?"

Mare began to tear up now that she had permission and safety to release.

"When I was very young, I was playing with a dollhouse. I tried to put all the furniture back into this box, but it wouldn't fit. I tried to cram it in forcefully. I got angry. My mother happened to come in about that time. She flipped out and spanked me. I was stunned. I cried and cried. A little while later she came back in and apologized. She was having a bad day or something and she tried to hug me, but a part of me blocked out her love. I think I decided then that if I expressed my feelings, especially my anger, I would get hurt. I have trouble expressing my anger."

Jane nodded and put her hands over the area. "Try to let it all go. You did the best you could given confusing messages in your childhood. You are a good person. You are a strong and wise woman. You can trust yourself."

Mare sniffed away a few tears and began to relax as Jane worked on different parts of her body. She teetered on the brink of consciousness, almost falling asleep, but about fifteen minutes into the session she felt something tugging in her uterus. It was like someone was pulling out cobwebs. Strands were being cleared away. Mare didn't even open her eyes, but she said to Jane, "wow, that is amazing," and she described the sensation.

"You must be very sensitive to energy. Most people would not be able to feel that at all, since I was not touching you physically."

Mare opened her eyes. Jane appeared to be sweeping out energy with her fingers and hands, but she was not touching Mare's skin or clothing at all. Mare could not believe it. She felt certain, before she opened her eyes, that Jane was laying her hands on her, but she could still feel the movement inside her and Mare could see that there was no direct physical contact between the two of them. *Hmmm ...*

"I believe I am sensitive to energy," Mare admitted. "This reminds me of a dream I had some time ago, Jane. I was in my basement, and spider webs were everyway. I was trying to make my way through them, pulling my hand through them. Do you think that was a message about the health of my body? I read that sometimes spiders can indicate ill health, and now it feels like you are pulling out cobwebs from my figurative basement."

Jane chuckled. "That's quite possible. It is an interesting coincidence. The body absolutely is able to send us warnings and signs."

"I would really like to do your astrological birth chart sometime. If you give me the information, I'll do something up for you."

"Sure, I'd like that. I've never done it before."

"So, I am cleaning out some of this stuff in here, which should help you conceive; however, I think you need to do some spiritual work to prepare yourself as well."

"Okay," Mare said, "like what?"

"I believe that we choose to come into this world, before we are born. I believe we select our parents and our life circumstances to come. We are more than just our bodies. We live many lifetimes. We have lessons to learn, so we set up our lives in a way that we receive the necessary challenges to learn what we came here to learn. Our souls evolve from life to life."

Mare nodded, listening.

Jane continued, "Have you talked to the spirit of your child yet? Told her you're ready?"

Mare imagined souls floating around looking for the right parents. "Ummm ... no, not really."

"You may want to put out a call to the spirit of your future child. I would recommend writing the child a letter. Create an image of the kind of soul you want to come to you and pick a name."

Though it sounded a little silly at first, Mare already felt a connection with her child-to-be. "I could do that.... write a letter to Olivia."

"You have a name for her already?"

"Yes, I want to call her Liv! I also like the O in the name. To me it represents completion and wholeness. I had a dream recently that I was diving in a swimming pool. At the bottom was a black and white soccer ball that I was trying to retrieve. Circles and spheres, and the colors black and white, have shown up a lot for me in the last year. I'd like to honor that by giving my daughter a name that begins with a circle."

"Okay, then write her a letter and invite her to come to you."

On the way home, Mare stopped at the gift shop to look for a card to offer to her daughter. She found an indigo background with a yin-yang symbol in the foreground. Yes, that's the one. It was blank inside. Plenty of room to write.

Later that night, after putting Cody to bed, Mare informed Pete that she was going to write a letter to their daughter, like Jane had suggested. His eyes widened, ever so slightly, and then he nodded. "Whatever you want to do, Mare."

Mare grabbed some scrap paper to start with. Then she transferred the final draft onto the card. She believed her daughter might be out there in the dream cosmos somewhere, waiting to be born. At the very least, it would be a neat keepsake for their daughter when she did ultimately arrive. *When she gets older, she might appreciate it.*

Dear Olivia,

I am reaching out to your spirit, on the advice of a friend, in hopes that you will make your way to us soon. Anxiously awaiting your healthy arrival, your father and I extend our open arms to receive the gift of your life.

You have been in my thoughts and dreams for so long; I feel I know you. I have sensed the presence of the wise, strong, playful and compassionate woman you are.

The last year has been a difficult one for us, to be sure. I am grateful that you paused until you had healthier energy surroundings. However, we have found peace, closure and completion. The final stage in our healing process is finding you. You, Olivia, will round out the circle; you will make us whole again. Your birth symbolizes our rebirth and re-creation. We are stronger, clearer and more open than we have ever been. We want you to know that WE ARE READY to welcome you, ready to provide for you and guide you, to learn from you and to love you with all our hearts, as we already care for one another! Until you join us, there will be an empty place in our lives.

For some months now, your name has been with us, especially with me— Olivia! I don't know quite how it came to us, but several signs certainly have affirmed it. I have only recently begun to pull the pieces together and now it makes perfect sense to me. 1) A passing stranger who in calling to a friend practically yelled the name in my ear, as if directing me to take notice. 2) I had a dream about losing, then finding a soccer ball and other balls and upon researching several sources found that the symbolism of the images consistently represented wholeness and completion. The exact stage we seem to be at. 3) I've been studying yin/yang energies as embodied in the T'ai Chi symbol, ☯ livia! I've been recognizing the elements of those opposing forces within myself and am trying to balance them in a natural way, to open both channels. Conception would be an indication of success in that, for me. 4) I've played with the sound of the name. Poetically scanning the stressed and unstressed syllables. Olivia Michele Lumen. It's got three Ls: Live, love, learn. 5) Os= the globe, a vortex: all powerful symbols. 6) Nickname: LIV!

I have always wanted one boy child and one girl to give balance and equality to our family. I've had dreams about a little girl also.

Cody is a warm, intelligent and energetic young man. He will be a kind and supportive brother. I believe you two will be very close friends. He will really enjoy having your company. He loves the outdoors, is athletic and so bright. He needs an equal partner in childhood and beyond to challenge and inspire him. You will have much to offer each other in times of conflict and in moments of joy! It would be ideal if the two of you were only a few years apart in age. We love Cody dearly and feel certain you will as well.

Your father and I have big dreams and you figure prominently into them! We are hardworking professionals motivated by creating things of quality, personal pride, financial security and altruistic goals of wanting to contribute to the well being of the world and the species who live here. We are on a constant quest for knowledge/truth in our lives and will certainly encourage and assist you in discovering your true self and what your life purpose is about. We are thoughtful and gentle parents who would like to help you express your own will. We will do our best to give you the freedom you need to assert your individuality, while providing an environment where you will be safe, feel nurtured/accepted and respected for who you are. We will likely make mistakes, but our intention will always be to provide the best circumstances we can for your personal development.

We value spiritual insights and though we don't subscribe to any one belief system, we are open to the wisdom of many cultures and hope to expose you to myriad philosophies, so that you may make your own informed decisions about your faith in a higher power.

In some respects, I guess this is an enrollment letter urging you to come be with us, so with that in mind I have promises to offer you and Cody. In addition to those goals I've already mentioned, we plan to:

- Take you to fun places (cities, museums, landmarks, waterslides, etc.)
- Participate in exciting activities with you (camping, hiking, canoeing, swimming, skiing, etc.)
- Allow you numerous opportunities to develop your interests and abilities (whether they be in sports, music, art, academics, etc.)
- Be as fair as we can be in our judgments and consistent in our expectations
- Show affection and let you know how important you are to us
- Be as honest as possible with you
- Praise you for quality/effort and guide you respectfully in self improvement
- Maintain a loving and committed marriage
- Take care of ourselves physically and emotionally, so that we can be our best for you and ourselves. We will be good role models.

- Expose you to the realities and "idealities" of life
- Love you unconditionally
- Listen to you and hear what you say
- Read wonderful books to you or listen to you read them to us
- Connect you with nature
- Help you with homework when you need us
- Avoid the words never and always
- Trust you and promote your trustworthiness
- Keep our word to the best of our abilities

So, dear child, we wait with eagerness for you to join us in this life. We assure you, we are ready! We love you infinitely and will be a close family. We have room enough and care enough in our lives for you. You are needed here now and always, Olivia! Complete our family circle. Make us one! Safe journey to you, love.

.Mom and Dad

The first card filled up so quickly that Mare had to glue another card into it. She showed the card to her husband. He read it and put his arm around her.

"Sounds good, honey." He flipped the channel to UPN. "Let's watch Janeway try to get *Voyager* back home. Eh? Seven of Nine is still try to reconcile her Borg and human selves. You love that shit. Personally, I like the catsuit."

Mare smiled, and settled in on the couch next to her husband. "Can you rub my neck a little?" she asked him. She sat down on the floor in front of him.

"Another headache, huh?" She nodded. He placed his palms on her shoulders and began squeezing. Mare tried to release any tension. She remembered the first time she had tried to give Pete a massage. He squirmed away from her. He had some resistance to being touched in that way.

"I've never been comfortable with massages," he had told her.

They watched the *Star Trek Voyager* episode.

"You know, Mare, your family is very much like the Borg." He put on a robotic voice. "We are Mahonia. Resistance is futile. Negotiation is irrelevant. We are right." He guffawed and slapped his knee. Mare had to laugh along with him. She knew that she and her family could be very bull-headed.

"That's right. We are. You remember that."

*   *   *   *

Mare was standing in her kitchen. A German foreign exchange student stood beside her. She began to cut up a tomato. She and Heinrich discussed how she needed to cut it. Perhaps she should separate it out into parts. Mare cut into the ripe red bulb very carefully. She removed white seeds and strips as though it was a red pepper, yet it was still a fleshy tomato.

"That's kind of crazy," he said jokingly, "you said you were going to keep it whole."

Mare replied, "You can't do that. You have to cut it like this."

Mare felt a small hand shaking her shoulder. He said nothing, but when Mare's eyes opened she saw Cody standing next to her bed.

"Hi sweetie," she said quietly. "Did you wake up?" She swung her sheets back and her legs over the side of the bed. "Let's get you back into bed." She took him by the hand and walked him to his room. She pulled the covers up to his chin and placed a loving kiss on his forehead. She stroked his hair, while the child's eyes closed. After a few minutes, Mare stumbled back to her own bed. She closed her eyes and the image from her last dream came back to her. *A tomato,* she questioned groggily. What does that have to do with anything? She blinked a few times; her eyelids heavy. It was about as ordinary a dream as dreams go. She would have forgotten it completely, if Cody hadn't awakened her. Her brain lightly ran through symbolic options. *Maybe I am ripe,* she entertained the thought, a grin slowly breaking over her sleepy face. *Ripe, reb bulb. Hmm ...* She laid there for a minute. *Maybe I am ovulating now.* She rolled over towards her husband. She placed an arm over him. *Maybe I should wake Pete up? No, that's ridiculous.* She kissed him on the shoulder.

She closed her eyes again.

A moment later, she found her hand wandering down over her husband's hip. She did her best to wake him.

"Mmm ... Mare, what's up?" he whispered.

"Ummm ... I just had a dream, Pete. A dream that may have indicated fertility." She paused. "You wanna have a little fun."

He rubbed his eyes and squinted at the clock. "Mare, it's three am."

"I know," she chuckled. "Still, what harm could it do, eh?" Her hand touched him enticingly, and it wasn't long before his arms were around her.

*   *   *   *

"You know, maybe you are taking this whole dream thing a bit too far, Mare."

"Could be. I know it seems a little silly." She gave him a mildly suspicious, sidelong glance. "Are you complaining?"

"Not at all."

Mare changed the subject. "Hey, the student council hired a couple to come and train kids how to swing dance at Winter Carnival activities on Friday. They are holding a night session that students, staff and spouses are invited to. I would really like to learn how to do the Lindy-Hop together, Pete. Then we could go out dancing and practice it in Portland. Will you come with me?"

"I don't want to, Mare. I really have no interest in it. You go. I'll stay home with Cody."

"But I won't have a partner to go through the moves with."

He said nothing.

"I miss going out dancing. We need to schedule some date time. We so rarely go out anymore now that we have Cody."

"Get Sophie to go with you."

You don't get it, do you? "Sophie and I have practiced it before together, but I'm not going to go out on the town with her. Tristan will dance with her."

"I'm not going, Mare."

So Mare went alone.

*   *   *   *

It was just after dusk, when Mare found herself walking away from town up the hill on a wooded trail that she vaguely recognized, from a dream perhaps? She was on her way to a party. She looked around at the leafy, mossy earth. The thin pathway meandered up the slope and she felt peaceful. The altitude steadily increased as the path wove a course around large pine trees. She placed each footstep carefully, avoiding rocks. Every time her foot made contact with the earth, a small pad would sound in the otherwise silent forest. Mare noticed her heart pumping more and more strongly after the rigorous climb, but she enjoyed the sensation. A mild perspiration rose like dewdrops on petals across her soft skin. She was quite warm, flushed. The hike felt cleansing and invigorating. She looked upwards on the trail, and then paused in her tracks. A grand house loomed above her to her left, and, in front of it, stood Austin Bean looking down towards her with a gentle smile.

She smiled back without a word, and began walking again, moving towards him. She followed the path which curved around to the left. When she was within a few paces of him, on even ground, she stopped again. The two stood face to face. Mare examined his features. *He is looking at me with such concern and affection,* she realized. He reached out to her and took one of her hands. They looked at each other compassionately, with love. His feelings seemed to mirror her own. She felt a longing arise in her. She wanted to embrace him, but she held back. *Somebody might see and assume something is going on that isn't. I shouldn't.* Instead, they simply stood there holding hands and comfortably looking into each other's eyes. Mare felt understood and appreciated. *He cares for me. And I care for him.*

A morning bird began to chirp a melody. Mare's head turned to follow the sound. All other sensations fell away, except a general calm.

Her eyes were facing a window and slowly she opened them. The melodious chirping continued.

Ohh … she murmured internally.

She closed her eyes again, trying to return to the gentle closeness she had felt in the dream.

As her waking consciousness returned, she heard a second voice. *Sure, your body feels happy right now,* it said. *But you need to stop dreaming about this eighteen-year-old.*

I know, I know. Go away.

Mare, it's not rational or right. Cut it out. Why do you keep having dreams about him?

I don't know. Please, I don't know. I just know it feels really wonderful. Is it so wrong just to dream?

Yes. He is too young, and you are married.

*   *   *   *

Kate and Mare were chatting by the stairwell, when Kate's attention was distracted. Mare followed Kate's gaze. Austin was walking by. Mare was wearing a slim skirt that stopped at her knees. Austin's eyes followed from her heels all the way up to her eyes. He didn't stop; he just smiled and nodded hello.

When Mare turned back to Kate, Kate was grinning mischievously.

"What?"

"Oh come on, I saw the way he looked at you. You are right. He likes you. And you, look at you … you are all glowing and flushed."

"This is not good, Kate. It's not funny."

"It kind of is." They walked to Kate's room.

"Some of them look and act like adults. And you are not that old, Mare. It's not that unfathomable that one of them would find you attractive, or that you would feel something for one of them. He's tall and handsome. He seems sweet. You've been through a lot. It's okay for you to enjoy his presence."

"As long as nothing comes of it."

"Right. Trevor and I have great chemistry too. You said you noticed it at the play. He comes in to visit me. We talk about things that most students wouldn't even understand. He's so much more mature. But, I know ... he's a senior. I am six years older than he is. We hang out, but that's it. I've even met his parents. We all really hit it off. They've invited me to dinner. Trevor and I did talk about our feelings the other day ... well, he did. I just said that we needed to keep our relationship platonic and professional, but I think he's hoping that when he graduates we might have a chance. I try not to think about it. Just having him around is nice. I gave him a ride home the other night. We were a little nervous about what people would think, so he crouched down after he got into my car. It's so silly. I ought to be able to give a student a ride home without it being a big deal."

"Teachers are held to high standards, and I think we should be, but I agree sometimes it goes too far. I know what you mean about feeling good around him though. I have been having dreams about Austin. When we pass each other in the hallways, I feel something. It's hard to describe. We never say much, just hi, but there seems to be so much more that's transmitted. I do like the way I feel around him, but I also don't want to feel that way. I can't seem to help it, but at the same time ..." She shook her head negatively. "Teachers aren't supposed to feel attracted to their students. I mean, I feel like an anomaly. Is something wrong with me? Do other teachers ever feel drawn to their students besides the crazy ones you hear about in the news?"

"You're not crazy. You are human. You work hard at school. You work hard at home. You try to be the best mom you can be. You have a two-year-old. I mean, my goodness. Then there's Pete." Her voice went into list-mode. "Your brother, and Walt and me. Need I say more? Mare, you need to put a little back in. You deserve a little happiness too, even if it's just a few moments of futile fantasy. Don't judge yourself too harshly."

"Thanks, Kate. I suppose you have a point. I have been feeling pretty spent. Austin does have a way of making me feel lighter when I'm near him. That affect he has on me is probably more powerful than the actual attraction to him."

Mare began to keep a dream journal and it was filling up fast. Each entry had a date and Mare gave each dream a title. The more attention she put on dreaming, the more her awareness and interest seemed to grow, the more vivid and memorable her dreams became. Not all of them made sense, however.

2/25/98—"Naked at Newberry's Store"

I enter a dream store I have been in before. Walking in, I declare out loud, "I'm having a deja-vu; I've been here. It's just like in my dream," I say, fascinated. I'm oblivious to the fact that I'm dreaming. My sister and mother are with me, and other patrons are milling around. The store is old. I realize that in my previous dream, I was naked. I look at the clothing and swim-suits on the racks and pick out a few things. I begin to experience the sensation of being exposed. My chest is bare! I self-consciously cover my right arm and hand over my exposed breasts. No one seems to notice. I tell my sister how strange it is to be reliving that dream in real life. Duh! She just smiles. Then I add, "maybe it is a dream," and I laugh. I walk into a large changing room with ceiling-high windows that face the street. Three windows in a half-hexagon. The curtains are sheer and I can see people walking by on the sidewalk as I begin to change. The woman before me has left a sexy, but rigid black bra in the changing room. I am excited and intend to keep it, though in reality I would never do such a thing. I try it on. A man is walking by trying not to look, but I know he wants to. He walks behind my field of vision. I feel he is looking back at me. I feel calm and confident, even though I have been covering myself.

Mare focused her attention on trying to gain lucidity in dreaming. She was tired of the rare and random nature of lucid dream. Everything she read she anyone could improve their abilities to remember and wake up in dreams. She wanted the liberty and excitement she knew was possible in conscious dream-ing.

One book discussed a type of blinder that could monitor REM sleep; a small red light would beep a couple of times when a dreamer hit REM. The dreamer could become conscious, without becoming fully awake. Some folks recommended looking at your hands periodically in the daytime and asking yourself if you are dreaming. Then in dreams when you would do the same thing, training yourself to notice.

Still it took her many months of attention and effort before she would begin to have lucid dreams regularly.

Often she would ask herself during the day, *am I dreaming*. Dreams are as real as "real life" sometimes. When Mare got to the point of asking, her sure test was to see if she could fly. If she could lift off, she was dreaming. Flying … fly-ing was something she hadn't mastered in the waking, physical world.

*   *   *   *

A few days later, Mare was at the airport waiting for a flight. She entered a store in one of the terminals and looked at the clothing racks. Her flight was scheduled to leave in one hour. As she flipped through the racks of discounted items, she came across a pale, mint-green, long gown. She loved the color and held the spaghetti straps up to her shoulders. *It is beautiful.*

She returned it to its original spot. *Even though it's a great bargain, I can't afford it right now, and when would I wear it?*

She left the store and entered a main corridor when she heard a crash behind her. A garbage can tumbled to the floor and rolled noisily. The woman who had run into it, looked behind her nervously and continued running. Two people followed her closely. The first screamed in terror. Mare moved towards the disturbance. *Is she okay*, she wondered. *Why are those people following her?*

From the other side of the hallway, Mare heard another shriek. This time from a man. Mare's head whipped around again towards the sound. Five feet from her, she saw a man whose hands were in front of his chest, bent at the wrist, like a dog waiting for a treat. Mare's brow wrinkled in confusion. He was looking directly at her. He smiled in anticipation, and, as his teeth began to show, she noticed the points of his fangs. *A vampire? That's ridiculous, what's going on?*

A low growl came from the man's throat and he moved toward her.

Mare took off running. As she did, she scanned the corridor in front of her. Had the world turned mad? Men and women were shouting. Some were hiding. Others were sprinting in various directions. It seemed that the whole airport was under attack. There were two groups: those who had been bitten and those who were "normal." In the beginning, it seemed that most of the people were with her, but gradually, more and more of the airport staff and patrons were turning into vampires before her eyes.

Mare glanced around and spotted a group of *normal* people who have gathered to fight the demons. She joined them. Using umbrellas and suitcases to hold off the bloodsuckers, the people ran, trying to gather together as many humans as they could. But there seemed to be so few left now. Mare noticed that Cody was with her. She must protect him! But how?

Mare grabbed a shotgun, as did a number of other people. *They won't attack as long as the weapon is aimed at them.* Mare's gun was raised at a group hovering in front of her. They looked pathetic, desperate, almost sad. Mare took a check of her own emotions. She was not exactly afraid. She remained tense during the crisis, but calm.

Mare was one of five people, all men except Mare, who had gathered into a protective circle. Her back was covered and she was helping to protect the others. *I am safe. I've got this under control.* The vampires stayed back; the small group held them off. Suddenly, Mare remembered … *Cody? Where is he?* Mare chided herself for losing him. *He was right here a minute ago.* Her stress level rose.

One of the vampires tried to talk to her. She could barely distinguish his words. She had little time to think as one of her companions threw her a shotgun shell with a dark green casing. Mare loaded it. The humans kept warning the fanged ones to back off, but one came toward Mare, and she depressed the trigger. She popped the vampire on the top of the shoulder. He was barely hurt. *My gun has misfired,* Mare thought in frustration. When Mare looked down at the gun, the trigger was only partially compressed. The ammo didn't get punched hard enough, and it only half exploded. Now Mare was out of ammunition. She felt a bump against her backside. She whirled around, ready to defend herself …

Pete's behind had nudged Mare's while he shifted his position during sleep. Mare opened her eyes quickly and blinked.

Immediately before waking she had thought that a vampire had gotten into the circle. But it was only Pete accidentally waking her up. She found it amusing.

An airport. Vampires. Shotguns. Her literary mind went to work on the metaphors. Hmmm … I am … trying to "take off." Makes sense. I am trying to "rise to a new level" but can't "get off the ground" because … "energy-drainers" are forcing me to protect myself? My "ammunition" or "weapon" doesn't always work? I do have allies. And also antagonists. I don't want anyone to drain my "life-force," and I don't want to become a "vampire." I don't want to give up my humanity. Her mind trailed back to the beginning of the dream. I am looking for "new clothes." I am drawn to the color green.

She explored the possible conclusions and interpretations until she became tired again and fell back into realities that were not so ordinary.

28

Confinements and Repression

Surely there is grandeur in knowing that in the realm of thought, at least, you are without a chain; that you have the right to explore all heights and depth; that there are no walls nor fences, nor prohibited places, nor sacred corners in all the vast expanse of thought ...

~Robert Green Ingersoll~

"I'm going to the hairdressers," Mare informed her husband.

"What are you gonna have done?"

"I'm going to get my hair highlighted and cut. Why?"

"I think you should go really blond this time."

Mare wrinkled up her nose. "It's hard to care for all-over color, and my hair's so fine that it can do a lot of damage. I think I'll stick with a few golden highlights to brighten things up."

"Suit yourself. I vote for blond though."

When she returned, he frowned. "I can hardly see the blond streaks. It blends in to your natural color."

"What's the big deal?"

"It's not a big deal."

"You just ... want me to be different?"

"No, I just want you to be who you are."

"No, you don't. I'm not as blond as you are asking me to be."

"I just like blond hair. Plus, ever since Cody was born, you look like such a teacher. Most of your clothes are so ... teacherly. I hate to see you hide yourself."

"Oh, so you meant you don't want me to hide my body."

"Well, why don't you show yourself off more? You've got the bod for it."

Mare's frustration was building. "Well, has it ever occurred to you that I would like to get noticed for things beyond my body sometimes?"

Pete said nothing.

"And in a practical sense, I wear my shirts a little on the baggy side because I still have a lot of clothes from when I was pregnant with Cody. We don't have a lot of money to buy new stuff at the moment, and I don't want to get rid of them until after I'm done with pregnancy number two." She looked him in the eye. "Plus, I like looser tunic shirts.... I can't really wear form-fitting shirts at school."

"Why not? There is no rule against them."

"No, but ..."

"But what?"

"Well, you know how my nipples are. I don't want headlights poking out through my bra; the boys have trouble enough concentrating as it is. They don't need to be looking at my breasts all day. That's part of the reason I wear looser clothing on top."

"Well, what's the harm with that? It would make class interesting." Pete began to laugh.

*   *   *   *

Later that week, Mare poured Sophie a glass of wine.

"I don't know, Mare. I want Tristan to be friends with whomever he wants to be friends with, but I am struggling with a little jealousy." She shifted her body posture, looking around at the noisy partygoers gathered for their friend Emma's birthday. Despite the fact that people were all around the room, the environment was noisy enough to afford the two friends some privacy. "Roni calls him quite a bit. I trust him, and she and I are friends, so I don't think anything would ever happen. Tell me I'm crazy, and that I should just not worry about it. That it's foolish to think I need to forbid him from spending time alone with her."

Mare looked out into the kitchen where Roni and Tristan were leaning against a counter, laughing. "Sorry, Soph, I can't do that. She flirts with him. She likes him. Give him free reign to stay friends with her, if you want, but if I were you, I'd keep my eye on her. Tristan loves you, but I don't quite trust them together either." Mare grimaced a little thinking about it. "Her personality is just ... very out there and expressive; perhaps her boundaries are also more open. Don't ignore your intuition."

Sophie squirmed uncomfortably. Mare placed a sympathetic hand on her friend's shoulder and then released it.

"Speaking of Roni, I get the feeling she doesn't like me. When I said hello to her tonight, she was rather cold and short with me."

Wiggling some tension out of her shoulders and taking a sip of her drink, Sophie confirmed her suspicion. "Tristan told me she doesn't agree with your involvement in the affair between Walt and Kate. She thinks you should have stayed out of it; it was their private business. But Tristan and I don't necessarily agree with that."

"Yeah, well, it's easy for her to judge; she wasn't in my shoes. She doesn't know the whole story."

"Right." Just then Emma came by with a woman Mare recognized.

She said, "Hey you two, there's someone I'd like you to meet. Mare, Soph. This is my sister, Renee."

"Yes, I recognize you," Mare said, extending a hand in greeting.

Renee nodded. A local newscaster, Renee's face was on the screen each night, reporting about the day's events and the area stories she had been researching.

"Emma!" Emma's husband yelled from the kitchen.

"Excuse me, will you?" she touched Renee on the shoulder, knowing her sister was in safe hands.

"Me, too. I need to go find Tristan," Sophie said. "Nice to meet you, Renee."

Renee smiled an acknowledgment and turned back to Mare. "How do you and Emma know each other?" Renee asked politely.

"I teach with her husband at Emerson. I grew up in the area, too. How do you like working the news, Renee?"

"I like it for the most part. It can be depressing sometimes, but exciting, too."

"I often wonder about that. I can't bring myself to watch the local news anymore. I get tired of all the bad news that seems to dominate the screen."

"Yeah ... I do get some human interest stories as well, and those keep me going."

"Renee, can I speak honestly about something?"

"Sure," she said with curiosity.

"My brother was in the news a lot last year. I'm sure you are familiar with the name. Seth Mahonia."

"Oh, right. Emma mentioned he was your brother. I'm sure that was a difficult time."

"It was … But the reason I'm asking about it is … well," she wasn't quite sure how to broach this topic. "In addition to depressing news, I often worry that it's … well, not accurate." She winced a little saying it. "I'm not criticizing you in particular, Renee, of course, but … the profession in general."

"I understand completely," she assured Mare.

"We all make mistakes, but sometimes the errors or sensationalism seem … excessive." Renee nodded. "In your experience … do you find that to be the case? I mean, I got so angry watching my brother's case on TV and in the papers. How distorted things got and how powerful the media was in affecting public opinion."

"I think a lot of people in the media do their best to get all the facts straight, but it doesn't always happen. Networks are definitely trying to get the most bang out of each piece, but usually reporters are trying to do a good job." This time, Mare's head bobbed respectfully. "But at the same time, too, we rely on the local authorities for information, and well … I'm sure you know … some are better than others at giving the facts."

"Yes, I am *quite* familiar with that."

Both women were silent for a moment.

"I'm curious, Renee. Have you ever read the book *The Path of Least Resistance* by Robert Fritz?"

"No, I don't think so. Why do you ask?"

"Well, I've always thought it was a perfect book for journalists to read. It's about how our thoughts create our realities. Fritz suggests that our lives are driven by certain learned patterns of thinking and behavior. And that these patterns form … mmm … sort of … ruts that are hard to get out of. To truly be able to create what we want, Fritz says that we have to form new, conscious patterns and get them to the level of becoming the new path of least resistance."

"Sounds interesting."

"It was one of the most influential books I've ever read. During my undergraduate work, I started an environmental group. We sponsored all kinds of events, and I remember having a conversation after one with our distinguished speaker. I was all fired up about how the environment was being destroyed, and he cautioned me about my language. He told me that the way to speak about it most effectively—if I wanted to create change—was to speak it in the positive—almost as if it already existed. I remember being very confused about it at the time, but intrigued. He encouraged me—if I truly wanted to bring about positive change—to read that book. He said that alarmist messages would only perpetuate the problem, and that the more inspiring and productive route was to speak the vision of it as I wanted to see it. That my words and thoughts would help to bring the vision into reality. I've never forgotten the conversation."

"Hmmm … wonderful," Renee said.

Mare continued, "The media has so much power to either re-enforce one vision or another." Mare shook her head a little. "I'm not sure if I'm making a lot of sense."

"I think I'm starting to understand what you mean," Renee encouraged her.

"It's just that … when I watch the news, it is so depressing. You've got a rape tonight and a murder the next, a kidnapping on Monday, a Thursday break-in and a multi-car accident on Sunday … If I watched it regularly, I would have to conclude that the world is going to hell in a hand basket, you know? I'd want to jump off a bridge, for goodness sake."

Renee grimaced in understanding.

"I'm not saying that there aren't some absolutely terrible things going on in the world and in our state. But, you know, I have a different idea of the world, and I want to hear more of the good stuff. I want to reinforce that the world is well, that people are generally good and that we are safe. There are many more positive things going on in the world, but we don't hear much about them. All the negative, violent stories are only perpetuating more of the same, aren't they?"

"I agree, but some would say that we'd be burying our heads in the sand regarding the truth."

"Yes, and I'm not saying that necessarily. But the news is already selective. You aren't just reporting the way things are because you are selectively leaving out a lot. I wonder how many journalists truly understand the enormous responsibility that comes with that power. Even the so-called "bad news" could be presented differently. Too much of the information that bombards us is designed to bring about a fear response, don't you think?" Mare looked at her in earnest, and she could see the woman wanted to agree, but felt rather helpless on her own to create sweeping change. Mare's vision drifted to the floor. She realized she was on the verge of a rant. "I'm sorry, Renee. This has all gotten pretty heavy."

"No, don't apologize. I've enjoyed this conversation," she said sincerely. "I think I'd be interested in reading the book and seeing the ways in which it might apply to my industry."

*   *   *   *

A hubbub filled the pre-performance ballroom. Mare was seated in the front row in a chair with the rest of the audience, waiting for the show to begin. The lights dimmed and the orchestra began to fill the room with the vibrations of their instruments. Several lines of dancers swept out onto the main floor, kicking, spinning and gliding their arms in coordinated movement. Mare appreciated their symmetry and flow.

Suddenly one line of dancers from the rear of the formation leapt boldly towards the front of the group. Mare saw Roni Ford and the celebrated Maine mime/performing artist, Tony Montanaro, within the "ranks." One of the dancers dropped out of the "formation" and started talking to Mare out of the blue. She did not recognize the woman, and no one seemed to notice or mind that she had stepped out of the show.

"Why are you here?" she asked a confused Mare. Mare sensed the woman wanted to help her, but she wasn't sure how. The question seemed important. "Why are you here?" she asked again.

"I teach drama and dance as part of my classes," Mare responded, which was only slightly true. Her brow wrinkled in contemplation.

Mare turned back toward the dancers. For some reason she was not happy with the arrangement of the dancers, so she reached into her jacket pocket and pulled out a small, skinny stick. She pointed it towards the front line of dancers and tapped it once. The line of dancers disappeared. Mare was pleased, as this had been her intention. Now that she had "cut" them out of the picture, she pointed the stick towards the back row. She wanted to "paste" them back into the rear of the group where they originally were. She flicked and flicked the wand, but nothing came out. She couldn't seem to paste them back where they started. They must be stuck in the wand. Mare tried to release them by tapping the wand against a chair without success. She kept shaking the wand, trying to get the row of dancers back into the performance. Embarrassment started to creep in. A neighboring audience member stood up and moved to help her.

When Mare later mentioned this strange dream at lunch, Bernard and Scott teased her about the whole "wand" thing. "Freud would have a field day with that," they joked.

Perhaps Freud would think the wand was some kind of phallic envy issue, Mare thought, *but it doesn't fit in my interpretation of this dream. Why did I want to relegate that row of dancers to the back? Do the dancers represent some part of me that is causing change, and I'm trying to go back to my comfort zone?*

*   *   *   *

"Here's something I think you should read, Mare." Joan handed her a copy of a letter that Rick had written and asked Joan to send to Seth.

"Seth wrote your father a letter. He wanted to know why just about everyone in the family had written to him in prison, except your father. I don't think he was trying to be mean, but he basically told your father how lonely he was growing up. He said that dad was out of reach and he sort of blamed your father for some of his messed up thinking."

Mare was concerned for her father. "Seth didn't?!"

"Well, he didn't directly, but he basically asked your father—where were you? I wanted more of you."

That Mare could understand. She always knew that her father loved them all, but he worked very hard and was rarely home. She understood the feeling of wanting more of their father; she had also tried to reach through to him. Mare always wanted to make him happy, but he seemed to her very sad below the surface. Rick's own father had left the family and moved to California when Rick was only seven. Rick said he didn't remember his father ever saying goodbye. The two did not see each other for another sixteen years. The next time Grandpa Mahonia came to visit was when Mare was born.

Mare opened the letter.

Dear Son,

You ask in your letter for me to explain to you who I am, because you don't seem to know. I feel I am a very loving, caring, supportive father of three beautiful, intelligent children, who I would give my very life to each of you if you needed it.

I grew up without a father or mother really. I had very low self-esteem. At times I felt I was a lower-class than some of the others in my school and social circles. I felt unloved by my father and unable to love my mother, because she was seldom around after Dad left. I was raised by my grandmother and grandfather, who I am sure loved me, but didn't show it by physical affection. I felt very lonely when I was a pre-teen/early teenager. I used to go up in the attic and read letters that my dad had written to my mother. He had left a chest with some of his personal belongings in it. I remember writing letters to some of his friends, trying to locate him, so I could talk to him. I guess it was to try to find out who and what he was. I remember when I was about six, I used to ride the milk truck with him. He used to buy ice cream and candy. One time he bought me a siren whistle that was the greatest, but I guess I drove him nuts with it. I remember little about him. He sent me a glove once. I guess I really missed him a lot. My brothers and I were sort of left at the farm. I don't remember minding it much, 'cause I liked it there. It was sort of a stable place. When they took my brother, Joe, to the institution (basically a prison for the handicapped), I cried a lot for him. Went to visit him a few times, but it was a very unpleasant thing, and I grew to hate to go to see him and have to leave him there.

I always told myself that I would never let my kids be without the love of their mother and me. I don't know whether I succeeded or not, but I always loved all three of you very very much! I always tried to set a good example of honesty and honor and respect for people who didn't have as much as us or were disadvantaged.

I don't know where or how I lost you, but it seemed that all of a sudden, I didn't know anything. I was wrong. You didn't need my help. You wouldn't listen. I was the bad guy and you wanted to hurt me any way you could.

You say you felt like an outsider. I also felt like that when I was a teenager and even now, I feel alone. Maybe I am basically a loner for some unknown reason, but I also need to feel loved and need to be reassured that I am loved. I guess everyone does.

I guess I am the most naïve person in the world, cause I couldn't see this happening. I saw you date Helen from the campground, and Liz, and I thought you cared about those women and just needed time, but it was just an illusion I guess.

You say it's because of what happened to you, but you won't talk to me or confide in me about what happened. You want me to explain me to you, but you shut me out. I suppose I am still in denial about all of this. This can't happen to us. This person is not the person that I love, that I raised, and taught what was right and respect for others' rights. I don't know this person.

Even now you reject me, and what I try to help you with or suggest. You rejected your family. You cut us out. You lied and betrayed our trust. You say it is not a choice, but it is a choice. Everything is a choice, and you have to make those choices, not anyone else. You have tried one way and it has devastated your life and the lives around you. Perhaps you should give the other alternative a shot. There is nothing greater than the love of a man and a woman. There is no way the alternative lifestyle is better or more fulfilling. It is full of tragedy and pain. I love you. You are my only son, the only one I will ever have. I know you have the courage to overcome this. You can't do this alone. We are there to help you, and we will get you help, but you have to let us help you. The secret of life is balance, I've been told, and God is part of that balance, maybe he can also help. He is always there.

Love,
Dad

P.S. I'll try to write more often.

Mare set the letter down in her lap and was silent. She wiped a drying tear from the corner of her eye. "That explains a lot. It was something I could always feel in him, but he never talked about it."

"I know; he never talked to me much about it either."

"Poor Dad." *I wish I could have helped him break out of that pattern.* "It's so strange that Seth's feelings mirrored Dad's own self-esteem and loneliness. It's another kind of cycle, I guess. Dad didn't want to leave us ever, but because of his own abandonment and low self esteem, he wasn't fully HERE either. Seth went looking for more overt affection elsewhere." Mare did not pause to consider that she had been searching for that male affection also.

Her mother nodded. "I don't agree Seth has a choice, though. I don't think you get to choose your sexual preference."

"Me neither, but I bet that Dad's emotional absence certainly influenced some of his decisions. I think everyone is affected to some degree by their own parents' attitudes, beliefs and fears. I know that Dad has a huge heart. I still remember some of the stories that Grammie Lexi used to tell. You know … how he came home one winter day without a coat. She asked him where it was and he told her he gave it to a classmate that didn't have one."

"Yeah," she put her hands on her stomach and thought about her husband. "My favorite is when he was playing basketball in high school."

Mare interrupted her, "Oh, I love that one, too. If one of the younger guys made a mistake, even if he was on the other team, Dad would go over and pat him on the back and offer him encouragement."

"Gram loves to tell those stories. She might not have always been there for her sons, but she was proud of Dad." Mare nodded.

Mare was proud of her Dad, too, even if he had struggled at times with his emotional availability. He was a great father.

Mare changed the subject. "So, in Seth's last letter, he said he'd been getting harassed some. People got hold of the newspaper articles on him and started passing them around the prison. They are thinking of moving him to a minimum-security facility, so he's around people who aren't so violent. He's already counting the days until he gets out."

"Yes, I spoke with him on the phone. Someone threw a tomato at him yesterday. They call him names—though he doesn't tell me specifically what they say."

Mare plopped down on the recliner. "He mostly sits alone at meals too. It doesn't sound very good." Mare got up and filled a glass of water. "He keeps asking me about the kids—Nate and the rest—how are they doing. Did so and so win the wrestling match and all that. I tried to do that for a while, but last time I told him that I didn't want to be a go-between like that. He needs to let go of those friendships. He says he understands his problem as a sort of addiction now. Then he needs to understand that he can't drink a drop. He can't have any contact with his former friends."

"Hey, Mare ... Did you know that Luke Matthews' mother wrote Seth a letter in prison? Luke is the one who is married now and in the military." Mare nodded, *how could I forget?* "She told him that, even though she wasn't happy about what happened, she could never hate him. He had done too much for Luke, and she could never discount that. She told him that she forgives him. That letter meant a lot to him."

When Mare got home, she found a letter from her brother in the mailbox.

Dear Mare,

Thank you for giving the box to Nate and for everything else you've done. I know I can never repay you.

I wanted to comment on your email to Nate. I told you his lie because I wanted you to call him on it and your letter to him certainly accomplished that. However, I am disappointed that you've cut off ties with him. I know I shouldn't care, but I do, even if he doesn't. Just because someone has made a mistake, no matter how terrible or angry it may make you, turning your back accomplishes nothing. Look at my mistakes, for example.

I know you have no obligation to him or his life, but when someone makes a mistake, they should have a chance to recover from it. If you expect him to apologize, he probably won't, but he should still be given a chance to better himself. I'm sure you think that Nate has manipulated me at times and maybe I can overlook people's faults too much, but he's a good and caring kid. I don't approve of his lying any more than you, but we all do it at one time or another.

Anyway, I don't know why I'm defending him, but he was my best friend and I do still care about and miss him. Your casual connection with him is all I have left of that. He and the others were everything to me. He and many of the others practically lived at my home as much as I did and they spent all of their free time with me. I know the bond I shared with them was as strong as any father-son relationship.

I know that you think I should just get over it, but it's the hardest part for me, as it would be for you. I'm only asking that you remember he's not a bad kid. We all make mistakes, and we should be given a second chance. After all, what he did was far less serious than my crimes and I hope (at least) that you have forgiven me.

I wish I could communicate with them. I've decided to stop writing to Ben and Jimmy, because I don't really know what they're thinking anymore. They were nice to me before I left, but I haven't heard from them since I've been here. I don't want to be a burden to them, if they don't want me to write them. I don't know anymore. Of course, they weren't involved with the abuse either. I've already gotten some nasty letters from some parents, saying—don't contact our children or us anymore. I guess a letter could be construed as harassment, but I was just trying to say I was sorry. I suppose I should just shut up. Nobody really wants to listen to me. I wish I could talk to Nate just one time. I'd like to try to explain some things that I've come to realize since my arrest, and I'd like to give him a chance to communicate with me directly too, whatever else it is that he might have to say. I'm not expecting friendship. I know that can never be again, but I guess, hopefully, forgiveness. It's very important to me. Well, I've said enough probably too much. You probably think I'm crazy living in the past, but right now the future seems incomprehensible.

Sincerely,
Seth

Mare sighed. Her brother had compared his problem to an addiction before, and she could see him struggle with the withdrawal. It wasn't the sort of withdrawal people would expect who only knew the stereotype. Her brother felt alone and misunderstood. Perhaps that is why any addict turns to his or her addiction.

*   *   *   *

Mare stopped by Jane's house to talk to her. Jane invited her into the main house on the lower level and poured her some tea. The house seemed different.

While the two women talked, Mare noticed the door to the living swing open. Her brother walked through and wandered towards Mare. He slapped his sister across the face and punched her in the stomach. She reeled back, stunned. Then he punched her in the chest. Seth slapped her over the top of the head, but the instant he made contact she ducked and ran to hide. She wanted to escape this vicious, seemingly unprovoked assault. *Who is this person? This isn't my brother. He is not violent?* He soon found her and began the attack again. She could not seem to escape the abuse. It hurt. She pushed him away and jogged up some circular stairs. She eventually lost him. Quickly, she gathered some blue plastic bags full of Christmas presents that she was supposed to give. Mare went downstairs again and entered what was now her parents' kitchen. Her parents entered and Mare frantically told them what just happened. Moments later Seth reentered, and Joan and Rick began to yell at and beat on Seth. *This is highly unusual,* she was thinking. *Why have all these normally kind people become so violent?*

Seth now appeared weak and victimized. Though confused, Mare felt safer. She took a few sniffs in through her nose. Something was baking. She pulled a tray of doughnuts out of the oven, grabbed one and took a bite out of it. As she was biting and chewing, it transformed into a bagel. It tasted fresh and delicious.

She felt a sudden bounce on the bed. Her heart was pounding in delayed fear. Evinrude began to purr and walk over her chest where he flopped down and began rubbing his nose against Mare's chin. Mare rubbed his head a little and rolled onto her right side, the cat still nestled under her arm. He loved to be snuggled in this way. The furry cat made her feel safer, calmer. With her eyes still closed, Mare revisited the disturbing vision. It seemed so real and vivid. *But what is this dream about. Neither Seth nor my parents ever struck each other like they did in the dream. We were not a violent family at all, except for a few childhood spankings.* Then Mare remembered her dream studies. Characters in dreams can represent part of ourselves. *What part of me might Seth represent? He was so angry. Am I that angry?*

Maybe by not expressing my anger externally, it is taking a toll on me internally?

*   *   *   *

Mare picked up the phone and heard her sister's voice. "I know that Pete has been wanting a dog. My friend, Judy, has a yellow lab that she needs to get rid of. Do you think you and Pete might want it?"

"Pete has wanted a dog for a long time. I'll talk to him about it. I'm sure he'll want to see it, and if he's a good dog, he'll want it."

As they were driving to Judy's house to see her dog, Clay, Pete's face beamed like that of an eight-year-old boy's. It said, "I'm going to get a puppy!"

Mare chuckled watching his reactions. He was so happy. It was as if a dog was about to complete his life somehow.

The pup was huge, and his tail was the longest Mare had ever seen on a lab.

"He's got some mix in him, but I'm not sure what it is," Pete said. "Looks like he may have some shepherd in him." The dog stretched his legs up onto Pete's chest. After a brief visit, Pete's eyes searched Mare's. She nodded. He turned to Judy and said, "We'll take him."

Judy slapped her hands on her chest a few times, and the dog complied with her signal, putting his paws on her and licking her face. "I'm going to miss you, Clay," she said tearfully.

Immediately, Pete got all the dog supplies he needed. A friend gave him a doghouse and he set up a runner off the back porch. He was thrilled. The couple talked about renaming the dog, but had trouble finding one that fit.

"How about Buddha?" Mare suggested.

Pete mulled over the idea, then rejected it.

Mare listed off some of her favorite authors. Pete liked the name Chaucer, and so the two decided that would work. Mare liked the idea of a literary name. Somehow, it fit the personality of the canine as well.

He was a wild, untrained pooch. Cody loved the dog, but he was such a big and clumsy animal that he often knocked the child over accidentally.

"He's not that old, but he's developed some bad habits already," Pete observed. He cut a piece of plastic tubing, folded it in half and taped it together. "My stepfather, Dale, used to train all of our dogs when I was growing up. He always used one of these for discipline. It works pretty well. We'll need to be very firm with him while he is training. He needs to stop jumping up on people—that is Judy's fault. She encouraged it. And he needs to stop running up the hill and chasing cars. I want to be able to take him outside without a leash, but he's hard to control. If he heads off into the woods and chases the deer, and animal control catches him, they will put him down. We've got to train him not to do that stuff."

Mare had never owned a dog, so she let Pete take the lead with Chaucer. She did, however, wince occasionally when Pete whacked the pup with the tubing. *I guess he must know what he's doing.*

*   *   *   *

Today one of Mare's friends was getting married. Mare joined a group of her high school buddies at a hotel to get ready. Pete was not in attendance. He had bowed out as usual. In the group was a dark-haired handsome mystery man to whom she had not been introduced yet. He seemed very polite and, though they had not been formally acquainted, they had made eye contact from a distance. Mare felt her heart flutter when he flashed her a smoldering, flirtatious gaze.

The ceremony was a lovely event and the reception was held in the corridors of a closed mall. Apparently, the groom's father owned the place. The band was loud and there was plenty of space to dance. Mare was invited several times to dance by single men. She loved dancing and missed going out to dance. She and Pete so rarely did anymore. The dark-haired man watched her for a while; Mare could feel his eyes on her. Then, when Mare stepped away from a dancing partner, the dark-haired handsome man stepped in.

"May I?" he asked, with hand extended.

"Certainly," she said.

"Do you know any ballroom dance," he asked her as the music changed.

"A little," Mare said.

Then he placed a firm hand around her back and began to move her around the dance floor. A flush of cool air brushed across her neck and blew through her air. It was an incredible, exhilarating dance. This man knew what he was doing. Not only did he guide her fluently around the floor, he looked her in the eyes. He connected with her. Sometimes his eyes were so intense she had to look away. At times on the dance floor, this man made her feel as though she were flying. The movements were light and she was responsive to his competent leading. They danced several songs together, drawing attention to their skillful pairing. Mare felt beautiful in his arms.

She was breathless when the music slowed and couples packed the dance floor. He led her carefully to the outskirts of the dance floor and pulled her closer.

"You dance wonderfully, Mare," he cooed.

"Thank you so much," she blushed. "You ... you are the one. You know how to lead."

Somehow he managed to pull down the spaghetti straps of her dress and expose her breasts.

Mare pulled her clothing back up, self-consciously.

"But they are so beautiful," he said with no trace of guile or guilt. He pulled the dress down again, almost in awe. The way he looked at Mare was not at all dirty, but pure, like he was honoring the powerful and beautiful woman that she was.

"You don't need to hide them," he said to her softly, running his soft fingers across the surface of her skin. "You don't need to hide yourself, my darling. You should stand proud."

Mare looked at him strangely and in appreciation for the sentiment. She was irresistibly drawn to him. She pulled closer to him.

A bell sounded abruptly. It was time to change partners. Mare was a little disoriented as her former dance partner was thrust aside and replaced by a heavy-set teaching colleague. "B?" Mare said. "What are you doing here?"

"I went to college with the groom," he said, as he pulled her closer and began to ogle her décolletage. Mare resisted his pull and looked around for her previous partner.

"You know, Mare, you and I should really get together ... you know hook ... up ..."

"Oh, god," she said. "Where is the other guy?"

She jerked back and her head bumped into the headboard of her bed.

*   *   *   *

March and April were months of intensive dreaming. The spaces between waking and dreaming realities became blurred. At times Mare's dreamscape was far more real than waking. During this time, she became fascinated with the idea of having an out of body experience. She read about it, got ideas about how to do it, and night after night, she tried to have an experience where she could look back at her body. Weeks after her initial efforts, she finally had a breakthrough.

It had been a sleepless night with Cody and the cats making a lot of noise and keeping Mare up. She slept lightly.

She had almost fallen back to sleep after the last interruption when she heard a sound, just loud enough to alert her consciousness. She opened her eyes, as she had many times that night. A loud, humming buzz filled her ears and head, and sent tremors down her arms and neck. Soon after Mare realized that, although she had opened her eyes to see, her physical eyes were actually still shut!

Mare thought, *All right! I am having a lucid dream!* She was excited, but tried to temper it, so as not to physically wake from too much stimulation. She tried with some effort to pull herself out of bed, out of her body. She felt like she was heavier than usual, that gravity was exaggerated. Eventually, though, she found success.

Once up, she looked back down at her sleeping body. She could see her face with eyes closed and Pete beside her. The humming was still in her ears. *Wow!* This was a first for Mare, at least the first that she had become aware of. She began to explore the room.

Things seemed quite ordinary. *Can I go through walls?* As she opened to the possibilities of *being* without her body, something vast and overwhelming loomed at the edge of her consciousness … and a feeling of fear crept into her.

She was teetering on the threshold of an immense void. An unknown realm, huge beyond measure. *I am afraid.* The great darkness of something beyond the physical plane threatened to swallow her up, or so it seemed. Like a newborn thrust out of the comfort and safety of the womb into a great unknown, Mare shuddered. Feeling microscopic in comparison to it, she pulled her consciousness away from the precipice, afraid that she might lose herself.

*   *   *   *

"Guys, I've been having some really strange dreams."

"Don't you know, Mare, that dreams are just a result of what you eat or other physiological factors," Tristan, the scientist, said.

"Maybe some, but not all. I'm noticing some very appropriate symbolism."

"Tell me about one, Mare," Sophie said.

Sophie and Tristan listened as Mare narrated a recent dream.

"I am at a party at Derek's house? My other teacher friends are there. You guys are there, of course. I don't remember very much about that. But in the next phase—I am a slave; we are all slaves trying to escape."

"Fancy that," Tristan said.

"Yeah, I know, kind of funny, huh? But anyway, it seems like we are in some kind of locker room or prison. With some effort, we manage to escape our confinement and find ourselves in the middle of an amusement park. This prison and the park exist in the same space somehow. I recognize this amusement park from other dreams. I am familiar with it. The mood is still serious, even when I take my friends on the roller coaster. It's almost as if this is a test. It is part of our ultimate escape from this place. I'm not sure who is trying to keep us within, but it's also as if something wants us to escape. At the edge of this park is a river. I lead my people to it and indicate that we must cross it to get to freedom. I am a leader. As we are swimming across the wide creek, I see a snake blocking our path. I grab it by the neck and let the others pass. At the opposite side of the water, I see what looks like guards waiting for these people.

I am a little concerned, but I feel strong and positive that we will get past them. I have helped them get to this point, but it doesn't seem like I will be continuing on with them … Isn't that wild."

"Ah, hah," said Sophie.

"You must have eaten a pretty good pizza last night, huh, Mare?" Tristan teased her.

Mare slapped him on the shoulder, good-naturedly.

"Notice any symbolism there?" Mare asked.

A mischievous glint came into Tristan's eyes and he was about to open his mouth again when Mare said, "Oh no, don't you start with the snake and Freud. Why is it you men always have to point out that? That's NOT what it represents."

Tristan grinned and shrugged.

Sophie looked thoughtful for a moment. "Well, the prison and amusement park seem like great metaphors for life."

"Right. I thought that, too. We are often trying to free ourselves in one way or another." She looked at Tristan. "And life can be an amusement ride, one that either frightens or excites."

"I'm not sure about the river though and the snake. I've had a lot of water imagery in my dreams and I know that often has to do with consciousness, particularly emotional consciousness, but …"

With tongue-in-cheek Tristan said, "I think it means that you need to get out of the house more, have some fun and spend more time outdoors. Go for a canoe trip."

"Very funny, Tristan," Mare smirked.

"I've got to go bring in some more wood," he said, putting on gloves. "I'll let you two figure it all out, but I'm telling you, be careful what you eat."

Mare rolled her eyes.

"He's a fat lot of help," Mare smiled. "How do you put up with him?"

"Good question," Sophie said, as she got up to grab the teapot and pour more hot water into their mugs. "I think that's an interesting dream, Mare. It's interesting that you are leading others in the dream. It does seem like the river crossing denotes some kind of passage. I'm not sure about the snake either."

"I know the snake used to be a sacred symbol of death and rebirth. The snake sheds its skin. In a sense it is reborn regularly. I don't associate it with evil as the Christian faith sometimes does. You know, with Eve and all." Mare realized that maybe she would want to approach that topic delicately, since Sophie was a firm Baptist follower of the Bible. Yet she also very liberal in other ways and appreciated symbolism, as a literature teacher. In many respects Sophie was a tough one to peg. She was enigmatic. Regardless, Mare appreciated the person she was. She saw Sophie as spiritual, honest and good. She didn't need to categorize her.

Mare changed the subject as her mind flashed through another dream. This one was quite short. "The other day I dreamed that I was in the courtroom again, but it was arranged differently than Seth's actual hearing. You were there. Remember how everyone was sitting on a particular side?"

Sophie nodded.

"Well, in this side the whole thing was flipped. The left and right sides were reversed. It was strange. I've been having a lot of dreams about trials and prisons and other kinds of confinements. I've even been chased by Godzilla. Think these are trying to tell me something?" she said with a laugh.

"Maybe. Are you feeling like you are being judged or confined?"

Mare's face turned more somber. "Either like I am or like I might be, if I'm not very careful. Sometimes I feel like I'm in prison with Seth. At least in spirit." Mare's eyes dropped into her cup of tea.

Sophie looked at her friend with compassion. "That makes a lot of sense."

Mare nodded, "Guess so." She met her friend's gaze. "Thanks, Sophie. It helps me to talk about it with people. It's been such a big part of my life lately, but I'm having a hard time finding some of the answers about it. Pete thinks I'm a crazy, which is okay, but there is only so much I can talk to him about it. He loses patience. He doesn't get that it's important to me. I wish I could just find someone who could help me fill in the gaps in my understanding."

"Yeah, I can understand how that would be hard. But I'm sure if you keep looking, you'll come up with the answers you seek."

*   *   *   *

"This is a call from the Windham Correctional Facility. You have received a call from inmate _____ (there was a pause, then Mare heard her brother say *Seth Mahonia*.) If you will accept this call, press one now." Mare did as she was asked.

"Hey, Mare."

"Hey, Seth. How's it going?"

"They've decided to move me from medium-security to minimum-security. They are hoping to prevent some of the harassment I've gotten here."

"Has it been any better?"

"Some days are better than others, but mostly I'm surviving. Thanks for the books you sent me."

"You're welcome."

"Did you see about the baseball coach who was sentenced recently?"

"Yes."

"I wrote to him. His family won't come see him. They've pretty much abandoned him. He seems like a pretty good guy though. He seems glad to have someone to talk to."

"That's good."

"Hey, I just found out that when I move to the new place I think I'll be able to do some group counseling."

"That would be really great, Seth."

"An outside agency runs a weekly program where I'm going. I'll be up near Bangor, near Uncle Carl and Pam, so at least they'll be able to come visit me some. I know it'll be harder for you, Mom, and Dad to drive the three hours very often."

"We'll get up there as much as we can." She remembered her first few visits at Windham. *It was a lot different than the local jail. Much more formal.*

Mare then listened as Seth got into a conversation about pedophilia based upon some of his reading. At the end of his reflection, he said, "Pedophiles don't want to hurt children."

"How can you say that, Seth? You don't know all pedophiles. Some people *do* physically hurt young people." Her mind ran through memories of stories about men molesting children in public bathrooms and people kidnapping, raping and killing children. Her irritation mounted. Finally, she said, "You can't lump them all into a group like that. Some are violent, and some don't care. There are people who snatch children right off the street. Some hurt their own children or grandchildren. Some are so full of self loathing, so out of control and out of touch with their own humanity, that they only way they can feel powerful again is to have control over someone else."

"Yes, Mare, yes … but that is not the majority according to statistics. Most pedophiles are like me … nonviolent, looking for attention and affection. Most do not re-offend once caught, and they aren't violent."

"Well, maybe the bulk don't, but be careful not to generalize. Not all pedophiles are like you. Maybe many are, but there are exceptions. Be careful of presuming to speak for all of you."

"Well, somebody needs to speak for us." He paused. "Look, I've been writing a lot lately, and I was hoping you'd read some of it and give me some feedback."

"Sure."

The conversation lagged for a moment.

"Mom said that you offered to get tested to see if you could give one of your kidneys to Rosie. I think that's really wonderful, Seth."

"Don't tell anyone about that!" he barked. "It might not even happen if we're a match. Plus, she may not want to take it. Who knows? I don't want the whole world thinking I'm offering just to make up for my mistakes or something. I just want to help, if I can. She's been waiting so long for one, and I've been thinking about it for a while. She's always been really nice to me. I'd like to help her, if we're compatible, but I don't want you to tell people about it."

"I understand. I'll keep it hush."

A few weeks later, Mare ripped into an envelope from the Charlestown Correctional Facility. Attached to some sheets of paper was a yellow sticky note that read … Mare, would you mind reading these? Let me know what you think. They probably need some work, but I don't expect anyone will ever see them anyway. Thanks, Seth.

She opened up the bundle and started reading.

My Life was Like a Mountain Bike Ride
by Seth Mahonia

Trying to compare my life to something visual may be the only way some people might grasp the reality of my life, maybe even understand a little, if understanding this is possible.

I picture myself back when I was a young boy, riding a mountain bike atop a large mountain. I found myself at an important crossroads in my life. At this crossroads there was a sign and on the sign read, *"THIS WAY TO FEEL IMPORTAND AND LOVED."* There was a young man standing nearby, inadvertently blocking another sign to a different path. He smiled and kindly asked me if I would ride along with him. Together, we road down that path of *importance and love.* What I didn't know at the time was that the hidden path led to a "normal life," and the sign I *did* read was altered to mask its intended warnings.

As we road together the man *did* give me the love, companionship, and feeling of importance I was searching for, but as the road began to go down hill, I found myself riding alone. However, I continued down and found much *love and importance* along the way. I was making a positive impact on the world around me and I felt goodness in my heart. This truly was a road to feeling *love and importance,* only I was naively unaware of the dangers that lie ahead.

I began to notice a rut was forming, and it was becoming difficult to steer. The road was getting steeper and the terrain much more difficult. The road back to a *normal life* was nowhere around and the top of the mountain was a long difficult ride back on an unmarked trail. I was lost. As the feeling of losing control began to encompass me, I called out for help but quickly realized there was no one around who would give me directions back to a *normal life*. From the outside no one could see the predicament I was in. It was then I realized the road to my future could only begin with the road from my past.

The rut seemed too deep to escape now, and the brakes failed to slow my decent down this ever-steepening mountain. Trying to ride as close to the top of this rut was the best I thought I could do. Unfortunately the rocks of depression and loneliness kept knocking me back down into the rut which now seemed bottomless. It had taken total control of the direction of my life.

As I approached the bottom of the mountain, I saw a large tree in the middle of my rut, and I had no choice but to slam right into it. In many ways I was glad my wild ride was over. Maybe now I could finally go back and find that *normal life*. My eyes followed up the rut, and for the first time, I realized that I had run down those people that meant everything to me. The kids, that along the way gave me their love and feeling of importance, were the ones lying in the devastation that my life's path had left behind. I looked on either side of my rut and noticed all the other people in my life who had become injured indirectly by the flying debris of my actions and my decision to take this now unchangeable path.

I stood there in a daze, watching my family, gravely injured, get up, dust themselves off, and hike down the mountain to help me ... to help me overcome the realization that I had severely injured the very individuals who had made my life worth living. My family stood between me and a cliff that lie just beyond that large tree. In many ways I did not understand their support of me after the turmoil I caused in their lives. It would have been easier for me, at least in that moment, if they would have left a clear, unimpeded path to that cliff.

Now that time has gone by, I realize I have to climb back to the top of that mountain, to try to find that *normal life* which even now lies beyond my comprehension. As I walk back up, I wish I could have an opportunity to somehow help those injured get back on their feet, brush themselves off, and tell them how truly sorry I am for not seeing the hurt of my actions, to ask for their forgiveness and hope that someday, as adults, we could again ride together, this time at the top of the mountain. We must first get back to the top, and I know how far that top is.

I frequently cry knowing the chances for myself and those who have been injured to come together again are unlikely at best.

I begin the first steps. Forgiveness cannot come about because of the things I say. It can only come from those who have been injured, yet still have the power and compassion to forgive. If the guys choose to forgive me some day, that forgiveness cannot be denied by anyone else. For their sake, as well as mine, I hope they are able to find that path for themselves. I wish them well, and only the best, even if they can't extend the same wish for me.

Mare considered the sentiments of the letter. She was still and could feel the beating of her heart. She knew that he meant it. She could understand how he had gotten lost in a pattern that was difficult to get out of. She hoped he could make the climb back up.

She shuffled through the other sheets, and found another letter.

To All Pedophiles

I know you are out there and, despite other people's perception of you, I also know that you're not necessarily the evil monster that society expects you to be.

If you are anything like I was, you are probably a caring, well-liked individual who believes that maybe society is wrong about the negative effects of adult sexual contact with minors. I know that hurting a child may be the last thing you think you are doing. You have probably done many positive things for the kids in your life and perhaps they look up to you.

You are probably thinking that if things were so bad, they wouldn't continue to be your friends and would stop coming around. You probably believe that you are somehow different than those people portrayed on the evening news.

Maybe, like me, at one time you tried to reduce the amount of time you spent with young people, only to find yourself depressed and alone without them.

Please listen to someone who has been there. We are not so different. The kids in your life, who now may feel there is nothing wrong with your conduct, will grow into adults who feel used because of your actions. The good memories you retain of your friendships will later be despised memories to these same kids. They eventually forget the good things you did and the love you may have had for them and remember only the acts, which they regret and are sickened that they were a part of.

But you think you are different. You intend no harm to them. You really care about those kids? Well, so did I. They were my whole life, but now they are gone from my life—every one of them. I am now crushed to understand the true effects of my actions. Those people you hear about on the evening news are people just like us. The news reports use words like—luring, grooming, sexual predator and assault. Some of it may be true. Much of it will be sensationalized hype. None of them will touch on the good things you have done in your life, because none of that will matter anymore. Of course, you think you are different, because you are different, and so are the rest of us.

Some of the young people you thought would never talk about your times together will someday come forward to tell stories that are somewhat (or very) different from the ones you remember. Police sometimes pressure impressionable young people to embellish their stories to "help put this guy away." It is unlikely that you will get a fair shake, because few will feel that someone like you and me deserve one. But you know what, what is true and what isn't won't matter when things start coming out. If you are like me, your biggest concern will be how the kids are getting through this. Your agony will be knowing that your friends were hurt by your actions. Once this happens, all the love in the world cannot take back the acts which have caused the pain.

I'd like to tell you to seek counseling; however because of mandatory reporting laws, seeking help will guarantee you jail time, loss of job, unrelenting media attention, loss of your home, loss of respect in your community, loss of all your friends, loss of all the kids you care so much about and a lifetime of all your neighbors knowing what you've done, no matter where you go. You will at that point, never be able to escape your past. To top it off, once in prison, you probably still won't receive counseling.

Do your best to avoid situations which could lead to a reoccurrence. I, like many others, was unable to escape on my own. Hopefully someday our society will understand that this is something that requires a treatment program to stop. Right now, there is no one out there that will help you. Good luck! You're on your own and no one cares until you are a front-page story, just like me....

Mare was confused by the letter and wondered how he would use it. She knew he wanted to reach out to others, and she applauded that, but how?

The ending bothered her. It was so ... hopeless. It gave no real way out. *Is there a way out?* Seth's letter made it seem like people couldn't do it alone, but also ... that there was no one to help. The picture of confessing looked so bleak ... who would ever seek help? She felt conflicted inside, and her mind began to add her own desires to her brother's thoughts. What would *she* say to people with her brother's problem? In her mind, she began to compose the sentences she wished her brother would write ...

... Being charged with crimes like this and facing the consequences of your actions is difficult and painful, but it does stop the craziness. After my arrest, I did begin to feel a sense of relief that at least now—finally—I didn't have to hide; I could be honest. I was able to find some help and begin the rebuilding process in a way I could take pride in again. The healing process is a long one, but the sooner you start, the sooner you can begin to build a new life for yourself.

Please don't hide. Even if others do not know what you are doing, it IS hurting the children AND it is taking its toll on YOU. You know this.

Mare's imagination could not stop. *How do we eliminate or at least reduce these kinds of crimes? Can't we say to offenders and potential offenders, COME GET HELP. Maybe we CAN find alternatives to prison and humiliation. We respect your honesty. We respect the fact that you admit you have a problem, and that you need support in overcoming it. We celebrate your courage and selflessness in turning yourself in, even if we may not fully understand how or why you do the things you do.*
We will help you because you are our brother ... because you are one of us. We have open enough minds and big enough hearts to help you. And we love our children; we want to keep them safe and healthy! We will do whatever it takes to keep as many of them safe as we possibly can ... even if we failed to keep you safe when you were a child. Please help us to keep more children safe! Be the rescuer that could have saved you. Give us the opportunity to evolve and forgive.
It is time to embrace ALL.

*   *   *   *

Mare sat down, her eyes filled with water, and wrote a letter back to her brother. All she could say was she thought he said a lot of good things in his writing. "I hope you get a chance to say these things one day, and that people listen."

That night, Mare helped Cody into his bed, and laid down beside him as she had done almost every night since he moved into his big double bed. They leaned their heads into each other, as Mare read the story *Goodnight Moon* to him. Because they had read the book so many times, occasionally Cody could supply a simple word to fit the end rhyme. This nightly reading ritual was their special time, and Mare treasured it. After reading, she would turn off the light and snuggle into her son, providing a feeling of safety and closeness. Every night, she would sing to him. His favorite song was *"The House at Pooh Corner"* by Kenny Loggins. "... Well, I wandered much further today than I should, and I can't seem to find my way back to the woods, so help me—if you can—I've got to get back to the house at Pooh Corner by one ... You'd be surprised, there's so much to be done ... count all the bees in the hives ... Chase all the clouds from the sky ... back to the days of Christopher Robin and Pooh ..."

When Mare awoke, she was still in Cody's room. All the lights in the house were out, and Pete was sleeping. She crawled quietly into her own bed, and wandered into the nightscapes of her dreams.

*   *   *   *

Mare was scoring papers in the back of the American Studies class, while her team-teacher, Norman—a history scholar—was leading their class through an exercise on the Vietnam War. Mare looked up when she heard a female student yelling.

"I don't want to do it, and I don't have to do it. This is such crap. Why do we have to learn about all these wars—who cares? It has nothing to do with my life."

Norman tried to reason with the girl and get her to sit down, but she continued her belligerent rampage. Finally, Norman's face got hard and angry. He pointed to the door, and said, "Go to the office, young lady! I've had enough of your mouth." Ally stomped out the door and slammed it. Fuming, Norman buzzed the guidance office and alerted them the girl was on her way.

Mare tried to turn back to her reading, but she couldn't. She was puzzled. She got up and left the room. A few minutes later, she found herself in the guidance office. She heard a loud voice in the back, so Mare followed a labyrinthine trail through the cubbies until she met up with the voice. Ally was speaking to Roger Beaumont about what had just happened. She was complaining about the teacher and angry enough to spit nails. Mare poked her head in and listened for a moment. Then she spoke.

"Ally, I can see that you are angry, but you know," she shook her head, "I'm having trouble understanding what just happened. You are usually so positive about school and respectful to your teachers. This doesn't seem like you." She paused, and looked at the girl whose demeanor had already begun to soften slightly, while Roger remained quiet and attentive to the conversation. "Is everything okay?" Mare continued. "I am worried about you."

The tenderness and sincerity of the question caused the young woman's defensive walls to crumble. Her hands went up to cover her face, and through the fingers Mare heard Ally cry, "Yesterday was my 16th birthday and no one in my family remembered. No one said one word to me about it," she wailed in obvious pain. "It was like I wasn't even there … no presents, no cake, not even a stinking *happy birthday*! Nobody cares about me."

"Oh, Ally," Mare wrapped a comforting arm around the girl. "I'm so sorry. No wonder you were so upset." She gave her shoulder a squeeze and looked at Roger, who was now grinning slightly at Mare's quick success with the girl. "That is very hard…. Well, maybe they just got really busy and forgot. Life can get kind of crazy. I'm sure they care about you, but you have every right to be disappointed. Did you say anything to them about it?"

"No. I mean, a birthday only happens once a year. It's supposed to be special."

The two women spoke a few minutes longer until Ally was calm. The girl was a different person altogether once she acknowledged her feelings. She had experienced a melting. Acknowledging her emotional wound seemed to release Ally from anger's grip. Mare thanked her for trusting them enough to share it, and headed back to class.

When Mare told her colleague the reason for Ally's stress and subsequent disrespect, his own frustration also melted and sympathy replaced it.

How quick we are to judge each other? How quick we are to take everything personally, when there is usually so much more going on that has nothing to do with us.

4/3/98—"Classroom Full of Light"

My classroom is at first small and cramped, but in this dream I am moved to a much larger room with lots of sunlight pouring in from a skylight. My students and I are having a celebration. I have brought food—spaghetti, pizza and orange Popsicles for my students. An older colleague enters the room unexpectedly. She is very traditional and doesn't like the way the teenagers are acting. She demands that one male student leave. She is disgusted by the wild behavior, but I am peaceful and happy. Eventually, she leaves and I begin to fly effortlessly and freely around the room. The ceiling is very high and the room feels spacious and supportive. I talk to my students and they ask me questions with interest while I am flying. They peacefully attend to their homework, while I soar around the upper realms of the room.

*   *   *   *

Mare's mother tossed the newspaper down in front of her daughter. "Read this," she directed.

Letter to the Editor
Pedophiles Among Us

Now that pedophile, Seth Mahonia, is in prison, parents in our communities can feel safe again. But what about the other pedophiles who surely still live among us? What about the one who might live on your street, that coaches your son's team or teaches at your child's school? We would be naïve to think that the problem is now solved.

Even if Seth Mahonia didn't understand the devastating effects his actions had on those kids, he certainly had to be aware of the consequences to himself. Why didn't this deter him? If this condition is some type of compulsion, then pedophiles should voluntarily seek treatment. Right? Most people don't know that doing so will guarantee jail time due to federally mandated state laws requiring the reporting of anyone seeking such treatment. At first, this consequence seems appropriate.

Five years in prison, public mockery, loss of friends, loss of the respect of the community, loss of job, loss of home—this is all well deserved without dispute. Certainly this should create the appropriate feeling of loneliness, isolation, rejection and depression for the perpetrator. Most people don't realize that statistically those are the same conditions that cause many to offend in the first place. So, does this effect really help keep offenders from re-offending? If nothing else, it is extremely effective in deterring voluntary treatment.

You might be saying, "Seth claimed he cared about his victims. If a pedophile really cared about them and wanted to stop, he would just do it." However, at the same time, we wouldn't expect an alcoholic, an addicted gambler or anorexic to recover without treatment and support, even if they truly wanted recovery. But this is a topic that makes us uncomfortable because it touches upon very private matters. Yet, this is part of the problem that keeps the cycle going. Pedophiles need help. How many of them are going to seek treatment if they are guaranteed prison time and the accompanying media frenzy that sex offenders always get?

Many pedophiles were abused as children themselves. Isn't it ironic that we hate pedophiles because of the psychological effects to young minds, yet when these same young minds, as adults, show signs of the predicted problems, we turn our backs? Pedophilia is a psychological problem often handed down from abuser to abuser. Many people do not understand that it usually has little to do with one's moral standards. It has more to do with emotions and thought processes. It doesn't mean you don't care about children. I know, because I am Seth Mahonia. I do care about those teenagers. They meant everything to me. I am devastated to realize the effects of my actions. But I am not seeking sympathy now. I am asking for your help.

In 1992 I tried to get help. I called a hotline. I spoke to a counselor by phone. But when I learned that by coming in the counselor would legally be forced to report my crimes, I decided not to pursue the treatment I needed and wanted. I tried to go it alone again. I suspect that the kids and parents affected by my problem *after* those calls would have preferred that I had received confidential treatment. Instead, I promised myself it would never happen again. Most of the time it didn't, but most of the time is not enough. Perhaps a rare offender will be willing to incriminate himself to get treatment, but we can't count on that. If we revise these mandatory reporting laws, it would not mean that an offender could never be prosecuted. Victims would lose none of their rights by altering these laws; they could still come forward. Society would lose nothing. The benefit would be that some offenders could get help. How many victims could be spared by allowing offenders access to treatment?

Pedophiles are out there who need and want help. For many of us it is not as easy as making a decision to stop. We are not all uncaring people. If I have touched a place of reason in you, please help this situation by clipping this editorial and mailing it to your state or federal legislators, so we can campaign to allow offenders treatment, so we can help decrease the number of young people who become victims. Statistics say that one in four girls and one in five boys are abused in this country. What if a pedophile came in contact with your child after he was denied treatment? I'm sure you do not want your child (or any child) to have to join those heartbreaking numbers. Please do something to help stop this hard-to-talk-about problem. The alternative is to hope that someone else will do something. We can't pass this buck. I was a victim once too. Let's take the next step together, away from hysteric reaction and toward prevention. We need to be willing to listen and talk and do something to redesign our society, so offenders can learn to think and act in ways that are healthy. Let's put aside our discomfort, and help keep children safe, healthy and happy.

Mare put down the newspaper. She was stunned. When she first started reading, she had no idea it was Seth. She wasn't happy her brother was stirring things up again. She didn't really want the community to be reminded of her brother's misdeeds. However, she knew that he had a point, and she agreed with his stance, but … what was it that bothered her? *Few people will listen to him. People don't want to contaminate themselves. They would rather stick their heads in the ground.* She let her mind trail through possible visions of the future ... *Okay, so a man tells a friend ... hey, I had a relationship with another man when I was thirteen, and I kind of liked it. I'm thinking I want to date males and not girls.* Or better yet, *you know, I have these urges of being with adolescent boys. What should I do?*

How would people handle a future where someone comes to them and tells them that they have fantasies that are taboo in our society? What if it were possible to suspend judgment and listen? Most of us have a strange fantasy at least once in our lives. Maybe talking about it would allow them to avoid acting on it.

Mare started to consider her own dreams about Austin. *Obviously, engaging in a physical relationship with a student is inappropriate. But is having romantic dreams about them wrong as well? Can we control our night dreams? We can control our actions, but can we control our feelings? Our impulses? What if I told Pete about these dreams and feelings? Would it help me? How would he react? Would it help us?*

Dear Mare,

Mom said you were upset about my latest letter to the editor. I'm sorry if it made you uncomfortable. I guess it's just important to me for people to understand. I've gotten nothing but positive comments, and I guess I'm not clear about the negative effects to you. I know working at school makes it more difficult for you, but is it only your anxiety about what people are thinking or might do? Is it the fear of something or is it something tangible?

I'm just trying to make a difference. It hurts me to know by trying to help, I hurt my family. I want my family to be proud of me, not to be hurt any further by my actions.

I have a lot of inner conflict and confusion about more than just my sexuality. It's not easy being me. I'm sorry if I hurt you again.

Love, Sincerely,
Seth

P.S. Maybe I'm so vocal because I know someone in the position I used to be in.

Know somebody? Mare wondered. *What does that mean?*

*   *   *   *

4/5/98—"Real Prison"

I am in prison. So are Seth, Pete and Hope. Supposedly, we illegally assisted Seth or were in violation of visitation rules. As I am walking around this prison, I get to see the different parts. I discover that prisoners' pets are here as well. The pets have their own cages. My animals: Evinrude and Choo Choo are here. All the animals look quite sick. I look around this dark place. I feel ill. It is almost completely dark—no sun—and the animals have little freedom to move around in their cages. I notice small vials and syringes scattered about the table my cats' cage is on. They seem to contain a dangerous substance. I do not touch them. I see Hope in the passageways once or twice. I am in a less-confined space than she. Her quarters are rough. Mom and Dad come to visit us, and they bring Cody with them. I am overcome with grief at seeing my son who is now living without his parents. He is only an infant in the dream—perhaps a year old. I miss him so much. I feel like I should be with him, that he needs his parents, but how can I get out of this place. It doesn't seem fair. I don't understand what I did wrong. Cody sees me, and cries out, "Mommy!" I weep and embrace him.

My area seems to be a temporary holding area. I don't know where I will be relocated to. One of my cats dies. I am afraid for everyone and angry. I want to be with my son. I want to help the animals in those little, dark cages.

*   *   *   *

Mare was in a parking garage with Cody. The rains have been very heavy and a hurricane was underway. She wandered through the passageways of the garage looking for safety from the storm. Mare held onto Cody's hand, so she wouldn't lose him. The water level in the building was rising. She picked up Cody, as the water rose to her knees. They were about to be submerged and perhaps carried off with the deluge. Mare tried to make her way to the stairwell to get to a higher level, when she noticed Austin standing at the base motioning to her. Austin grabbed Mare's hand and pulled her and Cody onto the stairs, just in time. He led them to safety. Mare was very relieved.

Mare awoke again with that comfortable, happy feeling that she had when having spent dream time with Austin. The second voice in her head chided her again. The internal battle raged on. It was time to do something. *I can't take these dreams and feelings anymore. I need to break out!* Mare said to herself upon waking.

29

Releases

"Stop eating that apple. God will be furious!"

—Marge Simpson (as Eve)

"You're pretty uptight for a naked chick."

Homer Simpson (as Adam)

For months Mare could remember vague snippets of dream memories about Austin. She was leaning on him. He held her and kissed her. Mare tried desperately to shake them off, and to refocus, but she found her attention being filled with thoughts of her eighteen-year old former student. She couldn't talk to him about these dreams.

A growing need was pushing its way out of her body, but she didn't know how to direct it, and she didn't feel she could contain it. *I don't want to talk to any of my colleagues about this. I need to talk to Pete. I need to get these feelings and thoughts off my chest. Then, maybe we can work on building intimacy in our marriage.*

She wasn't sure how to launch the conversation; her stomach was churning like a whirlpool, but she jumped in before bed one night.

"Pete, I need to talk to you about something."

He pulled the covers up to his chin and slid his arms behind his head to prop himself up.

"I'm listening."

Mare sat down on the edge of the bed, facing Pete, and crossed her legs under her. She looked down. "I've been having some recurring dreams lately that have been bothering me, and I figured that if I told you about them they might lose some of their power over me."

"O-kay," he responded slowly.

"I've been having romantic dreams about a student I had last year."

Pete paused to think.

Uncomfortably, Mare added, "No sex dreams. Just affectionate and caring stuff, but it's been bothering me, so I wanted to tell you."

"So, is this why you've been pulling away from me?"

"No," Mare said, defensively. "I think I'm having these dreams because I have been feeling lonely and misunderstood. We live under the same roof, but we don't spend any fun, private time together. You think groping me in the hallway is going to put me in the mood. The more you push me sexually and try to back me into a corner, the more I try to get away."

"If you loved me, you would want to be sexual. You're just not attracted to me anymore."

"That's not true. I want to be close to you. We've had a giant blow to our lives this year. I just can't jump back into things like nothing ever happened. Try to understand I've been changing. I want to have a good marriage, but right now, I feel like we're friends living under the same roof. I need some help getting into a sensual mood, but I don't feel like you want to waste the time building things up more slowly, and that frustrates me."

"Well, I don't understand why it's such a big deal. It wasn't a big deal before."

"Maybe not, but things are different now. We're parents, and I have a lot of demands on my energy. I think one of the things I find attractive about Austin is that he's playful. He likes to have fun. It's light with him. In the dreams I have I feel like he really gets me too. I don't think it's necessarily Austin who understands me that well, but my dream version of him does. I'm just realizing, Pete, that I have needs that aren't being met. I am asking for your help with them. I want to be healthy. I want to feel joy again. This whole experience has drained and emptied me, and I need to fill back up again. I just can't keep … putting it out without refilling somehow."

"Okay, okay." He started to slide over towards her. "So does that mean we can act out this fantasy, and you can be the pretty English teacher and I can be your hot little student?"

Mare laughed. Pete could entertain her when he tried. "Maybe. Do you like that idea?"

He nodded, and tried to pull her closer.

"So, wait—let's make a plan. Can we have more date nights or something? Maybe some candlelight or conversation? We just need to lead into it more slowly, okay? I would like to feel like we are emotionally close before jumping into immediate physical closeness."

"Okay, I'll try. Do you think you need to do anything else about Austin? Do you feel you need to talk to him?"

"Definitely not now. I'm hoping the dreams will go away now that I've told you about them. Maybe after he graduates, I can acknowledge something to him, if necessary, but not until then. I might not even need to do that." She smiled at him. "It feels really good to be able to tell you about it, and not have you get bent out of shape. It means a lot to me. Thank you!"

He started to kiss her slowly. Exposing herself the way she did seemed to turn her husband on. Talking about the fantasy also freed Mare of its burden. Both were feeling lighter and the two wrestled on the bed. It was a passionate evening.

*   *   *   *

Principal Tyler called Mare to the office at the end of the school day. He led her into the conference room and closed the door. "I need to ask you a couple of important questions, Mare."

"Sure, Todd. What do you need? It sounds serious."

"It's about Kate."

"Ohh ohh, now what?"

He sighed as if he wasn't sure how to begin. "Some staff and other folks have come to me with suggestions that Kate is having an inappropriate relationship with one of her students."

Mare knew the name that would come out of his mouth before he spoke it.

"Do you know Trevor Thompson? People have seen them together an awful lot. They seem close, and it has raised suspicions. I have spoken to his parents about it, and they consider Kate a friend to the family. They insist nothing is going on. Both Kate and Trevor swear that things are platonic between them, but you have been close to Kate, and I trust you, so I thought I'd see what you thought about it and whether you've seen anything."

"To be honest, Todd. I believe there is an attraction between the two of them. I know that they have spent some time together, and I think they care about each other, but I really don't think that they are having a physical relationship. I can't be sure, of course." *We both know I have been deceived before and we've certainly seen that Kate has some boundary issues.* "However, my feeling is that, I hope—she wouldn't be foolish enough, especially after everything else—to jeopardize her career by having a sexual relationship with Trevor while he is a student here. I don't think she has crossed that line, personally. I haven't seen any evidence of it." Then she thought, but didn't say ... *He's going to be graduating soon. If they are burning to be together, I think they are both smart enough to wait until he graduates, and he's no longer a minor.*

He nodded, "Thank you, Mare. I appreciate your input."

*   *   *   *

"They keep hassling me, and everybody looks at me as though I'm having an affair with him. I can't stand it, Mare."

"I can imagine it's very difficult. Do you think you will get a job elsewhere at the end of this year? I can't understand how you even got through this year with Walt around after everything you two have been through."

"I'm not sure. I'm going to look around at least."

*   *   *   *

While in the shower one morning, with the water pouring down Mare's head, she saw an image of Kate. A band of energy like an umbilical cord stretched from Kate to Mare. It was attached just above Mare's navel, and seemed to be draining her. *Kate has an unhealthy attachment to me.* Mare made a choice. *Oh, no ... I'm not giving away my energy without my conscious permission.* Then she imagined severing the cord between them.

*   *   *   *

Mare stood Cody on the toilet seat. "Smile, so I can brush your teeth, Cody."

He bit the toothbrush instead. "Come on, Code. I need your help." The two struggled for a few minutes. The two-year-old did not want to cooperate, and Mare had trouble getting him to understand. Her frustration mounted. She snapped at him and forcefully tried to brush his teeth.

Pete sent her a look of rebuke. "Ease up, Mare." Almost immediately she began to feel guilty, but her irritation would not abate.

Later on, she asked Cody to come to her, so she could put on his clothes. He ignored her. *How do you make a young child understand and obey you? If I ignore the behavior, won't that encourage him? He doesn't really understand time out yet. I can't get him to stay in his seat.*

As the child's stubbornness reached a peak, and when Mare could tolerate her son's disobedience no more, she decided to slap him on the behind.

Cody began to bawl. She did not want to spank him, but she was at her wit's end. Nothing else had helped Cody to change his behavior. She tried to make him understand that his choices had consequences. Some decisions can get you hurt.

*   *   *   *

Mare's mother dropped a bombshell. Seth had been involved romantically with the police chief and the deputy. Mare was so hurt and angry that she could hardly speak. She hit the wall and tried to scream, but her voice was weak. *Why did Seth protect the police,* she wondered.

Mare angrily got in the car and began to drive away, unsure of where she was going. She pulled into a parking lot. The building was now abandoned, or so she thought. For some time, she simply sat there. Soon, she noticed that members of the police department were all around. They were planning something. She started up her vehicle at the same time that the cops were going through some covert drill scenario. She pulled out and leaned over the side of her motorcycle. A bunch of orange suitcases sat in front of the building. They were being exchanged in an espionage-type training operation. As Mare drove by, there was one suitcase left. She grabbed it and drove off around the corner. She heard the police sirens fire up and start to come after her. Mare sighed and turned around before they even got to the corner. *I just wanted to mess with their plans a little and teach them a lesson, because I'm still mad.*

A female police officer took Mare into custody and led her into the building for questioning. Great tanks of gray and white speckled fish lined the front of the building. Apparently, the police had been studying their reactions to different stimuli. The woman walked Mare inside this large, two-story complex with high ceilings, which felt to her like a CIA or FBI operations center. There was much activity inside. The woman sat Mare down at a large table. *I haven't removed anything from the suitcase, I don't know what's inside,* she sighed. She explained over and over again why she took it. Mare was honest with her. The officer left her and went to a larger conference table on the other side of the enormous, open room to discuss the situation with her colleagues.

Mare waited. And waited. It seemed to take forever. She got sick of waiting.

Finally, when she could stand it no longer, she shouted, "I'm leaving! If you have enough to book me, then do it. Otherwise, I'm out of here!" She felt powerful.

The female police office, oddly, congratulated Mare. "Well done," she said. The rest of the place began to clap for her.

How very strange, Mare thought, still not quite catching on.

Next, the woman brought Mare out a different door on the other side of the building. They crossed a narrow walkway or bridge, which was suspended over another tank, a larger, open aquarium. Mare looked down and saw many more fish. The woman and Mare noticed that the fish reacted strangely to Mare as she passed over them. The two women decided to experiment. Mare lowered her body—legs and hips—into the tank. Both women were fascinated by the behavior of these aquatic creatures. The water felt warm around her legs and hips. After a few minutes Mare pulled herself back out of the tank.

The two women entered another building where they found a dark-haired man with whom Mare felt incredible chemistry. The female guide hugged the man goodbye. He then turned to Mare and encircled his arms around her. The contact between them was electric. She felt like she should know him. He seemed like the man in the wedding/dance dream that she had been so drawn to. After their embrace, Mare passed a mirror and noticed she was wearing only a black, strapless bra. This man and Mare communicated telepathically. He brought her to a couch. Mare thought, *I want to stay with him—our connection is mysterious, deep and incredibly sensual,* but she pulled away to leave. Again Mare passed the mirror and examined herself. *I look and feel great!*

When she awoke, Mare was feeling wonderful and free. The dream had caused a shift in her. She had shaken something. She had set some boundaries.

*   *   *   *

"Well, I've done your natal chart for you, Mare. It's a very interesting one."

Jane handed Mare a crisp sheet of paper with a wheel-type illustration on it and a bunch of numbers and symbols Mare did not recognize. She did recognize two horizontal, wavy lines that she knew represented water, but that was it.

Below the wheel were four groups, Jane pointed to the listings under Hemispheres. "What we're going to do here, Mare, is read your natal chart, and I'm going to teach you basic astrology using your natal chart, okay?"

Jane pointed to the paper before she turned on the audiotape to record their conversation. "What we see is a pie that is divided up into twelve equal parts. These pieces, which are numbered one through twelve, are your houses. If you think about astrology, whenever you see it in the newspaper, what you have are twelve different signs and in the newspaper it always begins with Ares. The first day of spring." Mare laughed and nodded.

"Which is amazingly confusing," Jane continued. "Why does it begin with spring?"

Mare knew, and she was sure that Jane knew, "earlier calendars started the New Year with spring, because the cycle of a New Year would begin, naturally, with the physical rebirth of the life." Jane nodded.

Mare was also aware that winter was associated with death and decay, just as spring was associated with the exploding green of new life. That is why years ago, before the birth of Christ (and after), everyone celebrated the Winter Solstice, because it marked the end of the longest day of darkness, and the return of the life-bringing Sun.

Thinking of her own sign, Mare said, "Aquarius is in the 11th house then, right?"

"Yes, very good. But what happens for each of us is … it isn't necessarily Ares that is rising in the place we are born, so we have something else going on here. What we have for you is that Pisces was rising the moment you were born. So you have a combination of Pisces energy in an Aries house, and, for you, Aquarius is in the 12th house, but they still have an Aquarian energy." She looked at Mare's slightly perplexed face and giggled. "It is a little confusing, at first; it'll make more sense as we go," she assured Mare.

"Basically I'm going to use the concepts of other lifetimes in reading your chart." Jane asked, calmly. "Do you have any difficulty with that?"

"No, that's fine with me," Mare said, tucking a wisp of hair behind her ear. "I don't think the universe wastes the energy of a soul. We are here to evolve, I think, and I don't imagine most of us can do that in just a lifetime or two."

"This is what I believe, also, and I believe we choose the time of our birth, as we choose our parents, as we choose the place. Okay?" She studied Mare's expressions gently and found no issue there. "There is a part of us that does the selection and we come into this sphere, into this plane, with a purpose. The moment we're born and the place we're born in sets up an astrology which is basically a blueprint for that lifetime. And this blueprint tells you what your journey is about, what you've come into this lifetime to do, what your tools are, what you have working for you, what your challenges are."

"I've got some challenges in there?" Mare giggled, sarcastically.

"Yes, I see some challenges in there. And ummm … so I'm going to read the chart from this perspective."

Jane continued by talking about the houses and Mare's balanced hemispheres, the planets, the sun and the moon. Mare tried to follow her words.

"Yes … so here we have an imbalance that comes forward. As you can see we have yin and yang. Basically now we're seeing something else being added in. We have our ten planets; we also have the ascendant. What constellation or sign was ascending the moment of your birth? It has a very important purpose.

We can see as we look, you have 8 plus ascendant as yin, or feminine energy, and two masculine. What that means is you're a very responsive, very sensitive and aware person. You're going to be picking up a lot of things. You're going to intuit a lot. But in some ways you may feel like a mouse that a kitten is playing with. That life is kind of moving you around, and that may not be appealing."

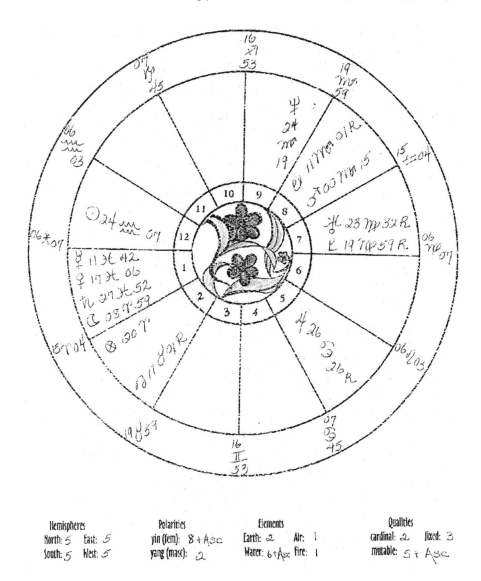

Hemispheres		Polarities	Elements		Qualities	
North: 5	East: 5	yin (fem): 8 + Asc	Earth: 2	Air: 1	cardinal: 2	fixed: 3
South: 5	West: 5	yang (masc): 2	Water: 6 + Asc	fire: 1	mutable: 5 + Asc	

"I do pick up a lot," Mare said, but I am also very … yang, tough, a tomboy. Was this a compensation because of the more vulnerable energy?"

"That's exactly what I was going to say. I was very surprised, knowing you, and seeing there was so much yin energy here. Yes, I think it's safe to say that you felt out of balance and so that masculine aspect felt like it needed to come forward."

"I probably didn't know how else to handle it."

"Yes, because you are going to feel like a pawn almost, carried here, carried there. But I want you to be aware of the blessings that come from having so much yin. There's a resilience in you; an adaptability, and just an openness and an awareness. Be open to letting that reign every so often."

Mare nodded with each statement. "In the last year, I have been trying to listen to that and let that side of me come out more."

"Uh-huh, you have. With that come a lot of gifts. If you feel you always have to make it happen, it's like with a square peg and a round hole. There's going to be a tendency not to allow the universe to just give to you. When you have a lot of yin energy the universe has a lot of gifts for you and part of having so much yin energy is—just allow it to happen. *Allow* it to happen. Sometimes by asserting a lot of yang, you might get in your own way."

Mare nodded at the accuracy of this statement. "Yes, Pete likes to call me the sledgehammer."

"This is going to be more of a trusting that there's a divine wisdom, and most of that, I would say, comes from within you. Just allow the gifts to come."

She patted Mare on the knee, and continued. "We're also going to look at the elements. All of the signs come with certain elemental energy to them, and as you can see here, yours …"

Mare broke out in laughter. "Water. That's me."

Jane smiled, "Yes, yours is water. As an Aquarian, you are an air sign, but you only have one air, one fire, and two earths. Your main thing … SIX planets are in the water element, plus your ascendant! That means that, even though at your core you are an air intellectual energy, a lot of you is emotion! A lot of you is feeling; a lot of you is intuition. So you read about Aquarian, and yeah, that applies to you, but … with all this water and strong yin energy you are picking things up all the time in your gut." Jane looked at Mare's face to see if this was true for her.

Mare was looking down at the floor and nodding quietly. Then she looked up and made eye contact with Jane. "Wow," was all she could say. "That would explain a lot."

"In your heart you just know things. You need to trust that, and almost use that powerful Aquarian intellect to take and transcribe the more nebulous things that are coming in to your feeling self."

Mare was feeling a great deal of confirmation of things she had never been able to put her finger on and explain. "Is this usual?"

"Ummm … a lot of times people have a few extra things here. But seven water signs … I thought I had a lot. You may feel afraid of this emotional part of you. You may feel afraid of it taking over your senses and your intellect. That it would create upheaval in your life. That the emotionality would keep you from being creative."

Mare squirmed a little in her seat.

"With all these worries comes a lot of energy being put into holding down the emotions."

Mare put her hand over her mouth and began to laugh.

Jane looked at her with a smile and said, "It's almost like putting this big watery feeling element that you keep hiding in the closet and locking it up."

"A man once told me, *you seem really tough on the outside, but that is not you. You are soft.* I felt like he had seen and exposed me, and I loved that. I do try to hide these emotions, sometimes not even consciously, because they come up so easily. Going to watch *Titanic* and then two hours later I'm still in the water with them."

"Yes, IN THE WATER … with the people!" Jane's eyebrows rose.

Mare's eyes widened with recognition and amusement. "Even as a child I remember being teased about my sensitivities. I cried during an animated Christmas special when the mother donkey died protecting and saving her baby from a sandstorm. I tried to hide it, but my family laughed at me. I am easily moved by acts of generosity and courage."

"A lot of deep feeling; it's not who you are; you're air."

"There's a conflict."

"The signs can either be cardinal, mutable or fixed. You can see again, there is somewhat of an imbalance in yours. Cardinality is the initiator; it gets things going. Fixidity is the stabilizer … the energy that completes things, and mutability is changeability. The interesting thing here again is that your core energy, which is your sun energy, is Aquarius and it's fixed. So, you are very, very stable at your core. Your moon is cardinal energy; that's another strength and that's emotional. So, emotionally, you're assertive and you can get things moving; you're creative. Okay, that's powerful! Right from your unconscious that energy comes. But basically the rest of you is into change, really likes new things, gets bored, is always looking for challenges and is very comfortable going from thing to thing."

Again, Mare felt like Jane had nailed her. It all came together.

"When you work, I bet it's difficult to sit and start and go all the way to completion."

"It is."

"I would see you with a few things going on at a time and needing to go from one thing to another thing and then back again, then to another thing and both from the water energy and from the mutability, and that's going to work best for you—don't judge it; make use of it, okay?"

She continued. "So while you are writing your book, you might have something else you're doing, about two or three other things and when you come up to a blocked place, it's better for you to just dance over or flow over to a different project or thing and then afterward, you'll just naturally flow right back. Does that make any sense?"

"You have no idea ... Does this ... ahhh ... have to do with relationships, too?" A train began to hoot nearby. She paused to listen to the rumble over the tracks.

"Yes, relationships ... at your core, you're this very stable, Aquarian energy. Basically the fixed signs mate, they're like wolves. They mate for life. That's their nature. They're focused on one relationship, but ... Six here are Pisces mutability—what you have is the emotional connecting, but two fish swimming in opposite directions. If any sign is emotionally fickle, it would be the Pisces energy. For you, this isn't who you are—you are an Aquarian, but there will be that tendency to be carried emotionally here and there. It doesn't mean that you're going to act on it."

Mare nodded; she had her boundaries, and yet the waves did toss her.

"You are not your thoughts; you are not your feelings; this is just what's occurring in your psyche."

"But it at least explains that I'm not crazy!" laughed Mare, thinking of her struggles around Austin.

Jane was familiar with this issue, and she understood. "No, you're not crazy. It's wonderful, because it affords you the ability to understand people at a gut level. You know, Aquarian energy is really the champion of diversity, not only do you champion that at your core—your feeling part is going to be able to support that—so you are going to be able to feel for ALL kinds of different people. Be moved by all kinds of different people. So, you are really bringing forward a blessing, particularly in your work, where these kids need emotional connection. That's wonderful, because, having that Aquarian core, you're not going to be carried away by emotions ... oftentimes you may FEEL like you are, but you are never going to be. You are able to maintain a good boundary, while you are still working from a place of love." She paused and both women considered what Jane had just said.

"Let's look at your 1st house. You can see this is where all the action is. This is called a "packed house." When you have three or more planets in a house it is *packed*. You have four. That indicates that your high self decided it was going to come into this lifetime and deal with some very specific issues. These issues come from many lifetimes of ... kind of tripping over something. Somewhere, in some lifetime, you had a different first house energy. There was some kind of trauma. Basically it set up a pattern, and that pattern defined you for many lifetimes, and now you've come here in this lifetime to work specifically on 1st house issues and to break through that pattern, to free yourself, to reclaim the energy, the power that got locked into that frozen place."

Mare asked her, "Am I here to *master* these particular issues this time around?"

"In essence, yes."

"What are the issues of the 1st house?"

"The first house is an Aries house. The 1st house is *who you are in the world*. The evolving I AM. So a lot of energy is going to be involved in terms of you OUT THERE in the world. How you appear—what you are like. You really want and need to be esteemed by the public. You really want and need that. I don't mean you want to be a celebrity, but you need and want to be held in high esteem, to be respected, to be seen as a person of power. I think that this was what was very, very difficult with your brother. In some ways, it was casting aspersions on you—which it really didn't, but which you would be very sensitive to. How does it make me look? That would be scary for you. How does this impact me and my family? And that's why I think it was amazingly important for you to write that letter to the community. That's what came to me as I looked at this packed house ..."

"Those *have* been my issues."

"Yes, and it's very emotionally charged because of all the Pisces energy. Sometimes it may get so important to appear in a true sight to everyone that you deny other parts of yourself, by wanting that appearance to be clear. And this is going to be one of the hard things, one of the challenges ... It doesn't matter what other people think of you."

Mare blinked in recognition. "You are right. Intellectually, I know this. In the last year, I lived with it. My integrity is very important to me and it would be regardless of other people, and yet I *do* want people to know that I am a good person."

"But see, what people think of you is important! This is one of your challenges. This is what you're going to be breaking up. The thing that's most important is who you are. It's almost like the incident with your brother was part of the teacher."

"Absolutely, it was a *teacher*. I have always cared what people think; it was almost paralyzing. I never wanted to make a mistake. It has cost some freedom and peace of mind. Even when I was in girl scouts I remember an incident that bothered me afterwards. We were playing some kind of circle game, I forget what. I just remember laughing a lot. I remember we were standing behind our chairs. At one point, I really had to pee, but I didn't want to leave because I was having so much fun. Every time I laughed I thought I was going to piss myself. I leaned my crotch into the chair to help prevent that from happening. I remember two other girls looking at me in disgust, like I was getting my jollies from the chair or something. I was very embarrassed afterward. I've always been concerned about the perceptions of others. I hate to think that people make assumptions without knowing the whole story, but I also don't want to go around explaining and justifying everything either. It keeps me a prisoner. I'm not sure why it has such a hold on me."

"That is understandable, but you will need to let go of your attachment to what they think. It doesn't matter. It only matters that you are being true to yourself. You can't always please the people around you. No matter how hard you might try. Public opinion won't always go with you, and it doesn't need to for you to get your soul's work done."

"I know you are right, Jane."

"When I see a packed 1st house like this what I see is a person who was out in a public position many lifetimes, might have been a politician, a ruler, maybe a prominent performer of some kind, where the public's view of you was very important. Now your lesson is that what's truly important is how I feel about me, and this life is going to keep challenging you in that way until you get it. Does that make any sense?" She paused. "A lot of your drive in life has been to succeed, a lot of your pushing in life, that Ram energy of the Aries just ramming and ramming, and a lot of that has been so people can see who you really are. *I'll show them*, and that can wear you out."

"Yes, it can. It does," Mare laughed with a little discomfort. Jane was hitting some soft spots here.

"Well, the thing is … one of the lessons you've been learning is that it's not important. The only thing that's important … the ONLY thing that's really important is how you see yourself."

Mare crossed her arms like she was cold, leaned back a bit, and nodded.

"You're just not going to need to push so hard," she said gently

Mare leaned in towards the tape recorder. "Did you hear that, Pete? He will like that."

"Just allow life to unfold. Where you have a lot of yin energy, you could have great success with your book, and it doesn't mean that you have to go beating on all the publisher's heads to have them take notice. What I'm going to ask you to do is trust more. Trust more for it to just organically evolve."

"I'm not anywhere near far enough to send it to publishers yet. I haven't been pushing it. I have some goals, but I haven't been making myself crazy."

"You have a lot of support to have that evolve organically."

"It's like T'ai Chi … yielding …" Jane nodded, seeing the connection.

"Your sun is in Aquarius and basically this is who you are at the core, as I said before. It is a fixed, air sign. Air signs deal with the intellectual plane. You are a thinking person, a head person."

"Big surprise, there, huh?" Mare grinned.

"But there's a steadiness in your thoughts. Some air signs are very flighty. Aquarius is the most stable, or rooted or grounded of all the air signs. You don't get lost in space. Aquarian energy is much more productive in terms of its thought. This is who you are. Your Aquarian energy is in the 12th house— the Pisces house—your sun is here. Twelfth house indicates past life issues. This core, Aquarian energy has come to assist you in letting go of these past-life, Piscean issues. This is very metaphoric. Aquarian is the water carrier. At your core, you can create the container needed for water. It's perfect that you have this emotional energy … all these watery feelings, because you are able to contain it, to create the container that it needs, so it isn't splashing out every-where and getting dissipated."

"I know what you are saying."

"So, that works well for you. Your moon—your unconscious or subcon-scious—is in Aries. That gives a lot of fire, and a lot of dynamic assertion to what you feel. It's almost like a Don Quixote energy. When you have a feeling that something is right, you are going to advocate for it with a passion, and the same as if you have a feeling that something is wrong."

Mare was nodding fervently.

"So, the way that your first house energy, the *I am*, is being defined is as the Champion, the Knight; you are in search of the Grail."

"I have been a seeker, and I want so much to contribute something positive to the world."

"There is a lot of will in the 1st house, and it's associated with the throat chakra." She paused. "That is interesting! You have been having problems with your thyroid, right?"

"Yes, I've been on medication for hypothyroidism."

"I would say it was from a past life. That sensitivity. In many lifetimes, I would say that you were martyred for speaking your truth."

With a touch of sadness, she said, "It *was* a pretty common thing in history."

"You were martyred for speaking your will. Yet, within you is that Don Quixote part that can't do anything else but … speak your truth."

"This whole thing about appearances is going to be a factor now that I'm sharing my writing with others. Sophie has been reading the first few chapters, which is all I have done so far, and she's been really great. I'm comfortable with her reading it. But there's this group of teachers at school who write and want to get together to share their work, and although I'm excited about it, part of me is intimidated, too."

"Tell me about the fear."

"This is a deeply personal book. I almost want to wait until it's all done, because my inner critic is always there on my shoulder. I don't want anyone else to tell me what's wrong with it until I take care of all the things I know are wrong with it first. At this point, I'm simply interested in feedback about the direction of the book … how it feels to a reader. Because it's a true story and so deeply connected to this local community that I live in, I panic sometimes. Many of the people who will be reading it will be local and familiar with the characters and events. That feels risky to me."

"You don't have to bring that book to the group."

"That is the only thing I'm writing at the moment, and I *want* feedback on it, and encouragement."

"You just need to control it, and make sure you are comfortable."

Mare laughed and thought about how comfort was overrated and how risk has its benefits. Then she said, "Okay, that's good, because I was thinking of just throwing myself in with the lions."

"*Throwing yourself in with the lions.* Good word choice, Mare. Think about it. Pisces is the martyr energy. I want to talk about this. This is what's really coming clear. You don't have to martyr yourself anymore to assert your will!" Jane's words brought to the screen of Mare's mind images of those who were thrown in with real lions. Her stomach overturned. She felt a strange tingling along the back of her neck.

"Somewhere along the line, you know, Mare, I say you were a political person, you were a leader. You might have been a leader in opposition to the norm, and the thing was, in order to assert your will or the truth, you had to be martyred. You don't have to do that anymore." Something about her words soothed Mare. "This is where the Aquarian energy comes in. This is the critic on your shoulder. You don't have to take your guts and lay them out there for the public, just as …"

Mare considered her words carefully.

"But I *want* to put it out there, once it's complete. Then I don't have any problem with it, because I've said what I need to say. I've said my truth and then if they want to have at it, that's fine. But until I get to that place where I feel like it's really speaking what my truth is, because I'm still searching."

"And I don't think of those people as lions either, but as a writer, anybody who puts a personal piece of writing out there probably has that fear of being attacked to some degree. I know what I want, the question for me is always how—there's a right way and a wrong way."

"Right, the thing is more trusting. Your emotions—your relationships with people—help define who you are. People are going to be drawn to you, in terms of perceiving you as an emotional person. They're going to be drawn to that softness and sensitivity, which you have, but they're going to be astounded when they hit up against the Aries moon and Aquarian sun. You spend a lot of time in the feeling world, but that isn't who you are. How does that ring?"

"It's true. One moment, I am a bleeding heart about something that's meaningful to me, and the next, what's significant to someone else seems minor or immature to me. I imagine I am sometimes hard to deal with."

"That's the water carrier, the Aquarian energy. The other is being impacted by Pisces. This is one of your life's challenges. How can I take this air energy, which is intellectual, which is masculine. And how can I have it exist with all this water energy, which is very feeling and feminine? How can these opposites come together, like oil and water? How do they mix? This is going to be one of your life lessons."

*   *   *   *

4/22/98—"Stolen Bus"

Pete and I are driving around in a bus we have stolen. We figure out how to drive it as we go. Numerous people try to stop us in town, and a few try to help us. The only purpose at first is to joy ride, but as we continue to evade

our would-be captors, it becomes more serious. At every turn, we are successful at giving people the slip. We try to get the bus up our hill. A few of my students help us. We get stuck in the snow and have to go back down a few times to get up speed and momentum enough to make it. We manage to acquire a second bus somehow, which puts us in more trouble. Something that started as light fun has now become dangerous. The stakes have gotten much higher. We keep trying to get uphill before we're caught. We eventually abandon the bus and begin to run. Cody is with us at some stages, I notice. Two other people are running with us, and a few fast runners are chasing us. A crowd has gathered at the bottom of the hill, so we cut off the street into the woods for a short way and onto another so we won't be detected. We are trying to get to the top of the hill, and, since we have been unsuccessful going this way in the snow, we try to circle around the base of it instead, by way of the lakeside, and take the road up the backside. Still running and being followed, we ask other friends to take Cody, since it's us the authorities are after. I see when I look behind me that Cody has been trying with difficulty to keep up with us. A two-year-old can't exactly move as quickly as we adults can. Poor Cody. How did we get into this mess?

*   *   *   *

Mare had just gotten home from work. She let the dog out, and she and Cody stepped outside to join him. They liked to play with the big dog. Like a bullet, Chaucer took off up the hill, chasing after a car. Mare yelled for him to come back. She would alternate between yelling harshly to him in an attempt to scare him into coming back and beckoning more softly to him to coax him to return. The carrot and the stick. When she could see that one failed, she tried the other. When that failed, she went back to the first. Neither was very effective in getting the dog's attention. He was a slobbering, excitable, spontaneous fool.

Mare's uphill neighbor, Mrs. Lashley, heard her calling and poked her head out her door. Realizing what the young woman was trying to do, the older woman tried to assist by calling the dog as well. Eventually the dog came galloping down the hillside lawn and onto the driveway, where Mare was waiting for him. The dog ran right up to Mare's fingertips, which were outstretched to him. Mare's flat hand struck the dog for his disobedience—once on the shoulder; then remembering her husband's instructions—twice on his haunches.

Mare looked up the hill when she heard her neighbor yell.

"That's not the way to get him to come home!" Mrs. Lashley shouted rebukingly.

Mare thought for an instant how to respond politely when she was feeling criticized and reactive. "Do you have another suggestion?" Mare asked from a hundred feet away.

"I hug my dogs when they come back."

"Do they learn not to run off? We can't get him to stop chasing cars and deer and running off into the woods!"

"Get him a runner."

"We have one and we use it, but sometimes we like to play with him. Other times, he sneaks out the door when someone's coming in."

"Tie him up; some dogs just can't."

"He's still a puppy, although a big one."

Mrs. Lashley did not reply, so Mare continued defensively. "I don't like to hit him, but my husband believes it's the best way to teach them at this age ..." Her voice faded off. She had the feeling that the older woman had gone back inside, or at least was no longer interested in discussing the matter.

Embarrassed and seething with irritation, Mare went back in. *Who does she think she is telling me what I'm doing wrong?*

Why is this bothering me so much—I thought I'd gotten over caring what other people think?

What is The Way *in a situation like this?*

*   *   *   *

"Mare, Seth got a letter from the State," Joan told her daughter. "Pete's step dad, Dale, is trying to get Seth's Maine Guide license revoked. He thinks that since he's a convicted criminal that he should not be able to keep his license, but the State told him no."

"Oh, really? He's very angry at Seth about what happened. His remarks have been very disparaging towards him, but I didn't know he had gone that far. I'm glad the State is letting Seth stay a registered guide."

"Well, Dale doesn't think Seth should be able to guide ever again."

"That's stupid. Seth isn't going to ever be able to work with young people again, and he shouldn't, but that doesn't mean he shouldn't be able to be a recreational guide for adults down the road, if he chooses to. Why would Dale do that?"

"He wants to make Seth pay apparently."

"Like he isn't already? I guess it will never be enough for some people, but Dale is my family too; you'd think for my sake at least he'd back off a little."

Mare had endured a few brief conversations with Dale about her brother. She had apologized to him as Seth's sister. She knew he had a right to be angry, since Seth had made a pass at his own teenage son many years earlier. But she hoped Dale would understand that this was her brother, and that she couldn't hate Seth as he did.

"Dale's brother works at school too. He said something to me this winter about how Seth deserved at lot worse than he got. I told him that I was sure that some people agreed with him, and I left it at that. No sense arguing about it. He doesn't care about fixing the problem, or how it came to be a problem in the first place. Out of fear, people like him and Dale just want to punish the perpetrators. Hurt them—make them pay for what they have done."

Joan added, "Kind of homophobic, too; aren't they?"

"Oh yeah," Mare said. "I think it's fear. Don't you? All they can do is lash out, just like Dale does at his dogs who misbehave. The only way they can feel any sense of control over the situation is to beat it." Mare grabbed her temples, "My head hurts."

*   *   *   *

Jane had invited Mare on several occasions to join a woman's dance group that she led about once a month. Today was the first day of a special workshop on the stages on womanhood. Jane pulled into Mare's driveway, and Mare climbed in. They talked throughout the twenty-minute drive. Jane asked her about childhood, since she was going to ask the group to look at it.

"I don't remember all that much about my childhood. It was pretty ordinary, kind of boring. I was a little bit shy. My parents were fairly good to me. We never had much money, but I always felt quite safe and loved."

"What else?" Jane prompted her.

"Well, you know, speaking of feeling safe, I remembered the other day when I was thinking an incident when I was in first grade ... I always walked a couple of blocks to school by myself when we lived in New Jersey. One day when I was doing this, a man stopped his car behind me and called to me. He was sitting in the front seat, but he had slid over and opened the passenger door. He tried to offer me candy. When I think about it now, I am horrified. I don't remember being scared, but I recall looking at him for a minute and then walking on. He did not follow me, and nothing else happened. I had forgotten about it for so long, but when it popped back into my brain, I was stunned at how close that situation could have been to something very bad. It scares me to think about it. It scares me for my own children."

Jane interrupted and said, reassuringly, "but you were protected. You did not go with him, and he did not come after you. You were quite safe. Something or someone was looking out for you. Your intuition was guiding you. Your children also have protectors and guides."

This thought immediately calmed Mare. "You're right. Something alerted my intuition, and not just the old warning not to take candy from strangers, it was much more." The more she thought about it, she envisioned some strong spirit who was with her—or perhaps a part of herself—who had scared the man away. It no longer seemed like such a close call to her. She had simply been guided on to her destiny.

When the two arrived at the stairway of the old building, they began climbing. They each took off their shoes and waited for everyone to arrive.

"Welcome, friends. I'm glad you could join us this afternoon for *Celebrating Lilith*. I designed this creative movement and improvisational dance workshop in order to help women celebrate their femininity. Women's bodies, minds, emotions, and spirits have for centuries been defined by a patriarchal system. This has affected the way we think and feel about ourselves, even the way we hold and use our bodies. Let's sit." She motioned the group of about twenty women to the floor.

"I'm not sure how many of you are aware of who Lilith is ... Many stories and myths about her exist, though in her most ancient form she was a Sumerian wind spirit and Queen of Heaven. However, as religions changed from being goddess-centered and Earth-based to male-dominated and technology-centered, she became demonized. Hebrew sources say she was the first wife of Adam, meaning she came before Eve. In Hebrew mystical texts, she and Adam began as one being within the same body, until God separated them. Thus, they were equals. It is said that she, being an independent woman, refused to lie below Adam. She demanded equality and the right to co-rule, but Adam refused, so Lilith left. She was eventually replaced by a more complacent Eve. Not that Eve faired much better." Jane smiled kindly, and the group chuckled, knowing how the church interpreted Eve.

"Because Lilith was vilified for her independence and labeled a harlot, her example has since helped to create an expectation that women should submit to male authority. Lilith is barely mentioned in the bible, conveniently enough, and if you look up the meaning of her name in a book of baby names, you are likely to find the definition "hated one." These interpretations deny her true legacy. So, we are reclaiming her positive associations and celebrating the wise spirit she was originally intended to be. We are going to dance; we are going to listen to our bodies and our hearts; we are going to write; we are going to explore the different stages of being a woman—child or maiden, mother and crone—and celebrate what it means to be women!"

Mare looked around the circle of women—all different ages, shapes and sizes.

Each woman introduced herself. Mare was reluctant to give her last name, though almost everyone else gave theirs, so she did also. She wondered if anyone recognized it from the news in the last year. She did not want to be pre-judged.

The first piece of music to play was a gentle one, slow and rhythmic. Jane began to move her body around the room, and guided her students through different movements. "There is no right way to do this, ladies. Simply listen to what your body wants to do. Just explore and trust yourself."

Mare wanted to be graceful. Students spread all over the wide room. Wooden floors creaked in certain spots, but were muffled by the sweeping violins. Mare caught glimpses of herself in the broad mirrors that lined some of the walls. Color was starting to come into her cheeks from the mild exertion. The light was low, and flattering to the reflection.

The tempo of the next song was quicker. Mare realized that she used her hands and arms very little in regular dancing. *Why is that?* She thought of Sophie who could flap her arms gracefully around like a flamingo. I tend to use my hips and shoulders, she noticed. She made an attempt to stretch into new areas of movement and expression. As she danced, Mare felt a warm energy rise up through her muscles. A range of songs filled the air, and with each one, Mare was called to move in myriad ways to accompany the pace and emotion of each. She became responsive to the flowing tunes. When a staccato tempo began to blare out, Mare answered its thumping instructions. Her body twirled and jumped with each crash of sound. She felt the urgency coursing through her arms. She felt the warm glow coming off from her neck. She let her anger dash out through her pores and in every direction her fingers pointed. Thoughts vanished, and she felt a unity. In this trance-like state, she allowed herself *to be* without question. She allowed whatever emotion each song triggered bubble up through the cells of her body and out in a vaporous release to the world. She felt free and alive and acceptable and beautiful and strong.

When the music began to slow again, and heart rates dropped back to near normal, Jane instructed the women to find a spot of their own and start writing. Mare's pen did not stop. She explored the state of her relationship to Pete; she examined her own attitudes and actions; she poured out her feelings onto the page. Words came dripping out of the pen as honey oozing from a spoon. She let them sloop out of her.

Finally a dance of me. Free. Flowing. I'm feeling like I want to live in the sunlight. This is why I've chosen this spot on the floor. A slice of sunlight is beaming onto it, and I want my cells to drink it in. I want to feel the warmth again. I feel like I've been hiding in the shadows too long. I want to express myself in every way. There has been sadness. I feel like I'm coaxing a little girl out to play. She's afraid; she wants to hide. She is only a part of me though. The other part wants to sing and dance in the warmth of light. I hope I don't slip on the teardrops that have spilled so copiously onto the floor. Where do I want to go with this dance, this opening? I'm not sure. The sound of the pen zipping across the page distracts me. My whole body is touching the floor now, since I am lying down on it. I'm becoming grounded, not just at this moment, but in every area of my life. I want to experience joy without restraints. I want to feel alive. Fully alive. To breathe. To love FULLY, without holding anything back. I have been withholding myself. Not so much from Cody, but from Pete. I've been stingy with him, because I've been trying to find a way to take care of myself while juggling the roles of mother, daughter, sister, teacher and wife. I want to share intimately, but I withhold. Sometimes I want to be left alone and I'm not sure where that comes from. Am I trying to protect myself? From what? I don't think it's worth the sacrifice. I want to connect to the world and those around me. I tend to keep myself separate. I've been strong and confident almost to an extreme. I want to start allowing my feminine or yin side to emerge again. I want to listen more, to be more patient, to allow myself to need others, to open up my heart.

You asked us to think about the love that was coming to us. What if I did allow others to love me? I feel many sources of love, now that you ask us to look at it. Some are unexpected. The funny thing is I notice that despite all the anger and hurt between Walt and I, we still care. Appearances are deceiving. He doesn't speak to me anymore, unless he professionally has to, but in his heart, I don't think he hates me either. There is love still.

When I look to feel the love and strength around me, the most powerful love I feel is from Cody and some of my friends. They've been sending a lot to me. The experience of accepting love is very enriching. God, how often do we reach out to feel that love?

I feel so cleansed and energized. I am present to myself and my surroundings. I can feel my heart beating when I am still. It is rocking me back and forth gently, subtly. I remember this from previous quiet moments. And I like it.

Each woman shared a piece of what she wrote with the group.

Next, Jane taped two big poster boards around the room. She asked them to generate a list of: 1. Joys—Pleasures—Delights of being a Woman. 2. Hurts—Challenges—Pain Associated with Being Woman. Each brainstormed a personal list for each question, and then got up and recorded them on the group poster. When all had recorded their responses, the group discussed the items …

Being A Woman (Hurts—Challenges—Pain)

- Shaving my legs
- Having to always "give"
- Periods and everything that goes with it
- The pain of childbirth
- Make-up and hairspray
- Objectification of woman (valuing the physical more than the rest)
- nylons and heels
- worrying about "bouncing" while exercising
- being looked over and past—don't exist
- apology in voice
- being on a diet all my life
- being THE CARETAKER/GIVER
- assumption that we must not have needs/desires of our own if we are "good"
- Less pay for "women's work"
- Being patronized by men—the assumption that I can't do certain things because I'm a woman
- Responsibilities—too many sometimes
- Looking in the mirror through my mother's eyes
- Cleaning up other people's messes (assumption that I'll do it because I'm the woman)
- Always having to begin the "issues" discussions
- Having my intuition considered "flighty" and his analysis scientific
- Being overprotected
- Being afraid—needing a man to protect me
- Guilt
- Being a man's anima—I'm a person
- Having to overcome stereotypes and expectations of our roles—what if I don't want to cook
- Not being taken seriously because "I feel it"
- Ever changing bodies
- "Weaker sex"
- the popular definition of beauty
- weak bladders
- having to keep my chest clothed
- competition with other women
- "men's looks"
- being talked down to by men
- Barbie dolls—I wanted legos!
- High heels and other uncomfortable fashions

Being a Woman (joys—pleasures—delights)

- The color pink
- Lots of "firsts" left for us to go for (1st female president, etc.)
- Feeling a baby kick and move and grow inside you
- Sharing with other women
- Singing voice
- Feeling breasts move as I dance
- Expression of emotion
- Dancing
- Birthing/Motherhood
- Flirting like only a woman can
- Growing
- Rounded figure (circles, circles)
- The ability to network and share feelings
- Powerful intuition
- Living on feelings
- Voice "crying"
- Orgasm (single and multiple) yeh! Ditto!
- Feeling pretty
- More variety in clothing and less limiting
- Enjoying sexuality
- Being able to wear a skirt and relish it
- Flowers and colors—bright colors
- Long, hot bubble baths
- Feeling sexy
- Freedoms
- Wearing makeup if want to
- Depth of feelings
- The rich, deep, healing blood of my menses
- We typically live long/endure!
- Vibrators
- Being in tune with surroundings/energies
- Sensuality
- "men's looks"
- surprising people with what I (a woman) can do!
- Small courtesies given to women and giving them back to men (opening doors, etc.)
- Having the chance to be a bride
- Being beautiful
- Giving self pleasure and others too
- Colorful clothing
- Expressing self through clothing

The group talked about being women—what they loved about it—what challenged them. They laughed that some items were on both lists. They embraced some of the feelings they shared in common. Then they danced for another hour.

As they went through a woman's stages of life, Jane asked them about their purpose on this planet. One woman complained that she wasn't sure what she was meant to do. A couple of other women echoed her sentiments.

I know, Mare thought. *I know exactly why I am here on this planet. I am here for a specific purpose. I am here to help evolve consciousness. I am meant to contribute through my writing. I am sure of it. I am being led on a particular path.*

At the end of the dance session, Jane had them stand face to face with a partner, holding their hands out in front of them. "Feel the energy coming off from your hands. Give it to the person in front of you. Feel the energy they are passing to you."

"Okay, Lightworkers, now stand side by side in a circle and let's pass energy through our hands to all our neighbors." She had the energy move first in a clockwise direction. Mare consciously passed energy from her right hand to the woman whose hand she was holding. She felt it move. She felt a warmth come from the woman's hand to her left. She imagined receiving it, and again moving it through her to the right. After a few minutes, Mare sensed a constant flow coming through her left and moving through her arms to the right all throughout the circle of women. It felt continual. It felt wonderful and powerful.

Next the women lay back onto the floor and closed their eyes, relaxing and noticing the flow of movement through their bodies. Before Mare closed her eyes, she looked up at the many lights that formed a circle over their heads. It was dark in most of the room, but a faint orange glow emanated from this circle overhead, a starry constellation of luminescent bulbs. Mare smiled and closed her eyes.

At the end of the workshop, Mare approached Jane to thank her. "It was wonderful, Jane!"

"I'm so glad you enjoyed it," the woman reached out to hug her. "It was a pleasure having you here. Come back again. Sometime I would like to have a class for couples, maybe you and Pete can join us then."

"I would love that, Jane. Let me know when you organize one."

*   *   *   *

4/24/98—"Quintuplets!"

I am trying to get pregnant. I take some blood tests, but all of the early ones come back negative. I live in the city in an apartment complex. I talk on the phone with doctors who inform me that the most recent test

has come back positive. I need to come in for an ultrasound, because the doctors suspect it will be a multiple birth.

In the ultrasound, it looks like I'm already three or four months along. We see two babies clearly. I am happy to be pregnant, but the thought of two scares me. Wait a minute, there is another. Wow, you are going to have triplets, he tells me. Let's look a little more. He moves my stomach around a little. Oh my, there are two more! Five babies in my belly?! That can't be! I already (in the dream) have two boys. I panic! I can't have five babies and two older boys in my life. How can I possibly work and take care of seven?

I talk to others including my friend, Emma, on the phone about what we should do. Pete seems less worried than I. I pretty much make up my mind to abort some for their health and my sanity, but how many? I feel pressure from the woman who just had septuplets to keep them all, but I can't imagine taking care of that many offspring.

What am I conceiving and "giving birth to" in my future? My book or books, maybe?

*   *   *   *

Pete and Mare took a vacation in Boston. They walked around the familiar streets happily, hand in hand. They did not get a chance to take many vacations.

Mare wanted to go see a show on the other side of town. It was a musical based on the book *I Know Why the Caged Bird Sings* by Maya Angelou.

When the train came up from the underground tunnel it had been following, a group of Asian men started to encourage all the passengers to lean to one side of the train. It was about to come to a famous curve in the tracks that followed along Comm Ave. They wanted everyone to lean to the right like a rider on a motorcycle might. Mare was worried they would tip the train over. She had no idea why they were doing this. She and Pete tried to lean the opposite way. The train began to go around a notoriously sharp curve, one at which many trains have been known to overturn.

Mare looked up toward the driver—a large, African-American woman. "That driver is purposely speeding up, Pete." The train barely stayed upright and Mare was furious at the woman's apparent carelessness.

She got up and marched to the front of the train.

"Why did you do that?" she demanded to know. "Are you trying to kill us all?" While Mare was trying to express herself, one of the Asian men near the door started grabbing at Mare's private parts. She pushed him away, highly frustrated.

He did it again. This chain of events repeated about four times until Mare forcefully threw him out the door and off the train.

A phone rang and the driver answered it. She handed the receiver to Mare. On the line was the powerful voice of another woman who sounded just like Maya Angelou. Mare told the woman this impression, but she simply laughed.

Maya's voice asked the woman, "Are you Mare Lumen?"

"Yes."

"Last time you were in the neighborhood you left some photographs on the train. Please go to the customer service office and pick them up."

Mare got off the train and went to the office by herself. Two women stood behind the counter. Mare spoke to the one on the right. "I was told you had some photographs for me."

The woman on the left answered, "I can help you."

It was her Aunt Becky. She hadn't seen her since she had divorced Mare's uncle when Mare was a child. During their last phone conversation, Mare had asked her, "Are you happy?" Her former aunt, having struggled through a couple of marriages, had trouble answering her question.

Becky flopped a gallon-size, zip-lock bag onto the counter. "Here you go. You left this on the train last time."

The baggie was full of her internal organs. She could see her heart beating. Many of the organs looked like raw chicken breasts, but Mare could see the heart clearly. She headed for the exit slowly, but she was thinking—*I have no heart inside me. How can I even move without my heart and internal organs?* This thought caused her movement to creak to slow motion. She asked the women to help her, which they did. With great difficulty, Mare crossed the street and heavily made her way towards the hospital on the other side. Instead of entering the front door of the hospital, her curiosity drove her around to the back of the building, down an alleyway. She saw a shiny, silver trashcan. She opened the zip-lock bag and spread her organs out over the lid of the metallic trashcan. She looked at her organs, amazed that they were not inside her, and yet she was still moving.

Another woman approached her and Mare quickly began to put her organs back into the bag, noticing simultaneously that some dirt had gotten on them in the process. Mare turned to see that the other woman had also pulled out a bag of organs. She spread them out on top of the lid as well. A man came by with his organs. Mare quickly tried to leave, feeling somewhat embarrassed and in a hurry. Yet, in some ways, she felt better. She had reclaimed something that was hers.

30

The Waves of Inner Life

Row, row, row your boat, gently down the stream,
merrily, merrily, merrily, merrily, life is but a dream.

—*traditional children's song*

Mare was hovering between lucidity and sleep. In this realm between waking and dreaming, images drifted through her mind. She had been training herself to remember her dreams, and this was the place to fish for them before they got lost in the undertow of her consciousness. The space in-between.

Stealth was required. She was a gentle hunter. Often she could grab the tail of the snake before it went down into its hole, lost forever. If she could grab the tail of the dream, the last trailing remnants of recall, she could usually pull gently on it—hand over hand, reeling it in to her, slowly, without force, so that its substance would remain intact. From the end of the dream, she could begin collecting fragments that would lead her through to the beginning. She hoped to capture each dream in as whole a form as possible. She knew from experience that the more she focused her attention on this, the more aware and alert she was to her dreams, and the more she could also become lucid within the dream.

Deep sleep is the one time of the day that the memory shuts down to rest. The in-between or hypnogogic stage of sleep is the place where the dreamer again has access to her memory, so that she can record dreams. The mind is also relaxed enough to sneak some of the dream content through. Mare straddled this gap, trying to pull content from one side over to the other. Mare wanted to be able to record dreams, so that she could better harvest their meaning and power. She understood that dreams served different functions,

302

and that the earliest dream cycles were generally clearance dreams, dreams whose purpose was to review the day, confront fears and stresses, and purge their negative impact to whatever degree possible.

Not all dreams held earth-shattering significance. On this she would agree with Tristan. Mare knew that dreams could reflect physiological stimuli, but she also felt certain that some dreams were bigger—spiritually derived and directed. She wanted to remain aware and awake to those possibilities.

Her dream journal sat on her nightstand, along with a pencil. Once she had grasped the tiny tip of the snake's tail, she would reach over to her notepad, eyes still closed, room still completely dark, mind quiet, and begin recording the fragments. She didn't see what she was writing; she just scribbled and tried to decipher the notes in the light of morning. An image. A feeling. A word. Sometimes a song that was running through her mind. Whatever was left of the dream, she jotted down.

Occasionally the dream was strong and clear and did not require a lot of detective work. Others were more slippery, and only left winding tracks in the dust of her consciousness. She would collect whatever remained, and place them into her basket. When she could find no more, she went to work on putting the pieces back together and extracting any insights she could glean.

Years later, she learned that writing the details of her own story would prove to be a similar challenge.

Life—from retrospect—is like a dream.

5/1/98—"Conception"

Background: It is the 17th day in my menstrual cycle, which is the time during my cycle that we believe Cody was conceived. Pete and I tried for a baby again last night.

I am outside in the backyard. My consciousness seems human in nature, but the actions of the other people and me in the dream seem "different." Many other "beings" wander and move about the yard. One word is in my head CONCEPTION. We creatures are all trying to conceive—to reproduce. However, there is nothing sexual in the process we go through in the dream. We are in a great hurry. We seem to be in competition to "get it done" first. And yet we also seem to be in cooperation somehow, as if it is important that at least one pair of us succeeds in reproducing. I race to construct a sort of egg-like sculpture. I put certain pieces into it in layers like a sandwich. I shape it. I add some sticky clear adhesive stuff and then enclose it within a shell. I do this two times. The first time fails. The sec-

ond time I race against time, and finish just in the nick of time. I am relieved and excited. I made it! I completed it in time before I died! (Our deaths had all seemed imminent.) In fact, one member of the group went behind a shed to die.

Note: I am perplexed about the whole death and urgency aspect of this dream. Was I going to give birth and then die? That didn't feel right. It did make me think of salmon swimming upstream to spawn and then die. Then I began to associate the dream with sperm. Had I somehow dreamt on a microscopic level of consciousness? Do sperm have any kind of consciousness, and could I possibly tap into that in dreaming? It seemed like the egg/sperm in my body were running out of time and had to form a blastocyst quickly before they all died. Can our bodies communicate with us about what is happening within it, and can that information be given symbolically in dreams?

Mare woke to Pete shaking her shoulder.

"Are you coming to bed?"

"Oh, sorry," Mare rubbed her eyes, and started to get up. "I fell asleep after reading and singing to Cody."

"Yah, I know. You've been doing that a lot lately."

Mare frowned in concern. "Sorry, I just get so tired that going through the bedtime routine with him gets me yawning and ready to sleep too. His bedtime routine has become mine. As soon as I snuggle up to him and my head hits the pillow, I'm out."

He nodded dubiously. Mare put a t-shirt on and crawled into bed. Pete slid over closer to his wife and started to kiss her neck and stroke at her breasts. Mare's body recoiled.

"What's wrong?"

"It was just kind of an abrupt transition, Pete. I was sleeping; you were angry. Now you want to get it on." She sighed. "My body and mind need some gentle coaxing first."

"You aren't attracted to me anymore. You don't love me."

Is this a setup or what? "That isn't true, Pete. You know I love you. I just don't like feeling backed into a corner. I mean, it's like you want to snap your fingers whenever you like and be serviced. I need more than that. I just don't want to feel like I'm being groped. I want to be ready. I want there to be some intimacy when we start to touch each other. It almost feels to me like you do exactly what you know I'm not going to like. Exactly the things I've asked you over and over again not to do."

"Well, I have to try something. Nothing I do ever works. I might as well give up."

"What is it that you want from me, Pete," Mare asked sincerely.

"I want my wife to want me. I want to feel loved."

"And how would you know if you were loved and wanted. What would I be doing?"

"You would respond positively to me when I touch you. You would want to touch me. You never initiate anymore."

They were reasonable desires. "I am sorry if you have felt neglected, Pete. I really am. I don't know how to explain what I'm feeling, but I want to. I just need a little attention that isn't sexual. We are parents, and we have many responsibilities as parents. I know that technically I have wifely duties as well, but I don't want my relationship with you to be based upon duty. That would feel too much like … like prostitution …"

"Great, now my wife feels like a hooker when she's with me. That's just fucking wonderful."

"No, no, you misunderstand. I want to be close to you. I want to be intimate. But the more you keep pushing me and pushing me about it, the harder it is for me to be receptive to it, or even initiate it myself. I want to know that I am more than just a body … that you know there is more to me than the flesh I'm wearing. I don't want to feel obligated to perform; I want to want it, Pete. I don't want to just go through the motions. I want to build a relationship of substance to go along with our physical intimacy. Does that make any sense?"

"Oh yeah," he said sarcastically. "Makes perfect sense to me. When are you going to talk to Austin anyway? Maybe you just need to get him out of your system."

"Pete …" she whispered.

Her husband turned off the light and rolled away from her.

5/1/98—"Knives in me"

I go into my "dream" apartment. I think someone, an enemy, is out to get me, so I am careful. (I think I am a man in the dream.) Indeed, another man waits for me. When I enter, he begins to throw small knives at me as I try to escape. When I run through the apartment, I pass a set of knives, so I grab some and I start to throw them at the offender. I am hit a few times, and the knives are still in me.

* * * *

I am one day late, Mare thought as she reached toward the shelf with the home pregnancy kits. She walked up to the cash registers and looked around to make sure that one of her students would not be ringing up her groceries. By the time her order was cruising down the mini conveyor belt, a teenage set of hands began filling her cloth bags. "Hi, Mrs. Lumen," the young man chirped.

"Oohh, hello, Charlie," she responded hesitantly, waiting for her pregnancy test to tumble into his young hands.

"I read those chapters you assigned."

"Great, great," she looked away as he picked up the box. In her peripheral vision, she noticed he glanced at the box, and then tossed it into the canvas bag. He said nothing, much to her relief.

At home Mare read and followed the instructions. She urinated onto the test stick and then let her bladder empty. She sat there. Waiting. *Was there more?* A feeling of fullness remained, even though she could go no more. A heavy need that she could not release, but she could feel being held back like a delicate treasure hanging suspended in a tightly woven net.

She sat down on the closed toilet lid and gathered her knees towards her. She could see the changes to the test stick from where she sat.

The affirmative red lines did not appear. According to the test, she was not pregnant. Her temples were throbbing.

Later that day, she began to bleed. Her uterus ached as waves of motion passed through it. She laid down on the couch in the fetal position and placed her cold hands over her hot abdomen. The first day of her cycle always came on strong. Her face was white as a sheet.

She wanted to let it all go out from her. She tried to concentrate on the pain as a friend had taught her. What size and shape is it? How much water would the space hold? What color is the pain? She cycled through the questions a few times to no avail. The pain continued. I need a release. Then the thought struck her. Orgasm. Sometimes that helps.

She ran upstairs and climbed into bed. Fortunately, Cody was shopping with his grandmother and Pete was fishing for the weekend with his father. She was alone. She slipped under the covers and grabbed her vibrator from the back of her bed. Technically, it was a back massager/wand, for external use only. A friend had encouraged her to buy one in college when she discovered that Mare had never experienced orgasm. The first time she came was a small sensation, and she thought, is that it? But later the experiences would intensify. Then Mare remembered a few dream orgasms she had experienced as a young woman. But never with a man. Pete had been the first, and only then by being crafty did he find success. They both knew it was a mental game. The strategy he finally settled on was to perform oral sex on her, and then stop periodically when he thought she was getting close. Reverse psychology. "Nope, don't come. I won't let you," he would say. He kept starting and stopping until she couldn't hold back anymore. Pete knew she wanted to, and that she wasn't holding back on purpose, but her rational mind would get in the way. The longer she took, the more pressure she felt and guilt. She felt guilty about receiving the attention for so long and not being able to produce the result they both desired. Using reverse psychology on Mare took away the pressure and appealed to the rebel in her—*go ahead and tell me I can't do it, and I'll prove you wrong!* It was a celebrated victory when they found success, and though it got easier for Mare to climax with Pete during cunnilingus, it was never easy. She never did have orgasms during intercourse—a fact that frustrated them both. He claimed she did once when they had been drinking, but Mare had no recollection of it, and concluded it was his wishful thinking.

Even alone with the massager, Mare had to fantasize to focus her mind on the pleasure. Yet most of her fantasies were from an observer standpoint. She was rarely *in* them. Often, she fantasized about Pete being with a porn star, actress or other character. It was almost as if she needed to remove her mind from the picture, and only through identifying with a woman who could experience the greatest passion and pleasure could she find the freedom to release her own. Mare found freedom in living out some alternate persona, though she didn't know why.

She would have given almost anything to climax easily and quickly, almost as much for her man's sake as for her own. *To be able to let go ... to trust that completely ...*

I wonder if the Big Bang was just God experiencing orgasm. Contract ... Expand ... Mare chuckled to herself, but then her thoughts turned more serious and sad. *I want to merge with Pete so closely that we feel like one. It goes beyond physical bonding. It's a spiritual co-mingling as well. Why does it seem so hard?*

*   *   *   *

Mare picked up the phone. "Hello."

"Have you heard about Chief Rolf? He's been asked to resign and it's all hush-hush. I wonder if the rumors were true about him getting the girl pregnant?"

"Hard to say. I heard something about him being caught with child pornography on his computer or some such thing. Who knows what happened, but whatever it was, the truth apparently caught up with him ... finally."

*   *   *   *

Dear Mare and Pete,

Got your card the other day. Thanks. As far as my fight goes I didn't punch anyone. I just threw him around a little. The other inmates were very surprised because usually I simply ignore them. Amazingly, no one hassles me anymore. People still yell shit when I'm walking away, but only when I can't see who it is. They're not afraid of me, but now I'm "unpredictable." They don't want a write-up any more than I do. So they've let up. I was looking for a couch, but threw him over a garbage can instead.

At first I was working everyday, but the last two weeks I've only worked one day. Part of that was because of my fight. Now I also have to serve a 10-day room restriction. That means no working.

Can one of you do me a favor? There's a doctor who's the director of the National Institute on Drug Abuse. He's doing research into the biochemical aspects of addiction, and I want to ask him a few questions. Could you see if you could find his address for me? Thanks.

I stopped writing my book for now. I think I was writing it for the wrong reasons, and I want to take it in a different direction. Plus, I get no privacy here; it's hard to concentrate. A computer would be nice too.

I guess Chief Rolf is going to get away with whatever he did. The town council had meetings about it, but they never reported the reasons for the investigation in the papers. Everybody has been talking about why he got fired, but officially they're keeping it very quiet. Apparently the town is not going to press charges. As much as I dislike him, I also feel sorry for him, because if he ends up in here, I know what hell he'll have to go through. A police officer, especially. There would be no end to his harassment. I wouldn't wish this on my worst enemy.

Mare, I have a question for you. If you were in my position and you knew someone who works for the school district who has the same condition that I have, what would you do? I ask because I am 99.9% sure I know someone, but I know not because I saw something, but because this person's life and mine run parallel to each other. It's not just a feeling—I know he is a pedophile. He interacts with kids exactly the way I did. Anytime someone goes as far out of their way to talk to kids as this person did the times I saw him, I would be suspicious. I could see in his eyes how his mood changed and how he seemed to "light up" when he was around them. I know whenever I was around the guys I always felt this kind of high. Like I was suddenly happier, more full of energy, move alive. That high has nothing to do with sex, but I became addicted to that "high" and without it I became very depressed, so I sought it out. I'm sure you've felt it before with someone who makes you feel that way, makes you feel like you are on top of the world, important and loved. I saw that in this person. Maybe he hasn't crossed the sexual barrier yet, but I believe he's in danger. You could say it's speculation, but it's more than that. Our paths have crossed a few times, but I've never been friendly with him. I won't report him, because I don't "know" anything, and for him to go to jail is not the answer to anything, in my opinion. I don't know what to do. Confronting him is not the answer. I was confronted dozens of times by parents and others. I was always cool, understanding of their concern, and very believable in my denial. The only answer is to educate him. Maybe schools could set up programs to talk to teachers and coaches, and have sex offenders speak. If it comes from anyone else, it will be discounted. This man is not a bad person, but he needs help, whether he knows it or not. We are not all the same, but most of us do care. Most of us care too much and get too close.

Everyone at my group counseling session cried when they told their stories, and all of us were seconds away from ending our own lives before we were ever caught. Setting up a program at school would not only educate this man I'm thinking of, but others who are in the system. Schools and camps are the "target market" for people with this problem. Almost all pedophiles are drawn to these positions, so that they can get their "high" on a regular basis. When I say high, I mean the feeling of love and importance.

I hope society will give us an opportunity to voluntarily get help without mandatory reporting. Anyway, I guess you've heard me say that before.

Take care,
Seth

"Did you read this letter Seth wrote, Pete?"
"Yeah, why?"
"Who do you think he's talking about as having his problem?"
"I don't know; do you?"
"I have a few ideas, but I'm not sure. I think he should write the person a letter or something, don't you? I mean, maybe if he starts a dialogue with this person, and if it is true, maybe he'll be able to get some help."
"And what if Seth's imagining things? He can't accuse someone of something like that, Mare, unless he's pretty sure. Plus, like he said, they won't listen."

Setting up programs at school systems ... How could that be done? It scared her to think about people with Seth's problems in schools, but the idea of getting people with his problem help did appeal to the mother and teacher in her.

"He did sound pretty sure. Intuition is something that shouldn't be ignored," she told Pete. "If Seth senses something, it should be checked out."

*   *   *   *

When Mare regained consciousness, she was lying on an examination table. A frightening creature beyond her ability to describe and almost beyond her ability to look at was leaning over her. He had cut her open and was tinkering with her organs. She now realized she was dreaming, and, as soon as she did, she had the power to escape and control her destiny. She released herself and left the mall-like chambers of her captivity. She returned home and took a bath to cleanse herself. Then she decided that she wanted to fly again. Going into the bedroom, she tried to rouse Pete, so that he could soar around town with her. She wanted him to experience flying. Groggily, he got up and tried to fly, but he couldn't get very far. He seemed to lack the energy. He went back to bed.

Next, Mare tried to get her sister to join her, but she made little progress with her as well. Then Mare remembered promising Roger that she would come and get him if she ever became lucid, so she willed herself to find him. She began to fly west in the direction of Roger's hometown.

A breeze was blowing through her hair as she flew over Lake Pennabago. She looked down. The surface of the two-by seven-mile lake was entirely covered with birds' nests! Each nest contained exactly three bright blue eggs. Every inch of the lake was covered with nests and in every single nest were three blue eggs.

31

Longing and Disclosure

Those who hear not the music ... think the dancers mad."

~Unknown

Mare splashed her feet in the water of the lake. It was the last day of school for seniors, and they were celebrating with the annual senior picnic. Bikini-clad eighteen-year-old women sunned near the waves, while the young men about to graduate tossed footballs around them. A few teachers wandered about, chatting with students who were moving on to college and jobs, saying good-bye, and trading laughs. Mare had asked to help chaperone the event. She was the class advisor for the juniors. Next year, she would need to help run the event for her own seniors.

But the real reason was that she wanted to be around Austin one last time. She wanted to ask him to stop by her room after the traditional senior count-down on this, his last day of high school. He smiled at her a few times, and after lunch, when other seniors were beginning to throw teachers in, as they did every year, Austin had gathered a few friends and former students of Mare's to toss her in the drink. She resisted and ran, but when they caught up with her and grabbed her arms and legs, she muckled onto them. She wasn't going in alone. Austin had her legs and Mare managed to clamp them around his hips. Her legs were strong and there was no way he was getting out of a soaking. Two other students had her thrashing arms, and she was able to encircle the waist of one of them with one of her arms. They tried to drop her, but two of the three guys went down with her. They all came up laughing, but Mare took off after the one who had escaped. She snatched his foot while he was taking off. He tripped and fell face first into the water. Satisfied, Mare began squeezing out her tee shirt and walked back up to the beach.

Now that she was already wet, she helped the teens nab the vice-principal and dunk him as well.

As kids were packing up and heading back to the parking lot to load up cars and buses, Mare tried to catch up with Austin. She had to speak with him before he left school for good.

Slightly out of breath, she touched his arm to stop him.

"What's up, Miz L?"

"Would you stop by my room after the countdown and before you leave? I have something I want to give you before you leave."

He gave her a look that asked *what have you been up to*. "Sure. I'll be there. Okay."

When Mare reentered the building, she could see that mob of seniors clustered around the front desk of the main office. Over the loud speaker, she heard the collection of voices count down their last seconds of high school.

Mare waited in her room, knowing that seniors were now roaming the halls, saying goodbye to teachers and underclassmen. Her heart was thudding hard, and her stomach was churning. *After all this time, I'm finally going to be able to say something to him.*

About twenty minutes later, Austin nervously poked his head through the door to Mare's room. "Hi," she greeted him. "Come on in. How does it feel to have finished your last day of school anyway?"

"Great!" he gushed. "And a little sad. I'm going to miss a lot of people here, especially when I move back closer to my mom in Louisiana."

"Well, we will miss you too. In fact, I got a little something for you to celebrate your accomplishments and to make sure you don't forget about us." She outstretched a gold papered-package with an enveloped taped to the top.

He looked at her with gratitude. "You didn't have to do that," he said tenderly.

"I know. I wanted to."

He opened the card first. The front of the card said, "Those who hear not the music think the dancers mad." Mare watched his expressions as he read her words.

6/4/98

My Dear Austin—

Congratulations! I'm sure you have been looking forward to graduating for a long time. Though I am happy for you that you are entering a new era in your life, I am myself pretty bummed at the thought of not seeing you around this place anymore. It won't be the same without your smiling face. Teachers aren't supposed to get too attached to students, but you are different. And I have to tell you—you have come to mean a great deal to me.

I've been trying to hold this in for a long time, but now there are a few things I want you to know before you go. You are aware of how difficult this last year or so has been for me. Truly, the most painful experiences I've ever had to endure happened during this time. My personal life has been in an almost constant state of chaos. I have learned a lot, but DAMN, it was hard! Why am I saying all this to you? Because I don't think you realize, at least not fully, how much you have helped me to survive this nightmare. Whenever I am around you—I'm not sure what it is—but I <u>feel</u> <u>better</u>! Somehow you lift my spirits and I always look forward to seeing you. Am I crazy?

I have wanted to acknowledge this to you for what seems like an eternity, and now that you're graduating, it seems more appropriate than before for me to talk about it, but even now I can't express what I'm feeling fully. I don't have the words for it or perhaps I lack the courage. My senses have been telling me that you and I have a special connection, and I won't ever forget it.

Your carefree nature, and your rebellious, yet playful spirit are qualities that I have really come to appreciate in you. Perhaps because I saw reflections of myself in you that I feared I was losing. I don't want to lose that fire.... Thank you for keeping that piece of me alive.

I will always be grateful to you for the role you played in this significant phase of my life!

Let's keep in touch. I want to hear that you are doing well, and that you are happy where you are going. Take care of yourself and your future! Before you go, I would really like to hear you call me by my first name. Hey! And you still owe me a dance. Nobody hears the music like we do! Have a wonderful life!

Fondly,

Me

His eyes lifted off the page and towards her. They paused on hers. Then he opened his arms and started walking to her. "Thank you so much," he whispered and paused, "Mare. That means a lot to me." The woman smiled to hear the words. He held onto her tightly, and she reveled in the hug she always wanted. As he was letting go, he added, "I am really going to miss you, too." His big brown eyes contained a warmth that filled her heart with comfort and affection.

"I meant what I said, Austin; you have helped me so much. Open the package. It's something to remember your friends here in Maine, particularly me."

He tore off the wrapping and opened the box. Within was a blue tee shirt with a handsome imprint of the State of Maine on the front. The words said, "Remember ME." The initials were intended to refer to Maine, but whenever he would wear the shirt, he would also have to think of her.

"Please don't forget me," she asked gently.

He hugged her again. "I could never do that," he admitted. They shared one more silent moment of eye contact as they sat on the desktops facing each other.

Austin said, "I've got some friends waiting for me out in the parking lot … so I need to go now. Are you coming to graduation?"

"Yes, I will be there."

"Great, my mom's supposed to be there. I would like for you to meet her."

"I'd be happy to. And I want a picture with you as well."

He nodded in agreement. As he was exiting her room, he suggested that she come and visit him this summer. He would be working out in the weight room quite a bit at school still. "We can talk a little more."

"Okay, I will. Enjoy your weekend. Please be smart and safe."

"I promise. See you at graduation!"

"Bye now."

Mare inhaled a few deep breaths after he left and walked over to the window. So many longings had been filled with the two of them just hugging each other. Her body had gotten a small satisfaction for its desires from the embrace. Mare hoped that now she could be free of it.

*   *   *   *

Pete talked Mare into blowing up the back end of a department store for fun. Mare's fingerprints were all over the place. She was almost immediately arrested. She talked to a female sergeant about Cody. The woman told Mare she would probably get three years in prison.

Mare was devastated. She looked for other ways around it so that both Pete and she would not be in jail at the same time, so that one of them could be with Cody.

"This is your fault, Pete," Mare said, watching her husband be led away in handcuffs while hers were being clamped on.

Pete cried.

I knew that I should be more careful about making mistakes. Now look at me. I'm going to jail.

*   *   *   *

"I gave Austin a letter, Pete, and thanked him for being a help to me through some of these difficult times. I didn't tell him about the dreams and everything. I just kept it vague. I mostly just thanked him for being who he was and for helping me through a tough time."

"Good. Do you feel better about it?"

"Yes, it was good to finally acknowledge at least a little of the truth. We may get together and talk about it a little more this summer. Would that be okay with you? Now that he's officially an adult, I am curious if he had dreams too. I feel like there was more that needed to be said, but we didn't have a lot of time. Maybe we could get together for coffee or something."

"I think you guys should just fuck and get it out of your systems."

"Pete, no! I told you that my dreams of him weren't sexual. I've only had urges to kiss him."

"Well, it seems like you need to do something about it."

"Well, it's not going to be that. I took vows, Pete, and I mean to keep them."

Maybe we could just go dancing or something. Watching him dance at these other events has made me want to dance with him.

At the end of the graduation ceremony, when all students had lit their individual candles from the common source, many of the 250 graduating seniors lit up cigars. Austin was still puffing on his when Mare found him, standing near his father, his ex-girlfriend Emily and her friend, Shauna. Mare greeted the girls and somewhat awkwardly asked if one could take a picture of her and Austin. Shauna complied. "Where's your mom?" Mare asked Austin.

"She couldn't make it after all," he replied calmly, but Mare could sense his disappointment. He had not seen his mother for almost a year.

"I'm sorry."

Austin's dad shook Mare's hand and asked her to pose for another picture with his son.

"Thanks for being so good to Austin," his dad patted a hand on her back. "You're his favorite." Mare smiled back at him.

"Well, I've got more students to see. Catch y'all later," she waved.

Mare wandered around giving more hugs and congratulations to other students. She found Kate taking pictures with Trevor's family and waved. Rites of Passage. This was one of the few. It was tough to see students come and go.

Later on, there was a great crowd of students was at Emerson High. Austin had Mare's hand and was leading her through the backstage area of the auditorium. Other students were milling about, and some noticed her and Austin, but because it was a dream, the two didn't seem to care. It felt so real.

*   *   *   *

Mare's mother offered to watch Cody a day or two each week during the summer, so Mare could write and have some time to herself.

Certain things made Mare feel better. Being outdoors was the big one … dancing, writing, those also helped. She was about to discover gardening as another path to healing, one that worked through her at a deep level.

Mare had gotten it into her head that she wanted to create a perennial flower garden next to the house. Pete had helped her prepare the space by rototilling. Mare laid out some hexagonal stepping-stones in a gentle curve from one corner of the area to the other. She bought a birdbath and placed it on the inside edge of one of the curves in the path. She knew very little about gardening, but she learned as she went. Mare drove her spade into the soil to make a place for a giant hosta her sister had given her. She positioned the plant right behind the birdbath. Digging in the dirt centered her. Creating a thing of beauty helped her to let go of the darker places within herself.

"I wonder how the birches are doing after the ice storm this winter." She walked around to the backyard to survey the lingering damage. She and Pete had a lot of work to do this summer cleaning out the debris. Many trees were cut in half. Large limbs were split like broken toothpicks. The white birches, which had bent over from the weight of the ice, were still alive. They had yielded to the weight, but had not broken. They remained arched over, however. The leaves were green and filling in, but Mare doubted that these particular trees would ever stand again.

She turned around and headed back to the front of the house. Despite the destruction in back, Mare was looking forward to designing the side garden and seeing what it would look like when it was filled and in bloom. Much of

Mare's summer would be spent digging. Most of the time she worked without gloves, so she could feel the beautiful earth in her fingers.

*   *   *   *

On one of the days that Cody was at her mother's, Mare put on some shorts, and then she added a little bit of makeup to her face. She went down to school to prepare some work for the next school year. She planned to swing through the weight room to see if Austin was around. She found him doing abdominal crunches with a friend.

"Hi there," she beckoned to him, and nodded to his friend. "Enjoying your summer so far?"

They talked briefly, then on the way out, Mare mentioned, nonchalantly, "you should stop by my room to visit before you leave the building."

About a half hour later, he showed up at her door.

"I want to give you my address in Louisiana," he said. "I'll be staying with my mom and step dad to start."

"Thanks. You mentioned you would like to continue our other conversation and I still have some questions for you. Do you think you could come over to my house sometime to talk?"

She could see him swallow slightly.

"Only if you want to…. I just want to talk."

He nodded. "Yes. Let's do that."

"Can you make Thursday at two o'clock?"

"I'll be there."

She gave him directions.

*   *   *   *

Five minutes after two, she heard his truck rumbling up the driveway. *He's here! Yikes.* She felt a thudding in her chest. *No big deal,* a second voice reassured her.

She opened the door and welcomed him. He was wearing a white bandana over his head with sunglasses over the top. He towered over Mare by about seven inches. Mare noticed he was beginning to grow a blond goatee. Mare felt slightly awkward at first. She told him so. "Thanks for coming, Austin. I thought you might chicken out. I'm sorry if this is uncomfortable."

He reached out and offered her a big hug. Both felt a little more relaxed.

"No, that's alright. It's just a little weird."

"I know."

Mare offered him a soft drink, and pulled a glass out of the cupboard. "So, what have you decided to do next year, Austin?"

"I'm going to a technical school near where my Mom lives. I'm going to get trained to do auto body work."

"Oh really, I know you did the program here at school this year. Do you like working on cars?"

"It's something I know I can do. I didn't get the best grades. I don't know what else I could do."

"You are smarter than you give yourself credit for. You could do anything you set your mind to."

"Yeah, maybe."

The two spent a good ten minutes talking about his plans for the fall and other more mundane topics.

Mare was leaning against the kitchen counter. She looked up at the young man. "Look, Austin, I'm not exactly sure why I asked you up here. I had a chance to tell you some of what I was feeling, but I guess I was wondering—for the sake of confirmation—if what I said struck any chords with you. I've been having dreams about you for almost a year now."

"You have? Really?"

"Yes, some pretty strong dreams that have really rattled me. I have felt a strong connection and chemistry with you for some reason, and I guess I'm trying to understand. I'm wondering if you have felt anything, or if I have just imagined all this."

"No," he cleared his throat and looked away for a moment. It seemed like he was pulling out his own memories. "It wasn't your imagination. I have felt it too. In fact, I have had quite a few dreams about you also."

"What were yours about," he asked.

"Well, in the dreams I felt like you understood me and that you appreciated me. I felt like you were an ally. The dreams weren't sexual that I remember, but they were very … affectionate."

"Oh," he sighed. "Some of mine were … sexual. I have to admit. This is weird, isn't it? I want you to know that it's hard for me to talk about this stuff. It's hard for me to open up and trust people. I don't even talk to my friends about personal stuff very often."

Mare nodded, "I understand. We've all been hurt."

"It isn't an easy thing to talk about, but I tell you—it makes me feel much better to know that it wasn't purely one-sided. I was hoping I wasn't simply delusional."

He laughed. "No, there is something about you that is very comfortable and … attractive." He held her gaze for a moment, then looked away.

"Thanks, Austin. This has been driving me crazy. You were my student. I am a married mother. I wasn't supposed to have these kinds of feelings about you, but I didn't know how to shake it. I talked to Pete about it …"

"You DID?" he reacted in astonishment.

"Yes. In fact, I also told him you were coming over this week."

His eyes swelled wide. "Wow. What does he think about all this? It's gotta be freaky for him."

"Yeah. When I first told him, he was really cool about it, but he's gone back and forth. Sometimes he jokes about it, without feeling threatened; other times, he gets very jealous and defensive. I never wanted to hurt him. I was just trying to make sense of the dreams I was having and what I was feeling. This last year has put a lot of strain on our marriage. Things have been missing in the marriage that I thought we could work on if I was honest with him about what I was feeling. You see, in some ways, the things that appeal to me about my connection with you are the things lacking in my relationship with my husband. I thought talking about it with him would help. Sometimes it did."

"I'm impressed that you told him, and amazed that he could listen."

"I want to rebuild our relationship, but first we have both felt like I needed to get you out of my system."

Austin shook his head slightly in disbelief. "It's so unreal. I think about you too, but … you know … the situation being as it is."

Mare nodded, indicating that he didn't need to elaborate. "Do you know, when I was nineteen … pretty close to your age … I lived with a man who was fifteen years older than I was? I was nineteen and he was 34."

"You did? How come?"

"He was a very active and attractive man. I didn't see the age thing as a problem. People are people, despite their age. He was older, but when I looked at him, I didn't see his age. I saw his vitality and strength. He was fifteen years older, but we were both consenting adults and neither of us was seeing anyone else. Your heart loves who it loves. We click with certain people … I don't know why. I can't quite explain the mysteries of what connects two people, but it happens. Your mind can tell you that it isn't right—that the person is too young or too old or married or otherwise off limits, but your heart has a will of its own." She looked at Austin and frowned a little. "I can't control my feelings or my dreams either … Lord knows I tried. I can only control what I do about them. I can control my actions. I have tried to be honest, not only with myself, but with those around me … to you and Pete, especially. I have tried to maintain my integrity and be true to myself at the same time. It hasn't always been easy to figure out."

Austin nodded like he could understand that.

Mare decided it was time to change the subject. "Hey, I got the pictures back from graduation." She pulled them out. "You've got that stinking stogey in your mouth. Can hardly see your face."

He covered his mouth and laughed.

"So you are going to have to pose for one more picture, so I can have a good one to keep."

"Okay."

Mare led him into the stove room and directed him to sit. She got out the camera and set it up for auto-timer. She realized the curtain behind the futon would need to be shut, so she climbed onto it to pull the curtains closed. She didn't want the sunlight to ruin the exposure. She felt Austin's eyes on her legs as she climbed up. She was conscious of the exposure of her thighs to him as she stepped down. The two sat shoulder to shoulder on the couch and smiled for two shots.

One of Mare's favorite songs came on the radio. "Uninvited" by Alannis Morrisette. "This song reminds me of you for some reason, Austin. Whenever I hear it, I think of you. It's from the movie *City of Angels*."

"Really? I love this song."

"Yes, this one and the one by Fastball … "The Way," I think it's called."

"Oh yeah, that one is cool too! Wow! That's bizarre!"

He studied her face like she was a mind reader or something. He put a finger to his lip.

"You know, Austin, I have this book, you might like. It's called *The Life You Were Born to Live*. I don't know whether I believe its claims or not, but I like the author, Dan Millman. He has some great books. He says you can add up the numbers from the day you were born." She grabbed a piece of paper. "What was your birthday again?" He told her. "You get another number that tells you about what you are here to work on in this life. Like I said, I don't know how it can possibly work, but I checked mine and it's very accurate. I'm a 29/11, which is double creativity and confidence. It talks about my need to be confident about expressing myself and that I have extraordinary energy to accomplish creative tasks when I am working in the positive."

"That's pretty interesting."

"Yes, did I tell you I am working on a book about my experiences?"

"No way, you are? That is totally cool! I look forward to reading it one day."

"Yeah, well, you are going to be a character in it, I imagine, so what would you like to be called. I have to change the names."

He considered the idea for a few minutes. "Hmmm …" He gave her a name. "How about that?"

"Great! That is the one I will use."

"Let's add up your numbers." He gave her the information and she added the totals. "You are a 34/7. Your primary focus is on issues of Trust and Openness. That's cool. You were just talking about that!"

"Hey, I want to hear more about that?"

"Sure." They skimmed a chapter or two together and talked about how accurate it was for him.

"You know, Austin, I'm not sure that Auto Body is going to be enough for you. You have great energy, and there's something about you that's very spiritual. You are sensitive to energy, from what I've seen. I think you need to work with people somehow, not cars. I think you are the kind of person who needs to help people. Maybe you want to consider the possibility of another career before you decide. I think you would be wonderful in the healing arts. You are great at bringing people's spirits up. You certainly helped mine." She smiled.

"I will think about it. Can I get a copy of this chapter?" He said with some enthusiasm for the idea.

"Sure, I'll send you one."

"Well," both were getting the impression that the visit was almost over. "So, is this going to be goodbye? Will this be the last time I see you before you move to Louisiana?"

"No," he crooned. "We should get together. Do something. This was fun talking. I'm really glad we did."

"You do still owe me a dance. We keep talking about it, but we've never actually had one. It's too bad you are not 21 yet; we could hit a pub and go dancing."

"I could get in."

"Well, you do look older, but I don't want you to get in trouble, especially not with me."

"I understand. Well, let's do lunch or something, if that doesn't work."

"Mmmmm, how about next weekend?"

"I may go camping."

"Okay, let's talk by phone sometime before then."

She looked at him again. "No, you are NOT going to want to do anything. It's crazy. We might as well just say goodbye now."

"No! I WILL see you before I leave. I promise I will."

"If you say so." Mare hugged him goodbye, and watched him drive off.

"So, are you going to sleep with him?" her husband asked later, somewhat playfully.

"Pete, will you stop saying that—no, absolutely not."

"Well, are you going to kiss him? Or let him get into your pants."

"Do you want me to kiss him?"

"Not really, but I think maybe you need to."

"I don't think so. I would like to just go dancing maybe."

For the rest of that week, Pete teetered between jealousy and amusement.

*   *   *   *

6/26/98—"Protecting the Cave"

I'm a military trainee of some sort. I talk with a general, as if he is a mentor. Although we are supposed to be learning, our unit has been tasked to regain a strategic site, a cave on the side of a mountain. One night, when the cave is back in our possession, I converse with the general on our way to protect it. He tells me the war was over a long time ago, except for this one hill/cliff/cave. This puzzles me. The general is killed or dies. I take it upon myself to finagle a truce. My rationale: we can't fight when our leader is dead. We must wait. I believe that the other side will respect this.

I have a flirtation with one of the other officers. When we return to base, we get together and plan to spend the night. He touches my breasts, but he is a bit cold and standoffish. I seem to want to get close to him, and yet, at the same time, he is very annoying and I know we are not for each other.

Note: The war theme is of interest. Do these two sides represent parts of myself? What does the general represent? The one that usually keeps order and gives the directions? I am leaderless in a traditional sense? More breasts!

*   *   *   *

Sitting in the center of Pizza Hut, sipping a Sam Adams, Mare confided to Sophie about her visit with Austin. Sophie was aware of the dreams Mare had been having, and was listening closely to what her friend was saying.

"Well, what do you want to do now?"

"I really want to see him again. I want to be friends and hang out a little."

"Is that all?"

"Well, I would like to kiss him too, but I think that would be going too far. That's what my body wants. My brain and my body are in conflict over this. Being around Austin makes me feel alive and happy. Why is that? I have been having trouble getting him out of my system, even though I know I should."

"My goodness, Mare, you've been through so much, and things haven't been easy with Pete. I'm not surprised you are feeling this way. Tristan and I have been worried about you this last year. You seemed to be so strong with everything, and yet I know you've been hurting."

Mare looked down. "I know. I'm not even sure that it's Austin specifically that's affecting me. I wonder if it isn't just what he represents. You know, youth and flirtation and playfulness. He knows how to have fun, and I want that carefree spirit that he seems to possess. I know my own is in here somewhere, and his calls to mine like they are long lost friends finally reunited. I don't seem able to control the feeling."

Sophie nodded with understanding.

"I walk around the halls and see these kids kissing and hugging and holding hands, and I miss that. I miss flirting. I miss first kisses. I miss the passion. I want passion in my life again, Sophie. I want to feel passionate again." She grabbed a saltshaker and fiddled with it in her fingers.

Sophie looked and her sympathetically, wondering how she could help.

"If I could have anything I wanted without worrying about the consequences, I would just kiss him and dance with him for one night out. But of course, I *have* to think about the consequences. I know it's stupid. Maybe he doesn't even want to hang out with an older woman like that. Perhaps he is just humoring me. It's just a fantasy. Why can't I let it stay a fantasy? Why do I feel compelled to act on it in some way?"

"You are only—what—twelve years older than he. You are a beautiful woman, Mare, and I'm sure Austin is well aware of your many positive qualities. He's an attractive guy, and he seems older than eighteen in some respects. Fantasies can be very overwhelming, especially when life has been hard. We need something to hang on to that gives us hope that gives us a sense of vitality and pleasure. Everyone needs that."

"But you don't think I should act on it either?"

Sophie hesitated, out of consideration for her friend, "I just think it would be dangerous for you to tempt yourself in that way. If you open the door a little, how do you know you will be able to stop yourself?"

"I have thought about that. I don't want to be physically unfaithful. I admit that in the last year I have questioned whether Pete and I are meant to be together. I don't think all of these uncertainties are coming from me.

Sometimes I have wondered if we were just meant to be together for the whole Seth crisis, since he was Seth's friend too. Now that we've essentially weathered that, things seem very different. I love Pete, and I want to keep our family together, but what we had before is no longer enough. I want more in the marriage. There's something about the way Austin and I relate that is missing with Pete. I want to be able to put in what's missing, but I haven't had a lot of luck with that. So I keep thinking about Austin. I think I would be able to draw the line with Austin. I'm not sure if Pete is helping or hurting this process either. He has encouraged me to sleep with him, which I'm certain I will not do! That line I'm positive I would not ever cross, but the smaller temptations—now that he's eighteen, and it would not be technically illegal—these thoughts are there and I don't know how to get past them! That is a little more of a gray area."

Sophie, never one to interrupt, waited until Mare was fully finished; then she formulated her words carefully as always. "Pete may say that, but I would be surprised if he means it. It may be a way of testing you. I think he would be very hurt if you did spend that kind of private time with Austin. Almost any spouse would be. Even if you just kissed Austin, Pete would be upset, I believe."

"You are right, I'm sure. How do I shake this, Sophie? It's got me. Maybe I just hang in until he leaves? When he's on the other end of the country, I won't be so attached to him."

The waitress set their pizza on the table and filled their water glasses.

"I think it's commendable that you are asking these questions and that you are trying to search for the right answers for yourself. Most people don't share such feelings. I can't tell you what you should do or shouldn't do, but be careful. I would hate to see you do something that you might regret. You are vulnerable right now." She looked at her friend with compassion. "I want you to be happy, and I'm glad that Austin has helped you to find some joy this year, but I don't want to see you exchange long-term happiness for a temporary feeling of relief."

Mare frowned and nodded. "Thank you, Sophie. You are such a good friend. I guess I will just wait and see. We are supposed to talk later this week. Maybe everything will fall through anyway, and I won't have to face the decision. I don't really want to make the decision. I wish someone would just make it for me, but I guess it's not that easy." Mare took a few bites of her food.

*   *   *   *

Later in the week, Mare called Austin. He must have had second thoughts also about the wisdom of them spending more time together. He apologized, saying he had plans to camp with friends. She could tell that at least one of his friends was with him, though he did not say so.

"I understand," she told him. "It probably wasn't the best idea anyway."

"But I would like to see you before I leave. I just can't do it this weekend. I will call you or see you before I leave. I promise." She had a feeling also that he wanted to protect her. He was going to make the decision for both of them. It was what she had asked for. Someone else to make the decision. Maybe that childhood protector is still with me, making sure that my life circumstances go as planned. Austin and Mare were meant to go no further. She felt a mixture of disappointment and relief.

"Okay, have fun, Austin. See ya." But Mare knew she had seen him for the last time.

7/5/98—"Austin's House"

I go over to Austin's house, even though I've never been there in waking life, to say goodbye. I give him back some clothes. His Dad is there, and he thanks me for being so good to his son. Austin and I get in a car and start driving. Cody is with us in his car seat. I steal a quick kiss. He is pleasantly surprised. I try to drive to Pleasant Pond, but people are everywhere and I want to talk privately. I bump into Pete and ask him to take Cody with him. Eventually we go back to Austin's house. Miriam and some police officers are there hanging out with Austin's father. I go back to the car, but then return because I haven't finished with my goal/hope of talking with Austin. One of the cops starts to accuse me of an inappropriate relationship with Austin, saying everyone has been suspicious for some time. I deny it. Nothing inappropriate has ever happened between us, I tell him sincerely. That my husband knows where I am, etc. He doesn't seem to believe me.

*   *   *   *

Mare looked for Austin's truck in the school parking lot. Something in her knew that he had left the state. For days, Mare felt desolate. He broke his promise. He didn't say goodbye. *I just wanted to be able to say goodbye.* She cried, and her mood did not escape her husband's notice.

After a day or two of despondence, she tried to put it all behind her. She decided to write Austin one last letter and be done with it.

Mare pulled out a piece of paper and started writing.

7/6/98

Hi Austin!

You know, it's interesting—you admit to having problems trusting people and opening up about your feelings—and I—can't keep mine from spilling out all over you. I'm sorry! Maybe I shouldn't have put you in the position I did. Lord only knows what you've been thinking since I told you about my intense feelings about you. Am I insane? Sometimes I wonder....

In reality, we haven't had many private/personal conversations. Yet—in the realm of my imagination (in my dreams) we've had a much more intimate relationship.—And I'm finding it difficult to distinguish between the two. The imaginal realm seems almost more vivid to me. (And is certainly very appealing.)

I think I may have been deceiving myself when I told your class that I have never done drugs. I'm beginning to suspect that YOU have been my drug of choice this year. Otherwise, how can I explain these feelings of withdrawal? God, what have you done to me? I've never felt so strongly pulled towards someone I've never touched beyond a friendly hug. (Aside from dream contact, that is.) I can hardly function now, because I don't know where you are ... here or in Louisiana. When did you leave? We should've probably said goodbye that day you came over. It would have been easier for me. I just need some closure, an official goodbye. I don't know whether you tried to contact me before you left, but I certainly would understand if you did not. I'm a married, thirty-one year old mother AND your former teacher to boot. What did I expect?

It's just that over the last year or more, I felt an emotional fullness towards you that has been building, and I have needed some kind of release for it. Telling you helped, and so did our conversation at my house. It meant a lot to me to hear that it all wasn't completely one-sided. It was a relief to me that you shared some similar thoughts. Thanks for opening up to me as much as you did. It must not have been easy. (I'd still love to hear about those dreams of yours. I won't ask if they were good—after all, we are both in our primes. ☺ Men hit theirs at eighteen and women in their thirties, supposedly.) Okay, okay, I'll stop.

Seriously, I do appreciate your humoring me as much as you did. It is probably a good thing I didn't get to see you before you left (I suppose, sigh ...). I think I would've been overcome with my desire to lay a soft kiss on you. Oh well, I guess I'll have to save that for my dreams. I hope I can still visit you there.

Well, I don't know what else to say. I've enclosed the photo I took—we DO look good together—and the photocopy of the numerology thing. I hope you find/have people in your life to open up to. It's a wonderful feeling to share yourself fully with another human being! I'm grateful that we got an opportunity to share a little with each other.

Though you weren't aware you were giving it, thanks for all your support! And since nothing else seems to work—I DARE YOU to call me sometime when you return to visit Maine. Maybe I'm asking for trouble, but a little trouble in life is good, isn't it? Keeps us alive.

I would welcome a letter or email too. Though I won't ask you to or expect it.

It must be tough for someone whose motto is—trust no one—to allow others to place their trust in him. It's okay to keep your word, darlin'. "I *will* see you before I leave." I'm not upset about that—(sniffle, sniffle). I just think it's an interesting connection.

Now that you've effectively turned my life inside out, I need to get on with it.

If you ever need a friend, you can count on me.

Best of luck to you!

XO,

Mare

Almost as soon as she dropped it into the mailbox at the post office, she regretted some of the things she wrote to him. *That was too forward. If this letter should ever come out, it won't look too good. But then, what is wrong with it? Is it wrong to tell someone how you feel? … That you care about them?* Mare told Pete about writing a goodbye letter, but she didn't tell him what it said. She didn't tell anyone. She was afraid of being judged. She was embarrassed about her feelings.

*   *   *   *

Mare tried to balance and make sense of her two worlds. In ways they were entangled, but in others, they were completely separate. The internal world, where she explored her dreams and fantasies, and the waking world, where she was still trying to repair her relationship with Pete and tend to her family. Somehow she needed to sort things out and reconcile the two realities.

Sitting in the local steakhouse with her Mom, Mare announced. "I'm finally pregnant!" Her mother was thrilled.

When they finished eating they headed to the coatroom to get their things. Mare discovered her baby girl left alone on the desk. "Why did Pete leave her here," she demanded to know.

Mare and her mother sorted through the many items in the lost and found box that was there, looking for some little girl's clothes to put on her. Mare felt happy to have a baby girl in the family now.

Later, she was driving to catch a boat with her two children, but before she arrived a blizzard struck. She tried to stay on the road, but her front end was pulled into a snowbank. Frustrated, she packed up Cody and the baby and a few belongings and walked to a nearby building, looking for help.

While a woman assisted her, she noticed that her babies were gone. Mare panicked. "Where are my babies?" She thought she'd been holding them close to her the whole time. However, the two women soon found them in another office. They were okay, but Mare was not so well.

The woman said, "You should not be so active after delivery."

Mare nodded, then fell over onto the floor. The nurse helped her up and into a chair.

"How was your delivery, Mare," the nurse asked.

Mare said, "It took **exactly** <u>four hours</u> from start to finish."

The nurse expressed amazement that it all went so quickly, but Mare slipped in and out of consciousness.

*   *   *   *

Mare looked at the four hours she had written in her dream journal the next day and decided to underline it. *When I do have baby number two, I'll have to turn back and see how long my labor takes.*

*   *   *   *

After Sunday breakfast with Mare's parents, they all made a stop over at the local flea market. Pete, Cody and Grandpa Mahonia scanned the tables for tools and gadgets, while Mare and her mother paused at other tables. Mare spent most of her time with her nose in the books. One unusual book cover caught her attention. On it was a picture of a glowing woman in a light robe. Behind her were three images of the moon in each of its phases. In front of her was a pool of water with her own image and that of the moons reflected in its glassy surface. The woman had a wand in her hand. The title was *The Power of the Witch: The Earth, the Moon, and the Magical Path to Enlightenment* by Laurie Cabot with Tom Cowan.

Then she read a line at the top that said, "A marvelous introduction to the magical and highly ethical world of Wicca."

Mare's curiosity piqued. *Ethical?* It was not a word she would have immediately associated with witches. *What is Wicca, really?* She wondered. *I know that witches have to be more than the Halloween stereotype.* She thumbed over to the Table of Contents.

"The Science of Witchcraft" … now that sounds fascinating. I wonder if she discusses principles of energy. She must. She skipped around through different pages. *"This woman is from Salem,* she noted with amusement.

The idea of witches brings forth all kinds of images and stereotypes. Mare reviewed them in her mind's eye. The torture. The burnings. The irony of Puritans seeking religious freedom, only to violently deny it to others whose beliefs varied. Mare recalled reading *The Witch of Blackbird Pond* in elementary school and liking it, though she didn't remember many of the specifics. The broomsticks. The warts. The newts and toadstools. *Give me a break, there has got to be more to it than that! Any group who is oppressed is generally misunderstood.* She looked up at the female seller, who looked a little shy and fearful, as if she might be caught or judged for possessing such a volume. Mare smiled at her. "I'll take these!"

*   *   *   *

Driving up Interstate-95, Mare and Pete talked about what they wanted to do during their weekend at his father's cabin. They would have a long weekend all to themselves. Mare hoped they would be able to have some fun and get closer again.

"Uninvited" came on the radio. Mare began to sing the words. Her thoughts turned absentmindedly to Austin. "Like anyone would be, I am flattered by your fascination with me. Like any hot-blooded woman, I have simply wanted an object to crave, but you, you're not allowed. You're uninvited."

Pete began to squirm.

Mare sang on and her head moved to the pulsing of instruments. "I don't think you unworthy. I need a moment to deliberate." There was a quiet pause at the end of deliberate, like the singer really was thinking about it all.

Pete interrupted by saying, "You need to liberate." It was a cross between a question and a statement of fact. He knew somehow that she was thinking about Austin, though neither said so, and he assumed Mare felt like a prisoner and wanted to leave him.

She looked over at her husband, and pointed out, "It's DEliberate ... not liberate. There's a big difference ... come on, Pete."

Pete let it go, and Mare shrugged and went back to tapping her leg.

After three hours in the car, Pete turned the vehicle onto the bumpy dirt road lined with pine trees. He and Mare unhitched the canoe from the top, and brought it down to the lakeside. Then they carried their belongings inside. Mare was planning to unpack a little and stretch her body after the long ride, but within seconds, Pete had his arms around her waist and his lips on hers. He was kissing her with great intensity, and Mare was so unprepared she could hardly breathe. She began to giggle, which caused her to pull away from the abrupt moment of passion. It was so shocking to her that it appeared funny.

Pete was indignant. "Oh that's fucking great. I try to kiss my wife and she laughs in my face."

Mare's expression changed instantly. He had her on the defensive again. "Pete! Good god, you practically attacked me. You didn't give me any transition time. You went from zero-to-ninety in three seconds flat!" Her own voice slowed down a little. "A gradual acceleration would have been nice. I mean, come on, that came out of nowhere!"

"Jesus, Mare. We come here for a little privacy, and when I try to get intimate with you, you laugh in my face, WHILE I'm kissing you! How is that supposed to make me feel?"

"Intimate?" Clearly their definitions of the word did not match. "Pete, I'm sorry," Mare offered with concern. "I didn't mean to offend you. You just took me by surprise. It wasn't like you grabbed me quickly and gave me a little kiss. You practically mauled me. That was intense!"

"This is just not going to work, Mare. I don't see how this is possibly going to work out for us!"

"Pete, what are you talking about?" At this point, Mare began to cry. "You are making a big deal out of something so small. I just giggled out of shock and discomfort."

"It isn't small that you don't love me anymore. You said yourself before, you think of me as a brother. That's just wonderful. I don't want to be married to my sister."

"I didn't say that; I said it felt like we were friends. Every marriage goes through cycles, Pete. You can't expect things to stay exactly the same always. Even a marriage has a rhythm to it. Every relationship has to grow to new levels."

"I have been trying, but nothing's working. You are in love with Austin, not me! How are we supposed to stay married?"

"I'm not in love with Austin! I never said that!"

"You were weepy for three days after he left town."

"It was a loss for me. I can't deny that. I was attracted to him, but we hardly know each other. I think it's more of an idea that I'm infatuated with. I felt something between him and me that I want to feel between us."

"Whatever, Mare. I've heard rumors. Dad's office manager has a daughter who is friends with Austin. She told her mother that something has been going on between you two."

"And you believe her? Pete, I have told you about the few meetings I've had with him. I confessed the dreams to you. Why would I have told you these things if I were fooling around? I have told you the truth. I have not been sleeping around. You know that."

"Well, maybe so, but other people think you have been."

Mare was dejected. "That sucks, but I can't control that, Pete. You know how rumors work, especially in Babylon. When I was in high school there was a rumor circulating around town that I had had an abortion too. My best friends had to work up the courage to ask me. It wasn't. Cody has been my first and only pregnancy." Her brain was getting sidetracked. "In fact, I would still like to know how that stupid thing started. My friend said her boyfriend's mother who worked at the hospital at the time told her that."

He brushed all that aside. "The simple fact is that you don't love me anymore."

"That's not true!" Mare's frustration peaked and she began to sob loudly. "How can I help you to understand?"

Pete stood in the kitchen with his hands placed angrily on his hips.

She looked at him with desperation in her eyes.

"Please, sit down with me." She dropped her body onto the couch. He followed reluctantly.

"I had a dream a while back. I followed a dwarf-like man through his life. He was so sad and mistreated. Something about it seemed to stretch across generations. I was only an observer in the dream, but when he looked in the mirror, it felt like I was looking at my own face. How can I make you understand? I feel like a shadow of my former self, Pete. Something is missing from me; a part of me has shrunken into dwarf form almost, and it has very little to do with you. I'm trying to find it again, and be whole. I'm searching for the answers."

Her husband looked down at the carpet.

"In the second part of this same dream a shy Japanese student followed me endlessly around a beach. I kept trying to ditch her, but she kept clinging. I asked her with irritation what she wanted from me. She said so sadly, 'I'm lonely.' These dream characters are showing me how I'm feeling, Pete."

As Mare confided to her husband, something in her seemed to melt. "She's a part of me, Pete. A part I need to re-integrate. My world has been turned upside down. I feel like I've died and now am coming back to life, but it takes time to reinvent myself. The things I used to be able to believe in and count on have been upturned. I have been trying to find my footing. I need you to understand. When I was young, I tried not to be a puppy-dog, like that Japanese student was to me in my dream. But that part of me is coming back quietly. She's unsure of how to let people in, but she is lonely and wants to. She needs me to be gentle with her."

His expression started to soften.

"Does that make any sense at all?" She examined his face for a reaction. "I know you feel like I'm rejecting you, but that is not my intent. I want to be a good wife, and I DO love you. I just have some personal work to do. I need to take care of her, AND I want to be here for you and Cody. I just don't know how to make it all work! I don't want to hurt you, and I know this has been hard. I am honestly trying the best I know how. I'm sorry if that isn't enough, but I honestly don't know how to do more than I'm doing."

Pete's eyes were red; tears were pushing against the wall of his defense, and had some success trickling over. "I love you, Mare. I want to help you. I'm also doing the best I know how."

Mare touched the back of her husband's head and pulled his forehead into hers. "I know you are, Pete. We are going to be okay. I trust that. I'm coming out of this. I am. I've just got a few battles to fight still. Can you be patient with me a little longer?"

He planted a soft kiss on her tear-covered nose and nodded.

With her hands on his cheeks, she kissed his mouth softly, slowly. She did love her husband. In that moment when he gave her the space, love poured out from her heart and surrounded them. The rest of the weekend was wonderful. They made love. They had fun. They relaxed, and listened to the loons call while the moon rose. The gentle breeze off the lake blew in through fluttering white curtains.

32

Magic and the Power of Words

Words do not label things already there.
Words are like the chisel of the carver:
They free the idea, the thing, from the general formlessness of the
outside.
As a man speaks, not only is his language in a state of birth,
But also the very thing about which he is talking.

Eskimo Quote

Sitting in a rocking chair on the cabin's porch, as the sun began to climb higher over the water, Mare read her new book and learned about the Wiccan religion. The author, Laurie Cabot, talked about the unity of life and the pattern and meaning that underlay solid matter. She discussed the significance of light (visible, X rays, ultraviolet, infrared and radar,) and the discovery that, when viewed from a subatomic level, all things are made up of energy, that they radiate and emit auras. She quoted scientific texts regarding quantum physics.

Mare had studied similar ideas before, and they had always intrigued her. She understood that experiments could be influenced by the expectations and intentions of the researcher. She also thought back to a concrete example in the novel, *The Celestine Prophecy*, where the characters talked to plants and influenced their growth. In it scientists were studying the effects of intention and love on the growth of the plants. Cabot continued, "Consciousness in all its forms—human, animal, plant, spirit—lies at the heart of the universe.

333

Consciousness lies at the heart of magic and is the reason that the power of magic really works" (147).

These words rang true for Mare. She could see the link between science and spirit. She knew that intention could influence the world in substantial ways. She understood that prayer, any positive or negative thought, could impact reality. She wasn't sure how far it could be taken, but she believed in the basic principle.

A student's negative thoughts, words or behavior can shift the room quickly into a negative space. The same is true of a positive student. They may not be consciously aware of it, but that doesn't change the result. Our thoughts do alter reality. "Good" thoughts and "good" words work a kind of magic. So do harmful thoughts and words.

That spring, Mare had noticed a poster on the wall at school. It was an advertisement for a student group working to eliminate prejudice and harassment of those who were different. The poster said, "Words hurt." It listed many negative impacts of words. "Words insult. Words humiliate," and so on. Mare wanted to pencil in, "Words heal. Words create. Words uplift and inspire. Words contain love. Words educate and inform. Words change the world. Words open our eyes."

Of course it's up to us which words we choose, in that, we are creators— whether we create or destroy with our words is up to us. In that sense, we are all witches.

Mare turned back to her book.

> "Witches are among the wise ones who participate in the work of creation in order to nourish the people and protect the earth. Magic belongs to no one culture, society, or tribe—it is part of the universal wisdom. Magic-makers in every century and in every culture have played similar roles and shared similar characteristics. Whether they were called Witches, shamans, priests, priestesses, sages, medicine people, or mystics, they knew how to heal the sick, summon the herds, grow crops, assist at births … Their rituals and ceremonies … [and] their prayers … were expressions of their oneness with the source of all life, the Great Mother of all living things (9-10)."

Yes! Mare thought. Something in her stomach recognized the truth of Cabot's words. *We are one.*

One of her favorite paragraphs was,

> "Just as the child loses its sense of oneness with the universe as it develops ego boundaries and learns how to protect its separate and distinct body from the rest of the world, human societies lost that sense of unity as they evolved away from nature. As men and women created societies more and more removed from the natural world, they found themselves working against nature, subduing it, exploiting it. In time they thought of nature as neither intelligent nor divine. Eventually they came to view it as the enemy.... But witches have never forgotten the basic truth about creation: The world is not our enemy; neither is it inert, dumb matter. The earth and all living things share the same life force; the earth and all living things are composed of Divine Intelligence. All life is a web of interconnected being, and we are woven into it as sisters and brothers of the All (13)."

The more Mare read, the more she respected the Wiccan belief system. It was ancient; it honored male and female manifestations of the Divine Source, but was especially Earth-centered. The book acknowledged the maiden/mother/crone female aspects; discussed European history of religion; talked about past and current persecution of witches and the causes of the fear behind the hysteria and misconceptions, how Wicca (in its true form) was not at all devil-worship, black magic or Satanism; it explained the meaning of the pentacle, the function and practices of covens, the wheel of the year, altars and rituals.

One of the final surprises for Mare, but only because it went against the Halloween stereotype of witches, was that true Wiccans followed the Witch's law that states, "If a Witch does harm, it returns to her three-fold." Wiccans believe in doing no harm.

Later that day Mare and Pete snorkeled the river again. Mare tried to recreate the peace and communion with the river that she had experienced the previous time. It was a pleasant day, but she couldn't recapture the feeling of being embraced by the river again. Perhaps the river would share its secrets with her once and no more …

7/9/98—"Uphill Sprint"

Pete, Cody and I are at the side of a house, gardening or working on something. Underneath the porch of this dream home is a long cage with animals in it. They are big "wild" cats. I reach through and stroke the

fur of one. I feel an affinity with them. Why have they been stuffed in this dark cage? I want to free them. The middle of the dream is blurry. At the end of the dream, Pete and I go running around the property. In an amazing burst of energy at the end of the run, I sprint strongly up a steep hill. (In waking life, it isn't even humanly possible to run as fast as I did). I feel exhilarated! I have conquered, or I will! The mood of most of the dream, especially in my reactions with Pete, is playful.

*   *   *   *

Scooping her hands in the earth somehow reinforced Mare's connection to it. The more she dug into it, the more grounded and centered she felt. Until that summer, Mare never knew that healing powers were buried in the earth. With each blossom that opened up, her heart rejoiced a little more. Pinks and purples and whites. Daisies and lilies and foxgloves and bee balm and bleeding hearts and bellflowers and delphiniums and globeflowers. Mare learned the names of as many as she could. She staked the tall and majestic pink peonies that must have been on the property for years. She picked the lilacs early in the season and let the smells fill her home. With each morning spent in her garden, she felt stronger and happier and clearer.

Life has seasons and cycles. Something is coming to a close, and something new is moving in. I need some kind of ritual to honor this process. Native Americans have ceremonies for things like this. In some cultures, I could give myself a new name or something. Why don't we have more rituals to honor the changing seasons of our lives?

The more she thought about it, the more she felt a need to make some kind of declaration for herself, even if it would be a private matter.

Mare wrote a letter to herself.

As Mare put down her pen, Peter Gabriel's voice blared over the speakers. Something about the song, "In Your Eyes," always moved her. She sang along to the lyrics

... All my instincts, they return/And the grand façade, so soon will burn/Without a noise, without my pride/I reach out from the inside ...

She had found the title to her book. Thank you, Peter Gabriel.

*   *   *   *

While Mare was trying to think of ways to free herself on a level of spirit, her brother was still dealing with physical bars. She got another letter.

Dear Mare,

I got your letter a while back, but I haven't been in the mood to write. I had a pretty bad week. I'm not sure exactly why, but I've just been feeling lousy and depressed.

I moved from Dorm 1 today, so far so good. My roommates were not too impressed, that was obvious by their reaction to seeing me when they returned from work.

One good thing, the two other offenders who I'm in group counseling with eat at the same time as me now, so I sit with them. They're both good guys.

You asked me some stuff about my life and the dates of major events. Well, I don't know what events you're referring to. I don't think you really know what the major events were or why I am who I am. If you could write down your questions, you could come interview me. Just me and you. I can't begin to explain on paper, but I want you to know why and I'm not ready to put it down just yet.

I've learned a lot since starting counseling and I realize things now that I didn't connect to my abusing others. While you don't know what those things are, you know some of them. Some of them I have never talked about with anyone. I'm kind of caught between wanting you to know why and not hurting others who don't realize that their actions affected my psyche. The things I'm referring to are subtle and to most people they would mean nothing, but to me, they were very influential.

When I look at the subtle things that influenced me I can only assume how my actions hurt the kids.... So many days I just want to die. It's so hard living with this. Some days I feel like I exist solely for the sake of Mom, Dad, You, Cassie and Hope. I want to die, but I can't hurt you guys anymore.

I feel like my life is over. I can never again be around kids and that just kills me. Their friendships were so important.

When I think about the future, I realize that even you will likely feel uncomfortable with me around Cody. Well, honestly, Mare, I don't believe I would ever touch him, but there are things that must never happen. One being that he not ever spend the night alone with me. This was always the time when I felt I had little control over my impulses. Anyone younger than twelve or older than 16 has nothing to worry about because I've never felt beyond my control with them. Those highest at risk, (I can say exclusively at risk) were between 12-16 and were in bed with the lights off. If they were younger or older or if the lights were on, nothing would start and those things have remained constant since I was 13. Those parameters I'm told will not change. I want you to feel you can trust me and the only way is to be honest with you and tell you what my weaknesses are.

I wouldn't want to be put in a position to test myself, not yet anyway. Most likely not ever.

By the way, today is day number 200. Only about 1070 days left. Doesn't sound like a lot, but I assure you it's a long ass time.

I know we haven't really sat down and talked about what happened in my life, but believe it or not, it helps me to talk about things. One on one is the most comfortable for me.

I'm anxious to see what you've done on your book. I would like to read it some time. Don't worry, I won't judge it, I just want to know your point of view.

Take care, love,

Seth

*   *   *   *

Mare was sitting in a circle with a group of women. They were all talking about women's issues and dreaming. They discussed how in dreaming and life we have guides or guardian angels and teachers and aspects of our higher selves who can help us along the way.

"I feel like I have people in my dreams who are helping me, but I don't know any of them by name. Generally I am not aware enough while I am dreaming to ask their names or more about them. I usually realize after waking up. I really want to meet my guides. I want to ask some questions."

Around the circle the women nodded in understanding.

At the end of the regular meeting, Mare spoke to many of them one on one. "Can you tell me anything about my guides," she asked the wise women. "I know I am not alone in the dreamscape. I know I have help and wisdom available to me. Certain individuals that I've never met in waking life keep showing up."

They could see she was frustrated.

Mare continued almost in a plea. "I feel like I'm going through some big stuff in dreams and life that I want help with. I have questions. I need some more direct guidance from someone who understands the significance of dreams. I have no one. No one around me who understands."

As Mare drifted out of the dream and back into an awareness of her sleeping body, the female voice assured her, "We are sending Danielle; she can help you."

*   *   *   *

"Pete, I had a strange dream before waking up. I was speaking to some women, and they told me they were sending Danielle to help me. Do we know any Danielles?"

"Not that I'm aware of."

*   *   *   *

Dear Mare,

I'm sorry I haven't returned your letter sooner. It's been another difficult week. The former town manager of Warburton committed suicide this week and it really bothered me. I guess because it reminded me how close I came to doing the same thing. He was about to plead guilty to child pornography charges, and I guess he couldn't face it. I know how he felt and because I was following his story it made it that much more real.

Sometimes I feel if only I had written to him, maybe having someone to communicate with who understands might have been enough to help him get through it. I know you guys had your share of suffering because of what I did, but you could never know how truly terrible it is knowing that you hurt your family and friends. It's so overwhelming you can never know. If it weren't for Hope, I would have ended up in the same place as the town manager.

As far as all the other stuff in your letter, I really don't feel like getting into it right now. I will tell you that no family members or friends of the family have ever acted inappropriate with me, so you need not worry about that.

As far as my own abuser, I haven't seen or heard from him since I was 13. Don't know where he is, where he lived or even remember his name. I only knew him for a week or two. As far as him abusing others, I don't know. One reason I don't talk about it is because I kind of initiated what happened. Because everyone wants to blame him it makes it difficult for me to say it was my fault. What happened to me did not determine who I became. If it wasn't him, it would've been someone else.

As far as what caused this condition I would say a lack of feeling love, lack of feeling important, a fear of losing my friends to their girlfriends, and a fear of being gay. There was nothing traumatic, just a bunch of subtle things which would require a book to understand. Maybe someday you can write my story for me.

Anyway, tell Pete thanks for taking the time to work on my television. Unfortunately, the cord is still too short and the TV itself is junk, but that's all right. Jail isn't supposed to be fun, I guess. Keep in touch.

Love, Seth

Mare said out loud, though no one was in the room with her. "It wasn't your fault. Even if you initiated physical contact, it was the adult's responsibility to define the relationship appropriately! You were only thirteen, a child, wanting to be embraced by love, wanting to feel special and important! That initial relationship was not your fault, even if you enjoyed it."

33

Motifs—By Land and Sea

It's so deep, it's so wide
Your inside
Synchronicity.

—The Police

With eyes closed, Mare fumbled for her notebook. She scratched out a few notes, then set her journal down and tried to go back to sleep.

In the morning, she began to transcribe the notes into a more complete description of her dream into her formal dream journal.

8/2/98—"Tall Man on Street"

All I recall from early scenes is eating warm bread, something I have often done in recent dreams, though I don't quite understand the symbol. I am walking "home" and heading through the town square. I feel I am a glowing presence—beautiful—not so much in appearance as in spiritual radiance. I am content and shining. A tall, handsome man (Hillerman or Hillman—seems to be a name associated with him? Isn't he an author?) is speaking to another man on the sidewalk. As I pass I feel his gaze on me, though I do not look at him. He is a spiritually aware person, and although others may not notice me as much, he is able to see the "true" me. He recognizes immediately my specialness and power. This makes me feel wonderful and charged. He quickly tries to catch up to me. He shares his feelings with me and takes my hand. He is very loving and sincere. He asks me to be his partner. The man's friend and I know I am married, but I haven't had a chance to tell my tall man. "The only problem with your attractive proposal is ... I am already married." We are both disappointed.

Another man is also around at the same time. He is pursuing me as well. I want someone to see me and want me in the way that this man did.

*   *   *   *

Mare felt a slight bump under her tires.

She backed up, to see if she had by chance missed the squirrel. To her dismay, he was stuck to the road, but still moving. Watching him thrash and try to move his broken body off the road, caused a pain in Mare's heart. *This is the second squirrel I've hit in the last week! What should I do?* She wondered. *He can't possibly survive those injuries. I hate to see him suffer. Do I just leave and let him keep struggling until he dies?* This idea did not hold a lot of appeal. *Do I run him over again and help him die quickly?* She didn't know what to do. In those few minutes of deliberation, a voice in her head spoke to her. "The squirrel … it has something to do with your book." *What would squirrels have to do with my book?* Then a memory popped into her brain. The chimney, Seth and Pete found the squirrels in the chimney! That was it. I will start the book with that scene. That's it! The squirrel had seemingly given her a sign, an answer to a question she'd been incubating. She looked back over to it in the road. He had stopped struggling, and given up the ghost. Mare silently wished him a peaceful passing, then put her vehicle into first gear and drove towards home.

*   *   *   *

It was August 11, 1998. Mare was sleeping when she heard noises. Her eyes were open and ears were listening in a flash. The ship was sinking. She climbed out of bed and went to the edge of the deck with the other passengers.

"It's going down. We have to jump," she heard someone yell.

Before she knew it she was in the water … in the very cold water … swimming towards a nearby island. Periodically, between strokes, she looked up to get her bearings. A giant beam was sticking out of the water and Nicole Kidman, the actress, was clinging to it. It appeared to be the remains of an old pier, because there were two rows and several beams on each row. Others were clinging to these as well, and many were either swimming to or already standing on the shore. Mare's legs were virtually frozen, tired and heavy with numbness. Her whole body shivered as she stepped out of the frigid water and onto the sandy beach. Someone was helping her, but she couldn't see who.

A few minutes later, she heard loud voices again. This time they were saying. "We have to swim BACK to the boat. All of us!"

Mare can't believe it. She doesn't understand why and she doesn't feel she can make it, but she follows the instruction and reenters the water anyway …

34

When the Student is Ready, the Teacher Appears

Life can only be understood backwards, but must be lived forwards.

~ Soren Kierkegaard~

After the "third-eye" dream and the dream Mare had of getting back her internal organs, she had written to author, Robert Moss, to ask him about her dreams, and what they meant. She also wanted to take one of his workshops. In August, she received a reply.

8/12/98

Dear Mare,

I am delighted to hear from you. I would love to welcome you into one of our dream circles in the Northeast.

I enclose my current workshop program, plus a flyer for the weekend workshop I'm leading in northern Vermont in September. This will be a fairly small group in a private, rural setting and might be a good place for you to begin if the drive is not too long.

I am very interested in the dreams you shared with me. The dream of your friend's energizing touch indeed has many parallels in the literature of ancient dream healing. In the temples of Asklepios, the god of healing or one of his emissaries (who sometimes appear under familiar faces, like those of "dear friends") often heals with a touch. If this were my dream, I would wonder if my "dear friend" is actually my personal angel, an aspect of the Higher Self.

I am especially intrigued by the dream in which you got back your internal organs. This seems to me to be a powerful dream of healing. This is surely a dream that asks to be dreamed onward. If it were my dream, I might want to talk some more to the unusual bus driver. I would certainly want to cleanse my "heart" and make sure it is where it belongs. In doing this, I may learn how to help others (a possible message in the appearance of other people carrying their own bags of organs). I think of shamanic traditions—and some personal experiences of self-healing—in which removing your organs and cleaning or replacing them (in non-ordinary reality) is central to healing and transformation.

Sweet Dreams,

RM

At the end of September, Robert was leading a course called *Dreamgates: A Journey into Shamanic Dreaming*. She read the handout about the course, and decided that if Pete was okay with it, she would go. She looked at a map of Vermont. *It's being held on Hero Island, near Lake Champlain. How cool. I am there!* Mare was intrigued by the idea of dreaming the organ dream on. She had many questions.

*   *   *   *

Bernard handed Mare, Miriam, Todd Tyler and Ted Alexander several stacks of resumes and cover letters. "We have ten candidates to interview for Kate's position. She got a job in the Portland area. Please look these over."

One of the women is married to our tech guy. Must be why Ted and Todd are here. They haven't attended interviews in previous years. Certainly they want to keep him here, so they are going to favor her. Her resume is excellent, and she was indeed impressive in person. Her name was Becky.

The next few candidates were so-so. None could give Becky a run for her money.

… Until the last woman. She was different. The interview started out ordinary enough. The woman was exceedingly polite. She was older than Becky and slightly smaller in stature. Her raven hair streamed down over her shoulders, and her eyes were as alert as a hawk's. The way she articulated her answers impressed the interviewers. Bernard asked her what the last book she had read was. After slight hesitation, she said she had just finished reading a book by

Carlos Castenada. *Hmmm ... I just finished a book by him too ... about dreaming,* Mare noted silently, observing several coincidences between her responses and Mare's own interests.

The more the woman spoke, the more compelled Mare felt to hire her. At one point, she and Miriam exchanged a look of collusion that said, "We like her." *She's very reflective; she realizes teaching English is more than teaching kids where to put commas.*

After all the candidates left, the five discussed the merits of each. Mare's two favorites were easily selected as the top two. After that it was tougher. Both were qualified, and both would be great. However, there was something about the second woman that made her stand out to the two female interviewers. Both women advocated passionately for hiring her. As expected, the principal and Ted supported the first woman, Becky. So, Bernard, the department chair, would be the deciding vote, but he couldn't yet make up his mind.

"I'll call their former employers and try to get a feel for each. Then I will cast my vote. They are both strong."

The group agreed and went their separate ways, except for Mare and Miriam. They had a private, post-interview chat.

"Isn't she great?" Miriam said.

"Yes, there is something different about her. Something familiar.... It felt like she was a spiritual sister or something. It wasn't even so much what she said, though she said some great and surprising things."

Miriam felt the same way. "I really want her to get the job, but I have a feeling that Bernard is going to be swayed by the other two. I wish there was something we could do."

"Maybe we should call Bernard this weekend, and work on him some."

"Do you think that would do any good?"

Mare grimaced in thought and searched somewhere inside herself. "You know, I know it seems like the younger woman is in the lead now, but somehow ... somehow I sense the second woman will get the job. It feels to me like she was meant to teach here with us. I'm not sure why. I just have this strong impression that we are destined to walk a similar path for awhile. Let's trust that and leave it be."

Miriam knew about intuition. "I think you may be right, Mare. Let's hope. See you later. Let me know if you hear anything."

Mare nodded and waved goodbye. She opened up the woman's resume again. She examined the cover letter again. Danielle Renard. Danielle?"

*   *   *   *

"Pete, you remember that dream I had where the dream women said they were sending someone who could help me understand?"

He thought for a moment, "Yeah."

"What was the name I told you?"

"Hmmm … Danielle, I think, wasn't it?"

"Yes, I think so. I'll have to check my journal."

"Why?"

"I believe we just interviewed her."

35

Intuition and Contact

Reality is merely an illusion, albeit a very persistent one.

~Albert Einstein~

As Mare trusted she would, Danielle got the job.

Since the two would be teaching a similar course load, Mare told Bernard that she would be happy to show their new colleague around the building and assist her with books and curriculum.

"That would be great. Danielle has also offered to join the district curriculum committee with you and Miriam."

"Wonderful!" *The three of us. Why does that not surprise me?*

*   *   *   *

"Thank you for your help, Mare. I appreciate the orientation."

"My pleasure. Miriam and I are especially happy to have you on board. Your interview really stood out."

"That's kind of you to say."

Mare wanted to gush to her that she felt they already shared some connection, but she didn't want to overwhelm the woman too soon. She tried to figure out a way that she could subtly drop hints about a possible dreaming link between the two. Mare didn't think it would be appropriate to broach a conversation about such a private topic too quickly. *How can I open a doorway?*

"You know, Danielle. I was fascinated in your interview that the last book you read was by Castenada. I have been reading his book, *The Art of Dreaming,* this last week, so I found the synchronicity of it to be very interesting. Perhaps we share some common interests."

The elder woman's eyes grew wide.

"I was wondering, which of his books did you read recently? I know he has many."

Mare studied her reaction, which seemed stunned and cautious. This amused Mare.

She swallowed hard, and then told her, "That is the book I was referring to, though it's not a very mainstream book, so I thought I'd leave out the title."

"How fascinating," Mare nodded, but she was not in the least bit staggered by the coincidence. It validated something that she knew in her bones. This woman had been sent to help Mare with her dreaming; she felt sure of it.

Mare showed Danielle to the book room, and said little else about it. She could wait—barely—for their common purpose to be revealed. She needed to tap into it slowly.

8/17/98—"Pre-School Dream"

It is the first day of the new school year. The kids are rotating through some sort of round-robin exercise. I have on a purple shirt and jeans. I feel underdressed and unprepared, and I check my schedule to see if I have time to shower and change. I take a shower, but the kids are all over the place. It's hard to keep them from seeing me naked, though I try.

*   *   *   *

Just before the new school year started, Mare asked Pete to read a letter she wrote to greet her students and preview the year.

"It's good, but it's dry. It doesn't sound like you yet. You need to put some of your personality into it."

"You're right. I need to make some changes. I've got all the right information down, but it doesn't communicate ME yet."

On the first day of school she handed out the revised copy of the letter. She tried to inject some of her personality into it when she rewrote the final copy. It read …

Dearest Student—

Welcome! How would you like this to be the best English-type class you've ever had? Yes, you say? Well, that's what I would like. Do I have a clue as to how that's going to happen? No, not exactly. I mean, I have some ideas, but it seems like a big task to me. Every one of your lives is unique in some way; your backgrounds, interests, skills and experiences are so diverse. How in the world do I set up a curriculum that meets everyone's needs and interests most of the time?

Let me get one thing straight. I am not here to waste your time. You are not here to waste my time. When I applied for this position, they did not advertise: Wanted—*Someone to bore students to death.* Now, with that in mind, you need to trust me. Trust that I will do my best to make this class interesting and useful. Does this mean that you will love every single stinking activity we do, piece of literature we read, or skill we practice? Of course not. However, you should know that this course is intended to achieve certain goals, so sometimes you are going to need to have faith in my judgment. I don't believe in assigning busywork, so you can count on that. That doesn't mean you will necessarily agree with all the educational choices I make. I *want* you to wonder why we have chosen to do certain texts or writing activities. Ask me, if you want—BUT do so <u>one</u>-on-<u>one</u> AFTER class, not in the middle of a lesson or activity. If I hear a whiney—"Why do we have to do this?" I might have to slap someone. Seriously, though, it IS rude to handle it in this way. Don't do it. Question the things we do, but do so with the confidence that there is a good reason for it, and then search for that benefit. It's there if you are willing to look.

Take ownership of this class. Be responsible for making it one of the best classes you've ever had. Not just because it will be fun (which I hope it will be), but because it will challenge you. Be here: in body and mind. NO ZOMBIES ALLOWED. You have a mountain of gold before you this year in all your courses. It's up to you to dig and find the nuggets. Some will be big, others small; but believe me, they are here! (Sometimes the good stuff is under a few layers of granite.) You've got to **be a prospector.** Brainwash yourself, "I'M GOING TO LEARN A LOT THIS YEAR IN ENGLISH." You could even convince yourself that you are going to enjoy it. Even if you don't care, **pretend** you do. You'd be amazed how much of a difference that small thought can make. You and I may both be geniuses (or not); however, a truly wise individual knows that there is always more to learn and that discovery can come in unexpected ways from unlikely sources. YOU have to be open to it. You have to have eyes and ears open, ready to SEE and HEAR.

To help build a community this year, we need to get to know each other. In the next week or so, I'm going to ask you to create a product that shares YOU in some way. I will give you some suggested formats in class. I want you to have some choice in the matter. Below are things I might be interested in knowing about you. These are not carved in stone; they are designed to prompt your thinking. You don't need to cover them all and there is certainly information to share that I didn't think of. It's just a guide.

To be fair, I guess I should disclose some personal stuff about myself too. Let's see, I like to run, hike, camp—just about anything that has to do with the outdoors. Sleeping is kind of fun. I am very interested in dreams and dreaming. Of course, I love to read and write … and listen and talk, which is all pretty important if you are going to teach English. Sometimes I have trouble finding time to write, but I'm hoping to set some goals for myself in that arena for this year. I have been working on a sort of "autobiographical" novel. Ummm … This is my third year of teaching. I have one son who will be three in December. I have other stories and tidbits to tell, but I'll save them for a rainy day. Zzzzzzz … YOU CAN WAKE UP NOW; I'M DONE TALKING ABOUT MYSELF.

With a little patience and teamwork, we will all be able to have a very rewarding year. I'm looking forward to discovering who you are and what you are capable of. Remember, oh determined prospector, bring your pick and hiking boots!

Ever So Fondly,

Mrs. Lumen

After her students read the letter, she asked them, "Okay, what kind of teacher do you think I'm going to be this year after reading this? What are your predictions?"

She heard words thrown out like "fun" and "cool."

"What makes you think that," she prompted them.

"Because you like to have fun."

"How do you know that? You just met me. Can you point to things in my letter that led you to those conclusions?"

"Yes, when you said *you can wake up now*. That was funny."

Other students pointed to other lines.

"Did I TELL you that I was going to be fun or cool?"

"No."

"You had to read between the lines, right? My words shaped your perception, and you also had to infer based upon my words. It's funny how powerful words are. They give shape to ideas. Words don't just report; they create! This year you are going to look at your own writing in the same way. How do you "show" your readers what you mean without necessarily telling them directly?

In addition to figuring out how to improve your writing, you will also examine what kind of reader you are. Are you making the connections actively? Did you notice your reaction to the letter before I asked? Do you let the writer lead you by the nose, or do you see his/her methods for grabbing and persuading you? What is it you are trying to accomplish when you write? That is very important to understand. What do you think MY main purpose was with this letter? I had more than one."

"To share a little bit about who you are ... to let us know about the year." Mare nodded.

"To entertain us ... make us laugh and keep us interested."

"Yes, I want to have fun, by the way ..." Mare acknowledged, "but I also wanted you to know that, *like anything in life*, YOU are responsible for having a positive experience. I'm not just going to stuff you full of knowledge. You need to take ownership of your learning process. You can waste this year or be miserable, or you can milk it for all it's worth. Your attitude. Your choice. It's up to you."

*   *   *   *

On September 17, 1998, at five o'clock in the morning, Mare awoke with an odd feeling of danger. Someone or something was in the house. She got up out of bed to make sure Cody was safe. She stopped in the hallway and looked towards the stairs. She could feel an intruding presence, and she knew that it was at the bottom of the stairs. Within moments, Mare saw a thin, black, shadow-figure ascending the stairs and moving towards her. She tried to remain calm. It had a candle-flame-like shape. It didn't seem to have physical form; it was more shadow. Her mind searched for a method of protection against it. A bit confused, the idea came to her that she should imagine a white light growing within her and emanating from her to keep her safe and her fear at bay. She followed this instructive thought.

As soon as she filled with this light energy—the entity jumped on her! Stuck to Mare, the shadow figure occupied the same space during this abrupt attack. Mare was immobilized by a low electric charge vibrating throughout her entire body. Her mind reeled. *How do I get out of this?* She tried to focus on keeping her light strong. She attempted to call to Pete, but her mouth could not produce any sound. In that instant, she realized she was in a dream state. Up to this point, she had believed she was wide-awake and fully conscious walking in her home. She resisted the shadow's presence. It didn't seem to like whatever she was doing, and almost as quickly as it had latched onto her, it let go and took off. The sudden release propelled Mare hurtling backwards into her physical body, which was still in bed next to Pete.

Her eyes opened instantly, and she got up and ran to Cody's room, wrapping her arms securely around him. She closed her eyes, and searched the house with her mind. *Is it gone?*

Cody and the house felt safe. Mare went back into the hallway and stood at the top of the stairs where the assault had just happened. Her heart was still racing. *That was real*, she said. *It was here. It just wasn't physical; it was energetic. But it was real!*

Once Mare assured herself that her home and family were really safe, she returned to bed, but couldn't possibly sleep. For a few days, she would be rattled by the experience.

Mare cuddled up next to Pete, and when he awoke, she shared her startling vision.

A spark of recognition entered his eyes as she told her tale.

"I've faced that same thing in this house in dreams, only I ran and hid from it. The way you describe it is exactly what I remember seeing and feeling when I came across it." He shared some of the details with her of where he hid and how terrified he felt.

"That is so weird, Pete. The funny thing is I felt it was more disrespectful than malevolent. I just remember thinking … How rude! Mostly I was concerned that Cody was okay. It felt so very real!"

Later, she recorded the following note in her dream journal … *My first thought was that it could have been some presence that Seth carried here. Jane confirmed this possibility. She said it could be a "thought-form." She said that our thoughts (and the thoughts of others), if they have enough energy, can take on form. Or perhaps it is connected to the house, since it is an older one. Jane suggested I "smudge" the place with dried sage to clear out unwanted energies.*

Mare couldn't wait to find a way to talk to Danielle about the incident. Perhaps she could shed some light on it.

*   *   *   *

Since the district had recently adopted a new curriculum development program, high school reps from each subject were invited to a training meeting. The trainer led them through various exercises and processes to teach them how the system was going to work. One of the readings the group had to look at was a science article on *Shadows*. Knowing that she needed to reach out to Danielle more, Mare remarked quietly that coincidentally, she just had a dream about a shadow figure a few nights before that. Mare noticed that Danielle perked up with interest when she said that. Mare didn't elaborate yet. In a more casual moment, when a handful of her more familiar colleagues were having a playful discussion about what they each wanted to "be" when they grew up, Mare purposefully and somewhat playfully noted that she would like to be a shaman when she grows up—a messenger and healer of spirit. Again, Mare noticed that Danielle practically choked on an ice cube when she spoke the word *shaman*. Mare grinned at the thought that she knew of their commonalities before Danielle did. Mare's friend, Nan, remarked that Mare would make a great shamaness.

Later, Mare got up the courage to finally tell Danielle that she had dreamed about her arrival beforehand.

"So, THAT is what's going on. The things you have been saying have been so … strange, so similar to my own path. It's funny; I was wondering how I ended up teaching again. I told myself before that I was going to stay out of it, and here I am. I did sense a familiarity around you."

"I have to tell you about this dream I had the other night. It was a big one. Would you mind?"

Danielle looked with caution around the hallway; no one was around. She motioned for Mare to continue. Mare narrated her shadow intruder dream. "What do you think," she asked Danielle.

With some reluctance, Danielle told her, "I think from what I've experienced of you and what you've told me, that you are pretty open and receptive to energetic goings-on. I would urge you to be very careful about what you invite into your space. Do you perform any protective rituals before you retire for the night?"

Mare shook her head negatively. I just feel safe, generally speaking.

"Well, you might want to consider adopting some practices designed to defend yourself from unwanted visitors."

"What do you think it was? I am convinced it was a real experience."

"Yes, I'm sure it was…. Well, you have read Castenada, do you remember what he said about inorganic beings? It could be one of those."

"My shadow creature didn't feel at all like Castenada's encounter. He had an affinity with his water spirit. This one felt very rude, though it did appear similar in form. Maybe it was more associated with fire."

"Do you remember what he said about the assemblage point? When you shift your assemblage point—your center of awareness—new perceptive abilities open up to you. Have you been doing spiritual work?"

"I guess I would have to say yes." Mare shared briefly her experiences with her brother in the last year. "It has changed me."

"Be careful, in opening up like you have been, you might accidentally invite other entities in who are drawn to your energy and openness. From now on, set your intent firmly that you will only receive guidance or visits from those who are here to contribute to your highest good."

"I will. Thank you, Danielle."

*   *   *   *

9/2/98—"Hard Rain/Missing Daughter"

I'm in our house. It is raining hard (both in waking and dream world). I have three children: two boys and a girl. The girl is not home; she's rarely there, in fact. I am very worried about her. Rain is leaking through the windowpanes. I try to and succeed in closing the leaks. Seems real. I feel an unsettling presence. I look up. A strange misty cloud is over me, some ghostly type of presence, and I sense negative emotional feelings in association with it. It feels yucky and I want it away from me. I keep fixing leaks.

*   *   *   *

Mare walked into Emerson High as she did everyday. But today something was different. She walked by the window of a classroom and was surprised to see Austin within. Through the glass he waved enthusiastically and indicated *I'm back*. She was happy to see him, but also wary. She had put him behind her already, but a familiar tug pulled at her heart. She shrugged and assumed she would talk to him later.

The hallways were busy with students.

Later Mare got a call to come to the main office. An administrator told her, "I'm sorry, Mare. Your father-in-law has had a heart attack. I'm afraid he didn't make it." He put a hand on her shoulder.

"What? Oh my god." She put a hand over her mouth as the information made its way into her psyche. *He seemed so healthy. How could he leave us so abruptly?* She began to tear up and sat down. Then she realized she had to get to her husband.

Driving to the hospital, her mind was reeling. *I just can't believe it. Poor Cody. He will barely know his grandfather.*

In the emergency room Mare checked in and waited for her husband and a doctor to see her. A doctor came out shortly. "I'm sorry, Mrs. Lumen. Your husband has also died … also of a heart attack."

"WHAT?!"

Mare wandered around the area outside the hospital. *How can this be? How can they both be dead? Pete was so young.* She drifted a few doors down and into her father-in-law's medical office. Pete had been using the basement as an office for his computer business.

Her emotions fluctuated like waves spilling over her from a stormy sea. Disbelief, confusion, and shock broke over her. *He can't be dead. They can't both be dead? How can that be? Both from the same cause. A heart attack ...*

My son will now be without a father. My poor son. My husband ... I loved my husband. The dreams I had for a family, for a family that stayed together. They are gone.

An alternating wave came. A feeling of liberation spilled over her and slid across the sand. *I am free,* she said out loud in confusion. *No more fighting. No more disappointing him.*

Do I really want to be free? I certainly didn't want Pete to die, even though I sometimes had doubts about the marriage. Oh, I can't believe my husband is dead. Pete, Oh Pete!

At school they held a memorial ceremony. The Transition Team helped organize and get Mare through the event. They also sang along with Mare as she performed the National Anthem in honor of her dead husband. After the ceremony, she kept thinking, "Wow, I'm a widow. A widow." She wept with her head in her hands. *Everything can change so quickly.*

Mare's mother brought Cody over to her after her song. When the boy saw his mother crying, he, too, began to bawl. Mare embraced Cody and sobbed even harder. *My son does not have his father around anymore. He doesn't even understand that yet. That will take time. He was not even three yet. Only two and a half years with his father. I am all he has left for a parent.* She hugged her son tightly and kissed his wet face.

President Clinton sent Mare a sympathy card. When she opened it, she saw some strange squiggly lines, which were indecipherable, but when her vision adjusted a secret code seemed to emerge. The lines got rearranged into a secret message that said, "I love you." *Weird!*

*   *   *   *

Mare felt the heaviness of sleep release her, and when her waking consciousness returned, she slid onto her elbow and reached for her husband to make sure he was still there. She felt a solid form beside her and could hear his slow, deep breathing. She was relieved.

Why did I have that stupid dream? A feeling of shame and confusion spread through her as she remembered the degree of relief she had felt in the dream.

No more struggle, no more conflict, no more uncertainly. Some other force has decided for me.

Some days Mare felt torn in two.

The dream stayed with her for many months. She kept looking for answers. Eventually, she would discover why she had dreamed that dream, but only time would reveal the secret.

*   *   *   *

"If I start to fall, lock off the belay device against your thigh with your brake hand, and hold it there," Pete said.

Mare nodded. "I think I can do it."

"I'll climb first, because this is a harder section."

He finished adjusting his own gear and double-checked it. Then he said, "Belay on?"

"On belay?" Mare said, remembering the proper command.

"Climbing."

"Climb on," she said.

Pete began to reach for the first hold and pulled himself up. He continued upward, placing a foot, stepping up, and then reaching for a handhold, while Mare looked up and took in the slack.

"Go a little slower, please," she asked, trying to make sure she was belaying properly. It was difficult because she kept wanting to grab the other part of the rope when she brought her brake hand up. *Don't let go of this part of the rope,* she had to keep reminding herself.

He paused and looked down. It looked like Mare was following his instructions, so he continued. When Pete was about three-quarters of the way up the face, he began to slip. Mare was bringing her brake hand up at the time, and in the confusion, let go of the rope with her brake hand to grab the outgoing rope. This was not good.

Pete lost contact with the rock, and Mare was holding onto the rope with both hands. Because she could no longer lock off with her brake hand, with the force of Pete's falling body pulling it, the rope began to fly back up through the belay device and her hands.

"Ow, ow," she said, her hands getting hot from the friction as she try to keep hold of it.

"Holy shit! Don't let go of the rope!" Pete demanded realizing, what had happened and scrambling for a foothold. He swung to the left.

"I'm trying," Mare winced, wanting to grab the other side of the rope again, so she could tie it off, but not being able to remove her hand now from where it was without dropping Pete. "Shit," she said.

Pete found a place to put his foot and quickly grabbed a slab just in time.

Mare quickly let go, grabbed the other side and tied it off. Pete was finally safe again.

Both climber and belayer were breathing heavily from fear and exertion.

"Jesus, Mare," Pete yelled when he had caught his breath. "You almost killed me!"

"I'm sorry! I just … I got confused and scared and … made a mistake."

*   *   *   *

Not long into their friendship, Mare began to dream about Danielle. She was about to discover a surprising and exciting possibility. The reason for Danielle's presence in Mare's life started to reveal itself.

Mare was sitting in a diner further North in Maine. It was a bridal shower, and a pretty blond woman was opening gifts at the main table at the front of the room. Her guests were scattered around at tables and booths. Four Native American women, along with Danielle, were in the back of the restaurant. Everyone was talking casually and watching to bride-to-be open her gifts. The bride was opening one of the gifts from one of the Native American women, and when she got to the card, she found it was written in a Native tongue that she had trouble reading. She tried to speak the words out loud, but she struggled with the pronunciation.

Though she was feeling a little like an outsider, Mare felt sympathy for the white woman. She turned towards the group of women at the back. "Maybe one of you could read it for her in English?" she suggested.

The women that Danielle was sitting with from the neighboring booth laughed, and Mare giggled along with them. The blond woman continued to open her gifts, but later she moved over to Mare and thanked her for trying to make her feel more comfortable.

At the end of the event, Mare helped get the tables back into order. She suspected that the Native American women owned the place.

*   *   *   *

Walking past Danielle's classroom after school, Mare turned in. Danielle looked up and said hello. Off-handedly, Mare mentioned that she'd had a dream about the woman a while back.

Danielle listened casually as Mare described the gathering at the diner and the women there. A look of alarm crossed Danielle's features. The woman got up slowly and closed the door.

"I had no idea you were conscious during that."

"What do you mean?" Mare asked, confused.

"I thought you just wandered in, like people sometimes do?"

Still, Mare looked perplexed.

"That meeting actually took place, Mare. There was a reception. The women did laugh at you. In fact, I thought it was quite rude."

"What do you mean? You went to a party, and I picked up on it intuitively?"

"No, I meet with these women regularly in dreaming, and last time, you tagged along."

"I tagged a ... what?"

"That's why they were laughing, because they didn't think you realized where you were or how you got there. They didn't think you realized you didn't belong there."

"Wait a minute. Let me get this straight. You were sitting with four Native American women at a table, women you know in waking reality, but visit whenever you want to in dreams. You are familiar with this dream diner?"

Danielle nodded.

"I never knew such a thing was possible."

"It's more than possible. People get together in dreams all the time, but don't usually remember anything about it when they wake up. That you were aware and could retain it is rare in these times."

"My family would never believe this."

"I don't recommend you go broadcasting it. I have learned to be especially careful about whom I include in my circle. I learned very young. Dreaming has always been powerful in me. When I was a child, I would tell my grandmother about the dreaming. She told me not to tell the nuns, and encouraged me to share them only with her. Even now, I stay very guarded about this part of my life. I'm not especially comfortable talking about it at school, or having people here know about it. Not all that long ago, people who had experiences such as these and talked about them could get stoned to death in Christian communities that were fearful of anything that seemed counter to their religious beliefs. People often fear what they do not understand and cannot explain. I do not take any of it lightly. I need to figure out why we are linked. I need to do some dreaming on it to figure out what to do with you. Apparently, I have come here in large part because of you, though I didn't know that when I applied. It's becoming clearer to me now, however. I need to seek guidance."

She turned to Mare. "In the meantime, I request that you not discuss this with anyone else. Anybody who knows could get pulled into dreaming with us. You must be careful of the links that are made with other dreamers."

36

Stuff the Cat into the Box, Honey—and Keep Paddling

Dreams give us the answers if we attend to them, because they come from a source that is deeper and wiser than the everyday waking mind. To attend means more than to listen; to attend, literally, is the "stretch" yourself.

—Robert Moss, <u>Conscious Dreaming</u>

"Mare, I have to talk to you. Privately." It was Danielle.

The two women found an empty conference room and sat down.

"What?" Mare asked in anticipation.

"Do you remember dreaming with me last night?"

"No, not last night. I slept like a rock, but the night before you brought me to a woman who guided me through the process of generating energy through my uterus and "lifting off" from that place in my body. I slowly separated myself from my body several times with her help. She also coached me about "intending." It was very empowering, although somewhat draining to practice it all as I did. I slept like a rock after that one. Last night, I don't remember any dreams from last night."

"Well, that's wonderful. But something amazing happened *last* night that I have to tell you about," Danielle started, clearly excited about what had transpired in the dreamscape. "First, I came to get you. I always knock or ask permission, and you were willing, so we went on a journey." Danielle had her colleague's full attention. "We traveled down into some underground caves. We saw places and met beings that I've never encountered, so I can only assume they are part of your personal guide system. Are you by chance from a Celtic tradition?"

"Yes," Mare said.

"I thought so. All around these tunnels and caves were … I'm not sure what else to call them … gnomes or brownies … little people with hats on their heads. They were working and talking and paying us little heed. You walked right up to one and began to talk to him. You knew exactly who we were meant to see. Does that happen to you often?"

"Well, I seem to have extra senses in dreams. Certain people stand out to me always. I am drawn or pulled to the right places and people it seems. I can't explain it. I also seem to have little control, at least consciously about where I go in dreaming. It seems to me like you are better able to influence or control your dream experiences."

"You knew exactly what you were doing last night. The small man you spoke to led us through some other passageways into one vast cavern. He was a guide. In the middle of this cavern was an elaborate and ornate chest. We opened it. It was filled with special coins and other valuables. You were instructed to pick a "sein fenn." I'm not sure how you would spell that." She was looking at a note sheet. "I only remember how it sounded. You absolutely understood what this meant (even though I did not), and you considered it carefully. The vision ended before you chose one. I don't know what that is— Sein Fenn. Do you? You certainly did in the dreaming."

Mare bit her lip. "No, I'm not familiar with that term, but it does sound Celtic."

"Yes, I've never dreamed of any of those places or characters before. Have you? It was very exciting. I want to go back."

"I don't have specific memories of that place, but I have dreamed about Celtic figures before. I am part Irish, as well as Finnish. It wouldn't surprise me if the settings were associated with me. I am drawn to things Celtic … music and images and people. In fact, Pete can't stand it when I start playing Celtic music, but I love so much of it. It calms me. Well, sometimes it riles me up, too. Depends on the music."

"Fey folk or faery kind in ancient times were powerful deities, but over time people's spiritual beliefs shifted to more monotheistic worship, worship that moved away from being earth-based, and these deities lost some of their power. Ultimately, they became more diminutive in size. These particular beings were clearly guardians of treasures of the earth. They were offering you a gift. I couldn't wait to tell you about it. It was a very special experience."

Mare nodded in reflection.

"I have to ask you, Danielle. Have you ever dreamed WITH students?"

"Yes, I try very hard not to, but sometimes they just pop in, sort of like you did at the diner. Most don't remember it though."

"I'm pretty sure I have dreamed with a few of my students before. I dreamed of this one student, Austin, a lot, and I have also had dreams of another student, Christian. Christian and I have become close, and the other night I dreamed he introduced me to his mother. I have never met her in person. I am curious to see if she looks the same as my dream. The ones of Austin were so strong I had to talk Pete about it. It was bothering me, and I was hoping that talking about it would help. I have dreamed of a few other students too, but none as strong as those two."

"It happens. Sometimes dreams are just symbolic, but others are mutual dreams, you are actually with the other person or people."

*   *   *   *

9/19/98—"Old Eggs in the Cupboard"

I'm in my house expecting a visit from my high school girlfriends. When they arrive I look through the cupboards for snacks. I am hungry. I come across hard-boiled eggs that one of these friends cooked for me a long time ago. "Wow," I think to myself. "These are old and no good now. Why didn't they get put into the fridge so they would last longer? I find even more, but I don't tell the girls because I'm kind of embarrassed about it.

Note: Are these old eggs my eggs? Is this why I am having problems with my fertility or is it just the fear of not being able to conceive?

*   *   *   *

On the home front, Mare and Pete signed papers on a mortgage for their home. The burden of the new mortgage and Pete's uncertain income caused more stress for the couple. Tempers were short.

"Pete, I would really like to start seeing a marriage counselor. Would you come with me?"

Pete, who had undergone years of counseling in college regarding his parents' divorce, responded simply and firmly. "It's YOUR problem, Mare; YOU fix it!"

Mare made the appointment without him, and poured her heart out to the counselor about her brother's troubles. She talked about the strain on her marriage; she disclosed the dreams she had about Austin. Additionally, she even talked about "playing doctor" with her brother as a child.

Surprisingly to Mare, he was very supportive about all of her confessions and struggles.

During their second session, the doctor told her, "You've had a hard time of it, Mare, but it sounds like you've done a lot of work to understand it. The dreams and fears you've acknowledged are very normal, given the circumstances. That you are aware of them, and can talk so openly about them is a very good sign. Many folks not only deny such things to other people, they kid themselves about it."

"Recently I had a dream that I was in our house, only it wasn't our waking house. I realized I was dreaming. I found Pete and I said to him, we are dreaming, Pete. Let's look around this house and see if it can tell us anything about our marriage. He agreed. The only remarkable thing about the house was that it was virtually empty."

After a couple of sessions, the doctor said, "We've done all we can with you alone, I think. I don't see a problem with the path you are on. A marriage takes two people. We really need to get Pete in here so we can figure out what's going on and how to fix it."

*   *   *   *

"Pete, the doc says that we really need two of us to come in to work on the marriage. I've already told him all my stuff. It's kind of hard for him to help our marriage if he only hears one side of the story."

He glared at her in anger, but said nothing.

*   *   *   *

Pete met with the counselor first by himself. Then the three sat down together. When the discussion turned to Pete's parents, Mare paid close attention.

After waffling for a moment about diving into the muck again, Pete started, "I was ten. My parents argued a lot and I didn't understand why. They would yell and throw stuff at each other. Later, when they divorced, my whole world fell apart. My two younger sisters and I moved out of our house into another one with my mother that was twenty minutes away. My father and Margaret and her two children moved into our old house. It was really weird."

Pete told them of how his mother found out about his father's affair with Margaret, and how his dad had accused her of fooling around. "Who knows," Pete said. "My dad and mom fought over custody for many years. When I would go over to my Dad's, he would try to convince me to come live with him. I was his son, and he wanted me with him. I was the only boy in the family. It tore me apart to be stuck in the middle. I remember wanting to die. In fact, I was hospitalized when I was in high school. I got some weird infection."

He turned to his wife. "Mare has heard this story. I had been in the hospital for a few days, but my condition was not improving. I prayed one night for God to send me a reason to live. That night I had a dream that I was riding a horse on a beautiful beach. Enormous boulders were standing up out of the sand. In front of me was a woman riding her own horse. I couldn't see her face, just her dark blonde hair flying behind her. I knew she was my wife. I always thought that God showed me a piece of the future to give me something to live for … that I would eventually find happiness. After that, my condition rapidly improved. Once Mare and I got together, I always believed she was the woman of my dream."

"I see," the psychologist nodded. "That's very interesting."

Then, Mare added cautiously, "When Pete and I first started dating, his esteem fluctuated a lot. At times, he was very confident, and others he felt he was not loveable and he would push me away. We talked about it before we got married. I tried to reassure him how loveable he was, but it is a deeply buried fear for him, it seems" she added carefully, not wanting to make her husband mad. "He told me once that whenever things get really good, he starts waiting for the bottom to drop out."

Pete flipped a hand into the air, as if saying, "Yup, that's basically it."

"In college, more than one of Pete's girlfriends was unfaithful. I think it is still hard for him to trust me, to trust our life, given the betrayals he's experienced in the past." Mare looked to her husband. "I tried to tell him that I'm different, that the others snuck around behind his back, and that I have taken the risks to talk to him about my feelings…. But the more insecure he feels about us, the angrier he becomes. I feel like we are trapped, like I'm fighting a losing battle with it. He's made decisions about me, about us, that make it harder to repair our marriage. We both feel drained."

"Do you want to be married? Do you love each other?"

One by one, each answered yes.

"So we need to figure out how to fix this now that the cards are on the table."

"What do you feel like you each need?"

Both spouses shared their thoughts, as they had done before. The three hammered out a skeleton of a plan, and made an appointment for another session.

Pete asked her later that night while they were getting ready for bed. "Maybe we should stop trying to have another baby. What if we don't make it?"

Mare looked at him with concern. "Pete, we are going to make it. Have faith in us. I do. We just need to break out of our bad patterns with each other. We need to build in some respect again."

"But what if we don't? What if we can't? Shouldn't we wait?"

"I would rather live as if we know we are going to make it and commit to that outcome. Cody is almost three now, Pete. Don't you want to be a family? Don't you want him to have a sister or brother to play with? I don't want them to be so far apart that they can't play with and relate to each other." She looked to him for some response. "I thought you wanted two children like I do? Even if we somehow fail to pull this together, I would still want Cody to have a sibling. I want to have two children, and I don't want to have a child with anyone but you. No matter what happens in our marriage, I think it's important that Cody have a full-blood sibling to grow up with. Even if we were to get divorced and go our separate ways, Cody would always have another who was in the same boat as he was ... someone who would understand all the ups and downs of his family. He needs a brother or sister."

Mare climbed into bed next to her husband. "Besides, we aren't going to let this family drift apart any further. We are reclaiming it. We made a commitment, and I intend to do everything in my power to keep our word."

She snuggled into him. "I had a dream recently that we were paddling down this river and the cats were with us. They kept getting out of the box we had them in, and we kept putting them back in. Then I noticed that there was one side of the box that was completely missing. It was no wonder they kept getting out."

"What do the cats have to do with us?" he asked puzzled.

"One of the dream dictionaries I trust suggested they represent marriage. We can repair this, Pete. I know we can."

Pete hugged her. Something seemed to shift in him. He seemed ready to move ahead. If Mare was so hopeful about them, maybe the relationship could be salvaged.

*   *   *   *

Mare sat in the chair, while Cindy got the needle ready. Pete sat in the chair next to her while the other technician prepared his arm.

"I'm warning you, Cin, lab techs often have trouble with these little veins," Mare confessed.

"I'm a pro. I'll get it the first time. Don't you worry."

"How are your parents doing now that things have settled down a little? They were pretty stressed when we saw them at New Year's."

"They are better, but they've been through a lot. It takes time."

"That's true," she concurred as she slid the needle into Mare's forearm. "It's a good thing they have a strong marriage. A difficulty like that tears many couples apart. But they've been able to rise above it, it seems."

Mare nodded quietly. "Yep, some couples don't make it through such ordeals." *What about Pete and me? We have had to be strong too? We have done well to keep it together.*

"Okay, so you know how this *Glucose Tolerance Test* works, right. You ate nothing this morning?"

"We ate nothing."

"Good, next you drink the sugar drink. You come back every hour, and we test your blood sugar level. Let's see if we can't figure out if low blood sugar may be part of the reason for your low energy and related symptoms."

"'Kay. See you in an hour."

Mare was looking for any explanation that might account for her low interest in being sexual with Pete. She had even checked with her OB/GYN. She knew that she loved Pete and that he was attractive. Why wasn't she more interested in sex?

Each time Pete and Mare came in for the test, Pete complained of dizziness. The medical staff commiserated with him that he must certainly be hypoglycemic. In the end, however, the couple discovered that, though they each had low blood sugar problems, Mare's readings were lower than Pete's.

*   *   *   *

On happy hour Friday, Mare and the crew from Emerson High went to the Pub after school, as they did most weeks. While beer and wine streamed steadily into tall glasses, teachers talked about all of the things on their mind.

"Have you heard about Connor Rand?"

"Oh yeah, that's that kid who is always getting into fights."

"I have him right now in American Studies," Miriam told them. "He's so angry. He scares me."

"I had him last year too, when he was in school, that is; he was always being kicked out. He is one troubled dude," Joel said. "That kid has some serious problems."

"Yes," Miriam continued, "he's been expelled this time. The school board voted that he can't come back. He keeps violating his probation and breaking school rules. I wish we could find a way to help students like Connor, but it just seems beyond schools to do it. As teachers, we just don't have the power to save them all, though it seems like society expects us to."

"It's his parents' fault," someone else interrupted, "that boy has been seriously abused. He's angry and he wants to make the world pay."

"Yes, but what do we know about his parents, maybe they had rough lives too."

"Oh, come on, we are all responsible for the choices we make. You can't go beating the crap outta someone just because your mother drank and your stepfather was mean to you."

Nods ran around the table. Tristan took a swig of his drink. He was getting a buzz on, Mare could tell. She chuckled as she sipped her own drink. The conversation shifted into separate, smaller discussions.

"So what are we up to this weekend?" Mare asked Tristan.

He turned to her, and answered, slurring ever so slightly, "Roni and I are going to a dance performance in Portland."

"Yeah," Roni added her two cents, "a couple of friends of mine are lead dancers."

"You going, Sophie?" Mare looked at her friend.

"Nope, not this time. I'm going to stay home and get some work done."

"You wanna come, Mare? You should come with us. You like dance," Tristan encouraged her.

Roni hesitated a moment, then added, "Yeah, Mare, come along, if you like. We can get an extra ticket, I imagine."

"Thanks, I'd love too, but Pete and I are going to stay home and rent a movie tonight."

The noise level in the restaurant was pretty high, as Tristan got up to go to the bathroom. Sophie and Roni chatted.

A woman in high heels crossed in front of Tristan, and Mare watched him check out her legs as she slinked by.

He looked back at Mare with raised eyebrows and a devilish grin while he waited for her to pass so he could get through. "High heels are really sexy, don't you think?"

Mare was amused, but slapped him playfully on the back as he continued on his way to the men's room. *That is unlike him.*

37

The Goddess, the Bear, the Tree, and the Dragon

When we energetically and dramatically encounter [the] mythic realm and the beings who dwell there, we begin to understand that our individual lives—our personal stories—echo the events and truths of their lives and stories. We reflect these mythic beings and they reflect us ... We begin living with the doors and windows of ordinary life wide open to the depth world.

—Jean Houston, The Hero and the Goddess: The Odyssey as Mystery and Initiation

Oranges, yellows, and reds flickered past Mare's vision, as she sped along the rural routes of Maine and New Hampshire on her way to the dream workshop in Vermont. It was a glorious time to be driving through the mountains and forests of an autumn-cloaked New England in late September. Orchards, ripe with her favorite Macintosh apples, flashed through her windows. The Kangamangus Highway of New Hampshire with its colorful mountain passes looked like an artist's palette.

A feeling of freedom and exhilaration trailed her as she made the three-plus-hour trek towards Lake Champlain.

Danielle had been nervous to learn that Mare was attending a workshop on dreaming. "You can't always trust people who dabble in dreaming."

"I'll be careful," Mare assured her new friend. For Danielle, dreaming was a private matter, not something to be discussed with a group of strangers.

*   *   *   *

"Hi there!" Mare greeted the workshop host, Cheyenne, at the door of her lovely old farmhouse. "So nice to finally meet you after talking on the phone all those times."

Since Mare was trying to save money, Cheyenne had offered her backyard for the woman to camp.

"Do you want to join us for dinner and a drink? This used to be a colonial tavern back in its heyday."

"Really? How cool! I would like to get my tent set up and everything ready for tonight before it gets too dark. Would that be okay?"

"Go for it."

Mare got to know Cheyenne and her fiancé over dinner that night, and the next morning they offered her the use of their shower.

"How'd you sleep last night?"

"I slept well. It was windy and I kept dreaming that I was surrounded by teepees. I could see a silhouette of a Native American woman. She looked over to me, and the wind fluttered her hair."

Cheyenne nodded, "I'm sure you did. They used to live on this land. They pop up in my dreams too. If you happened to have dreams about a leprechaun-type character, he lives here too, and a few fairies like to check things out occasionally too."

"Okay, I'll keep a watch out for them," Mare chuckled. She wondered if people could actually see such things. She hadn't, except in dreams.

"I'm sorry. I'm losing my voice for some reason," Cheyenne said. "This is a bad weekend to get laryngitis. I hope it passes."

During their phone calls, Cheyenne had told Mare that she was Native American and that she was a shaman. Mare knew little else about her, except that she worked with animals.

Other workshop participants began arriving, along with Robert, who would lead them through the weekend's activities. Mare wondered what they would do. Robert laid out a beautiful purple cloth in the middle of the floor and began placing items in the middle that held special meaning and power for him. Candles, stones, some small statues, a large feather, and other items speckled the surface. He invited participants to place their own items on the cloth.

Robert had white hair that surrounded his crown like a flame. He was tall and imposing; his voice powerful and theatrical. Mare was impressed by his vast knowledge of ancient history, mythology and various cultures. He wove entertaining stories into lessons in dreaming.

After the small group of participants introduced themselves, Robert asked them each to think of a dream they had experienced recently and to give it a title. Through the course of the weekend, each person would have a chance to share their dream, formulate questions they still had about it, and hear feedback from Robert and the group regarding it. Robert stressed to the group the importance of saying, "If it were my dream" or "in my dream of your dream" … this is what I see.

"Each of you is your own dream expert. Perhaps we can help shed some light on darker areas, however."

Robert invited Mare to share a dream. She gave the title "Recovered Organs." She narrated the dream through once. She told them about the bizarre train ride. The scary corner. The man who kept trying to grab her. The large, powerful and black female driver. The phone call about picking up her pictures. Standing at the customer service desk. Receiving her bag of organs. Walking slowly to the door and across the street. Being in the back of the hospital and spreading the contents of the bag on the trashcan lid. Noticing the speck of dirt on her heart. Hearing others approach and replacing them in the bag. Watching as others did the same thing she had just done. When she was finished, she placed her hands in her lap and look around at the other participants.

The group asked her clarification and detail questions. As he did in his letter, Robert suggested that this dream needed to be dreamed on. Mare agreed.

"You've got a lot of great imagery here with the train ride, the unusual driver, the bag of organs and the trashcan. It should be easy for the group to go back in with the guidance you've given. Well, are you ready to go back into the dream?"

"I guess so," Mare responded, "but I have a question. Will I actually see the dream like I do when I'm sleeping, or is it more of a visualization?" Mare always wanted to know the how of such things. She didn't want to do it wrong.

"It could be either. Let's just see what happens, shall we?" His eyes glittered.

Outside Robert unfolded a large blanket and laid it out carefully on the grass. "Mare, let's have you in the center, and each one of us will pick a spot around you."

"Now, remind us what we are going in to find out."

Mare said, "I want to know why the bus driver turned so hard and almost crashed us. Train driver … whatever she was." Sometimes it seemed to Mare like she had been on a bus, sometimes a train. "I want to know why I placed my organs on the trashcan, and mostly I want to get my organs clean and back inside me where they belong." Robert nodded.

Taking his hand drum by the cross bar frame in the back, Robert said, "I am going to begin drumming in a minute. Drumming has been a tool of the shaman for thousands of years. Many cultures ancient and contemporary have used percussion to shift their awareness so that they may journey into non-ordinary reality, the place from which dreaming emerges. Here, a shaman or a dream traveler may receive knowledge, spiritual guidance or healing, either for themselves or for others in their community." He let the beater dangle with his arm, as he provided the academic background for drumming. "If you know anything about brain waves, you might be familiar with the patterns of alpha, beta or theta rhythms. Normally, during waking hours, our brain waves oscillate anywhere between 13-30 cycles per second. This is *beta*. At this state, your mind is alert. When your brain is in a mild trance state, like when you are first waking, it beats a little slower in an *alpha* rhythm, which is about 8-13 cycles per second. During deep sleep, your brain waves register at the *theta* rate of about 4-7 beats per second. Scientists have studied the practice of drumming in recent years, and they understand that if you beat a drum at a rate of about 4 beats per second, your mind tends to synchronize with the drum beats and can slip into a brainwave pattern that is similar to deep sleep. The repetition and rhythm of the drum or a rattle, or even certain kinds of singing and dancing, can put you in this altered state of consciousness. This is a good way to consciously go back into a dream state and do what you need to do."

"Okay, lie down and cover your eyes with your bandana. When you hear an alteration in my drumming, I am calling you back. Wherever you are and whatever you are doing, return to the sound of the drum." Robert began to thud the beater against the deerskin surface.

Mare let her mind follow the thumping of the drum. She waited for images to enter her mind. She thought back through the dream. She was on the train with Pete. The travelers leaned. The driver cut sharply. The train almost tipped. Mare stomped to the front and spoke to the driver. She threw the harassing man off the train. She got the phone call telling her about having forgotten to pick up her pictures. She went to the office. Got the bag and was surprised when she discovered her own organs. Started walking out. Struggled to move. Pulled the liver off her tongue ... a memory she had forgotten in the earlier retelling. Went across the street, behind the hospital, laid her organs on the silver lid, saw the dirt, heard people coming, packed up the organs. Then she walked into the hospital and asked a doctor to put them back in. When her organs were back inside her she didn't know what to do. She flew a ways. She stopped at an old woman's campfire, and began a conversation. Then she heard the call back.

She kept her eyes closed as Robert finished calling back the participants. While she waited, with her awareness back on her body, Mare wondered if she had been successful. It wasn't as vivid as dreaming for her. She had trouble seeing things. She wondered how much her mind had simply made stuff up along the way. She knew the mind was a powerful thing; so perhaps even making it up would affect the healing process. She wasn't sure.

When she opened her eyes, Mare noticed that Cheyenne, who had been on Mare's right with her head against Mare's arm, was now standing close to the house, coughing.

"How are you feeling," Robert asked.

"I'm not sure. Pretty well, I think."

Robert invited the other participants to share their visions of Mare's dream. Cheyenne started, "I'm sorry I had a coughing fit and had to move away from the group."

"I didn't even notice," Mare admitted, a bit surprised.

"Good," Robert said, "I was concerned about that too, so I moved into her space. How interesting that you weren't aware of the coughing and motion."

Cheyenne continued with slight difficulty, "I spoke to a beautiful woman in pink. She said that two spirits wanted to be your child, but that your body was unable to carry twins. I'm not sure why. Both of the spirits were girls. I spoke to one. Are you trying to have a baby?"

"Yes, I have been. And I want to name her Olivia … Liv. I wonder if that is at all connected with the liver on my tongue?"

The woman who had been at Mare's feet asked to speak next. "Speaking of giving birth … While I was in the dream, I felt an enormous flood of energy coming from you, almost as if you *were* giving birth. It was like I was in the delivery room with you. I think a baby is coming for you."

"Yes," Robert interjected, "in my dream of your dream, you are going to have a daughter as well. Isn't that fascinating. This particular topic hadn't even come up during the preliminary conversation."

"We have been trying for over a year now, without success."

"That is about to change, I think. What other messages did you bring back for Mare?" Several other people shared their visions of Mare's dream. Some spoke to the characters.

"The people near the trash can told me they thought you might be able to help them get their organs back in too. They came for your help."

Mare listened to each story.

Robert rounded out the discussion by saying, "Well, I would like to share the powerful vision I had of your dream. In my dream of your dream I spoke with the driver. She's no ordinary driver. She reminds me of a female African deity I'm familiar with who is an embodiment of the earth with the powers of creation. She's a powerful goddess. She is steering your course, and she knows she is taking you by surprise. She's a character, let me tell you." He bellowed a hearty laugh.

Mare was not very surprised by Robert's vision. "She has shown up in other dreams of mine. In another, she was totally and unabashedly nude and singing in a nightclub. I was embarrassed for her."

Robert's eyebrows rose in delight and he nodded. "She is mischievous, but I believe you can trust her. The woman on the phone is another goddess figure who visited you. Two in one dream ... quite unusual! I was not surprised to see the spirit of the bear enter the drumming circle. The bear in Native American tradition is a very powerful healer. This bear is the one I saw clean and replace your organs." Mare asked some questions and Robert filled in more details about his experience of entering her dream.

She had many images of bears around her home and had recently purchased a tiger's eye necklace in the shape of a bear. Tiger's Eye was one of her favorite stones. She loved the shining browns and blacks of it that seemed to blend together so fluidly.

"I think we need to do something to honor your big dream, Goddess." He had come up with a new title for her after her dream. So, now they had a queen and a goddess. No one else had been "blessed" with a nickname yet. He called her "Goddess" for the remainder of the weekend. She *did* feel like a Goddess.

"What do you suggest, Robert?"

"I think before we go to dinner, we should take a walk down to the lakeside and pay a toll to the earth goddess for her assistance."

"How do we do that?"

"I will show you."

On the way down to the water, the group was joking around and talking. Mare and Robert hung back and strode side by side.

"This last year has been such a transformational one for me, Robert. So much is happening and I have so many questions. Not long ago I had a dream about a shadow figure that entered my home. Do you know anything about such things?"

"During the drumming, I did see some shadows."

Mare confided to him briefly about her brother and how she was writing a book about her spiritual awakening that seemed to be accompanying the struggles.

"Perhaps I will write about this weekend one day."

"It is clear to me that you are undergoing what is called in mythical circles *the dark night of the soul.* I'm pleased to hear you are writing about your initiation experiences."

The sun was getting lower in the horizon when they reached the water.

"We need to find a good tree that has some kind of opening in it." He began to scan the area for candidates. "Then I want you to deposit the coin you brought in the hole. It'll be a symbolic gesture to honor your dream and give something back to the Earth in return for your own fertility."

Mare giggled and moved to a nearby Oak. She looked up at the trunk and started laughing. Within seconds, the whole group was rolling. At about the level of Mare's chest on the tree trunk, was a five-inch, twisted slit. It looked exactly like a wooden vagina, labia and all!

"Only too appropriate, isn't it?" Robert grinned. "Perfect. I think you found the right one."

When Mare stopped choking on her laughter, she said, "That whole piece of bark that surrounds it is barely touching the tree. If I put a quarter in there, it's not going to stay. It's going to drop right through."

"Try it," he urged her.

With the quarter between her thumb and index finger, coupled with some embarrassment as to the sexual suggestiveness of the act, Mare inserted the coin into the opening. She waited for it to drop out the bottom of the disconnected bark. It did not. Mare pushed on the slab of bark slightly to see if it had gotten snagged. Nothing happened. The coin had disappeared into the tree.

Mare looked at Robert with raised eyebrows. His amusement was obvious by the elfin grin on his lips and the twinkle in his eyes.

One of the women took a picture of Mare with Robert and the tree.

Later that evening the group went to a local restaurant for dinner. The woman Robert called "Queen" noticed from the menu that a hundred years earlier it had been a brothel. The table was lively with animated conversation and laughter. A short while later, a leather-clad man in his thirties stopped at the table, a drink in his hand. He addressed the whole group and tried to flirt with Queen. Feeling a little uncomfortable with his presence, she tried to subtly and politely get the man to leave. Robert's temper flared, and he gave a more direct instruction to the man who then stumbled off in a huff.

"I apologize, folks," Robert continued. "The tiger in me gets very upset about such flagrant rudeness to women." In a moment he was completely calm again. He added, "Often spirits who have not moved on will frequent places they spent time at while they were living. If this truly was a brothel, perhaps the spirits of some of its former patrons still linger, attaching themselves to weaker, troubled souls who wander in. Then they get to behave the way they did while they were living."

The group thought about his words. Mare said,"I think there is also a high energy coming off this group. We are radiating. He could have been drawn to us like a moth to a flame."

"Very true, Goddess. Very true."

*   *   *   *

That night the wind picked up, but it was not enough to dampen the campfire they started. One of the women had brought her guitar and a few women sang songs.

Robert suggested they go through a little ritual. "Decide upon something you want to get rid of. We'll burn it in the fire. It can be something physical, but more likely than not, it'll be something intangible. Feel free to write it on a slip of paper. Then toss it to the flames." He gave a few further recommendations to them, and in a few minutes announced what he wanted to part with.

"I let go of my ego's hold on me. I release my concerns relating to vanity and pride … again." He said a few other things then flung his paper into the fire. He spit on it afterwards, which apparently dispelled any negative spiritual attachments that came with it.

Mare went last. Not everyone said what she was letting go of. Mare announced with certainty, "I am letting go of my sorrow and my loneliness. I let go of my anger and fear. I will be joyful and free. It's up to me." She expelled a quick breath of air onto the fire, symbolizing the discharge of the things from which she wanted release.

Since the wind was howling and her tent was flapping furiously, Mare accepted Cheyenne's invitation to stay upstairs in her office. Other participants were staying at a local bed and breakfast. Robert slept on the living room futon. Mare brought in her sleeping bag and pad, and placed them on the floor in the upstairs office. It had been an eventful day, and she was exhausted.

Mare slept fitfully. Strange visions and sensations entered her dreams. In the morning, she was tired, but feeling happy. She went downstairs where Robert and Cheyenne were waiting for her. They were both smiling when they saw her.

"How did you sleep, Goddess?" Robert asked mischievously.

"I dreamed of both of you," Mare said with some enthusiasm and a little confusion. "I don't remember much in terms of plot, but I remember a dragon came to me. It was like he was made of fire. I think he placed a spirit inside me," she said somewhat awkwardly. "I feel like I joined with another last night, like there was a spiritual conception. It feels like my daughter is with me now in spirit." Mare knew it was a bizarre report, and she barely believed it herself, but she couldn't help sharing it.

Both Cheyenne and Robert nodded in understanding.

"Yes, it *was* a spiritual conception. You are going to have another baby."

Thrilled, Mare inquired when Robert thought it would happen physically.

He shrugged, not really wanting to answer the question. "It depends, but I would say not long, maybe a couple of months."

Mare beamed with excitement and fulfillment.

"This is going to be a very special child, Goddess. Very special indeed. I would be honored to be Olivia's godfather, if you should be in need of one."

A little surprised, Mare responded, "I am flattered by your offer, Robert, and I will talk it over with my husband. Thank you. For everything."

Later in the day after working with more people's dreams, Robert took them outside for a short exercise in raising their consciousness to a higher level. "Spread out," he told them.

When each had found a spot he told them, "Think of a tree that perhaps is particularly special to you. Picture that tree in your mind."

Immediately, Mare imagined the old maple beside her porch.

"Imagine," Robert continued, "that you are inside that tree, your arms stretching to the sky as all your branches are."

The wind was still blowing furiously. Mare's eyes were closed and for an instant she lost herself in the wind again. Swaying in the swirling air.

"If you ever want to journey into the upper world, just use this tree to transport you there. The World Tree in ancient traditions links the human world with the world of spirit. Your consciousness can move into a higher level of consciousness through this relationship. Remember." Mare barely heard his words, nor would she have quite understood the idea of an upper world. Her consciousness had moved elsewhere for the moment.

*   *   *   *

That evening, after the drive back from Vermont to Maine, Mare wrote Robert a letter.

Dear Robert,

The most amazing thing happened while I was driving back from the work-shop. I just have to tell you. I was "ushered" home by the most spectacular dis-play of heat lightening I have ever seen! It started before St. Johnsbury, VT, and didn't stop through all of New Hampshire and into Maine. It was like fire-works—no, it was more like popcorn, in frequency at least. I swear, during the entire 2 ½ hours (or more) of these brilliant flashes, it did not pause longer than ten seconds between blasts! Forgive the sexual reference, but it was like the sky was having multiple orgasms. Ha!

Pete told me that it hit our town about a half hour before I arrived home. It continued for an hour after I pulled into my driveway. I called my friend, Sophie; she claims that she has only seen one other storm in her life that was as luminous or powerful.

They were no little specks off in the distance. They were huge, explosive bursts of light that splashed across the night sky, always to my front and/or left (from the North). There was no mistaking or overlooking it; it demanded that all take notice. I can't believe it tracked the same path I did. It would have been unremarkable if it had lasted a half hour and then moved off in a different direction from me. Instead, I'm convinced it followed me through three states!

I thought you might get a chuckle about it, though I doubt you are sur-prised. I wasn't. So much happened that amazed me this weekend. It just seemed to fit with the rest. I felt like it was all for me, or for my child at least. It was wonderful.

With love,

"The Goddess"

About a week later, she received his response.

To: The GODDESS c/-Mare

O Radiant One,

I was thrilled to read your account of the homeward journey, illuminated by heat lightening. I wonder if the Magi saw light effects of this kind as they followed their star? Some of the old Persian accounts suggest that it was a pillar of light and/or a traveling radiance in the sky—rather than a distant stellar phenomenon—that guided them to and from the birthplace of the Holy Child.

I hope you are well in all ways. It was a joy sharing all our dreams and adventures on the island.

  Love and sweet dreams,

RM

*   *   *   *

"A dragon?" Danielle questioned suspiciously. "Do you know anything about this dragon or these people? How do you know it is associated with your highest good?" Danielle barely tried to stifle her concern, but even with her brief comments, Mare could see that Danielle did not trust any of Mare's workshop experiences or the people who were part of it.

"I know that Robert is human, with human failings and challenges, but he is interested in bringing about the highest good," Mare said. Remembering that he threw into the fire, she added, "I think he struggles with some ego issues, like we all do, but his heart is in the right place, I feel certain. He has many gifts to contribute."

Mare knew that Danielle's experiences were more private, and that she was quite guarded about certain esoteric practices. Mare had experienced difficulties getting Danielle to open up about much of her own experiences.

"Well," Danielle looked at her dubiously. "Here." She scribbled some words onto a sheet of paper and handed it to Mare. "Before you go to bed each night, I want you to say this. Say it aloud if you can, but if Pete is there, you might just want to think it. Set your intent firmly on it."

"It's a prayer. It was taught to me by a dear friend, who was a dance mentor and a Ba 'Hai for 60 of her 93 years. I substitute "creator" for gender-identified words. I find if I recite it slowly and solemnly by the time I'm done I've arrived at the first gate."

Mare thought back to some of her readings. "I'm not sure I understand what you mean by the first gate."

"I keep forgetting. Dreaming has happened spontaneously to you. You haven't had any real instruction. Some other day, we'll get together and talk about it. Now that I know that I have been called here in part by you, I need to re-deploy my energies so that I can manage the different tasks in front of me. I need to get rid of a few things. When I'm finished, I will be more ready to help you. I would like to do two things. I am hoping to gather a small group of dreamers I know together to meet and dream together. In the meantime, when is your birthday?"

"February 13th ... why?"

"I'm going to make you something. I need to dream and get guidance on it, but I should be able to have it by your birthday."

Mare couldn't imagine what it would be.

"Also, I would also like to gather a group of women, maybe some of our young students too, to dance. I used to be a dance instructor. I would be willing to organize it to start."

"Sounds great. My shoulder has been bothering me a little, so I haven't been able to do T'ai Chi lately. Dancing would be a great way to get my energy going."

"How has *your* dreaming been lately?" Mare asked Danielle, hoping to tap into some of the mysteries she felt Danielle had been keeping under wraps to this point.

"It's been fine, except I keep being confronted with repeat images of water that scare me. I'm not feeling overwhelmed by anything in my present daily life so that apparent symbolism doesn't feel appropriate. Last night I dreamed I was in a coastal area and enormous waves were breaking close to me. It feels like I'm being invited to enter, but I don't dare. I almost drowned as a child. Rough or big water like that is frightening to me."

"I love water," Mare said. "Water is my element. Jung says that water is representative of the subconscious or collective unconscious. Perhaps by diving into it, you will be able to explore yourself in a new way. I've had a lot of water dreams in the last few years."

"Perhaps, but I haven't found the courage yet."

"I've also read that the medium of water can act like a portal in dreams."

"Yes, I sense that it is a medium or conduit or some type of transformative medium, but I don't understand what to. I find myself looking into and through the water, sometimes realizing that I'm looking through a curtain of sorts and that I'm on one side and *something* is on the other beckoning me. I don't have a trust of the *something* at this point. We'll have to see. Maybe I'll have to come get you next time and you can help me experiment with it. I don't feel safe around it."

"I'd be happy to." Mare examined the petite but powerful woman. "You know, I think we were brought together because our strengths and weaknesses compliment each other. Perhaps I need to be more cautious, and you need to let go and trust a little more."

Danielle returned the gaze, uncomfortable. "Perhaps. I've got to get going. I'll see you soon."

"Talk to you later." Danielle left. Mare looked at the prayer in her hand.

> *Oh Creator, refresh and gladden my spirit,*
> *purify my heart and illumine my powers.*
> *I lay all my affairs in thy hands.*
> *Thou art my guide and refuge.*
> *I will no longer be sorrowful or grieved,*
> *I will no longer dwell on the unpleasant things of life.*
> *I will be a happy and joyful being.*
> *Great Spirit, thou art more friend to me than I am to myself.*
> *I dedicate myself to thee, oh creator.*

38

Secret Places and the Spirits Who Reside There

Suffering and joy teach us, if we allow them, how to make the leap of empathy, which transports us into the soul and heart of another person. In those transparent moments we know other people's joys and sorrows, and we care about their concerns as if they were our own.

~Fritz Williams~

After a brief shopping venture in a large department store, Mare, Pete and another couple headed out the front entrance. In the breezeway of the store, which was surrounded by glass walls, Mare stopped to look at a few sales racks. She picked up a coat she liked that was priced at $50. It had a 70% off tag. Under the coat itself was a sharp-looking, suit-dress. It was a complete set. It was an above-the-knee getup, and Mare told the others she was going back in to try it on.

In the center of the giant store Mare found a smaller sub-store with a counter. The man behind the counter was ready to assist, Mare sensed, but she moved past him into the dressing room. Mare tried on the outfit and looked into the mirror at the brick-red colored suit. She liked it. It fit well and looked great. She decided she would need some shoes to match, so she went back out the glass door of the dressing room area to look for some. She took a left out of the door and noticed another door on her immediate left that said EXIT. It was almost in the exact center of the large store. Mare felt a curious pull towards it, and yet there was something forbidden about it. She got the feeling she might be trespassing or violating some rule to go through it, but she couldn't resist exploring it further. Bringing her nose closer to the glass, she tried to peer through it to the other side. Only a hallway lay beyond. Nothing more could be seen. *Not many people pass through this EXIT.* Despite her reservations about whether it was right or not, Mare's sense of adventure and inquisitiveness urged her on. She opened the door.

She felt a slight chill as it first swung open, then closed behind her. Something was very different in here.

She began walking down the long, narrow corridor. It had many turns, but no doors. The further she explored the more unsure she became about whether she was supposed to be in this secret place. Eventually the walls opened up into open rooms. The corridor continued, Mare could see, but now there were these couple of side rooms. About waist high were barriers, almost as in museum exhibits. Inside these side rooms were images of floating energy. Atomic generation or radioactive molecular studies are thoughts that passed through her mind. It looked like a secret science lab. Matrix was a word that popped into her awareness when thinking about this place. This seemed a place that touched the source of all … The building blocks of life.

Mare glanced down the hall. It went on further than she could see. She sensed a vastness that seemed somehow familiar … and frightening. Maybe she was venturing too far?

Her fear of getting caught doing something she wasn't supposed to be doing overtook her initial feeling of courage. She needed to go back. She did an about-face. On the return walk, she passed an older man. Mare half-expected him to scold her, but he barely noticed her presence and said nothing.

She hesitated. He's going in. Part of her wanted to turn back to see where he was going, but the vast unknown was somewhat unnerving and the voice of fear won out.

Soon she came upon the original door and re-entered the store. She took a deep breath and sighed. Mare got it into her head that she wanted some Native American moccasins. She looked around again. On the way to the shoe department, she saw some very unique coffee mugs. One in particular caught her eye. It had a cloudy background with a deer and a bear on it. Mare thought it was something Pete would like. Examining it, she noticed that it was a sort of hologram, changing as she turned it. The wild animals changed into cows. She never did find the traveling shoes.

*   *   *   *

"Danielle, I had this bizarre dream the other day." Mare told her about her mall/exit dream.

"You have such fascinating imagery for the other side."

The other side? Mare pondered that for a moment. "It was amazing. I really want to go back in and talk to the man in the dressing room. I know he could have helped me. He was a guide, but because I didn't realize I was dreaming, I didn't think to ask him. He was definitely the one. They don't reach out unless you ask, I guess."

"Ah hah." Danielle nodded. She paused a moment. "Speaking of gateways … I had another water dream last night. The gigantic waves were a hundred feet high." Mare's attention was fully with her. "You were with me this time. I was petrified, but together, we went through the watery curtain on a journey. You were correct. It was a gate."

"What happened? I don't remember being there."

"I'd rather not talk about this at school. You need to come over to my house some time. We'll go for a walk and talk about it in more detail."

10/5/98—"Angels and Ghosts"

I am near a warehouse/old mill beside a lake. In the sky, I see a man with beautiful wings, but he looks like he is in some kind of trouble, like he is doing battle. The scene looks like it could come from a painting. Am I on a field trip with students? We enter the building. The kids with me are younger now, elementary, not high school students. One is throwing up on the stairway. I want to help her and I lean over her to see what I can do. Unsettling spirits are around in cloud-like form. I wonder if this is why the child is vomiting. I, too, try to shake off the unpleasantness of my surroundings. A woman/a seer who is more like a benevolent spirit covers my body with hers to protect me—to act as a barrier—against the ghostly negative presences. She does not want them to touch me. She is familiar somehow. This is a dangerous place.

*   *   *   *

In early October, the national news reported the murder of Matthew Shepard, a young gay man who was lashed to a fence post, brutally beaten, and left to die. Mare's heart sank. She was sorry for Matthew and his family. Sorrow filled her that mankind could hate a stranger out of fear of what he represented.

The same month at Emerson, a student group was started—*the Gay/Lesbian/Bi Alliance.* Club members wanted school to be a safe haven for all students. They asked to speak to faculty about what it is like to face discrimination. They had stickers made to put on the doors of any faculty member who would accept a student regardless of his or her sexual orientation.

Mare put the sticker on the corner of her classroom door. *You will find kindness here.*

*   *   *   *

10/21/98—"Hiding the Sprite"

I am inside my enormous Maple beside my home, visiting with the fairy who lives there. Someone knocks on the door. I take a magic wand and sprinkle something over the fairy so my visitor can't see her. The language arts curriculum chair, Natalie Dugan, who is also a friend, comes in and looks around as if she feels something more is there, but can't identify it. I just smile innocently.

*   *   *   *

Mare recognized the blue envelope when she picked up her mail. It was another letter from Seth.

11/5/98
Dear Mare,

Thanks for the letter. Please understand that I have been taught from a very early age that people who are gay are to be laughed at. That they should be made fun of and that there is something wrong with them. Even now society bashes gays and churches bash gays.

Look what happened to Matthew Shepard. What harm did he do to them? Still, just because he was gay, he was hated enough to be murdered. People are afraid of us. Why? Last night my roommates were degrading a fag on *The Jerry Springer Show.* Strangely, it's hard for me to take offense to the language because I was raised with it. I, too, have been taught to believe it is not normal. It's a contradiction inside my head. Hard-wired almost. Nothing you can say can change that feeling, because I learned it growing up, and it has been continually reinforced to this day.

It's difficult enough at the moment being homosexual, but just imagine being a homophobic homosexual. Throw in a little pedophilia and you can see how messed up my life really is.

Thank you for caring and trying to help, but I'm afraid there is little you can do to change the way I feel about the stereotyping and stigma of homosexuality.

As far as what happened when I was a kid, that is only a part of it. A small part. The problems with my sexuality don't come from that. They come from my belief that society doesn't accept homosexuals. Pedophilia came about because I couldn't deal with an adult sexual relationship with a man. I needed someone to love and someone to be loved by and by avoiding an adult relationship it left a huge emotional hole which I filled with the lives of my friends. I thought that was all I needed to be happy, but it was never enough, unfortunately.

I don't blame anyone for who I became. Many factors were involved. I can point to everyone I know and say that something they did or said made me feel a certain way about a certain thing that made it easier or harder for me to deal with that part of my life. But the truth is, it wasn't something that happened, it was the way I reacted to it in my mind. I was drawn to kids for emotional needs. Take my abuse away, and that need would have still been there.

I don't know what the future holds. The past is the past, and can't be changed, no matter how much I want it to be different. I just hope I can cope with everything, and find a way to be happy again. Doesn't seem possible right now, but I'm hopeful. Tell everyone I said hello.

*   *   *   *

Mare was laying in bed in the middle of the night, halfway between sleep and wakefulness. As she began to drift closer towards sleep and dreaming, Mare sensed there were other people in her bed.
She noticed she was wearing a bra and that things were hot and heavy in the bed around her. A picture of Danielle's face came into Mare's mind and almost as soon as it did Mare tried to let go of it. She sensed she was interfering and didn't want to. She tried to detach herself from it all, but it was too late. Into her mind's eye came an image of Danielle and a man. Suddenly, despite Mare's best efforts to escape it, an intense, fast, icy-hot feeling swept her into a spiral of energy, a tunnel. Everything was tingly, especially the sides of her neck. Her ears were ringing.

The next morning, on the way to a curriculum meeting, Mare, with a sly grin, asked Danielle, "What in the world were you up to last night?"

The older woman began to blush.

Mare recapped her experience and apologized. "I tried to break away from it; it was just like getting caught inadvertently in a current that overpowered me, like an orgasmic whirlpool. Seemed like you were having a fun time though."

*   *   *   *

Mare was copying a homework assignment onto the board near the end of class. Her students were talking quietly.

Then a voice rose in volume over the others, "You don't know anything about it. You're ignorant, that's all."

Mare turned around to face them. Her eyes asked, "What's going on?"

"You better be careful, Sean," another student warned. "She might turn you into a toad."

Laughter spread from desk to desk, except for a few girls who sat somberly.

Lori's dander was on the rise. "Oh, that's SO funny, guys. Not."

Mare saw the pentacle dangling from Lori's neck, and was beginning to put the pieces together.

Another female student said, "You are just afraid of us, that's all. You wouldn't bother us at all, if you weren't afraid."

"Yeah, well, who knows what you will do; you probably go out and sacrifice cats or babies or something."

Mare could be silent no longer. "That's enough, gentleman! I will tell you right now." Her voice was stern, but not unkind. "I do not allow harassment of any kind in this classroom. If these young ladies consider themselves to be Wiccans, that is their right. What do you know about the philosophy of Wicca? Do you think they just ride around town on a broom? I have done some research on the religion myself, and although I do not consider myself a Wiccan, I respect those who practice it. True Wiccans are not Satanists. They believe in doing no harm." Her eyes moved around the room, but fell on no one in particular. "It is a highly moral belief system, very respectful of nature, and just because you don't understand it or agree with it, does not give you the right to disrespect a person. You don't have to believe what they believe, but there'll be no language of hatred in this room. In here, we are all human, and we will treat each other with respect, regardless of our differences." A few of her students put their heads down slightly in shame.

Mare sighed in frustration. There was so much she wanted to say, so much she wanted to teach them. She thought about Hitler, Skinheads, gay-bashing, anti-semitism, racism … it was all the same to her. Peace begins on the smallest level—from one person to another. No, even before that. It starts within, with a person's relationship with him or herself. It was not a small conversation. The bell was about to ring.

"Let me tell you something," she added, more calmly and compassionately, "I teach English because I love reading stories about people. I like walking in someone else's shoes for a while. It gives me a broader perspective of life, because I know that my own perspective is limited." She looked around into some of their eyes. "So, please, treat others as you would like to be treated."

After class, the two girls who believed themselves witches came up to thank her. "That was really cool, Ms. Lumen."

"I'm proud of you two for standing up for yourselves. May I ask?" she replied back. "How much do you really know about Wicca?" Mare asked, afraid the girls themselves were drawn in by stereotypes of being different. If they were going to declare themselves Wiccans, that was fine, but she wanted to make sure they were also educated about it.

"My grandmother taught me some stuff. I have a book of spells."

"Have you read any books about it?"

"No," Janet said, "I haven't." The second girl indicated that she hadn't either.

"Well, I've got a couple I'd be happy to lend to you. Learn about it; really know what you are talking about."

"Sure, that'd be great. I didn't know there were books about it."

"You know maybe we can design an assignment for you where you create a brochure or something that educates people about the Wiccan belief system. It could be distributed to schools—teachers and students. I'm sure a lot of people don't understand it, and where there is ignorance, there is fear."

"That would be so awesome!"

"Great, so do some research yourselves. I'll bring the books in tomorrow."

*   *   *   *

Later that day, Mare bumped into Sophie. "So, do you and Tristan want to help with our haunted trail at our Halloween Party?"

"Definitely, it sounds like a lot of fun. You heard that Roni is having a dance party before yours at the studio?" She squirmed a little.

"Yes, I'm not going because I need to take Cody trick or treating. He's going to be a cowboy. He has the cutest little cow-pattern chaps. Then I need to get everything ready for our party, but we were invited to Roni's."

"Is Pete going with you?"

Mare nodded her head no. The two held eye contact for a moment, and then Sophie nodded.

"Alright, I guess we're going over there first, and then coming to your party."

"Okay, cool." She studied her friend's face. You don't seem very happy. Is it Roni?"

Sophie nodded. "I've just got a bad feeling. Roni's doing this holiday show. She wants Tristan to be part of it. He's been spending a lot of time over at the studio practicing the dance they are going to do. I hate feeling jealous, but I can't seem to shake it."

"What do you want to do about it?"

"Honestly, I'd like to forbid them from spending time together, but how can I do that? She is my friend, and he is my husband. I want to be able to trust them. I don't know what to do."

*   *   *   *

At about 9:00 Sophie arrived at the party. She was dressed like something that just stepped out of *A Midsummer Night's Dream*. She had on a brown leotard, and small branches and leaves were coming out every direction. "I'm a tree," she told Mare with a limp smile. Something was bothering her.

"You look very natural and pretty," Mare put an arm around her friend's shoulder and led her further into the party. "Where's Tristan?"

She looked a bit uncomfortable or stressed. "He's still at the other party. He said he would be here shortly. That party is closing down, because it was for students and teachers, so folks who are coming from there should be arriving now. Looks like there are already a lot of people here. Hey, cool pirate costume, Mare." Sophie was trying to be upbeat.

"Thanks. Come on in. We've got a witch and the Queen Mother and Queen Elizabeth. A cowboy and cowgirl, a sheik, a cat, Pete's a Klingon, let's see what else? Would you like some wine?"

Music was playing. People were laughing and talking. Mare went around snapping pictures.

Mare's colleague, Dave, showed up, along with his wife, Emma. Emma was clad in a witch's dark garb with black makeup around her eyes. She was such a lively, intelligent woman. Mare wanted to get to know her better. She did not know it yet, but they would become close friends in the years ahead.

Roni's husband showed up next, along with a Russian colleague. Tristan and Roni soon thereafter. Roni had chosen a pirate's costume similar to Mare's. Neither was especially pleased by the duplication. Tristan had dressed up as a woman. With his shoulder-length, strawberry blond hair, long legs, scarlet lipstick, and heels he was quite a knockout. Mare ribbed him about it. "You are a gorgeous woman, Tris!"

He and the Russian had been drinking vodka for a few hours now. They were both pretty hammered, but Tristan was showing the signs more.

"Did you hear about Kate Maguire?" someone asked a small group gathered around him. "She and Trevor are living together in Portland. I guess the rumors were true."

Sophie looked at Mare. Mare shrugged.

"You've always supported her and stood behind her innocence," Sophie said to her privately. "Has she been in touch with you since she left Emerson?"

"No. I found out from Bernard she had quit, but I knew she would go if she got another offer. I don't blame her for wanting to leave."

"Did she ever say goodbye to you or anything before she left?"

"Nope ... but you know, I'm not surprised. We had begun to drift apart." Mare thought back to when she had severed the cord. She adjusted her eyepatch, so she could see better. "I won't ever know the truth about them. Even with this news, I would rather give them the benefit of the doubt. They're adults. It's their choice."

At about ten o'clock, Mare and Pete announced that the Haunted Trail behind their house was ready for courageous travelers. Mare led small groups through the trail behind the pond. The night was pitch black. Tristan banged on a barrel to scare the living daylights out of the people who came close to his spot. Other characters jumped out and startled their cohorts. Tombstones were scattered along the pathway and skeletons hung from the trees.

"Hey, the haunted trail was great, Mare," Nan said. "It was very spooky. Tristan about gave me a heart attack banging on that barrel."

Tristan stumbled in towards the group and said, "Speaking of being spooked ... you ever been to a place that gave you the willies? Certain places that just felt different? A little unsafe."

Several people jumped in with stories. Mare relayed one of her own.

"That was your fairy senses," Joel said. "We do have an extra sense that picks up on stuff like that. I always trust mine."

"That's a great way to describe it," Mare said. "Our fairy senses." *I think my fairy senses are pretty strong*, Mare thought to herself as she took another drink.

When Mare's party started to die down, Roni and some of the crew wanted to head into town to a local dance pub. Pete chose to stay home. Mare went anyway, joining Sophie, Tristan, Roni and a few others. By midnight, Mare had consumed nearly a bottle of red wine. She had another glass at the tavern. The group danced hard for an hour or two, closing the place down. While dancing, Mare had left her wine on the table unguarded.

On the dance floor, she felt so uninhibited. She let the rhythm of the music wave through her. She noticed that Roni kept one eye on her, perhaps surprised that she was letting loose to that degree. Roni was a dance instructor. She had the moves, but tonight, Mare didn't feel threatened by that. She sensed some tension, but she didn't pay it much attention.

When the tavern's doors closed, Mare, Roni, Sophie and Tristan went back to Sophie's house. Tristan and Mare both were extremely intoxicated. The four collapsed onto the bed, and Tristan put his arms around the girls. "All of my favorite women are here," he sighed contentedly.

With what lucidity Mare could gather, she considered his statement. She looked with fuzzy perception at the two other women. Each one of the trio had a very different personality. Mare and Tristan had a friendly, competitive camaraderie. They had fun, wrestled, debated, could tease each other. They were almost like siblings. Similar in many ways. Roni who had studied dance around the globe was worldly, expressive, sensual, and liberated. His wife, Sophie, was spiritual, grounded, athletic and wise. You could not find a more solid, loyal ally than Sophie. Each woman was beautiful in her own way—both inside and out. Each had her strengths and her challenges. Her mind wandered to the most famous trio of Greek goddesses: Athena, Aphrodite and Artemis. Each of the women had attributes similar to the goddesses. She could see how Tristan admired them all.

Mare was getting dizzy. She ran to the bathroom and launched whatever was in her stomach. She stumbled for some towels to clean up some of the mess she had made. She could barely stand. "I'd like to go home now," she said. Roni gave her a ride home.

That night, Mare had more troubling dreams about ghostly presences. The veil between the worlds is the slimmest on Samhain, or All Hallows Eve, according to legend. Mare felt that either she had slipped into it, or those from the other side had popped over to visit her. It was not a pleasant interaction.

All the next day, Mare was ill. She couldn't even get off the couch.

"Why didn't you come out dancing with us?" She groaned with effort.

"I didn't feel like it. I was tired."

Mare looked at Pete sadly. Then she changed the subject. "I feel like I have died. Every cell in my body aches! I've never been hung-over this long. The whole day. It seems unnatural. Do you think someone might have slipped something into my drink at the tavern?" she asked Pete.

He shrugged. "Dunno. It's a good thing it's Sunday, so you have time to recover from this."

"I called Sophie a while ago. Tristan has never gotten sick from alcohol in his life. He did last night. He was really trashed. *Must be something about turning 30.* Mare remembered her own 30th. *People's lives get turned upside down.*

*   *   *   *

It was a dark night. Mare, Pete and Cody were on the run. People were after them. A great catastrophe was about to happen. They narrowly escaped being caught at several places. Sometimes they were on land, sometimes on water.

They found a car and jumped in, escaping to a hilltop. Pete needed to fix something so people could live. The whole world was in danger. Mare's father, Rick, followed them in another car as they drove up a trail. The group had to stop several times, although they were in a great hurry to get to safety. Just in time, they made it to the highest point. A protective casing automatically closed around them, like a venus fly-trap closes its two jaws. They were now safe in this womb-like place, no matter what happened outside. Explosions had begun. Mare knew outside was Armageddon.

*   *   *   *

The phone rang twice. Mare picked it up.

"Mare, it's Sophie. Can you come get me?"

"What? Sure. Are you okay?"

Her stability in her voice couldn't belie the restrained emotion behind it. "I will tell you when you get here. Can you come right now?"

Mare looked over at Pete who was typing at his computer. He could watch Cody.

"Yes, I'm on my way out the door."

"Thank you."

Mare pulled into Sophie and Tristan's driveway. Before Mare had stopped the car, Sophie opened her front door and walked stiffly and nobly down the porch and over to Mare's car. She climbed in, and Mare noticed her posture was very upright. Almost in a forced show of pride. Mare knew enough to pull out of the driveway and start down the street. Sophie was silent. Mare looked over at her with concern.

"Let's drive to the lake," Sophie directed, not wanting to get into it until they could stop and do it privately.

Neither woman said anything more while Mare drove through town and out to the lakeside. She parked in a rest area beside the cold, but not yet frozen body of water. The wind was blowing strongly. Mare left the engine running for warmth. Then she turned her attention towards Sophie who began to cry.

"What's wrong? What happened?" She suspected, but she didn't suggest a reason for her friend's despair.

After hyperventilating a few breaths, Sophie said, "I ... I ... found a letter." She put her hands over her eyes. "It fell out of Tristan's pocket when I picked up a shirt. From Roni."

Mare frowned, winced, and put a hand on Sophie's shoulder.

"It was a love letter, obviously." She told Mare a few of the intimate sentiments it expressed.

"I confronted Tristan, and he said that—yes—they had been getting closer. Apparently, Roni's husband found a letter too a few weeks ago, too, but he didn't tell me. Roni and Tristan have gotten it into their heads that they want open marriages. He wants me to let them be together. They've already been trying to talk her husband into buying the arrangement."

"You've GOT to be kidding. He wants to be able to sleep with Roni, and have that be okay with you?"

"Well, Tristan has said that he does not need to sleep with Roni, but that he would like a physical relationship with her."

"But he has been physical with her—to some degree—already?"

Sophie nodded with difficulty.

"Yes, they have thought this whole thing out for months. They see no reason why I should be opposed to it." Again, she sniffed back the tears. "Essentially, he wants my permission to continue seeing her."

"Yes, well the mind works in funny ways. They have had time to rationalize it. The good thing is that if he's asking you at least he hasn't slept with her yet. That's a good thing. At least he respects you enough to do that."

Sophie paused for a moment, looking into Mare's eyes briefly, and then looked out the window at the dry and dead November landscape. *Has she promised Tristan that she would not tell me certain details?*

"Sophie, I am so sorry. How can I help?"

"Can I stay with you for awhile?"

"Absolutely. You are always welcome. Stay as long as you need to."

"Thanks, I hope it's only for a day or two. I can't understand it, Mare. How can he think that I might be able to go along with such a hair-brained plan? I am a Christian. He knows what my morals are. I can't condone what he is proposing. I pledged myself to one man for the rest of my life. He did the same. I can't even imagine having to share my husband with another woman, especially one who claimed to be my friend ... I knew something was wrong. My intuition was sounding the alarm. I don't know what to do now."

"Oh, Soph, go easy. It's a lot to absorb. Give yourself some time. You will find your way. So will Tristan. He's no dummy. He will realize his mistake." She put a hand on her friend's shoulder. "It's part of his journey. He's facing temptation. Most of us have had to experience it. It doesn't mean that he will throw away your life together."

Sophie's thoughts turned to Roni. "She reeled him right in. And you know how she did it?"

Mare waited for her to continue.

"With flattery. 'Oh, Tristan, you are such an awesome dancer. You have a great stage presence; you're a natural!' She has tapped into the man's pride … puffed him way up. What man wouldn't love such an ego stroking? They've got the whole thing worked out in their minds. They see nothing wrong with the idea. Somehow, Tristan thinks that he can love and have a physical relationship with both of us. Well, I won't stand for it. He'll have to choose. It's Roni or me!"

Sophie grabbed a chunk of her chin-length brown hair and pulled it to her lip. "What am I going to do, Mare? If he leaves me, I will be alone for the rest of my life. It's part of my upbringing and integrity. When I married, I pledged myself for life to Tristan and Tristan alone. I cannot remarry, even if he does. I don't want to be alone."

"Sophie, you can't think like that. Stay in the present. None of us can see that far. Don't worry about something that hasn't happened and may never. Draw solid boundaries for yourself, like you have done, and stick to them. You can get through this."

That night Mare talked it over with Pete, while Sophie rested in the room across the hall. Both Sophie and Tristan were dear to Mare; she wanted to help. Maybe, since she was one of "his favorite" women, she could reach out to him.

The other two women were intimately involved. Maybe Mare could hold up a mirror for him. She wasn't happy with him for what he had done, but part of her understood what Tristan was going through. She didn't hate Roni either, but she was angry with her. *Following your heart is one thing, but what about integrity?*

You don't violate your marriage vows. You don't date a married man. You don't pursue someone who is in a committed relationship. You just don't hurt a sister like that.

Mare could understand the feelings of temptation because of her struggles regarding Austin, but such conscious betrayal of a friend was nearly beyond her ability to comprehend.

*   *   *   *

After a few days staying with the Lumens, Sophie returned home to figure things out with Tristan. She put her foot down. If he wanted to stay married to her, he could not see Roni at all. She forced him to make a decision. At first Tristan resisted and fought her ultimatum, trying to get her to see his way.

Most days after school, Sophie would come down to Mare's classroom to talk. Mare listened, and when Sophie was struggling to figure out her husband, Mare tried to explain through her own example. Each time Sophie talked about how she felt rejected, Mare thought of Pete. In many respects, Sophie and Pete were in the same boat. So were Mare and Tristan. The struggles of the one couple acted as a mirror for Mare to look into. She could understand the man's longing. In addition, Sophie articulated her feelings in a way that helped Mare understand Pete's insecurities. After a few conversations with Sophie, Mare wrote Tristan a note.

Dear Tristan,

You are probably tired of reading letters after this weekend, but I feel the need to chat. Let me start by saying that I'm not here to attack or judge you in any way; I hope you know that. You both mean a lot to me, so naturally I want to see you work this out! Of course, I also need to be honest with you about where I'm coming from and/or how I see the matter as a semi-objective semi-outsider. I know this matter is between the two of you, but I want to help you both in any way that I can. So, please hear me out this one time; then I hope you will feel like you can talk to me. It may be helpful for you to think this through with someone other than the two women involved.

Man, this has to be one of the toughest issues a married couple has to face … I don't really know how you're doing or feeling, but I'm sure this has to be very difficult for you. I have talked to Sophie a lot and it kills me to see her suffering the way she has this weekend. Although, I have to admit, I think she is coping with it in a very mature way. Her dreams and entire future are at risk, or if she were simply to go with your request, she would have to give up her own integrity and personal belief system, which is something none of us can live without. Yesterday, Sophie seemed to think that you were angry with her about the way she was responding to the circumstances; I hope this is not true. Although Sophie had fears about this, she was really not prepared for your declaration/confession. She is dealing with it to the best of her abilities, as I'm sure you are.

Remember, you have had several months to rationalize this matter to the point where you believe you are pretty clear about it from your point of view.

However, I would be willing to wager that you came to this point over time, probably after some personal turmoil. Not only that, but the one person (I know of) with whom you have discussed this *has a vested interest* in the decision going her way. How can you get a clear perspective on this situation when you have some hot chick breathing down your neck? It's tough to think clearly under those circumstances, wouldn't you say?

I understand perfectly how you could come to feel the way you do about Roni. She's an attractive woman. Most of us have felt charmed by people outside our marriages. Like I told you, I have struggled with some of the same issues myself this last year. Marriage *can* be a drag. Think of the fun—we get to: pay bills together and worry about how to make ends meet; listen to each other's worries, fears and complaints; see the same face every morning; cook, clean and do laundry/wood/trash for the household—you name it. You just don't get to share those things in a casual relationship. But, there are also some great things about marriage too, like the comfort of knowing someone intimately, of being able to count on another person, of the security of a committed relationship, of learning and discovering the world together, of sharing dreams and watching them come true, of connecting on a deep level.

On a physical level, it's almost impossible for a spouse to compete with the hot rush of energy you get when you first kiss someone, especially if that person is in some way unavailable. That makes it even more attractive. This is what I most miss about married life: flirting and the first passionate kisses. I think about this sometimes with longing and I remember the experiences I've had that fit this description. But, you know ... I've been there; I've done that. In fact, Pete and I had that fire when we first dated. (We still have our passionate moments, but it's not the same as in the beginning. And can never be quite that way again, which is kind of sad. Unless we break up, get back together; break up, get back together. However, we are up to bigger things than playing such games with one another.) We are in it for the long haul; we promised each other and we meant it. Now we are free to explore the deeper experiences of love, the lasting love that is exciting in a different kind of way. The fleeting impulses of a relatively new relationship can't hold a candle to that.

Pete and I have a prediction about your relationship with Sophie. And this isn't easy to admit, although we share it with the best of intentions.... Here it is: It's probable that you will stay together for a while, until your desire to see Roni again becomes more than you can resist. You leave Sophie, since knowing you are sleeping with Roni will be more than she can bear. After a time, a time in which you likely enjoy your indulgence, Roni will tire of you and run off with some intriguing new man. Either that or when you are away from Sophie for a time, you realize that any other woman is shallow in comparison to her. Then you will regret your decision to leave your wife. But, by then, it will likely be too late. This is not what we hope happens, but it is what we fear may happen.

I keep thinking about Odysseus and the Sirens. They looked appealing from a distance. Their song was mesmerizing. They beckoned seductively to sailors. But, as the men drew near, the appearance of the women changed horrifically—only it was too late then to save themselves! Tristan—Odysseus didn't jump into the ocean after them! He trusted the warning and saved himself certain doom. He tied himself to the mast, and only listened to their song.

This situation frankly scares me, for both Sophie's sake and yours. Of course, my opinion doesn't count for much, but I personally believe that you and Sophie are soul mates. You seem to complement each other perfectly. I'm afraid that if you pursue a relationship with Roni, you will lose a woman who is one of the strongest, most selfless, compassionate and rooted women I have ever known. She's expressive; she's playful; she possesses wisdom beyond her years.

Please, if you can shake yourself from Roni's grasp for a moment, think back to your early relationship with Sophie and what drew you to her. You may find that you were building a pretty excellent kingdom together after all, and say to yourself—"What was I thinking?!"

Truly in Friendship,
Mare

Within a few weeks, Tristan decided he needed to take a leave of absence. He was going home to England. The official reason was a *family emergency*. Only a handful of people close to the situation knew what was really going on.

Tristan would have three weeks without either woman to make his decision.

*   *   *   *

11/14/98 *"Pandora's Train"*

My ears are buzzing, and I am going through tunnels. I realize I am dreaming. I am in a moving train. A man with curly black hair and a pockmarked face is holding a gun in front of me. I am not scared, because I know this is a dream. He shoots me in the abdomen. I am unaffected. I say to him, "You can't hurt me. This is a dream. I am all powerful here."

He takes off running towards the front of the train, going from compartment to compartment. I pursue him in a quick flash, but ultimately lose him. In the last car, which I believe is the engine, I stop. The car is empty. I decide to look around. I see lettering on one of the walls of the train car. I move closer to read it. It says PANDORA. I am puzzled by the reference to the Greek myth where the woman's curiosity opens up many troubles for mankind.

*   *   *   *

"Mare, I had a dream last night. Roni and I were facing off. She stood in front of me and said, 'You are never going to have a family! Tristan is coming with me. You will never have the children you always wanted.' I said nothing and neither one of us budged."

"Oh, Soph! Do you think it's just your fear expressing itself? Either that or it's Roni haunting your dreamscape to scare you into stepping away." Mare smiled half-heartedly. She had discussed a few of her dreaming discoveries with her friend, though it was hard for Sophie to acknowledge the possibility of mutual dreaming.

Sophie was strong on the outside, but Mare was concerned for her. After Thanksgiving, Mare, Pete, and Cody brought Sophie with them to look for Christmas trees on her uncle's property. A light snow had dusted the woods, so the group had a good time getting into the Christmas spirit. The four walked, and tried to find trees that would look good in their living rooms. Sophie did not know if they would be spending the holidays together when her husband returned, but she moved on with life as if she were going to. The air was crisp and cool, and the combination of being outside along with their physical exertion, brought color to everyone's cheeks.

"Do you want help decorating at your house, Soph? Or would you like to join us in decorating ours? We would love to have you!"

"We have hot chocolate," Pete grinned trying to coax her to stay.

"Thank you, both. You've been very sweet. I think I'd like to just spend some time alone this afternoon. I had a great time with you though."

Both Mare and Pete hugged Sophie goodbye.

"Have you heard from Tristan yet?"

"Not yet, and I don't expect to for a while. He needs to be alone too, to get his head on straight. I'm not planning to phone him either."

"Call us if you need anything, or if you want some company," Mare urged her.

When the three weeks were over, Sophie drove to the Portland Jetport to pick up her husband, still unaware of his decision. She later told Mare that the hour long ride home was filled with only casual conversation about his trip.

When they arrived home, he told her, "I choose you."

Mare heard all the details at school the next day. She was cautiously happy. They still had a challenging road to travel.

"That's wonderful," Mare threw her arms around her friend. "He would have been a fool not to choose you! He's not a fool. He knows what you're worth!"

Sophie smiled.

"Do you know what happened while he was there? Did he share his thought process with you?"

"A little. It was his friend in Scotland who made the difference. Before he went to Scotland, his family and friends in England kept encouraging him to stay with me. He visited his Scottish friend and told him about his dilemma. His friend said, 'Sounds like you've made up your mind already ... just go with Roni ... That's what you're telling me.' Well, I guess that shocked Tristan. As soon as he was encouraged to go with Roni, he realized that he didn't want to lose me. That *wasn't* what he wanted."

"Hmmm ... that's very interesting. Reverse psychology sometimes works wonders. Give the person the freedom to leave ... *really* give them the choice ... sometimes the desire to leave goes away."

"Just one recommendation," Mare offered. "Take your time. Expect some bumps along the way."

"We've been spending a lot of time wrestling. I think it's our way of transitioning slowly into more intimacy. Plus, it lets us get our frustrations out. I know it does mine. He's telling Roni today after school. I want to speak with her too. Now that Tristan has chosen; I have a few things to say to her."

"I'm sure you do." Mare's eyebrows rose.

"Would you come with me?" Sophie asked her.

*   *   *   *

"Do you really think you should get involved, Mare?" Her husband asked.

"She asked me to. Maybe she's afraid one or the other of them is going to lose their temper."

"I can't wait to hear what happens!" Pete said. "Cat fight!"

*   *   *   *

Mare drove Sophie down to Roni's studio. Mare felt a mixture of excitement and trepidation. Part of her wanted Sophie to let Roni have it, to confront her about the betrayal of their friendship. But Sophie was not a volatile personality. She seemed very calm, although Mare knew her heart was pounding. "What would you like me to do?"

"We agreed to this time, so she knows I'm coming. I think maybe if you waited in the hall outside the main room, just in case."

"You got it."

Sophie and Mare ascended the staircase to the studio. Sophie entered, while Mare remained outside a little lower on the stair. She wasn't sure how long this might take, so she found a folding chair stacked up against the wall and brought it down to the landing between floors. Just as she sat down, she heard the door reopen and Sophie came out.

"You done already?" Mare asked her.

"Yes."

Mare quickly brought the chair back up and left with Sophie.

"What happened?" she asked when they got back to the car.

"I told her that now that Tristan has made a decision I expect her to respect that and stay out of our lives for good." She stopped.

Mare waited.

"That was it?"

"Yes, I didn't feel the need to say more right now. I just wanted her to stay away from my husband."

"What did she say? How did she react?"

"She just kind of rolled her eyes and said, 'whatever … fine.'"

Mare grinned and said, "I would have loved to see her face when you looked her in the eye. I can't believe that's all that happened. I expected yelling, or some bitch-slapping or something!" Mare laughed. "You are a better woman than I. I think I would have had to tell her off."

"I'm done with her. I'm not going to waste that kind of energy on her. He's my husband; he wants to stay married. That's that."

Mare continued driving down the road. She thought about the dream where she had cut and pasted Roni and the row of dancers that came from the back to the front of the performance. She told Sophie about the dream.

Mare confided to Sophie, "I'm angry at Roni, but I also see myself in her. In dreams, I think Roni represents the part of me that wants liberation and freedom of expression, the part that seeks a sort of unrestrained joy. When she started to dance her way to the front of my dream, I felt threatened. I wanted to put that part of myself back in the rear of the show, but I couldn't quite manage that either. She is like a mirror for me. Perhaps that's why she doesn't like me either. Maybe I am her mirror. We are opposite extremes of the same thing. I need to stretch myself and let go more, and perhaps she needs to learn to set some boundaries and maintain some integrity."

Then Mare said, "I see all these mirrors around me. You and Tristan reflecting Pete and me. Danielle and I seem to also be like two sides of the same coin. It's really cool. It makes me think that there are no accidents. We have things to learn from one another about ourselves."

Sophie nodded thoughtfully.

"When Pete and I married, we found a vow that I liked, but I didn't quite understand at the time. We promised to be a 'mirror to our true selves'. I think I understand it better now. I want to hold up the highest mirror I can for Pete. I want to see him the way he would truly like to be seen."

39

Affirmation vs. Judgment

Mare's class began watching some of *The Power of Myth* with Joseph Campbell talking to Bill Moyers. They had been learning about mythology.

> Joseph Campbell: ... Transcendent means to "transcend" or go past duality ... The Garden of Eden is a metaphor for that innocence that is ... innocent of opposites ... Good and evil are relative to the position in which you are standing ... The way to awake [from the nightmare] is not to be afraid, and to recognize that all of this, as it is, is a manifestation of the horrendous power that is of all creation ... And you play your part, not withdrawing from the world when you realize how horrible it is, but seeing that this horror is simply the foreground of a wonder ... I will participate in the game. It is a wonderful, wonderful opera—except that it hurts.
>
> Affirmation is difficult. We always affirm with conditions. I affirm the world on the condition that it gets to be the way Santa Claus told me it ought to be. But affirming it the way it is—that's the hard thing ... The hero is the one who comes to participate in life courageously and decently, in the way of nature, not in the way of personal rancor, disappointment, or revenge ...
>
> So Jesus says, 'Judge not that you may not be judged.' That is to say, put yourself back in the position of Paradise before you thought in terms of good and evil. You don't hear this much from the pulpits. But one of the great challenges of life is to say "yea" to that person or that act or that condition which in your mind is the most abominable.... Once in India I thought I would like to meet a major guru or teacher face to face. So I went to see a celebrated teacher ... and the first thing he said to me was, "Do you have a question?"

The teacher in this tradition always answers questions. He doesn't tell you anything you are not yet ready to hear. So I said, "Yes, I have a question. Since in Hindu thinking everything in the universe is a manifestation of divinity itself, how should we say no to anything in the world? How should we say no to brutality, to stupidity, to vulgarity, to thoughtlessness?"

And he answered, "For you and for me—the way is to say yes."

We then had a wonderful talk on this theme of the affirmation of all things. And it confirmed me in the feeling I had had that who are we to judge? It seems to me that this is one of the great teachings, also, of Jesus.

... Mythology suggests that behind that duality there is a *singularity* over which this plays like a shadow game ... There is the plane of consciousness where you can identify yourself with *that which transcends* pairs of opposites ...

—Joseph Campbell from *The Power of Myth* with Bill Moyers (video or pgs 47-50, 65-67)

"Now that you've heard Joseph Campbell and Bill Moyers speak about some of these mythological topics, what things stand out in your mind?" Mare asked her freshman honors class. She had instructed them to write down at least five important points in each of the first two videos in the series.

A student raised her hand. "Nobody ever talks to us about stuff like this. We don't really know how to operate in the world. I wrote down a quote here ... 'One of our problems today is that we are not well acquainted with the literature of the spirit.' And then later on he says, 'What we're learning in our schools is not the wisdom of life.' Like he said, many teenagers are getting to that transcendent experience by way of drugs. I think he's right. Very few people talk to us about what it means to be alive. We don't get much training in how to be a human being and how to deal with pain."

"Nice job, Melanie. Would anyone like to add to that, or does anyone feel differently?"

"I have a lot of problems with some of the things he said because I believe that the Garden of Eden and the things in the bible are to be taken literally."

"Okay," Mare responded carefully, *it is hard to bring up issues of spirit without stepping on some religious toes.* "You absolutely have the freedom to choose what you believe. I want to make that very clear. But ... what if you could entertain the *possibility* of some more metaphorical interpretations; it might open up worlds of knowledge to us that aren't available by a strictly concrete reading of the stories. It's just a different place to stand and look at things. Consider his words, but believe nothing unless you have done your own original thinking on it. If you don't like the perspective from that place, you can always move back to the original one. Different ideas and discussions are good. You don't have to believe them to hear them. You are free to keep whatever thoughts you entered here with. Thank you for bringing that up, Jennie. What other thoughts do you have, folks?"

Jeff said, "I never really thought about rituals before. How does a person know when he or she is an adult? I mean, we graduate from high school, but does that mean we are now grown ups?"

"I know plenty of adults," Joanna added, "who don't act or feel like adults and plenty of younger people who are way more mature."

"Good point," Mare kept the conversation moving.

She pointed to a hand at her left.

Another boy said, "It's cool that these myths show life hasn't changed much really. The lessons are pretty much true for everyone all over the globe, no matter what kind of culture they came from, no matter the time period."

"Excellent," Mare praised them. "The stages of life are generally the same ... we go from childhood to adulthood to being married to getting ready to die. A lot happens in between, but we still have tons in common with all other human beings now and across the ages. Yet it's our differences that are usually emphasized. I'm not sure those are as important as what we have in common."

Laura's hand went up, although she didn't wait to be called on. "I liked Campbell's discussion about marriage. Man and woman are separate, yet in marriage, if the marriage is truly a partnership, the couple becomes one. To some degree their individual egos have to vanish or at least take a back seat to the concerns and benefits of the partnership."

"Wow, that is very insightful, Laura! If only these kinds of conversations could be had more often. Nice work. Is that the way most marriages operate?" Mare prompted them.

She saw a variety of nods: some up, most down. "So it depends on the individual marriage?"

"It depends on whether the spouses have reached the second level of marriage that he talks about. Are they really committed? Do they have what it takes to become *one*?"

Mare nodded. "What about the whole idea of non-judgment? Can we embrace those people and things which we abhor?"

Her students struggled to respond. "Is it possible," she continued. "That, even if we don't agree with someone's actions or beliefs, we can still feel compassion for them? Is it possible to include them still as part of humanity and forgive them, even if they've made grave mistakes?"

"No," Jeremy insisted; "why should someone who killed someone else get any compassion? They messed up. They should pay!"

Mare was expecting this. She nodded. "I know, Jeremy. A lot of people feel that way. And I'm not saying you are wrong. But—don't we all make mistakes? It doesn't mean we have to condone their mistakes or eliminate consequences, but what if we could still accept them as human beings and wish them well, even if they had wronged us? What if that were possible?"

"That is hard to do, Mrs. Lumen," a female student added. "Look at the world. Why is there so much fighting going on? We have not had much success with that, have we?"

"No, we haven't." She paused.

"Most of the great wise people of different religions have pushed this one point, even though their words are often skewed over time ... Who are we to truly judge another human being? What if we could see into the core of each individual and really experience a sense of his or her goodness? If the yin/yang principle we learned about earlier this year is true, then no person is all bad OR all good. Are you perfect? I'm not."

She walked to the other side of the front table. Campbell talked about Buddhism being a potential religion for the future because it did not exclude anyone, seeing *all* beings as 'Buddha beings.' What if all creatures have a piece of the divine within them? As Campbell says, 'Each [of these religions] needs its own myth, all the way. Love thine enemy. Open up. Don't judge. All things are Buddha things.' How would we treat each other differently if these things were true? Do you remember the Greek idea of hospitality? The code was to treat each guest as if he or she were a visiting god or goddess in disguise. What if "we treated every single person we came in contact with as a visiting deity? What if people treated you that way? How would that alter our world?"

∗   ∗   ∗   ∗

Mare found herself in a huge governmental complex with a male friend she did not recognize on waking. The majority of this facility was off-limits to civilians, but Mare and her companion were on a mission; they were looking for something.

Sneaking through the hallways, they avoided guards and a computerized security system. In some rooms, which felt similar to hospital rooms to Mare, were "floating" computer images hanging in the entrances. If Mare and her partner were to walk through these 3-D images, they would trigger an alarm. Despite not having triggered any alarms, the pair knew that security was aware of their presence in the facility, and guards always seemed to be just a few steps behind them. The guards could not find them. Mare and her companion were skilled at run, duck and hide.

Within the complex was a small store. The two entered it, still concentrating on their final goal. Mare looked around at the magazines, toothpaste and candy bars. She and her partner separated as they walked through the shop. Mare was in a different aisle when she heard urgent voices and a shuffling of footsteps. Immediately, she crouched low and closed her eyes, imagining that she was invisible from the eyes of the security guards. She blocked out all images and sounds as she focused on vanishing. She soon realized her partner had been captured.

They did not detect Mare's presence, however. After they left, realizing it was now all up to her, Mare resumed her search. *A cause—larger than myself—is counting on me*, she reminded herself when her fear intensified. The problem was that she was not exactly clear about what she was looking for. She only knew she would realize it when she found it. That was the guidance she had received.

She made her way to higher and higher areas in the building, always aware that her pursuers were not far behind. *I can do this.*

As she ascended to higher levels in the complex, she found one section that was more like a home or apartment. Peeking around a corner, she saw two people sitting at a dinner table having a conversation. Her heart increased its rhythm. She had to get past them. She had to go through this room. She made a break for it, spinning around the corner and sprinting as fast as she could through the center of the apartment. She didn't look around to catch their reactions; she just bolted through to the other side, around another corner and up a set of steep stairs. She was fast. But it wouldn't be long now before her pursuers would find her.

She heard running footsteps behind and below her. They did not want her to find what she had come there to discover. Mare sped through a tangle of rooms to a back corner. She felt something tug at her intuition. Looking up, she saw a semi-concealed loft, seemingly the pinnacle of the enormous complex. She felt a tug and recognition. She quickly climbed up into it.

A feeling of calm spread over her. Her heart rate eased. She knew that she was going to be safe here. They could not follow her into this sanctuary. This was the secret room she had been searching for.

Scanning the room, not with her eyes, but with her intuition and feelings, she tried to sense exactly where and what the treasure was that she had been sent to find. Before she located it precisely, she woke up.

The next morning, feeling fresh, centered and alive, she recorded the information into her dream journal: *12/6/98—"Fortified Room of Treasure."*

*   *   *   *

Cody took a deep breath and blew it out onto his three candles. His parents and grandparents clapped and cheered for him when he accomplished his task. He clapped his own hands and smiled. Before long his face was covered in vanilla frosting and brown clumps of chocolate cake.

When all her guests were gone, she scooped her son up, carried him to the upstairs bathroom, and turned on the water.

From her knees on the bathroom mat, Mare reached across the tub and washed Cody's blond locks. He loved water, and he was giggling and splashing her. His mother let him play for a few minutes with his squirty bath toys, while she watched him thoughtfully from her perch on the toilet seat.

The light of his playful spirit shined. Mare marveled at his innocence and beauty. Naked and unselfconscious, lying back in the water, grinning from ear to ear, blowing the bubbles from his face, this precious little boy smiled at his mother. It was infectious.

This wonderful little spirit! He was so dear to her it made her heart ache. *How do I keep him safe from the world? I can do everything in my power to protect him, but I can never protect him absolutely from harm.* The thought pained her. She thought back to the conversation she had not long before with Jane about the man in the car offering her candy all those many years ago.

"But you remained safe, Mare," Jane had reassured her. Even though your parents weren't with you; something was protecting you. You walked on. You walked the path you were meant to in this life. Trust that. Your son will as well."

Then after a moment's consideration, she thought about her own pain and an epiphany was born. *I cannot protect him absolutely, but I wouldn't want to do such a disservice to him even if I had the power! Who am I to shield him from living? How unfair that would be.*

My own mistakes and pain have helped me to grow. How can I deny him that? I can keep him as safe as I can, but he will need to be given the freedom to live, to experiment with the world, to overcome obstacles. He will have to face whatever pains and challenges come his way.

Cody's splashing caught her attention again. He would grow up, and he would learn the lessons he came to learn. She began to understand the idea of surrender, of letting go and trusting.

It is not for me to judge experiences as good or bad. The last few years have cracked me open and brought compassion to my heart. Now that I've survived it, I wouldn't give it back if I could. I don't regret any of it. It had a purpose. Mare thought of her own travels. *I am protected. I am not alone. Neither is Cody. He is protected too. He will walk the path he was meant to.*

While she was deep in thought, Cody aimed a small slice of water at her. On making contact with his mother, the child erupted into a cascade of giggles. She dropped back down to the floor and splashed him back. Their smiles held the whole world in them.

40

Winter Solstice

Therefore we pledge to bind ourselves to one another to embrace our lowliest, to keep company with our loneliest, to educate our illiterate, to feed our starving, to clothe our ragged, to do all good things, knowing that we are more than keepers of our brothers and sisters. We ARE our brothers and sisters.

~Maya Angelou~ "Black Family Pledge"

Peace is not a relationship of nations. It is a condition of mind brought about by the serenity of soul. Peace is not merely the absence of war. It is also a state of mind. Lasting peace can come only to peaceful people.

~Jawaharal Nehru~

The second annual winter solstice hike up Quarry Mountain was another cold one. However, the sun shone upon the hill in all its richness, so the temperature did not seem so bone chilling. The same four attended as the year before: Sophie, Tristan, Derek and Mare. Again, they plodded up the slippery peak. Tristan crossed a wide slab of granite that was covered in ice. He slipped, and his behind acted as a toboggan until it hit a patch of underbrush on the trailside. When they could see he was okay, the other three howled in laughter. He grabbed onto some tree limbs and pulled himself up. All four reached the top and started running around in the few inches of snow that covered the plateau. Derek dropped four Clementine oranges in a pile on the snow as he had done the year before. Then Tristan started a little fire next to them, and the foursome played Frisbee around it. They ran to keep their blood warm and flowing. They chased each other until they were panting, and then Derek launched into Sophie's sun song. They ran in circles around the glowing branches in the center. Out of breath, they plopped down onto the ground and stared into the flames. Mare placed her mittened hands out in front of her to warm the frozen bones. Then she glanced to the orange pile beside her.

"Hey look, the Clementines have multiplied. Now there are five!"

Sophie laughed and Tristan grinned.

"They gave birth," Derek announced. "We have increased our number!"

"When did you toss the extra one down there, Derek? I didn't see you do it."

"I didn't do it. I only brought four."

"Come on! You had to."

"I didn't. It was magic. Ooooo."

"Okay, it was magic." Mare stood up and turned her body, so she could warm her bottom.

"So, we are about to start a new cycle," Derek observed. "The days are going to start getting longer; the sun is returning. Any parting thoughts about this last year, or the year to come?"

Tristan burst out, "Yes, I'm glad it's over! Shit. It was a hard one." His long strawberry blonde locks trailed over his parka.

Sophie chuckled, "Me too. I'm ready for a new beginning," she glanced at her husband.

Derek reflected, "I have learned that I need to set boundaries with regard to my involvement at school. I'm done putting in all kinds of extra hours. I need to spend more time taking care of myself some. I still plan to work hard, but I need more balance. I want to spend more time with friends. More time relaxing and having fun, like this." He clapped his gloved hands together.

"That's great, Derek," Tristan reinforced. "Good for you. You have been working too hard."

"How about you, Mare," Sophie asked. "What's your take on this last year?"

Mare was silent for a moment. She thought about her brother. She remembered back on Walt and Kate, and Austin, and more recently Sophie and Tristan. "I've learned that … I have nothing to hide. I don't need to be ashamed about the qualities that make me human, and I don't need to hold them close and keep them secret. I know that I—that we all—have a darker side. But where I thought there were shadows, like in the example of my brother, I have also found light." *Yin and yang make a whole circle,* she thought to herself.

The wind blew a handful of hair across her nose, and she pulled it aside. She looked up into the eyes of her friends. "I have seen myself in others every time I have looked. I've discovered that we have more in common than I could have ever known. I have experienced a deep sense of feeling connected to others, and I want that to grow. I hope that Pete and I find healing and intimacy. I see my garden coming into full bloom next summer. I am anxious to see what the bulbs look like that I planted this fall. I am excited to continue writing. There's only one thing left that needs to happen." Mare looked down at the orange Clementines. "It will. In the meantime, I have started to let go." She hesitated, and the others were thoughtful. "The last couple of years have been excruciating, but you know—I wouldn't trade them for anything. I am happy with who I am and the way I continue to evolve. Without those painful moments, I would never have found this place or this understanding. I am grateful for the lessons I am learning."

* * * *

12/22/98—"*Catching the Little Blond Girl*"

I am flying through city streets. I am aware I am dreaming. I ask for guidance about where to go. I see a train and I fly down for a closer look. Some of the train cars are open, and I can see people standing in them. I see a little blond girl in one of the cars looking at me. The train is going very fast, but I leap for her. She catches me.

* * * *

For Christmas Eve, Mare and Pete hired one of Mare's students to do a private violin concert for the Lumen family annual gathering at John and Margaret's. The white lights sparkled in the tree branches, and the children hovered around the gifts, hardly able to contain their anticipation at finding what was inside. Mare was calm and happy as she watched. She slid over next to her husband on the sofa, put her arms around him, and planted a kiss on his neck. He put an arm around her and smiled. "I like the blond," he said. His wife had finally caved and fully colored her hair.

A photographer arrived to take a Lumen family portrait. He positioned John and Margaret first. Then he pointed for Margaret's three daughters to take a seat. Pete's sister and her husband and daughter sat on one side. His other sister's black velvet dress stretched over her ripe and bulging belly, and she and her fiancé stood behind her father. Pete, Mare and Cody took their places as well. Everyone smiled.

"You look radiant, Mare," her father-in-law hugged her afterwards.

"Thanks, Pop. I'm feeling good, just a little tired."

"Maybe *you* are expecting too?"

Mare put her hand over her abdomen and grinned, "Maybe."

She leaned over and stuck her nose in the boughs of the Christmas tree. She inhaled the fragrance of balsam. The spirit of Christmas was here.

End of Book One

To be continued in Book Two: <u>Jumping the Abyss</u>.

Questions for Discussion

1. In what ways does Mare find healing?

2. What lessons does Mare take away from her painful experiences?

3. Point of view is an important aspect of *Reaching Out*. Although the primary perspective is Mare's, she tries to put herself in other's shoes at times. What kinds of things does she/the reader discover through this exposure to the "other side," particularly to her brother's situation? Did your awareness or point of view as a reader change through the course of the story? How did your perception shift through the reading process, if at all?

4. Is there a villain or villains in this story? Where are the true conflicts and how, or how well, does Mare reconcile them?

5. Evaluate Mare's relationship to Pete. Is there hope for them? How and why does their relationship decay, and what is it that each wants in this relationship? Are those desires reasonable and/or attainable? What truths are spoken here of the marital experience? Is anyone/anything to blame for their struggles? What keeps them together, and what threatens to tear them apart? Were you rooting for them to stay together or to separate?

6. Why does Mare share her dreams about Austin with Pete? Did she make the right decision? What did you think about Pete's reactions to it?

7. Do you recognize any parts of yourself in Mare's character? How about the other characters? What do we, as humans, share in common as revealed through the story?

8. What role does longing play in the novel? How did the characters handle their feelings of longing? Could you relate to these emotions, and how do you handle such feelings?

9. The author uses a number of symbols in the novel. One important one is the yin/yang or T'ai Chi symbol. How does the idea of duality impact this story? How does she weave this theme through the various chapters? Discuss the idea of good/bad and right/wrong as it applies to the story and life in general.

10. Mare teaches her students about choice in relationship to slavery? How much choice do we have as humans? What choices does Mare make along the way?

11. To what degree does place affect this story?

12. Why does the author begin the book with the lines from Homer's *Odyssey*? What do these two works have in common? What are the connections between Mare's many dreams and the mythology she and her students study?

13. Why does the author choose to integrate some of the dreams into the narrative, while, at other times, she uses journal entries? What effect is she creating by integrating them the way she does? How do these choices affect the reading experience?

14. In what ways are people judged in this story? Where there any places where, as a reader, you noticed judgment come up? What times in your life have you have judged or felt judged?

15. What do you think the author's purpose was in writing this novel? In what ways could the writing or reading experience have been cathartic?

16. What role does Nature play in the novel? Could this work have been written without it? Do you have special places or activities associated with Nature that influence your life?

17. Are dreams important? How so? Did you have any of your own epiphanies or discoveries about dreaming through the course of reading this book?

18. What purpose is suffering/trial playing in Mare's life? What have you suffered through and what are the lessons in those difficult experiences?

19. Speculate about some of the things that may happen in book two. What happens to Mare and Pete? Is she pregnant? What abyss might she be referring to? How will their lives be different? What will happen to Seth?

20. What gifts did this book share or make to you as a reader? Is there anything about this book that you are grateful for? In other words, what did you appreciate?

Works Cited

Cabot, Laurie, and Tom Cowan. <u>Power of the Witch</u>: The Earth, the Moon, and the Magical Path to Enlightenment. New York: Delta, 1990.

978-0-595-45425-9
0-595-45425-9

Printed in the United States
95259LV00004B/70-999/A